"ONE OF THE LEADING MASTERS OF EPIC FANTASY."
—*Publishers Weekly*

ACCLAIM FOR DAVE DUNCAN AND HIS PREVIOUS WORK

"Dave Duncan is one of the best writers in the fantasy world today. His writing is clear, vibrant, and full of energy. His action scenes are breathtaking and his skill at characterization is excellent."　　　　　　　　　　　—*Writers Write*

"Duncan excels at old-fashioned swashbuckling fantasy, maintaining a delicate balance between breathtaking excitement, romance, and high camp in a genre that is easy to overdo."　　　　　　　　　　　—*Romantic Times*

"Duncan can swashbuckle with the best, but his characters feel more deeply and think more clearly than most, making his novels . . . suitable for a particularly wide readership."
　　　　　　　　　　　—*Publishers Weekly* (starred review)

Also by Dave Duncan

The Dodec Books
MOTHER OF LIES
CHILDREN OF CHAOS

Chronicles of the King's Blades
PARAGON LOST
IMPOSSIBLE ODDS
THE JAGUAR KNIGHTS

Tales of the King's Blades
THE GILDED CHAIN
LORD OF THE FIRE LANDS
SKY OF SWORDS

A Man of His Word
MAGIC CASEMENT
FAERIE LAND FORLORN
PERILOUS SEAS
EMPEROR AND CLOWN

A Handful of Men
THE CUTTING EDGE
UPLAND OUTLAWS
THE STRICKEN FIELD
THE LIVING GOD

THE
ALCHEMIST'S
APPRENTICE

DAVE DUNCAN

ACE BOOKS, NEW YORK

THE BERKLEY PUBLISHING GROUP
Published by the Penguin Group
Penguin Group (USA) Inc.
375 Hudson Street, New York, New York 10014, USA
Penguin Group (Canada), 90 Eglinton Avenue East, Suite 700, Toronto, Ontario M4P 2Y3, Canada
(a division of Pearson Penguin Canada Inc.)
Penguin Books Ltd., 80 Strand, London WC2R 0RL, England
Penguin Group Ireland, 25 St. Stephen's Green, Dublin 2, Ireland (a division of Penguin Books Ltd.)
Penguin Group (Australia), 250 Camberwell Road, Camberwell, Victoria 3124, Australia
(a division of Pearson Australia Group Pty. Ltd.)
Penguin Books India Pvt. Ltd., 11 Community Centre, Panchsheel Park, New Delhi—110 017, India
Penguin Group (NZ), 67 Apollo Drive, Mairangi Bay, Auckland 1311, New Zealand
(a division of Pearson New Zealand Ltd.)
Penguin Books (South Africa) (Pty.) Ltd., 24 Sturdee Avenue, Rosebank, Johannesburg 2196,
South Africa

Penguin Books Ltd., Registered Offices: 80 Strand, London WC2R 0RL, England

This is an original publication of The Berkley Publishing Group.

First edition: March 2007

Library of Congress Cataloging-in-Publication Data

Duncan, David, 1933–
    The alchemist's apprentice / Dave Duncan. — 1st ed.
        p. cm.
    ISBN-13: 978-0-441-01479-8
    1. Nostradamus, 1503–1566—Fiction. 2. Prophets—Fiction. I. Title.

PR9199.3.D847A77 2007
813'.54—dc22

                                        2006026659

PRINTED IN THE UNITED STATES OF AMERICA

10 9 8 7 6 5 4 3 2 1

THE
ALCHEMIST'S
APPRENTICE

1

It was the wettest day since Noah. It also happened to be Saint Valentine's Day, but I was not in a loving mood. The saint himself would have cursed the weather.

Maestro Nostradamus had been even snarlier than usual all morning. Then, halfway through the afternoon, he rattled off a list of reagents he needed for his experiments and ordered me to go out and buy them. I complained, reasonably, that he already had stocks of all of them on the shelves above his alchemy bench. No, he needed more and right away. Worse, since Giorgio, our gondolier, had been given the day off to attend a nephew's wedding, I would have to go on foot.

I came home when the stores closed, two hours after sunset. I was wet, cold, tired, and late for supper. I found the Maestro in his favorite red velvet chair, dangerously close to the fireplace, with his nose inside a book. As always he was wearing his black physician's gown; the straggly hair dangling under his hat shone silver in the candlelight.

"Cinnabar," I said, setting the packets in a row on my side of the big desk, "birthwort, hellebore, realgar, aconite,

nux vomica, and powdered stibnite. Two ducats, five soldi."
I counted out the change.

"No dried virgin's glove?"

"Not a speck of it in the city. Old Gerolamo says he
hasn't carried it in ten years. Yes," I added before he could
ask, "I checked every herbalist in Venice, and every apothecary. I even tried the Ghetto Nuovo."

He grunted. "You paid too much."

"That was the realgar. It's a good piece. Make a nice pen-
dant on a lady's breast." I put the coins in the secret drawer
where we keep the petty cash.

He sniffed disapprovingly. His disposition had clearly
not improved while I was out. "Go and get dry. You have
work to do tonight."

I said, "Yes, master," politely and headed off to my room.
By the time I was toweled and dressed, the Angeli family
had returned from the wedding—Giorgio, Mama, and their
current brood. I ate in the kitchen, where the children's excited jabber and two helpings of Mama Angeli's excellent
sardoni alla greca soon restored my normal good humor. I
strolled back along to the atelier to learn what my master
wanted of me, wondering whether I would get any sleep at
all.

You think an astrologer's apprentice is accustomed to
staying awake all night to aim cross-staffs and quadrants at
the stars? Then you are wrong, because the celestial science
is pursued by day, with pen and paper at a desk, calculating
aspects and ascendants from ephemerides. I admit I sometimes have to waste valuable sleeping time up on the roof
recording the Maestro's observations of comets and other
meteoric phenomena, but not often. Besides, that night the
rain would have blinded us.

I do not mean that he never keeps me up to ungodly
hours. He does. Seeming to need almost no sleep himself, he

loses track of time. He may spend a long evening instructing me in arcane lore until I am cross-eyed and all reasonable men have gone off to bed—and then decide to dictate lengthy letters to correspondents all over Europe. When that happens, he is quite capable of keeping going until dawn. I, on the other hand, do enjoy my sleep. When I stay up all night by choice, it is for pleasure, not business.

I was surprised to find the big room deserted and dark, the fire dwindled to embers. The Maestro had said he had work for me, but there were no written instructions on the desk. He had not just gone to the privy, because he had doused all the lamps except a single candle, but that one stood on the slate-topped table holding the great globe of rock-crystal that he uses for prophecy. It had been draped in its usual velvet cover when I was there earlier, but that had now been removed, revealing four lines of text scrawled on the slate itself.

Now I understood his curdled mood. Clairvoyance is exhausting and drains him. He had not had time to go into trance while I was changing and eating, so he had done it while I was out. I wondered if he had sent me off on that wild, drenching trek around the apothecaries' shops just to keep me out of his way, but that seemed unnecessarily callous even for him.

One of my many duties is to copy out his prophecies in a legible hand, for his writing is atrocious at the best of times and execrable when he is foreseeing. I fetched two lamps, my writing implements, and the big book of prophecies. Transcription proved unusually easy, which implied that the events it foretold were near at hand. I had known him to produce much worse cacography and was confident that I was reading it correctly. Nevertheless, when I covered the table, I left the writing in place so he could approve my reading in the morning.

When Death puts up Death upon a vain course,
The Serene One moves and is unmoved;
Wisdom has departed and Silence is deserted,
So the brave Riddler must guard the treasure.

The Maestro's prophecies are always couched in imprecise language, but this is not trickery—he is often as mystified as anyone, for he retains no memory of writing them or what he has foreseen. We have spent days trying to interpret some of his gibberish. By comparison, this quatrain seemed positively lucid, and he obviously expected me to reach the same conclusion he had, at least about the final line.

When I was growing up in the parish of San Barnabà, most of my playmates were sons of impoverished nobles. Having no wealth, they would brag instead of their ancient lineages. Venice has been a republic for nine hundred years and some boys could claim descent from very early doges. I could always end their arguments, because my family name is Zeno. The Zenos of Venice have produced one doge and many great heros, but I would claim to be a descendant of the philosopher Zeno of Elea, of the Fifth Century BC, who was known for his riddles. Then all the rest of them would pile on top of me. It did end their arguing, as I said, but did me no good, other than eventually teaching me to keep my mouth shut. There are other Zenos around the city, but we are not on speaking terms. I am the Maestro's guardian. The *Riddler* was me.

I had intended to bottle and label the reagents I had purchased in the afternoon, but the quatrain's warning seemed more urgent. In search of a second opinion, I locked up the atelier and went back to my room. There I unwrapped my tarot deck and took a reading, laying out the spread on my bedcover. It almost made my hair stand on end.

I favor a simple five-card cross, which the Maestro scorns

as simplistic, but which usually gives me good short-term guidance. It begins with a face-up card to represent the question, the present, or the subject. If the first card produces nothing significant, you can try once or even twice more, but a third denial risks desensitizing the deck. My deck was very well attuned and right off gave me the jack of cups, which always means me, the alchemist's apprentice. I dealt four cards around it, face down, to make the cross.

The one below represents the past, problem, or danger, and there I turned over Justice reversed. The card on my left—which is the subject's right, of course—denotes the helper or path, and there I found the Emperor reversed. The card at the top of the cross tells the future, objective, or solution, and was Death, also reversed. The fourth arm of the cross is the snare to be avoided, which in this case was the four of swords. The presence of three of the major arcana implied a very strong reading and the overall spread was definitely a warning, especially the reversal of Justice. I admit I did not understand the counsel it was offering. The Maestro was clearly missing and the reversal of all three trumps suggested no clear-cut solution. The four of swords was worrisome, although not as frightening as either the three or the ten would have been.

Certainly tarot has its limitations, but the overall indication of personal danger was obvious. I gave my deck a kiss of thanks, wrapped it again in its silk kerchief, and tucked it back under my pillow. Then I retrieved my rapier and dagger from the top of the wardrobe.

The house was quiet. I locked the front door behind me and trotted downstairs to find old Luigi, the Barbolanos' toothless night watchman. Luigi would be less help than a broken ankle in any sort of fight and is also a notorious gossip.

"Have you ever," I asked him, "in your long and distinguished service, known anyone try to force a way into the

Ca' Barbolano?" Although I am a natural optimist, the tarot's four swordsmen seemed excessive odds, even to me.

A guard dog should have teeth, but when Luigi smiles he shows mostly gums. "Never! Is not our beloved Republic the most peace-loving place in the world?" He had not even noticed that I was armed.

"And we are protected by our noble lords of the night!"

He cackled at my sarcasm. The *Signori di Notte* are young nobles elected to lead the local constabulary, whose general incompetence makes them little less dangerous than the criminals they are supposed to catch.

"I am expecting a visitor," I said. "If you want to keep your eye on the back door, I'll take the watergate."

We make this same agreement quite often. He always assumes that I am waiting for a lady. Regrettably he is almost always wrong in that, and the visitor is some nervous client with a clandestine appointment to consult the Maestro. Luigi went shuffling off happily to his kennel at the back, where he would no doubt enjoy a few hours' illicit sleep. The servants' entrance there leads out to the walled courtyard, which in turn opens into a narrow, winding *calle* that will take you eventually to the *campo*, with its church, bell tower, and parish well, but the gate is locked at night. No visitor of consequence ever comes to the landside door anyway.

The watergate is a three-arched loggia, whose floor is barely above the surface of the Rio San Remo at high tide. That night the tide was out, exposing a slippery carpet of weed on the watersteps. I topped up a lantern with enough oil to burn until dawn and hung it in the central arch. Then I went back in and shot all the bolts on the big doors.

Ca' Barbolano is not the largest of the great family palaces in the city, but it is not the smallest, either. Mostly I kept my lookout from the mezzanine windows above the watergate, but sometimes I stretched my legs with a stroll along the *androne*, the single long hall that extends from one door to the other. Its high walls bear tribute to centuries of sea trading by Barbolano ancestors—cobwebbed banners and great bronze lanterns from ancient galleys, arrays of cutlasses, crossbows, and scimitars. Storerooms line both sides, but the glow of my lamp flickered on other wares left heaped on the floor: bales, boxes, and barrels, intermixed with oars and cushions from the gondolas outside, brought indoors for safekeeping.

Out on the canal, wind and rain continued their wild dance. At times the downpour was so heavy that I could barely make out the lanterns on passing gondolas. The light outside our door continued to burn brightly and so did the one outside Number 96, next-door, but even 96 was attracting little business in such weather. Once or twice I saw a light moving on the building site directly opposite, but I could not tell if it was carried by a conscientious watchman or the thieves he was supposed to deter. Midnight came and went. The last of 96's customers departed. Its windows darkened and eventually a servant took down its lantern and carried it away indoors, leaving me the whole world to myself.

Nothing happened for another hour. I had almost come to believe I had misunderstood my instructions when I saw a light approaching. I could not even make out how many men the boat held, but it pulled in at our watersteps. I raced downstairs, my lamp throwing wild shadows on the walls.

Before they banged the knocker and wakened Luigi, I flipped open the peephole. "Who goes there?"

The night growled, "Visitors to see Doctor Nostradamus." The speaker was standing with his face in shadow. His voice was familiar.

"He is not at home." *Wisdom has departed.*

"Open this door, Zeno!"

"I have orders to admit no one. Anyone else you wish to speak with, I shall be happy to fetch. But the Maestro is not at home."

Then the speaker edged back so the light was on his face. "Open in the name of the Republic!" said Raffaino Sciara.

The night was now much colder. In theory I could have demanded to see his warrant, but if I delayed him any longer, Sciara could set his men to work on the big brass door knocker, and the last thing the Maestro would want would be a clamor to rouse the household and let the Barbolanos learn that he was in trouble with the government.

"At once, *lustrissimo!*" While I was hauling on the bolts, my mind chased its tail puppy-wise, wondering what could possibly have provoked this invasion. As soon as I had one flap open, I grabbed up my lamp again and backed away. I smiled a toothy welcome at the *fanti* as they entered—four of them, just as my tarot had warned. *Fanti* wear no armor, but they carry swords concealed in their cloaks.

It was the man behind them who gave me intestinal cramps. Raffaino Sciara is tall, stooped, and cadaverous, with all the lovesomeness of a serpent. He bears an uncanny resemblance to the image of Death in my tarot deck. His cloak of office is blue, but otherwise put a scythe in his hand and he would be dressed for Carnival as the Grim Reaper. He is *Circospetto*, chief secretary to the Council of Ten, which plays at the capital crimes table.

I bowed gracefully. "Welcome to Ca' Barbolano, *lustrissimo.*"

The death's-head inspected me with a sneer that would curdle spring water. "Where is your master, boy?"

"He is not here."

"I can see that, Alfeo."

"Can I assist you in his absence? Read your palm? Cast your horoscope?"

The Maestro might have accused me of childish babbling to conceal fear and for once I would not have argued. The Venetian Council of Ten runs the finest international spy network in Europe, but it also knows everything about everyone within the Republic itself. Its members come and go, but its secretaries remain forever, and Sciara must have more secrets fluttering around inside his memory than San Marco has pigeons. Whatever personal hopes or motives he may have are hidden behind a mask of absolute loyalty to the state. I suspect he has been dehumanized by all the uncountable death sentences and forced confessions he must have recorded.

"He never leaves this house."

"Not *never*, sir. Just rarely. His legs—"

"Did he go by boat or by land, Alfeo?"

"I honestly do not know." Innocence glowed in my countenance, I hoped. "I deeply regret that you should have wasted a journey on such a horrid evening—"

"Where is he?"

"*Lustrissimo*, I have no idea." I love telling the truth, because it needs so little effort. "Did you hope to catch the world's greatest clairvoyant unawares? He foresaw visitors looking for him tonight and instructed me to make sure that nothing was stolen in his absence."

"Ha!" Sciara's breath was as sour as his face. "You have two choices, Zeno. You can take me at once to your master, or you can come with me."

I would be astonished if the Ten ever issued a warrant to search a nobleman's house, and if they did it would not be served by *Circospetto*, but by *Messier Grande*, the chief of police. On the other hand, Sciara and his four henchmen could certainly take me in for questioning, and questioning can be the least pleasant of experiences.

"I swear I do not know where he is, *lustrissimo*."

Circospetto showed his teeth in a death's-head smile. "Show me." He nodded to the *fante* with the fanciest silver badge on his belt. "Guard the door and try not to steal anything."

I said, "This way, then," and headed for the stairs.

Yes, I was shaken. Officially the Ten investigate major crimes against the state, but they will meddle in anything they fancy. I must trust that the Maestro had acted upon his own warning and departed. I was certain that he would not be found if he did not want to be found. Although I had been his apprentice for years, I still did not know the limits of his powers.

The first flight of stairs brought us to the mezzanine landing where I had spent most of the night. Doors there lead into two apartments occupied by the Marciana brothers, who are *sier* Alvise Barbolano's business partners. I raised my lantern in passing . . . "Such a shame you did not come in daylight, *lustrissimo. Sier* Alvise just acquired this painting, *San Marco Blessing the Fishing Boats.* Quite a rarity. By Sebastiano del Piombo."

Sciara did not spare it a glance. Philistine!

Another flight brought us to the *piano nobile,* the Barbolano residence itself. The doors there are twice my height and can be opened wide enough to row a galley through. They were shut, of course. I did not draw our visitor's attention to the Tintoretto on the wall. His continuing silence did not seem to be from lack of breath and the old skeleton had no trouble keeping up with me, although I had a forty-year advantage.

The last two flights brought us to the top floor, which the noble Alvise Barbolano puts at the disposal of the celebrated Maestro Filippo Nostradamus. I unlocked the door and stood aside to let my companion enter, striding in like a de-horsed horseman of the Apocalypse. Our two lanterns did very little to raise the darkness, for the *salone* runs the full length of the building and its ceiling is twenty feet high; it takes a lot of flames to illuminate it. The statues glimmered spookily and stars twinkled from gilded cornices and picture frames, from chandeliers of Murano glass.

Sciara seemed unimpressed. "His bedroom?"

I led the way across to the appropriate door. The Maestro had prophesied that he would not be there and I believed him.

"Open it!"

"It is not booby trapped, *lustrissimo*. Once in a while I will balance a bucket of water on it just to make him laugh, but—"

"I told you to open it."

I opened it gently and raised my lamp. Then I walked in.

The Maestro earns a lot more money than he ever admits, but he could not support the upkeep of one broom closet in Ca' Barbolano. His bedchamber alone is fit for a king, but everything in it—furniture, paintings, tapestries, chandeliers, statuary—is owned by *sier* Alvise. The bed, standing on gilded columns, displayed undisturbed bedding of silk and lace. The Maestro might be hiding in one of the marquetry chests, but Sciara seemed to consider that possibility as unlikely as I did.

"Where does his horse sleep?"

"Horse, *lustrissimo*? He owns no horse that I know of."

"You know who I mean! The mute."

"Ah!" I led the way along to a smaller room—a comparatively humble room, although some of the richest men in the Republic sleep in worse. I marched in, not bothering to be quiet, for Bruno has been stone deaf since birth. Stretched flat out across two beds put together, the giant was snoring loud enough to raise waves on the lagoon. Being very close to naked, he was an impressive sight. "There is more of him," I said, "but we keep the rest in storage."

I did not draw *Circospetto*'s attention to the Veronese Madonna on the wall. It is only a small one, but Bruno likes it.

"Your tongue will strangle you yet, Zeno. Let me see the study."

I led the way again, going a little slower as I worked out what to do. So far so good—the Maestro had gone, leaving Bruno behind. *Wisdom had departed and Silence was deserted.* But, although Sciara had visited the Maestro's atelier before, he had never had a chance to snoop around there at will. Now the brave Riddler must guard the treasures. My first problem was that I had not only locked the door, but also warded it, as I always do at night. The one time I forgot to disable that curse, it threw me halfway across the *salone* and tied me up in an agony of cramp. What had disabled a healthy youngster like me might well kill a man of Sciara's age.

I unlocked the door, but then I hung my keys back on my belt and turned to face him, folding my arms. "First you must give me your oath that you will not remove anything."

"Stand aside."

I said, "Gladly," and did so. "But I warn you, *lustrissimo*, that if you touch that door handle you may receive a very unpleasant surprise."

Lantern light turned his osseous smile into a sigil of crooked shadows. "Are you threatening me with violence, *messer*? That is a serious criminal offense."

"Warning you of danger, merely."

"Open the door, or you will come back with me and explain your refusal to the magistrates."

"I expect *sier* Alvise Barbolano will lodge a complaint with the Council."

"What the nobleman may choose to do is not your concern. Open the door or fetch your cloak."

I was damned either way. My refusal might even be all the evidence the Ten would need to issue a formal search warrant. I knew of evidence in there that could be used to hang the Maestro and me with him. Among his papers were prophecies, letters written in cipher from people all over Europe, horoscopes for senior members of the government, and many other documents that could be regarded as evidence of treason or heresy.

Furious, I turned my back on the intruder to conceal my hands. I made the passes and muttered the incantation needed to remove the wards. Then I led the way inside.

The room was dark and unoccupied, but the poisons I had brought back the previous evening still sat in full view on the desk. Both Gerolamo the herbalist and Danielle the apothecary had warned me to be careful with those. Sciara made a methodical circuit of the room, starting at the alchemical workbench with its mortars and alembics, lingering to look at the scores of jars on shelves above it.

I stayed very close, prepared to grab away anything he tried to pocket.

He took even longer at the wall of books, raising his lantern to scan the titles—books and more books, all bound in embossed leather and lettered with gold leaf. The Republic is the greatest center of printing in Europe, so the Maestro's collection is far from being the largest in the city, but it contains many rarities—manuscripts and fragments centuries old. More to the point, no library in Europe contains more works on the arcane: cabalism, demonology, alchemy, Gnosticism, and other heresies banned by the Church. Venice pays much less attention to the *Index Librorum Prohibitorum* than the rest of Catholic Europe does, but just because a law is rarely applied does not mean that it cannot be, so forbidden books are never displayed. Some have been rebound and incorrectly titled. Others are hidden inside other books, hollowed out for the purpose, a few are locked away in secret compartments behind the walls behind the books. Books are rarely evidence of treason, but they can suggest heresy or witchcraft. Sciara was looking at enough evidence to send the Maestro to the stake, if he wanted to. He would have to find it first, but he had all the time in the world and unlimited resources.

He ignored the velvet cloth over the crystal ball, as if to imply that he would not be distracted by hocus-pocus. He passed the fireplace and came to the big double desk near the windows, littered on the Maestro's side with books and on mine with the packets of reagents I had left there, plus the letter I had been working on when I was sent shopping. Sciara reached for the paper.

"I should warn you, *lustrissimo*," I said, "that that is a confidential document addressed to the Pope."

He read it anyway, then turned his skeletal smile on me. "This is your side of the desk, your writing." He had noted the gold inkstand and the bronze one, the location of the windows, and the fact that I wore my sword on my left side. He had drawn the correct conclusion.

"I am the only person who can read my master's."

"Was he dictating to you, or do you presume to advise the Holy Father on medical matters?"

"The Holy Father's physicians wrote to consult him. He told me to recommend his standard treatment." Which I knew by heart, papal hemorrhoids being much like any humble sinner's.

Sciara glanced over at the great armillary sphere, the terrestrial globe from Gerardus Mercator, a celestial globe that is reputed to be by Nicolaus Copernicus but probably isn't, the equatorium, cross-staffs, and so on, but did not bother to go closer. "Where is Filippo Nostradamus?"

"I do not know, *lustrissimo*."

"You swear that?"

He might be hiding in the apartment. He might be hiding elsewhere in the house, and it would take days to search that. He might have gone out, although he could not travel far without riding on Bruno's great shoulders or employing methods I dare not mention. I did not know.

"I swear by Our Lady and all the saints."

"May they give you strength in the days to come. Get your cloak, boy."

He was serious. I have fallen into frigid canals often enough and recognized the feeling. "On what charge?"

Sciara curled his lip. "Practicing sorcery on a door knob."

"Rubbish! I was trying to bluff you. You didn't think I was serious, did you?"

"What matters is what the Council believes. Cloak or not, you come with me."

2

When he found the atelier door unlocked, the Maestro would know I had not left the apartment willingly; I repeated the message by leaving my sword and dagger in full view on the bed. My cloak was still damp, but a mere apprentice is lucky to own even one good cloak and mine is of finest kidskin, a gift from an admirer. As I went downstairs with my baleful guide, I asked leave to go and waken Luigi, so he could lock up behind us. The secretary sent one of his flunkies instead. The manner of my departure was to remain as secret as possible.

The two boatmen had been sheltering inside the loggia. I followed Sciara down the slimy watersteps to embark, and joined him on the cushioned bench in the *felze*, leaving the boatmen and *fanti* out in the rain. I spared a charitable thought for convicts sentenced to the galleys, chained to their oars and exposed to the weather day and night. We are never more than a few feet from seawater in Venice, but a galley bench would be too much close.

The city slept. Rain roared on the *felze* and painted golden haloes around the lantern on our prow and the little

shrine lights that mark the corners of the canals. We passed
no other boats and the only illuminated windows told of
people sick, or dying, or giving birth. Oars creaked, ripples
splashed sometimes, and one of the guards had a worrisome
cough, but otherwise I could brood undisturbed.

Life as a galley slave is still life, and the punishment for
sorcery is death by burning. Despite the weather that night,
I had no desire to become toasty warm while chained to a
post between the columns on the Piazzetta.

Like his celebrated uncle, the late Michel de Nostredame,
the Maestro is both astrologer and physician. Those are
honorable professions—the cardinal-patriarch himself employs an astrologer and the Pope has several. It is the Maestro's dabbling in alchemy and other arcane lore that teeters
on the brink of the forbidden. He had often been pestered
with accusations of witchcraft and fraud, which obviously
could not both be true, but so far his many clients in the
nobility had always stood by him and none of the slanders
had ever been taken seriously. If the Ten had decided to
charge him with magic or demonology, then it would have
sent *Missier Grande* to arrest him, not a glorified clerk like
Sciara.

So I kept telling myself, anyway.

That did not explain why I was being abducted. Sciara
flatly refused to answer my questions. The Council of Ten is
notoriously secretive. Its judgments cannot be appealed.
I had no right to counsel, or even to know who had accused
me of what. I could expect to be tortured. There was a famous case once of a doge's son being tortured to make him
confess to a crime that, as it later turned out, he had not
committed.

The Council of Ten is so named because it consists of
seventeen men, except when it is increased to thirty-two.
That is typical of the tangle of misnamed and interlocking

committees that govern the Republic. All members of all committees are noblemen, those whose names are written in the Golden Book. Commoners cannot be elected to office, but the most senior citizens, whose names are recorded in the Silver Book, are eligible for appointment to bureaucratic posts. Sciara is one of those.

As a fanatical optimist, I tried to convince myself that things could be worse. I might have been arrested by the Three, the state inquisitors. "The Ten can send you to jail and the Three to the grave," says the proverb. But the Ten can burn or bury you just as easily, and for all I knew I *had* been summoned by the Three. I could only wait and see.

We came at last to Rio di Palazzo, the narrow canyon between the towering walls of the Doges' Palace on one side and those of the New Prisons on the other. The New Prisons are not yet in use, so the only lights visible were those marking the watergate to the palace. Our approach had been noted, and as the boat pulled up at the wide double arch, a pair of armed night guards appeared there to help us up the slippery steps. Sciara went first and I followed, aided by the grip of a powerful, calloused hand. The *fanti* from the boat joined us in a clatter of boots.

The Doges' Palace is one of the wonders of the world, a huge building blending the most sublime with the utterly squalid. Although we were not in the sublime part, at least we were out of the rain, standing in a wide, pillared passage leading through from the canal to the central courtyard. On the left, light spilled out from a guardroom door and I had no doubt there would be a brazier and other comforts in there. A closed door in the opposite wall led, I knew, to the most squalid part of all.

Another fancy helmet saluted *Circospetto* and asked what

he could do to help the *lustrissimo*. Alongside his sword hung a matchlock pistol, which is a useful weapon if you want to club someone to death.

"This," Sciara said, "is Alfeo Zeno, apprentice to the philosopher Filippo Nostradamus. You should tuck him away somewhere safe where we can find him again when we need him. A charge sheet will be drawn up in due course."

The captain regarded me with little interest. "In the Wells, *lustrissimo*?"

Sciara pretended to consider, watching me with amusement, his face more sepulchral than ever in that gloomy, lantern-lit crypt. "Well, despite his humble garb, he is NH Alfeo Zeno, so perhaps you should find him something more befitting his rank. As I recall, the Leads have been honored by his presence in the past."

I ignored the mockery. It is true that I am entitled to put the letters NH before my name; they stand for *nobile homo* and mean that my birth is recorded in the Golden Book, as Sciara's is not. Perhaps that rankled, but at least he had not publicly accused me of sorcery. The captain nodded to one of his men, who went into the guardroom and returned with a lantern and a jingling ring of keys. He crossed the passage and unlocked the door to the Wells.

"If *messer* would be so kind as to follow me?" The captain led the way.

The ground floor of the palace is put to mundane uses. The stables are there, the guardrooms, and two sets of prison cells. The Wells are by far the worst of the jails, small stone kennels without windows, damp and dark and airless. They stink most horribly.

That eastern wing is very old and the stairs that lead from the Wells all the way to the top of the palace are steep, narrow, and oddly haphazard, as if they have been reorganized many times over the centuries. They are not intended to impress, because they are never seen by anyone except the *fanti* and their prisoners. Winding back and forth in the near-darkness, I had to concentrate on where I was putting my feet and soon lost count of what floor we were on.

The second story is mostly occupied by the bureaucracy—the High Chancellor and his staff of secretaries and notaries. The Golden and Silver Books are maintained there, for instance, and another office will issue the permits you need to do anything more than breathe. The third floor belongs to government, for it includes the doge's apartments and meeting rooms for magistrates and many councils, including the appeal courts and the Great Council itself. The fourth story is where the *Collegio* and the Senate meet, and also the Council of Ten.

Above those are attics containing the prison cells known as the Leads because they are directly under the great sheets of lead that cover the roof. It is not true, though, that the inmates bake in summer and freeze in winter. These cells are used for gentlemen prisoners, mostly political offenders, and they are not uncomfortable as prisons go. The room to which I was conducted was spacious enough, although utterly barren. I scanned it hastily by the light of the guards' lanterns. The walls were of heavy planks and the only furnishings, if you could call them that, were a bucket in one corner and a crucifix hanging on the wall opposite the door. A small grilled window admitted sounds of rain. The lights were withdrawn, the door banged, the lock clattered, and I was alone in the dark.

Most inmates would be terrified at that point. I was merely furious. My tarot had warned me of Justice reversed. Deciding that the floor was the best place to sit, since I had no other choice, I huddled myself down in a corner, as small as possible. I hated to dirty my cloak, but I was shivering too much to think of removing it. The vermin that swarmed in summer were mercifully absent.

My next decision required more thought. I had two options—I could wait there in my cell until I was taken down to appear before the tribunal, taking the risk that it would send me straight back up to the torturers. If that happened, my ensuing experiences were likely to be both unpleasant and prolonged, since I had no idea where my master had gone and to confess to assisting him in the black arts would be suicide.

Or I could leave.

Here I must digress to list the three laws of demonology, with apologies to those of you who already know them. Firstly, you can summon and direct a fiend if you know his true name and a few simple precautions. Secondly, being evil incarnate, the demon will do anything he can to defeat your purpose; he will always strive to deceive and betray you. And thirdly, accepting favors from a fiend will weaken your hold over him and let him gain power over you. That is how Faust was damned. The only defense against being possessed is purity of purpose.

After teaching me those rules, my master told me the name of a minor demon. I shall not repeat it here—it is unpleasant to say, leaving a foul taste in the mouth, and writing it down might cause the paper to go on fire. I shall refer to him as Putrid. Putrid is not especially powerful as fiends go, but I could command him to whisk me to anywhere in the Republic, either within the city or in the territories it controls on the mainland, or even to foreign states beyond its borders. There I should have to make a new life for myself. Any life that came from Putrid would be nasty and brutish. Understand?

In my present circumstances, I had even more problems. The Maestro might have called on demonic aid for his escape from Ca' Barbolano; he knows the names of many fiends more potent than Putrid. I hoped he had used some other sorcerous technique, one that did not risk his immortal soul, for he has many arts that he has not yet shared with me.

Putrid was all I had, though. I had no means of inscribing a pentacle, which is a sensible precaution, although neither essential nor foolproof. The crucifix on the wall would make a summoning difficult at best, perhaps impossible. I concluded that Putrid had better remain a last resort for the time being. I wedged my head back in the corner and went to sleep.

The bell tower of San Marco stands just across the Piazzetta from the palace, and I was jarred awake by the clang of the great *Marangona* bell announcing the start of a new day. The first light of a winter dawn was creeping in through the grilled window. A few minutes later, the lock rattled again and the door creaked. So did my neck.

"You are summoned!" the guard announced.

"How about some breakfast?" I grumbled.

"There might be some left when you return, if you're still hungry."

Back down those dark, contorted stairs I went, stumbling after my solitary guide's lamp. Before we had gone far, he threw open a door and I was dazzled by a blaze of daylight. There, in a fine meeting room where magnificent paintings hung on leather-covered walls and others shone overhead in gilt-framed ceiling panels, a man sat on one of the benches, obviously waiting for me. He rose to greet me; then he tilted his head slightly and regarded me with distaste.

"There has been a mistake," he said with hauteur. "I was expecting a *sier* Alfeo Zeno."

"Your prayers have been answered," I said.

In Venice people are defined by their costumes. A trades-man does not dress like a shopkeeper or a courtesan like a lady. It mattered that I was stubbled, tangled, and rumpled but it mattered much more that I was dressed as an apprentice, not a nobleman. He, on his part, looked both splendid and ridiculous, because his beard was streaked with white and he had to be at least fifty, yet he was decked out like a youth. His spindly calves were enclosed in full-length silk hose, his gaudy tunic and fur-lined brocade surcoat barely reached to his thighs, and his bonnet bulged almost as high as mine. He even sported a ruff. Fair enough—he was wearing the livery of the doge's equerries, who are normally youngsters from no-ble houses. It was not his fault that the doge had appointed at least one older man to keep the rest of them in line. But he did look silly. I knew most of the sixteen equerries by sight, but not this one.

"This is the right man, *clarissimo*," the guard said.

The equerry shrugged. "Well, His Serenity did mention something about an astrologer. Obviously astrology doesn't pay well."

He was sneering. After an unearned night in jail, I re-sented that. "And obviously you fought at Famagusta."

Bull's-eye! The equerry started. "How do you know that?"

"From the stars. Are we keeping the doge waiting?"

He shot a worried glance at the guard and crossed him-self. "If you would be so kind, *sier* Alfeo . . ." He gestured at the door, very nearly bowing.

I did bow. "Do, please, lead the way, *messer* equerry."

A cheap trick, yes, but as my master says, *Sometimes a cheap trick is all you can afford*. Of course I had been lucky. I do not recall my grandparents, but I had met enough of their friends to hear a trace of Cyprus in the equerry's *Veneziano*, and the way he had angled his head when he looked at me reminded me of one of the Maestro's patients who had suffered an eye injury. The doge had distinguished himself at the disastrous siege of Famagosta, so it was reasonable that he would have given a sinecure job in the palace to a man who had served under him back then, and had since, likely, fallen on hard times.

I followed my chastened guide through another grandiose meeting room and across the third-floor landing of the Golden Staircase. We were now in one of the areas designed to impress visitors and I felt a great deal more cheerful. My arrest had been absurdly unorthodox, I had not been properly charged or booked in as a prisoner, and now the doge had sent a senior equerry to fetch me at such a bleary hour that we were very unlikely to meet anyone on the way. Doge Pietro Moro has a reputation for being impatient with rules.

The entrance to the doge's personal apartments is through the equerries' hall, which is large and imposing, furnished with benches and couches and a few tables. In the past I had spent many hours in it, waiting on His Serenity. The paintings had been changed since my last visit, but I could hardly demand time to inspect them. A couple of the inmates—both much younger than my keeper—were sitting by the fire, playing a game of tarot. They looked up and frowned at the squalid company their colleague was attending. I smiled politely as we passed through.

"*Sier* Alfeo Zeno, sire." We had reached our destination. I walked around the equerry into a dressing room where the doge was having his hair cut by a valet. I doffed my bonnet and bowed low. We Republicans do not kneel to our head of state.

"Thank you, Aldo."

The door closed.

Our most serene prince, Pietro Moro, is large and grizzled; he has a rheumatic back, is of the sanguine temperament as defined by the immortal Galen, and at that time was in his late seventies. It is rare for a man much younger than that to be elected doge—Venetians favor rapid turnover in the supreme office of the state. At the far end of the room stood a row of mannequins draped in different versions of the state robes, one of which was being vigorously brushed by a second valet. The doge goes garbed in white and ermine and cloth of gold; he wears a brocade cap called the *corno* because it rises at the back in a horn. This protuberance bears a marked resemblance to an oversized nose, so it is regrettable that the present incumbent has been known all his life as *Nasone*, Big Nose.

Keeping his head still for the scissors, he squinted at me out of one eye. "You seem to be in trouble again, lad."

"I suspected so, Your Serenity. I don't know why."

"An old friend of mine died yesterday."

I could not see where that led. "I offer my humble condolences. I heard the bell tolling yesterday and was informed that a procurator had entered into grace." Danielle the apothecary had told me.

There are nine procurators of San Marco. They are state trustees, managing endowments, caring for widows and orphans, supervising trusts. The office is unpaid, but brings such honor and precedence that the procurators are recognized as the "grand old men" of the Republic, the only officials other than the doge who are elected for life and are permanent members of the Senate. When a doge dies, the electoral college will almost always choose one of the nine to succeed him. I had no idea why the death of one of them should imperil me.

"Bertucci Orseolo."

"I do recall the name, sire." He was not one of the Maestro's patients, but he had been a client. I could recall transcribing his horoscope a couple of years ago. I could also recall the trouble I had had extracting payment for it.

Silence, except for the faint snip of scissors. Was it still my turn?

"I have never heard a bad word said about him." Apart from some I had uttered myself, that was.

"I have!" The doge chuckled. "Many. But he was a great fighter in his youth. And a fine servant of the state, a credit to one of the oldest families in the Republic. Older than yours, even."

I was never sure whether Pietro Moro was shocked or amused that his doctor's assistant was listed in the Golden Book.

"I am proud of my descent from the forty-fifth doge, Your Serenity, but my branch blew off the family tree a long time ago." I stand fourteen generations from Doge Renier Zeno. Although I do have rich relations, they were never close and they all became much more distant after the Turks stole Cyprus away from the Republic and ruined my grandparents.

The doge said, "Hmm!" which needed no reply.

Wealth is not the same as nobility. Most European aristocrats are descended from warrior barons, but the ancestors of our Venetian nobility were all merchant princes—sailors and traders, not fighters. Three hundred years ago the ruling families closed the Golden Book to newcomers, and since then many distinguished families have fallen into poverty, just as some outsider families have grown immensely rich. And yet, as long as a man is of legitimate birth and does not descend to manual labor, he can retain his designation of *nobile homo* and write NH before his name. The poor nobility are known as *barnabotti*, after the parish of San Barnabà, where most of them live, and they are numerous. In theory, when I reach the age of twenty-five, I will be eligible to take my seat in the Great Council and begin a career in politics, but a man without fortune or family cannot hope to be elected to office without endless kowtowing to his betters. The prospect held no appeal. One cranky master was better than twelve hundred of them.

The doge said, "I am almost out of the unguent." His back pains him, especially in damp weather.

"I have a note on my calendar to mix more and deliver it to Your Serenity next week. Should I do so sooner?"

"No. You will have more important things to do. Your master has a copy of *Apologeticus Archeteles,* does he not?"

"Er . . ." We were not alone. Either or both of the valets could be a spy for the Three or the Church. Pietro Moro shares the Maestro's passion for old books, but no one except high church officials may read books by the notorious Protestant heretic Ulrich Zwingli. Was the old man trying to trap me? Or test me? If he was just playing games, juggling sabers would be safer. Yet only the wiliest politicians ever get to wear the *corno*. Gruff and overstuffed though he was, Doge Moro was as wily as they come, and he must have some reason for his dangerous question.

Such problems are too complicated to analyze on an empty stomach.

"I do not recall any book by that name, sire. I will look when I get home." *If I get home.* "He is always happy and honored to lend Your Serenity works from his collection."

The valet was reaching under the massive ducal nose to trim minute amounts of hair from the ducal mustache, ending the conversation for a few moments. I was happy to wait. Attending the head of state's levee was more pleasant than rotting in his jail.

When the scissors had been put away and a comb run through the doge's beard, he could turn to frown at me. He raised a leg so a kneeling valet could drag a stocking over his varicosis. "Procurator Orseolo took ill suddenly at a private party on Valentine's Eve."

Sweet Lady defend me! Orseolo! My memory reported for duty at last.

"And about, er, two years ago I think, the Maestro cast His Excellency's horoscope . . ." I write out all his horoscopes in fair. I cast many of them, too, although the Maestro would do that himself for a procurator. "As I recall the problem, there was a conjunction of Venus and Saturn in Aquarius, his birth sign. The Maestro's exact words were that His Excellency should 'beware the coming of the lover,' sire."

His Serenity snorted. "You are wasted on that old fraud. You ought to be serving the Republic. There are ways to get a man of your age into the Great Council, you know."

"Your Serenity honors me greatly." I could also apply for a posting as a gentleman archer on a galley, which would certainly be more pleasant and likely safer than the free-for-all political games of the Venetian aristocracy.

"Bertucci died yesterday." The doge pushed a massive arm into the shirt a valet was offering.

Saint Valentine's day. "My master will be chagrined to learn that his warning was not heeded." I knew he would also be delighted to have his prophecy meet with such a spectacular and public fulfillment, although of course he would not say so, even to me.

"Oh, he knows! He was one of the guests in the Ca' Imer."

"A *guest*, sire?" Mere physicians are not invited to the nobility's frolics, not even physicians with international reputations. If they were, everyone would still exclude the Maestro, who has the social skills of a porpentine and either insults people or bores them to death.

The doge raised his chin so the valet could fasten his shirt buttons. "He was present, at least. You did not know?"

"No, sire." I had gone to my weekly fencing lesson and then squired a certain young lady to Carnival on the Lido. The Maestro had not told me that he had been out also, because he hates sharing personal information with anyone. He trusts me, it's just the principle of the thing. Bruno had not told me because Bruno does not talk.

"Of course," *Nasone* said, "when the procurator was stricken, the learned Nostradamus attended him. He advised that the patient be carried home immediately and his own physician summoned."

"Did he venture a diagnosis?"

"No, but everyone else did."

I had enjoyed very little sleep in the last two nights, which is my only excuse for being so obtuse that morning. That comment finally blew away my mental fog.

"Lord have mercy!"

"Amen to that!"

"Your Serenity cannot possibly believe—"

"No. No, I don't," the doge said grumpily, heaving himself to his feet. "I don't believe in claptrap about stars and birth signs, either. I do believe your master is the best doctor in the Republic, but he is also an outrageous charlatan with his almanacs and horoscopes—drivel from beginning to end; vague, shapeless, ambiguous, meaningless bombast. I'm sure he swindled dear old Bertucci out of a scandalous heap of gold for a scrap of parchment whose only value was to demonstrate your excellent calligraphy, *sier* Alfeo Zeno. But I do not believe Filippo Nostradamus would poison a man just to make one of his own rubbishy prophecies come true."

The valets had turned away to hide grins. Our beloved doge is an atrocious skeptic, as bad as any Protestant or

Freemason. His doubts are not confined to astrology; they extend to all supernatural matters, perhaps even to the spiritual, although even he would not dare admit that.

I could say nothing except, "I cannot believe it either."

"But the rumors have started." The doge shrugged to adjust the weight of the massive brocade robe his valets had just hung on his shoulders. "I think I can hold the hounds back for three days. No longer. You should be able to get safely away in that time, both of you."

"He won't go." I spoke automatically. The Maestro was old and almost crippled and stubborn beyond measure. I simply could not imagine him running away from a senseless, trumped-up charge of murder. *Wisdom had departed*, but I was certain he had not, and never would, flee from Venice.

The doge was scowling. "Then you'd best go without him, lad, because poisoning is classed as witchcraft. If he burns, you'll burn too."

"How do you know it was poisoning, sire, not just apoplexy? Even if it was murder, there were other people there. Don't you have to prove my master did it?"

The old man shook his head scornfully. "It's obvious because he was the only alchemist present. No, I don't believe that matters, but many people will, and the Three will certainly investigate any suggestion that a procurator has been murdered. I am one among many in the Ten; I have no control at all over the Three. I am taking a risk even telling you this. You have very little time. Get your master across to the mainland and safely over the border." He took a lurching step and winced. "Yes, I would appreciate a jar of the unguent as a going-away gift."

I bowed. "Today, sire."

The doge nodded and took another couple of steps. "Give him a lira, Jacopo." He spoke off-handedly, because that was his usual tip, then he chuckled. "No, make it a ducat this time. Sciara was a little over-zealous."

Before I could express the magnitude of my gratitude, he turned back to glower at me. "But I want my *Apologeticus Archeteles* returned. It's mine. I loaned it to him months ago."

"You did?" I said bitterly. That was not how the old rascal had told me to catalogue it. "Then I will find it and deliver it to Your Serenity."

3

I hurried along the loggia, down the giants' staircase to the courtyard, and out through the Porta della Carta, the main gate. The rain had stopped, but a chill wind still blustered across the Piazza San Marco. Clerks were hurrying to work, beggars were already on their stations, and hawkers with baskets on their heads called their wares. It was too early yet in both the day and the year for the gawking foreigners who usually abound. Normally I would have enjoyed walking home, along winding alleys and over innumerable bridges, savoring the beat of the city's great heart, but that day the situation was critical—had the Maestro truly fled the city? That seemed beyond all belief. The Ten would take it as a confession of guilt. I would be off to the torturers in no time and *sier* Alvise would hurl everything the Maestro owned out into the canal, cleansing his palace of the taint of murder.

I headed across the Piazzetta toward the Molo. Public gondolas are expensive. I cannot afford them and the Maestro won't, as he already owns one of his own and employs a man to row it. That day the expense seemed well justified.

Besides, I was a ducat richer. The Maestro provides my room and board—very sumptuously, I admit—but he is sparing, even miserly, when it comes to a clothing allowance. Almost all my spending money comes from the tips his clients and patients give me for performing my arduous duties—opening and closing doors, for instance, and bowing them out. That is the reason I do not flaunt my "NH." Some people are embarrassed to tip the nobly-born a *soldo* or two, or else consider my rank an excuse not to. You'd think they would reward me more, not less.

Yesterday's events now made perfect sense. Bells ring in Venice all the time, but the Maestro, already worried, must have recognized the tolling for Procurator Orseolo and known that his peril was now much greater. He had sent me off to chase wild geese while he consulted the crystal. A very fine prophecy, too—*Death* the murder causing *death* the death penalty to break cover but go after the wrong suspect. Venice as *La Serenissima*, the Most Serene Republic, is feminine. The *Serene One*, in masculine, would be His Serenity the doge, who had *moved* to send warning and remained *unmoved* by my protests. The *wise* Maestro had departed, leaving the *mute* Bruno behind. Very succinct!

There were dozens of gondolas tied up at the Molo. I picked out a man with arms like a Barbary ape and began haggling, accepting his second offer on condition he sing to me the whole way.

A few strokes of his oar swung us out into the choppy and iron-gray Basin of San Marco, a February desert. At other seasons it teams with great ships swaying at anchor, best seen all sparkly in misty morning light. Here the convoys gather for voyages to distant lands—Seville, Egypt, Constantinople, or far-off England and Flanders—hundreds of galleys, all identical, all state-built and state-owned, rowed by freemen mostly, not criminals, and every one captained by a Venetian nobleman. Here they return with exotic spices, sulfur, wine, olive oil, raisins, currants, timber, and dozens of other cargoes. As a child I dreamed of being the captain of such a ship and sailing to such places. Some days I still do.

Regrettably that morning there were almost no ships, my gondolier had the throat of a Barbary ape, and I was distracted by my worries about the Ten. I was not convinced that the doge could hold them back as he said he could, and I could see no possibility of persuading my master to flee the city. Nor could I imagine myself ever deserting him and running away. A man has to cherish his self-respect. I was caught in the jaws of a dilemma.

The quatrain had been magnificently fulfilled, so far as I could see, every line, but it gave no guidance on what was going to happen next.

When I paid off my gondolier at the Ca' Barbolano, I found the great doors open, and the Marciana family army busily loading a boat. I slipped by with a few cheerful greetings on the wing. Jacopo and Angelo Marciana are brothers of the citizen class, and partners of NH Alvise Barbolano in a type of arrangement that is quite common in the Republic: *sier* Alvise provides space in his palace for them and the business, plus certain hereditary trading rights that the nobility reserved to itself centuries ago. The commoners do the work and provide the capital. The Marcianas also supply the muscle power of a dozen sons between them. The profits are divided.

I ran up the stairs and was again lucky, in that I did not run into old Alvise himself, for he lies in wait for me whenever he wants a medical consultation with the Maestro, or celestial advice on his business dealings, or something to poison the rats, or just something. I must always be on my best behavior for our landlord.

The only person I did meet before I reached our door was Bruno, coming down with the usual love-the-whole-world smile all over his face. I have rarely seen anything as welcome as that smile. If the Maestro had mysteriously disappeared, Bruno would be out of his mind with worry.

From the dust on his shoulder, I could tell that he was in the process of ferrying firewood, of which several bales had been lying down at the quay. I have seen him run all the way upstairs with a load I can barely move. As I mentioned earlier, if Bruno were twins, they would still be too big. Sighting me, he grinned even wider and cracked his usual Alfeo joke, which is to pick me up and kiss me on the forehead. Resistance is futile. I have very rarely seen Bruno anything but happy, but when vexed he ranks with the primeval forces of nature. The Maestro invented a sign language for him and a written equivalent, so he can converse with us and even write us simple notes. In consequence, he absolutely worships the Maestro and is delighted to carry him wherever he wants to go.

When he set me down, he flashed the signs for *Happy— you—here.*

I signed *Happy—come back.* With a further exchange of grins we parted, me up and he down, but I was saddened to think that that was all Bruno could ever know of my midnight adventure.

Arriving at the apartment, I found Giorgio mopping the floor with the help of two of his sons. Giorgio is our gondolier, but he has many other talents, including an extraordinary fecundity. I have lost count of his children and would not be surprised to learn that he has, also. Some are out in the world making grandchildren already, yet new ones continue to appear regularly. He nodded a welcome to me, his silence somehow conveying relief that I was safe.

As for his assistants—Corrado and Christoforo Angeli are twins, although not identical, and at that time were engaged in a furious race to see who could produce a real mustache first. Never have so many sneers been directed at so little. Having to help with household chores ranks lower than being flayed alive, of course.

Corrado produced a lecherous leer. He said, "You had a good night, Alfeo?" and ducked so expertly that his father's hand whistled uselessly through the space his ear had just left.

"Very memorable," I said. "Would you tell the Maestro I'm back, please?

"And run!" his father said.

I poked my head in the kitchen. Noemi, a younger member of the Angeli brood, looked up from kneading dough and beamed at the sight of me. The current youngest, Matteo, lay under the table sucking on a bone. Their mother cried out a prayer of thanks and came for me with a bloody hatchet she had been using to chop veal. I returned her hug and bent to endure her kiss. Mama is as wide as Bruno but only half as high. She was due to produce another little Angeli very shortly.

"You are safe! Luigi said the night watch came. We found your sword on your bed. We were so worried!"

"No need to be. But I must shave and wash."

"Have you had breakfast?"

Of course not, and food is Mama's cure for anything and everything. I said, "What do you have ready?"

Instantly Mama rattled off a dozen choices while Noemi filled a jug with hot water from the kettle on the range. Mama is very efficient; it is she who keeps the Nostradamus household gliding along as smoothly as a gondola. She has been known to produce dinner, twins, and supper in the same afternoon. Settling for a *small* cup of soup, I headed off to my room to make myself respectable.

I had barely removed my shirt before I heard a familiar thumping and the Maestro hobbled in, wielding his staff. He avoids all unnecessary movement, so I was touched that he had made the effort to come and inquire after my well-being.

"Who was ransacking my atelier?" His voice tends to become shrill under stress. Acerbic, brilliant, cantankerous, duplicitous, and encyclopedic, Filippo Nostradamus has a great reputation and a large head, but the Good Lord skimped on the rest of him. Short and scrawny sums him up, and he wears a foolish goatee, which he dyes. His knees and ankles give him much pain, so he would do better leaning on two canes, but prefers an oaken staff taller than he is, inlaid with cabalistic signs in silver and topped by a large crystal. It impresses some people.

I sighed. "No one ransacked anything. Raffaino Sciara read the letter on the desk and took a quick look at the book shelves. Would you care to prescribe a soothing unguent for the lash marks on my back and the burns under my toenails?"

"Why did you let him in here?"

"Because he threatened to arrest me if I didn't."

"And then arrested you anyway? Bah! He was bluffing."

"Four swordsmen are no bluff."

"Arresting people is *Missier Grande*'s job. What did Sciara want?"

"He wanted to tell you something. It can wait." I turned my back and opened my shaving kit. The oaken staff thumped a few times on the terrazzo, then the door boomed shut.

I made a fast toilet, washing away as much of the prison frowstiness as I could while considering what I was going to wear. Between yesterday's rain and today's jail, I was running out of fresh clothes. I decided to poultice my wounded self-esteem by trying out my newest outfit.

Venice is the most beautiful city in the world, a fairyland of islands and canals set in an opalescent lagoon; it boasts a hundred great palaces and as many glorious churches, all of them treasure chests of incomparable art. Curious, is it not, that the people dress mainly in black? Lawyers, doctors, and widows wear black, as do the hordes of priests, nuns, monks, and friars. A nobleman wears a black robe, black bonnets, and a strip of black cloth, a tippet, draped over his left shoulder. Admittedly nobles holding high office bloom in reds and purples and everyone dresses up for Carnival. The only real exception to the prevailing drabness, though, are young men.

I cannot afford to dress in the silks and satins of the true aristocrats, but I emerged from my room resplendent in red knee britches, white stockings, a linen shirt with a modest ruff, puffed sleeves, and lace cuffs, a waist-length doublet striped in blue and white, ornamented with acorn-shaped buttons, topped off with a shoulder cape trimmed with squirrel fur and a bonnet like a gigantic blue puffball. On my way back to the kitchen I had to go by the mop-wielding slave gang, and I noted the gleam in Corrado's eye as I approached. The moment I passed, he predictably muttered something admiring about buns, and then yelped as the back of my hand cracked against his ear. Christoforo squealed with laughter.

Even Giorgio grinned. "Let that teach you not to sass swordsmen," he said. They are all impressed that a mere apprentice like me can take fencing lessons, but the Maestro pays for them because he is physically very vulnerable and works a dangerous trade. I have known him advise wives to stay away from their husbands for their own protection, for example, and that is an excellent way to make enemies.

Predictably, Mama had provided a bathtub-sized bowl of

pidocchi soup and a cannonball of mozzarella cheese, my favorite. When I let myself into the atelier, the Maestro was seated at his desk, peering into a book. Three more were stacked within reach, and I recognized them all as herbals. He scowled as I laid down my tray. He has so little interest in food that I keep track of his meals to make sure he eats at all.

"I can take it to the dining room if it bothers you," I said, "but on reconsideration, I think my news is urgent."

He pouted. "Sit, then." He pouted even more as he studied my appearance. "A gift from your friend?"

"Certainly not!" I pirouetted, to increase his enjoyment. "Most of last year's income and half of this year's. An apprentice who fails to flout the sumptuary laws reflects badly on his master." I sat down and tied a napkin around my neck to protect my freshly starched ruff.

The big double desk works well for us. We can pass documents back and forth readily. He is left-handed, I am right-, so we can both have light from the windows on our work. Noting that the medicinals I had bought the previous day had been removed, I started in on my delicious *pidocchi*, made from the sea louse, which is not as bad as it sounds, being a type of shellfish. Soup is easier to eat while talking than most things are—except when it is scalding hot, and Mama does make her dishes hot.

"So what was this message?" the Maestro demanded.

"I paid the gondolier five *soldi*."

His eyes glinted. "That's your privilege if you're too lazy to walk."

"True. But then I can't be here for another twenty minutes."

I spooned soup, smacking my lips to decorate the silence. I'm never quite sure when his crabbiness is genuine and when he's just staging a fit of pique for our mutual amusement.

This time he conceded the point. "Enter it in the ledger, then."

"Oh, thank you, master! Most generous of you. As you foresaw, we had an important visitor about an hour after midnight. I congratulate you on the quatrain. Admirable personification, antanaclasis, and metonymy." I gulped and winced my way through my soup and the events of the night while the Maestro never took his eyes off me. He kept his book open and his finger on the place.

"It was a charade, of course," I concluded. "The doge is the only permanent member of the Ten and Sciara has been *Circospetto* for years, so they must know how to work together. They want to give you a chance to escape before they are forced to open a formal inquiry. Sciara was mad that you were not here for him to bully. That's all."

"If you believe that, you're even more naive than you look." My master smiled, meaning he bunched up his cheeks and stretched his lips sideways without showing his teeth.

With saintly patience, I said, "If you had been home last night, Sciara would have given you the message and left, taking his guards with him. You weren't, so he made the point more forcibly by scaring me half to death. But the doge is insistent—you must flee!"

I could guess what was coming from the jutting angle of the goatee.

"No! I'm too old to start over somewhere else. There is my wealth—" He waved a hand at the bookshelves. "Will you carry them for me? And where will I find a new clientele, a new palace to live in, new printers for my almanacs?"

I sympathized. I did not want to run away either, to be a homeless vagrant. But the risk was appalling.

"Can you prove that Procurator Orseolo died of apoplexy or hemorrhage or anything other than poison?"

The Maestro removed his finger and slammed the book shut. "Of course not. As soon as I examined him I knew he had been poisoned."

I burned my tongue and spluttered. "Did you say so?"

"You think I am an idiot?"

"Not until now. It wasn't your doing, I hope?"

"No, it was not." The fact that he answered the question at all showed that he was worried. He could see his predicament; it was the solution he rejected.

I cut myself a hunk of bread and a wad of mozzarella. Needing some chewing time, I said, "If you didn't poison him, who did?"

"I don't know." He seemed to shrink slightly, unaccustomed to admitting ignorance. "Ottone Imer is an attorney of citizen class and a bibliophile with more taste than money. Alexius Karagounis is a book dealer from Athens. He had some rare volumes to offer—looted from some Macedonian monastery, no doubt. Imer invited a few of the city's most prominent collectors to view them at his house."

In this case *prominent* meant *wealthy*. The Greek would face tax or licensing problems if he tried to sell the books openly in the Republic. Imer had acted as official host in return for a commission, and the learned Doctor Nostradamus had been hired as a consultant to testify to the works' authenticity. He was a prominent collector too, but he could not compete with the truly rich. This all made sense.

"Did he have anything worthwhile?"

"Three or four minor pieces." My master sighed piteously. "An almost complete Book Ten of the *Aeneid* written in an uncial hand that cannot possibly be later than Eighth Century. Incredible condition, but unmistakably genuine. Possibly the oldest copy known. Then there was something that *might* be one of the lost plays of Euripides."

I gulped down my cud to ask, "Worth killing for?"

Another sigh. "If genuine it would fetch thousands of ducats."

"I would kill for that."

Nostradamus ignored my repartee. "I arrived early," he continued, "so I could view the books. I met Imer and Karagounis, and they showed me the manuscripts, all laid out on one long table. I inspected them and agreed that they all appeared to be quite genuine. I remained in my chair—and the Greek stayed with me as if he thought I might grab his treasures and run away with them! I resented his supervision at the time, but now I welcome it, for I cannot be accused of tampering with the wine. I was never near the wine! When the guests arrived, most were shown into the *salotto*. The prospective buyers came into the dining room to inspect the books with their glasses already in their hands. Eventually our host realized that I had not been offered refreshment and ordered the footman to bring me the wine of my choice."

"Then the books were auctioned?"

"Nothing so crass! Discreet negotiations were to be held later in the evening. When everyone had expressed admiration, we joined the ladies and other gentlemen in the *salotto* so the servants could lay out a supper in the dining room. Eventually we all went back there, but we had not even started on the antipasto when the procurator was stricken and we all went home." Again he sighed and his eyes grew quite misty. "The Greek still owns his books. But he is a foreigner. They will suspect him first." He was conveniently forgetting that he was foreign-born himself, although he had been granted full citizenship as a bribe to move to the city, many years ago. The Republic is notorious for luring all the best doctors in Italy to come and live in Venice.

I said, "The Greek is not an alchemist, and you are. Sudden death always provokes rumors of poison and most people cannot distinguish between poisoning and witchcraft. That was why you were so crabby yesterday. Also why you sent me out to buy half the poisons in the pharmacopeia—nux vomica, hellebore . . . You are planning to test each one to find out which creates the same symptoms? Shall I ask Giorgio to bring in his children?"

"Fool! I do not know why I put up with you. I knew at once." The Maestro leaned on his elbows and put his fingertips together, a sure sign that I was about to be lectured. His hands are as delicate as a woman's. "The patient was an elderly male of choleric temperament. He limped slightly on his right leg and had old trauma scars on his right hand, with some loss of mobility. These were likely related to his reputation as a former war hero. I detected minor flashes of irascibility and hints of dysphasia, which I posited as the onset of *dementia senilis*. They would not yet be obvious to the layman. His family probably just regarded him as testy. He began to show signs of distress at the supper table— profuse sweating and salivation. I was not at all surprised when he excused himself and got up from his chair."

"Nausea? Urination? The company would forgive an elderly man's need to visit the closet, surely?"

"But he stumbled as he turned. A footman caught him and of course I went to assist. I detected an extremely rapid and irregular heartbeat; also some vomiturition. The patient displayed confusion, not recognizing me although we had spoken only minutes earlier. He asked me several times why I was blue." The Maestro's little cat smile meant that it was time for me to interpret.

"Oleander poisoning?"

He nodded grudgingly. "A not unreasonable hypothesis. Many physicians would make the same mistake. But oleander induces retinal toxicity only in chronic cases."

So the blue illusion must be significant, but it was a new symptom to me. I thumped my brain to spill out whatever it knew about diuretics and expectorants. Nothing relevant appeared, but Gerolamo the herbalist had mentioned a laxative that might be appropriate. I made a guess.

"Virgin's glove?"

The Maestro's nod of approval was intended to mask annoyance. His hands withdrew into his lap. "Very good! Continue."

"Also known as fairy thimbles or witches' gloves or foxglove. In his celebrated *De Historia Stirpium Commentarii*, the learned Leonard Fuchs named it digitalis." Which was how it was labeled in the Maestro's collection—so why had he sent me to buy more, and under another name? "As I recall the medical uses of foxglove, the fresh leaves, when bruised, are efficacious in the treatment of wounds and the juice is used to relieve scrofula. Internally it can be taken as a laxative, but is unpredictable and dangerously toxic. What treatment did you advocate?"

He pouted. "I suggested that his own physician be summoned at once, as he would be more familiar with the procurator's regimen."

The first treatment for suspected poisoning is to induce vomiting, but the patient had been retching spontaneously without ejecting any matter. A rapid pulse would suggest that the patient should be bled, but he was elderly and might have unknown ailments. Even sips of water might have been dangerous. The Maestro had diagnosed murder and seen his own danger; any advice he had given would have been suspect. I could not blame him for taking the path of caution in this instance.

"Can you estimate when the patient ingested the poison?"

He shrugged. "He had obviously not eaten recently."

"You imply that he must have been poisoned after he arrived?"

"An obvious hypothesis. And whatever the toxin, it must be extremely potent to be concealed in a glass of wine. The learned Paracelsus wrote that anything is poisonous in sufficient dosage."

Worse and worse. "So there is no hope of laying the blame on tainted food in his own household?"

"No, and he had certainly not been munching on a salad of oleander. The dried and powdered leaf of digitalis can be prescribed for internal use, as a laxative, and it is rumored to soothe a raging heart. Possibly he took an accidental overdose, in which case we need not fear a murder charge. The man's doctor must be interrogated."

I said, "He's probably a Jew, in which case he has likely been arrested already. If I were one of the state inquisitors, I should now be putting Imer's servants to the question, especially the footmen who served the wine."

"But you are not!"

"Then why don't you offer one of the servants an enormous bribe to run away and take the suspicion with him?"

He shook his head, still angry. "No, we can ignore the servants, so—"

"Why?"

The Maestro matched up his fingertips again for another lecture. "Why should an attorney's footman want to murder a procurator? Only if bribed to do so by someone of high rank, and if he is fool enough to be still in the city, then the Ten can catch him and torture the truth out of him. The doge would not be warning me away if he expected that to happen. But even the Three will not question the gentry rigorously without good reason to do so, certainly not torture

them. The courtesans may not fare quite as well as the nobility, but even they——"

"Courtesans?"

He pouted. "There were several there. Your friend was
one of them. Is she capable of poisoning a man, one who insulted her, say?"

"Certainly. I'll ask her if she remembers doing so." Vio-
letta is a neighbor and the most prized courtesan in the city.
The lady and I are friends, but I do not employ her services.
One night with Violetta costs more than I earn in a year.

The Maestro pulled a sour smile. "Then you now have
two reasons to help me find the murderer. If I had the birthday and time of birth of everyone who was present, their
horoscopes . . . but the law will require palpable evidence,
either eyewitnesses or a confession."

"Denizens of the infernal regions must know."

"Don't be absurd!" He glared at me. "Beg my life from
a fiend? Don't you hear anything I teach you? I can't do
that."

He was hinting that I could. For me to try to save him
would be altruistic and therefore less dangerous. Not safe,
just less dangerous. Summoning is best done after dark,
when demons are more active and there are fewer people
around to catch you at it. I would decide then whether to
take the risk.

I thought of another problem. "How much foxglove
would be needed? And what does it taste like?" I rose to
reach for the *De Historia Stirpium Commentarii* that lay on his
side of the desk. "Would wine disguise its taste?"

"Sit down. You think I have not consulted the herbals?
Most poisons are vile-tasting, as you know, because they are
tainted by the Evil One. Foxglove is so bitter that livestock
will not graze it, whereas they do die from eating oleander.
The taste and dosage would depend on how the essence was

extracted. Steeping in water may be enough, or spirituous extraction followed by reduction. I shall conduct some experiments."

"If you have any sense at all," I said, "you will throw your entire supply in the canal and destroy the label on the bottle. Yesterday you sent me out to buy every nasty thing in the pharmacopeia. Was that a wise action?"

He bunched his cheeks. "I wanted to discover if digitalis is presently available in the city. Since only the murderer and I knew the poison used, I preferred not to advertise its name."

"Even if Gerolamo and the rest do not stock it, surely foxglove can be grown in any little garden plot. It likes sandy soil, as I recall."

As a feat of memory that remark was pure show-off, and his wizened little eyes tightened to show that he knew it. "But that would still be evidence of premeditation."

And oleander was common enough. "So anyone could acquire the plant. But who," I asked innocently, "could possibly have the arcane knowledge to extract and concentrate the venom? Or is this where we began this conversation?"

The Maestro scowled, because Italians are notorious as the poison experts of Europe, the Venetian Council of Ten has the same reputation within Italy itself, and the Council of Ten has been known to consult Maestro Nostradamus on such matters. And that, I realized, might well be what it was up to in the present instance, except that it was putting the demand for assistance in the form of a personal warning from the doge. That would explain why Sciara had felt justified in dragging me off to jail.

I opened my inkwell. "You will, of course, now write to the Lion's Mouth to report your suspicions that Procurator Orseolo died of an overdose of medicinal digitalis. You will have to sign it."

The *bocca di leone* is any of several drop boxes available in the palace to accept accusations of treason or other major crimes. Anonymous tips are supposedly ignored, but no one believes that.

The Maestro grimaced. "No. I despise men who work in silence and darkness. Very few people could have committed the crime. It must be possible to work out which one did. *Then* we can report to the Ten."

There is no use arguing with him when he sticks out his goatee like that. "We have two days." The doge had given me three, but I was allowing one for travel. I opened a drawer and selected a quill and a sheet of our best rag paper. "The attorney, Imer, is the man to start with. He must be quaking in his dancing pumps."

Maestro Nostradamus said, "Faugh! You still don't know how bad this is. Take a cheaper sheet."

I changed the paper.

"There were about thirty guests in all," he said, "but not all are suspect. Only the procurator was affected, so the poison was not in the bottle. It must have been put in his glass. It acts quickly but not instantaneously—I know that but the Ten do not. So the only persons who matter are those who came in to look at the manuscripts."

He leaned back wearing an expression of extreme smugness like a suit of plate mail. I plodded through his logic and decided it would have to do for now. I could not possibly question thirty people in two or three days.

"Clear crystal glasses, or colored?"

"Murano ruby glass. You could not tell what anyone else was drinking, and if the poison made the wine cloudy, that would not show either."

"And what sort of wine?"

"We were offered a choice of three: refosco, malmsey, or retsina. I had the refosco. It was a good jar."

He fancies himself as a connoisseur of wines. I plan to study them when I am rich.

"Refosco is red, malmsey a sweet white. The other one is Greek, yes?"

He made a steeple of his fingers again for a sermon. "Yes. Retsina is most vile, flavored with resin. Served in honor of the Greek merchant, I suppose. It is pungent enough to hide the taste of lye or vitriol, but few Venetians would touch it. Malmsey is so sickly it might suffice. Refosco would not. Let us review the suspects. I proclaim my innocence, and in any case I was seated behind the table. I could not have put poison in anyone's glass without standing up and stretching across, which would have been a very conspicuous action. Write my name in the first row.

"The Greek was in the room all the time. Our host came and went. As organizers of the affair, they must be suspect. Imer and Karagounis in the second row."

He closed his eyes to think. "I was early, as I told you. Imer and his wife greeted the guests as they arrived and saw that they were given wine. Most went to the *salotto*, only the book collectors came into the dining room. The first buyer to enter was Senator Tirali. He wished me well and at once walked the length of the table, on the far side from me, inspecting the goods. I felt like a shopkeeper!"

"I believe you, master." I knew of another Tirali, the senator's son. Neither was a patient of the Maestro's.

"Close behind him came Procurator Orseolo, leaning on a cane. He and Tirali greeted each other coolly. They were old rivals as collectors."

"Put Tirali in the second row?"

"I suppose so, but I doubt if their rivalry ran to murder. Orseolo had a woman attending him. I didn't hear her name and she stayed close to him. Next came a foreign couple, who did not introduce themselves to me. They spoke in French with barbarous accents, questioning me about the books. They knew nothing about books. All they were interested in was price."

I added them to the second row: *two foreigners.*

"Two footmen poured the wine. We should include them in the second row, if the Three have not gotten to them first." The Maestro opened his eyes. "Then *sier* Pasqual Tirali, Giovanni's son. With your friend."

I wrote Violetta's name in the first row and started a third for Pasqual Tirali, vowing to send him to the torturers for prolonged interrogation. I get twinges of jealousy sometimes, when I think of her evenings.

"They were the last to arrive. There was one other before them, Pietro Moro. First row."

I stood my quill in the inkwell, laid my forearms flat on the desk and glared belligerently across at my master. "You are hallucinating!" The nightmare had just turned into sheer terror, as nightmares do.

He shook his head smugly. "I warned you that you were being naive."

"Master, before a doge is crowned he has to swear an oath known as the *promissione.* It is no trivial matter. He swears to shun each and every mistake and crime of all his predecessors in the last thousand years. The *promissione* is read to him every two months during his reign to remind him. He can barely blow his nose without his counselors' consent. He must not leave the ducal palace without their permission. He must not meet with foreigners! He . . . I cannot imagine all the promises the doge would have broken if he went to that supper party!"

"He wasn't wearing his ducal robes and *corno.* I expect that's another. But Moro is a fanatical collector of books."

"Then why did the sellers not offer him a private viewing in the palace?"

The Maestro scowled horribly. "I do not know the answer to that. But I don't suppose for a moment that Moro is the first doge to slip out for an evening incognito, playing Haroun al-Raschid."

"And somebody tried to assassinate him? Is that what you mean? The poison went to the wrong man?"

The Maestro pursed his lips. "I wondered how long it would take you."

Even more aghast now, I said, *"The Serene One moves and is unmoved?* The procurator got the wrong glass and the poison meant for the doge? Is that what it means?"

"Possibly. A hypothesis to keep in mind. Even if not, do you see why I cannot write to the Lion's Mouth? The Council of Ten must not have cause to investigate the procurator's death, not officially. A suspicious death involving illicit acts by the doge may bring on a constitutional crisis, just when relations between the Republic and the Turks may be boiling up to another war. What you got this morning was not a warning, it was a cry for help!"

I stared down at my list, although I was seeing nothing. I did not want to see old *Nasone* either murdered or deposed, but all doges have political enemies. "Did everyone see him there?"

"Probably not," the Maestro conceded. "He came in, looked at the books quite briefly, and spoke with Orseolo. Then an argument broke out with the foreigners. I think he left then. He was not at the supper table later."

"What sort of argument?"

"The foreigners had not been invited. Imer told them to leave. Probably the doge had not been invited either. Faugh!

Moro has always been impulsive. He champs under all the restraints of his office, the eternal committee meetings. Read me the list."

Present and not suspected:
Dr. Nostradamus; Procurator Orseolo; madonna Violetta;
Nasone

Possible suspects:
Attorney Imer; Karagounis; Senator Tirali; two foreigners; a
woman; two footmen;
Pasqual Tirali

"You assume too much. Move your friend to the list of suspects."

I protested, "Did you see her tipping poison into the victim's wine glass?"

"Bah! Of course I didn't. I didn't see anyone doing that. I very much doubt if anyone did. It would be too obvious."

That had already occurred to me. "You said Orseolo had a crippled hand and used a cane. He must have laid his glass down when he wanted to handle one of the books? The others would too, perhaps, but he must have done so more often?"

My master nodded. I could see that he had been hoping to point that out himself.

"So," I said, "the murderer unobtrusively poisoned his own drink and then switched it for the victim's. Did you see that happen?"

"No," he admitted sourly, "but I was constantly being distracted by stupid questions. It is likely that somebody did. Tell Angeli you need him shortly."

I went over to the door and stuck my head out to tell one of Giorgio's brood to warn him. When I returned, the Maestro was staring fixedly at the window and tugging his beard.

I know better than to interrupt him when he is thinking on
that scale. I took up my knife to sharpen my pen.

Eventually he sighed and looked at me as if wondering
where I had been. "A letter."

I took a sheet of rag from the drawer and dipped the quill.

"About ten lines," he said, so I would know how to place
it on the sheet.

"Italic, roman, or gothic?"

"Italic, of course. 'To the exalted chiefs of the noble Council of Ten. Usual bootlicking . . . It is with deep sorrow that
I most humbly bring to Your Excellencies' attention certain
evidence pertaining to the despicable murder of . . .'"

4

Giorgio was ready in his standard gondolier costume of red and black, so we trotted downstairs and embarked. He is a wiry man and not tall. Standing in the stern of the gondola he looks far too slight to move a thirty-foot boat at all, but he is as proficient with his oar as he is at making babies. We skimmed off along the Rio San Remo, sliding between the traffic. The sun was shining with as much enthusiasm as it ever musters in February; bridges and buildings had a well-washed look. Women on balconies were hanging out washing, peeling vegetables, shouting conversations across and along the canal, lowering baskets to vendors in boats or on footpaths below them. Often they were singing. So were the cage birds, which had been brought out to enjoy the morning and tantalize the cats. Seagulls flapped clumsily or just stared. Almost all the boatmen were singing, too, when not fluting the odd cries they use to warn on which side they intend to pass. They say we have ten thousand gondolas in Venice.

"Is it true the Maestro was at the supper where the procurator died, Alfeo?"

Mama does the talking in the Angeli family. Most of the time Giorgio says little, although his silences have an uncanny knack of prompting other people to tell him secrets. He would not question me unless he were seriously worried.

I said, "He was taken ill at the supper. The Maestro went to help, as you would expect. The procurator died yesterday, at home, tended by his own doctor."

"Oh." Apart from returning hails from other gondoliers going by, Giorgio wielded his oar in silence for a while.

"The Maestro didn't poison him."

"Alfeo! I never said that he did! That's a terrible—"

"That's the rumor. It's a lie. Last night I was called in to the palace for a consultation. I was not arrested, not questioned. My arms are no longer now than they were before. Don't worry about it."

A man who has to support a two-digit family must worry about his employer's fate. Giorgio slid the gondola through a minuscule gap beside a farmer's boat already on its way home for the day. He ducked as we shot under a bridge. Then he had time to speak again.

"You are not nearly as good a liar as the master, Alfeo. You are worried, so I am."

"Then I confess! I'm on my way to tell the Council of Ten I did it."

The whole boat shuddered. "Don't make jokes like that, Alfeo!"

It was less of a joke than he thought, although I had no intention of posting the incriminating letter I carried. "How was the wedding?"

Family is one topic on which Giorgio will talk, and talk at length. His children are outnumbered only by his brothers and sisters; Mama has even more; add in aunts, uncles, nephews, and nieces and the wedding party must have outnumbered the Turkish army on campaign. Giovanni from

Padua and Aldo from Vicenza and Jacopo and Giovanni from Murano . . . He was still reciting the guest list when we arrived at our destination.

Ottone Imer shared chambers with several other attorneys in the maze of alleys in San Zulian, just north of the Basilica of San Marco. That the house included living quarters and premises grand enough to entertain thirty guests I took on trust from the Maestro's account. It is an expensive part of town, so either Imer had family money behind him or he was successful professionally. So why was he dabbling in the used book trade?

The black-clad clerk who peered disapprovingly at me over his glasses looked somewhat dusty and dog-eared himself, as if he needed to be taken down off his shelf more often. He conceded that the learned attorney was in, but that was all he would concede. If I wanted to get any closer to his employer, he suggested, I must state my business in some detail. The learned attorney was not, he implied, about to stop doing whatever he was doing to oblige a mere apprentice, even if, he hinted, the apprentice's master was a well-known charlatan dabbling in shady arts. I could make an appointment for next week, or Lent, or next summer, he intimated.

Attorneys do not usually turn down business sight unseen, but attorneys rarely have important nobles collapse at their supper tables in a hiss of dangerous whispers. Was Imer hiding from everyone or just from anyone connected with that unfortunate event?

I shrugged. "Then I must take the matter higher up."

The watchdog's manner grew even chillier. "Take it as high as you wish."

I produced my letter and held it where he could read the inscription. "Is this high enough?"

He had seemed pale before. He turned ashen and stumbled to his feet.

"Run," I said sweetly, and he very nearly did.

In moments I was ushered into the private office of Attorney Imer, which was dim, cramped, and untidy. The owner stood beside a desk heaped with ribbon-tied bundles of paper. Briefs seldom are. He was tall, severe, fortyish, and had an unfortunate tick at the left corner of his mouth. I wondered if it appeared when he addressed the bench, or if only mention of the Ten set it off.

I bowed. "At the *lustrissimo*'s service."

"My clerk said you had a letter to show me?"

He did not invite me to sit, so I sat. He remained standing, eyes icy, mouth twitching. He looked down his chin at me. Lawyers are very highly thought of in Venice, especially by other lawyers.

I said, "My master was the first physician to attend Procurator Orseolo when he was stricken, two nights ago. He was disturbed by the symptoms he observed—so much so that he believes it may be his duty to draw them to the attention of the Ten. He takes this step reluctantly, as you may imagine, knowing the suffering it may cause to innocent people. He is aware that there may be other explanations for what he saw, and invites you to go and discuss the matter with him."

Roses bloomed on the attorney's cheeks. "Blackmail? He plans to extort money from me?"

I have never known the Maestro to turn away money, but to say so just then would have been indiscreet. "*Lustrissimo*, I would not serve a master who committed such crimes."

"You prefer selling horoscopes?" Evidently Imer was a skeptic, like the doge. "Yes, the procurator took ill here, in my house. He died at home, I assume in his own bed. He was old. Old men do that. What is left to discuss?"

I stood up. "Evidence of poison. I thank you for your time." I started to turn, then had second thoughts. "Just out of personal curiosity . . . Is the servant who poured the wine your employee, or did you hire him for the evening?"

"You can take your personal curiosity to hell with you, boy, and keep it there."

"And the man with the big nose?"

The attorney's mouth twitched violently four times. "Let me see that letter!"

I passed it over. It was not sealed. He twitched six times while reading it. "Extortion! If your master wants to come here and ask some questions on a professional matter, I shall try to make time to see him. Ask my clerk to set up an appointment."

I shook my head. "My master has difficulty walking, sir. My orders are to take you back to visit with him or else drop his letter in the *bocca di leone*. You may come and watch me do so if you wish. My gondola is waiting."

"Blackmail, I say!"

"May the Lord be with you, *lustrissimo*." I held out my hand for the letter.

"Very well. I will come with you, so I can personally caution Doctor Nostradamus that he is violating serious laws."

He shooed me out ahead of him in case I tried to rummage through his briefs.

Imer might be doing well for an attorney, but the Ca' Barbolano overwhelms almost anyone. Sheer size, to start with. In a city squeezed onto a hundred man-made islands, space is the ultimate luxury and the Maestro's *salone* is enormous, stretching the length of the building. Huge mirrors alternate along the walls with paintings by Veronese and Tintoretto, chandeliers spread crystal foliage overhead, and the inhabitants on view are built to scale. Michelangelo's *David* from Florence stands nearest the door. Beyond him are

Sansovino's *Mars* and *Neptune* from the giants' staircase in the Doges' Palace, and the *Laocoön* from Rome. More titanic sculptures loom beyond these. All of them are copies carved in chalk, but the ones I can vouch for are very good copies; the rest are certainly impressive.

Ottone Imer made a cynical effort to shrug off the vista he saw from the doorway, no doubt assuming that Maestro Nostradamus could not possibly own all this and his real quarters were probably some servant's kennel under the roof. But when I showed him into the atelier, its display of books, charts, quadrants, alembics, globes, armillary sphere, and the rest told him at once whose territory he was on. There was no one there. I gave him a moment to gape at it all. *First impressions last*, my master says.

Belief begins with the wish, is another of his.

I conducted Imer across to the fireplace and the two green velvet chairs facing the window, the two reserved for visitors.

"The Maestro will be here directly." I went to the red chair, adjusted its position slightly, moved the candelabra out of the way, looked past our guest, and said, "*Lustrissimo* Imer, master."

"Good of you to come, *lustrissimo*. My legs are—"

Imer almost jumped out his seat. The door was across the room to his left, in plain view so he knew it had not opened, and the old man had not been there a few moments before.

Another cheap trick, alas. The old mountebank *can* move quietly when he wants, even with his staff. He would have had Corrado or Christoforo watching for our return. The wall of books is divided in two by a central alcove, which contains a huge wall mirror—a beautiful piece if your taste runs to the syrupy, being oval in shape, with a wide frame of mosaic cherubs and flowers. It turns on a pivot, providing access to the dining room—not truly a secret door, just an inconspicuous one.

He greeted his visitor with a twisted bow. I saw him comfortably seated and leaned his staff against the fireplace where he could reach it. He enjoys deference when we are alone and insists on it when we have company. Then I went to sit at the desk, where I could take notes if required or just watch the visitor's face.

Imer was scowling. "Trickery!"

The Maestro smiled ingratiatingly. "Of course, but effective." When he wants to, he can seem very old and small and vulnerable. "My sympathy on your supper party the other night. A most unfortunate—"

"Your apprentice threatened to denounce me to the Ten. I am contemplating lodging a complaint of attempted extortion."

Without turning to look at me, the Maestro said, "Alfeo, did you threaten the learned attorney?"

"No, master. I asked him if he would help you clear up a mystery before innocent people became involved. He agreed to come and see you." Just as I had agreed to go with Raffaino Sciara.

Imer's mouth twitched. "Criminal investigation is the responsibility of the state inquisitors, nothing to do with you!"

"We all have a duty to report evidence of crime," the Maestro said. "Are you sure there was a crime? Let me explain. When the procurator was overcome, I hurried to his aid as fast as I could. I detected symptoms characteristic of a certain poison. However—" He raised a tiny hand to forestall an interruption. "The substance in question is also a potent physic. The procurator was old and perhaps forgetful. If he accidentally took his medicine twice, or if he had an unusually severe reaction to the drug, which is possible, or if he had just opened a fresh preparation that happened to be a little stronger than intended . . . then there was no crime. We need to know if the procurator's own physician had prescribed this particular physic for him. You must know who was sent for that night? So will you tell me the doctor's name?"

"And then what will you do? Blackmail him as you have tried to blackmail me?"

The Maestro dropped his pathetic-old-man mask, shedding ten years and dropping his voice an octave. "Alfeo, you brought me an idiot. Put him back where you found him and give that letter to the lion." He reached for his staff.

"Wait!" Imer snapped. "I withdraw that remark. It was uncalled for and I apologize. What exactly are you proposing?"

The Maestro leaned back and studied him with distaste. Eventually he said, "I am proposing, *lustrissimo*, to wind up the medical case on which I was consulted in your house two nights ago. If I can satisfy myself that the patient died by misadventure, I shall so report to a certain senior magistrate who has already asked me, unofficially, to investigate the matter. It is my hope that the authorities will then be content to let the matter rest. If I do not, a formal inquiry will be launched. Then you, and I, and a great many other people, will be seriously inconvenienced, embarrassed, and disturbed. If that is what you prefer, then go away and stop wasting my time. If you want to have your skull crushed in a vise, you will be on the right track. Otherwise you should give me your full cooperation."

Twitch . . . twitch . . . "I shall answer any reasonable question, but without prejudice and only in strictest confidence."

My master sighed testily. "In a murder case? You know that you are talking rubbish. What was the name of the deceased's personal physician?"

Imer's face shone red with fury. He was a curiously bad actor for a man who must impress panels of hard-bitten judges for a living. Perhaps that was why he had gone into the used book trade. "I do not know. You were there also, so why don't you know? Senator Tirali took over, you will recall. He ordered *me* to go and fetch a litter! I sent a man to find one and then tried to calm the ladies, some of whom were very upset. Orseolo was taken home and everyone left."

"Not helpful."

"The best I can do. You want me to invent answers?"

"Was anyone else taken ill?"

"Not that I am aware of."

"Who was the servant who poured the wine?"

"There were two—Giuseppe Benzon and a man I heard called Pulaki, a servant of the merchant Karagounis, whom you met. Benzon has been in my employ for four or five years."

"Indeed?" the Maestro murmured. "Karagounis is from Athens, in Turkish Greece. Is this Pulaki also a Greek native?"

"I don't know."

"If so he would be a subject of the sultan. You let a subject of the sultan serve wine to, er, *Nasone*?"

Imer had seen that one coming and did not faint or cry out with horror. He looked as if he wanted to, though. "I did not invite that man to my house! His arrival was completely unexpected."

"But . . ." The Maestro shook his oversized head sadly. "Why don't you begin at the beginning and explain how you got yourself into this swamp?"

By now Imer was ready to clutch at any straw. "As you know, I am an authority on old manuscripts." Then why had he shown no special interest in the Maestro's book collection since he came in? "The foreigner Karagounis came to me with some interesting items he wished to sell. All looted from churches and monasteries, I'm sure. Since the Turks conquered Greece and the Balkans the Church there has been . . . not suppressed, but it doesn't flourish as it used to."

He babbled for a few minutes, telling us things we already knew, how foreigners were forbidden to trade, and how wonderful the Greek's manuscripts were. "You really doubt that *Meleager?*"

"Lost works by Euripides turn up all the time," the Maestro said sourly.

"But not with poetry like that! Several of the prospective buyers seemed to think it was genuine. It would have fetched a fortune! I couldn't possibly afford to buy it, but I did agree to help him in return for one of the lesser pieces, which he withheld from the sale, and I intended to bid on a few of the others. I approached the top ten collectors in the Republic . . ."

The Maestro turned steely-eyed at not being ranked in the top ten, but did not interrupt the flow.

"Eight were interested enough to view the collection. Six said they would make offers. Procurator Orseolo and Senator Tirali both said they would come in person. The others appointed agents to bid for them. I asked a few friends . . ." Imer had invited some people he wanted to impress and his social triumph had turned into nightmare. "And yourself, Doctor." He dried up.

"The doge was one you had shown the books to?" the Maestro asked.

"And his agent was there. I never expected him to come in person! He didn't stay long."

"And the foreign couple who spoke French?"

Imer shook his head. "I have no idea. They seemed to think it was a public gathering. When I realized . . . I ordered them to leave. The man was abusive, but they left."

"You offered three wines."

"There were to be others at supper. Karagounis provided the retsina. He said it was better than any in the city. Vile stuff. I never touch it."

I was careful not to show any reaction and the Maestro certainly did not, but he chased the ball.

"Who else drank retsina?"

"How should I know?"

"What happened to wine that had been opened and not finished?"

"I expect the servants stole it. They usually do."

"What do you know about this Karagounis?"

The attorney squirmed. "Not very much. He is planning to marry a local girl, so he can become a resident. He is taking instruction in the Catholic faith and plans to abjure the Greek heresy . . . So he says. I warned him it would be better if he did not come to the viewing, but he turned up anyway."

"Has he chosen a bride yet?"

"I believe so." The attorney colored, which suggested that the bride was part of the deal, some niece or cousin, no doubt. He was not old enough to have marriageable daughters to dispose of.

But that seemed to be that. The rest of the Maestro's questions produced nothing of use. Imer had been dashing back and forth between his books and the main party and could not say who might have been close enough to tamper with the victim's drink. If he was representative of the Republic's attorneys, I hoped I would never need to sue anyone.

"Well, we may be worrying needlessly," the Maestro said. "I must track down the procurator's physician. My boat is at your disposal, *lustrissimo*. Alfeo will come with you as a witness when you question your servant."

"Benzon? Why?"

"If we learn that other people drank from the same bottle as the procurator, we can eliminate one unpleasant hypothesis." The Maestro stretched his lips in a smile.

The attorney grimaced as if he had a serious toothache.

Giorgio rowed us back. He sang a couple of romantic

ballads in case we wished to talk confidentially, but Imer said absolutely nothing, except to tell me Karagounis's address when I asked for it.

The moment we entered his chambers, he ordered the old clerk to fetch Giuseppe Benzon, an order that obviously surprised the old man. This time I was invited to sit in a client's chair. Moving like an old man, Imer walked around the cluttered desk to his own.

"If we frighten Benzon so much that he runs away, we shall be in grave trouble."

This was precisely why the Maestro had specified that Imer ask the questions, not me. I said, "You are entitled to interrogate your own servant, *lustrissimo*." If the servant did flee, that admission of guilt would rescue the Maestro from suspicion, but might not help Imer much.

Benzon was about my age, a stocky, honest-looking lad with a smear of jewelers' rouge on his hand to suggest that he had been cleaning silverware. He looked reasonably scared already by the unexpected summons. He bowed and was told to shut the door, but not told to pull up the third chair.

"As you know," Imer mumbled, "one of my guests took ill two nights ago. All he had consumed in my house was some wine, and the doctors are wondering if there was something wrong with that particular bottle. Do you happen to remember which wine the procurator chose?"

"Yes, *lustrissimo*. He laughed and said he would take the retsina."

I was already impressed by Benzon. His eyes were quick and he did not fidget.

"Thirty-two guests and you remember what every one of them drank?"

"No, *lustrissimo*. But he was only the fourth or fifth to arrive, and I never served a procurator before." Procurators wear marvelously ornate purple robes and tippets.

"Did anyone else take the retsina?"

"Three or four, *lustrissimo*. I had to open a second bottle."

Imer's glance at me was a comment that the first bottle was therefore not available as evidence, and I nodded.

"Pulaki brought six bottles. Where are the others?"

"His master told him to take them when they left."

"Well, apprentice? Have you any questions to ask?"

I could think of several. Being neither a state employee nor a doctor in the case, I had no right to ask any of them. Procurators do not joke with other men's menservants.

"My name's Alfeo, Giuseppe."

Benzon eyed me uncertainly. "Yes, *lustrissimo*."

"Just Alfeo. How many glasses could you fill from a bottle?"

"About six, if the glasses were all empty. Topping them up, I would get more, of course."

"That's good. Thank you. You said the procurator laughed. Did he come alone, or who was with him?"

"A young lady."

"Hot?"

Lechery flickered in his eyes. "Fiery!"

"Courtesan?"

"No, er, Alfeo."

I met Imer's frown. "Any idea who she was, *lustrissimo*?"

He shrugged. "I forget. Granddaughter? Niece?"

"No further questions, thank you."

5

I told Giorgio the Karagounis address, which was close by, in the Greek quarter of San Giorgio dei Greci. The Greek ought to be even more susceptible to bullying than the attorney had been, but I had very little hope that these interviews of the Maestro's were going to do any good at all. Had I been present at that book viewing and seen two people exchange glasses and one of them had then died, I would not admit to noticing anything at all—not at this late date. Had I poisoned one of the glasses myself and switched them deliberately, I would be even more taciturn. But an apprentice does what he's told. Maybe my master would come to his senses in a day or so.

When we arrived at the door—Giorgio knows every building in the city—I shouted up to a woman drying her hair on a second floor balcony.

"Top floor," she said.

"You watch out for her, sonny," said one on another balcony. "She lies in wait for the young ones."

The first countered: "No, you stop in at her place, handsome. She's the one who gets lonely."

"You can share me," I suggested, earning whoops of approval from spectators at other windows.

Giorgio said, "Good luck. Their husbands carry knives, you know."

"Husbands or not," I told him. "I won't be long." There were other gondoliers waiting nearby, so I knew he would not lack for conversation.

The stairs were dark and narrow, smelling of urine and unfamiliar cooking, as tenement stairs usually do. I met no husbands and no one lay in wait for me. Top floor was four up, and I slowed to a walk for the last flight, so I would not be short of breath when I arrived. I had a choice of three doors. The first did not answer my knock. Nor did the second, but a woman shouted from inside it, and then told me to try the one opposite, which was the one I had already tried.

Either Alexius Karagounis was out trying to sell his books elsewhere or he had already fled from the Republic. I went back down again. No lonely housewives or knife-bearing husbands detained me.

When we returned to Ca' Barbolano, the Maestro had already retired for his midday nap, having skipped or just forgotten dinner, as he often does. I carried an armful of books into the dining room, where Mama delivered enough food to feed a galley crew after a long day: marinated anchovies in caper sauce, rice with peas, and tuna with polenta. Then she asked what *dolce* I wanted.

"I cannot possibly eat all this," I complained. "I had that *pidocchi* earlier, remember?"

"Eat it! You are too skinny!" Compared to her, everyone is too skinny.

"I am not as skinny as Giorgio."

"Bah!" she said. "Forty years I have lived in this parish and never a fat gondolier have I seen."

"He doesn't get enough sleep."

She shook her fist at me and waddled out, chuckling. I ate alone, reading everything known about digitalis.

I went to my room, bolted the door, and changed into shabbier clothes that I did not mind dirtying. My room is not the largest or grandest I could have, but I enjoy the view from its three big windows, which look out across a forest of chimneypots towards San Marco. Most houses are two or three stories high, so the churches, bell towers, and palaces stand up like islands in a stormy sea of red tile roofs. More particularly, my windows overlook the roof terrace of Number 96, and that scenery becomes spectacular on warm days, when the residents sun themselves there. They wear hats with wide brims and no crowns, spreading their hair out to bleach it without browning their faces. That day the terrace was deserted, except for some laundry drying.

The *calle* between the two buildings is very narrow and little used because it is a roundabout way of reaching the campo, while the wider one on the far side of 96 is straight and also leads to a bridge. Although my windows are about fifty feet above the ground, they are secured by stout iron bars. I opened the center one and peered out, provoking an explosion of pigeons. Three of its bars can be removed just by lifting them out of their sockets and leaning them against the sill—inside the room, of course, so they cannot fall out and drop like iron javelins to impale passing citizens. I wriggled through the gap and set my feet on a hand-width ledge just below, while keeping a firm grip on the bar that does not move. Then I made one long, death-defying stride to the steep tiles opposite, where I could sprawl forward and grab the rail around the altana to stop myself sliding off and making a nasty stain on the ground.

Yes, I could have gone downstairs, out the watergate of Ca' Barbolano and in the watergate of 96—there is no real pedestrian *fondamenta* flanking the Rio San Remo, but there are ledges along both buildings just above high water and the manoeuver is not difficult for an agile person. I prefer my secret route, though, and like to think I am deceiving the Ten's spies. Besides, a man must keep up his reputation.

I unlocked the trapdoor and trotted down several flights of stairs without meeting a soul. Number 96 is owned jointly by four ladies, although many more live and work there. Violetta occupies the best suite, in the southwest corner, and I have a key to its servants' door. Peering into the kitchen, I found Milana struggling to iron a bulky brocade gown that probably weighed nearly as much as she did. Milana is small and has a twisted back, but she is fiercely loyal to her mistress and I have never seen her unhappy.

She jumped. "Alfeo! You startled me."

"I do it just to see your smile. Is she up yet?" Courtesans go to bed at dawn, like the gentry. I also wanted to know if she was alone, of course, but that went without saying.

With a doubtful frown, Milana said, "Just a moment and I'll see," and disappeared. In a moment she returned, smiling again. "No, it's all right. I told her you were here."

I thanked her and went through to Violetta's chamber, entering just in time to catch a tantalizing glimpse of bare breasts as she pulled the sheet up—her sense of timing would be the envy of any high-wire sword juggler. Her room is vast and luxurious, decorated with silk and crystal and ankle-deep rugs, plus gilt-framed mirrors and erotic art.

Other nations denounce Venice as the most sinful, vice-ridden city in all Christendom, claiming that we have more prostitutes than gondolas. Such talk is sheer envy. We are just less hypocritical about our follies, that's all. Noble ladies see nothing wrong with a young blood squiring a courtesan to a ball or banquet—they would much rather he flaunt his current plaything in public than debauch their daughters in secret. Many noblemen never marry at all, supposedly to protect the family fortune from being divided between too many heirs, or else just to avoid the fuss and bother.

Harlots to suit every purse are available at Number 96. Violetta is not one of them. She is witty, highly educated, a superb dancer and singer. The stage lost a great actress in her, and it is tragic that Titian did not live long enough to immortalize her beauty. She is not available by the hour or the day, rarely even by the week. She accepts no money, only gifts—an emerald necklace here, a dozen ball gowns there—and the state treasury itself would not buy her favors for a man she did not fancy. Violetta dresses as well as any dogaressa or senator's wife, and owns more jewels than the Basilica San Marco.

I am not and never have been one of her patrons, but we are friends. We are frequently *close* friends, especially during siesta, when we both have time to ourselves. Love was not what I had come for that day and I saw at once that it was not immediately available, for she was Medea, teeth and claws, green eyes smoldering. In truth her eyes were not, and never are, green. They are all colors and no color. They change all the time, but at that moment they had a greenish tinge, which is a danger sign. I seated myself on the end of the bed, safely out of reach, and smiled stupidly at her glare.

"Who was that slut I saw you with on the Lido two nights ago?"

"I wasn't there," I said. "It was some other man. I was masked, so you couldn't have recognized me. And she is not a slut. Michelina Angeli. Her mother asked me if I would take her there as a treat for her fifteenth birthday. She will be betrothed soon and wanted to see Carnival on the Lido."

"A *virgin?*" Medea asked with disbelief like a blast of Greek fire.

"I didn't ask her. If she isn't, then it won't look like me. Besides," I added, "how did you recognize me?" I had certainly not noticed her among the hundreds of masked revelers.

"I would know those gorgeous calves anywhere." She laughed and melted before my eyes, becoming Helen. Helen of Troy, that is. Violetta does not play roles, as an actress does. She truly is several different people by turns. She says she cannot control her changes, they just happen, but I have rarely seen the wrong persona appear for any given situation. Medea's voice is hard and metallic, Helen's low and husky. Even her face is softer, more rounded. As Helen, she is the most beautiful, desirable, and skilled lover in the world. As Medea she is as dangerous in bed as she is anywhere else.

Helen held out her arms to me. The sheet dropped, of course. Encrusted in her finery, Violetta can be the cynosure of a ducal ball. I cannot begin to describe her appeal when she is still warm and drowsy and flushed from bed, still smelling of sleep, wearing nothing under a silken sheet. Her natural hair is middle-brown, but she bleaches it to a reddish gold. For formal affairs she dresses it in two upstanding horns, but then it hung tumbled loose in thick waves. I wanted to plunge into those waves and drown.

"Please!" I begged. "Business first."

"You are *not* business, Alfeo Zeno! Don't you dare be business! You are strictly pleasure. Every wife in the city has a *cavaliere servente*. Cannot I?" Her eyes were dark with promises of unimaginable delights.

I needed digitalis to soothe a raging heart. "Very soon, beloved, you will have the finest lover in the Republic all over you, but I do need some serious talk first. Noble Bertucci Orseolo died, did you hear?"

"And people are whispering that he was poisoned by your master to fulfill his own prophecy. I sent him a note yesterday. Didn't he tell you?"

"Not directly. I was out shopping."

"It's absurd! An old man drops dead and everyone suspects poison."

"It was poison."

Helen sighed. Reluctantly she pulled the sheet up and straightened her legs. Her face and voice changed again. She become thinner, and I recognized the one I call Minerva, after the Roman goddess of wisdom. The Greeks knew her as "Owl-eyed" or "Gray-eyed" Athena. Violetta's eyes were gray and the mind behind them blazed. "That is terrible news. Can I help?"

"We think the venom was in his wine."

"A poisoned glass substituted for his?" Typically, she had worked that out faster than I had. Minerva may be even smarter than the Maestro.

"It would have to be done that way, we think. I know you can take one glance at a ballroom and describe every gown to the last stitch. Can you tell me who stood next to Orseolo at the book table?"

She did not deny my exaggeration. "Let's see . . . I came in on Pasqual's arm. Don't pull faces. You know how I earn my living. We were on our way to the Lido, but his father was going to be buying old books. Pasqual wanted to make sure the old man wasn't blowing away the family fortune, he said. We stayed a few minutes and then left.

"As we came in, the viewers at the table all had their backs to us; your master was opposite, facing us. On my left . . . a footman was refilling glasses for the procurator and his companion, or offering to. Of course he was the one who collapsed later, Orseolo. Then that awful English couple—"

"Ah! The ones who spoke in French? Do you know their names?

Stars twinkled in her heavenly eyes. "I do know their names, Alfeo, but Parisians would not know their French. He is *sier* Bellamy Feather. Her name is Hyacinth. They have rented an apartment in Ca' della Naves over in San Marcuola. Protestant heretics, probably spies."

That was bad news. If even Violetta thought they might be spies, the Ten's informers would be crawling around them like flies on a dung heap.

"Next to them was the swarthy Turk . . . and an old man wearing senatorial scarlet. He had a big nose. Next to him there was a gap and then Pasqual's father. We went to the gap, of course, and Pasqual asked if he was going to buy Cleopatra's diary." She smiled knowingly. "I pretended not to recognize the nose on my left. He kept his eyes on the books and ignored me."

"Then he's older than I thought." In fact, having access to Pietro Moro's medical files, I knew that he still engaged in sex, although not as often as he would like. Doge or apprentice, some problems are universal.

"You knew *Nasone* was there?" Violetta asked.

"The Maestro told me. It is a complication. Have you ever seen him skulking around incognito before?" She had been to a thousand balls and banquets for every one I had.

"Never."

I tucked that piece of information away to deal with when I was less distracted by shadows through silk. "The Turk you mentioned was probably the book seller, a Greek named Alexius Karagounis. You did not know Procurator Orseolo, so you did not know the lady with him?"

Minerva-Violetta shook her head. "A girl. No older than your alleged virgin. Not a courtesan."

"A lover or a relative?"

Violetta would certainly know. The Maestro had not noticed her, but if Orseolo had recently acquired a lover, that would have fulfilled the prophecy in his horoscope. And she would have been close enough to switch glasses.

"Most likely a granddaughter. If they were lovers, she would have had to work hard."

"You are an amazing witness!"

Minerva was amused by my praise. "People are my business, Alfeo dear. They moved around, though, and I can't remember all the moves. Our host came in briefly and left again. Orseolo and the girl walked down to the far end to see what was there. And there were the two waiters. Don't forget them."

"I heard there was just one footman in the room."

"Now you know that there were two. One was stocky, about your age, with eyebrows almost as sexy as yours, and the other middle twenties, slender, dusky, looked like a Moor. Ah! Yes!" Her eyes grew as bright as they would be when she put belladonna in them that evening. "When we arrived, we were offered a choice of three types of wine. You think the poison was in the retsina?"

"Probably. But other people drank it, too."

Her eyes went out of focus for a moment. "I think . . . Yes, when they offered refills, the waiters came around with a bottle in each hand. Yes, I'm sure. Two waiters, three wines, four bottles. Does that sound suspicious?"

"You amaze me. You should be elected to the Council of Ten!"

Minerva said, "Only if I get to choose the other nine," with a hint of Helen in her voice. "Alfeo, suppose the Moor is a spy for the sultan and tried to poison the doge?"

"By the Moor you mean the dusky footman with the unsexy eyebrows?"

"His brows were moderately sexy, just not to be mentioned in the same sigh as yours."

I had not realized how much my eyebrows contributed to my celebrated good looks. I made a note to examine them some time. "Assassinate the doge and the Great Council will at once elect a replacement."

Violetta is the supreme courtesan because she is whatever woman her current companion requires. Mention politics and she is Aspasia. Where Minerva is imperious, brilliant, all-knowing, and tolerates no disagreement, Aspasia is cultured and subtle, her voice infinitely persuasive.

"The doge does have a significant influence on the conduct of foreign affairs," Aspasia said, "although the Senate can overrule him. Pietro Moro is respected and has a following. He is standing up well to the saber-rattling from Constantinople, so his successor might be more malleable, but that certainly would not be true if the assassination were exposed. Then the explosion of anger in the Republic would guarantee the *corno* going to an even harder-liner, and the Sultan will be worse off than before. Of course that might be the purpose—faking a botched attempt on the doge's life to win support for his policies. I wonder what England's position is in the current crisis?"

"That's too complicated for a simple apprentice boy. Which wine did you drink?"

"The refosco. An indifferent brand. Pasqual took the retsina."

I hoped his share had contained a slower-acting version of the poison. "You have been a great help. I have to speak to everyone who was in that room to find out what they saw, just as I have heard the Maestro's version and now yours. If the Ten—" I was silenced by an irresistible need to yawn.

"Too much Carnival?" Aspasia asked sympathetically. "How much sleep last night?"

"Very little," I admitted.

"Reclassifying your virgin, I suppose? Hard work."

"No! I kept dreaming of you and waking up weeping that you were not there at my side."

She hoisted a skeptical eyebrow. *"Iuppoter ex alto periuria ridet amantum."*

"Ovid. 'Jupiter laughs on high at the perjuries of lovers.'"

"Not bad! When do you ever get the time to read Ovid?"

"Never. You quoted that to me the first time we met."

"Oh, of course!" Her smile was Helen's. "I was bleaching my hair on the *altana* and a madman came leaping across the *calle*. Before I could even scream for help he vaulted the rail and knelt at my feet to offer me a rose."

"And told you that you were the most beautiful thing he had ever seen."

"He was young and quite beautiful himself."

"He swore to love you forever. And he has not touched lips to any other woman since."

She was pleased, not convinced. "None?"

"Not seriously. I had to fight off a lust-maddened virgin two nights ago, but I thought of you and lost interest. Jupiter has stopped laughing. He weeps for me."

I waited breathlessly to see who would respond to my plea. Minerva is intellect incarnate, sprung from the head of Jupiter, eternal virgin untouchable. I did not feel strong enough to deal with Medea, who is daunting, demanding, and deadly. Aspasia would either talk me out of it or cooperate for her own purposes while despising my animal lusts.

"What nonsense! Go home. This is siesta and you need to rest."

"I have urgent work to do," I agreed, but my feet were

already kicking off my shoes, because that had been Helen's voice.

"I will waken you." She threw the sheet aside.

The rest of my clothes hit the floor in a blizzard and I had her in my arms. When we paused in our kissing to draw breath, I said, "You are very generous, giving charity to a poor apprentice."

"Charity? With other men I must serve, but with you I can just be myself and enjoy. I need you to keep reminding me that men can be lovable. You know," she murmured, turning her lips away as I tried to claim them again, "what I love most about you, Alfeo darling?"

"Tell me." I nibbled her ear.

"That you aren't jealous. That you never judge. That you never nag me to reform."

Reform and marry me, a pauper? Live by selling off her wardrobe over the next ten years? I loved her because she did not try to buy me, as she so easily could. If she insisted I become her pimp, I would have to obey. If she thought I was not jealous, she was crazy. She was crazy, but I learned long ago not to yearn after things I cannot have.

"I would probably die if you did reform," I said. "And while you sin, I want to sin with you. You can have all of me, my darling, every bit. I will settle for as much of you as you can spare."

6

A man can have few experiences more pleasant than being wakened by a kiss from a beautiful girl when he is lying naked in her bed. Before I could get my hopes up, though, I realized that the woman bending over me was wearing the habit of a nun of the Carmelite Order. Some houses dress less strictly than others, and in this case my initial mistake was understandable, for her veil hid nothing and her bodice not much. I screamed and grabbed for the covers.

"Whatever is wrong?" Deviltry danced in Helen's dark eyes. "I have never known you to be shy before."

"I thought I was about to be raped. What time is it?"

"Time for you to meet an important witness. After you collapsed and left me to amuse myself, I recalled that Alessa used to know an Orseolo. So I went and asked her, and he belonged to the correct branch—Enrico, Bertucci's son."

I slid off the bed and began to collect my clothes. Alessa is a former courtesan who retired from the profession when she turned thirty or so, and is now one of the co-owners of Number 96. She runs the on-site business, a stable of a dozen or more girls.

"How much did you tell her?" I asked nervously. If my interest became widely known, whispers would start that the Maestro was worried by the whispers, and that would do his reputation no good.

"Just that you were upset by the rumors and wondered if there was anyone who might have wanted to kill the old man. Alessa is clever, though. She guessed right away that you were moved by more than idle gossip."

"I know and love madonna Alessa, and have great respect for her sagacity and discretion." I dragged Violetta's hairbrush twice over my tangled mop, gave up, and stuffed it all inside my bonnet. "Lead the way, Sister Chastity."

We went along the corridor to Alessa's corner of the house, where we found an Ursuline abbess laying out sweetmeats and glasses. Alessa is still on the bouncy side of forty and a very appealing woman, somewhere between buxom and statuesque, well worth a cuddle. The cut of her habit was no more discreet than Violetta's.

"What has caused this shocking outbreak of piety?" I demanded, and gave her an endearing kiss. My enthusiasm must have been convincing, because she cooperated until Medea began making menacing throat-clearing noises.

Mother Alessa recovered her breath and said, "Our new Carnival costumes were delivered and we decided to try them on. How do we look?"

"Inestimably pure and holy. You will drag saints down off the steps of the Throne of God."

"Vi, we should set him up as a friar. We could tonsure him!"

"Or a Turk?" Violetta suggested. "We could get a rabbi from the Ghetto Nuovo to—"

"No you couldn't!" I said firmly, sitting down and accepting a glass of Alessa's excellent marsala. "I like me just the way I am. I have to get back to work. Reverend Mother, please keep this a secret, but the Maestro believes that the procurator was indeed poisoned, as the gossip says, although definitely not by him. What can you tell me about him?"

Alessa is another lost actress. She raised her gaze to Heaven, clasped her plump, soft hands, and began to speak with a sonority worthy of Holy Writ. "Bertucci was a very upright man, honest and devout, a generous benefactor to the Church and the city. A *good* man! He won great distinction in the Cypriot war. He was widowed years ago. He is survived by his son, Enrico, and two grandchildren. I have been trying to think of anyone who might hate him enough to murder him and honestly cannot."

"You were close to Enrico?"

"He kept me generously for several years, until his father heard about our nest. He disapproved and insisted I leave. Then he arranged for Enrico to be elected rector of Verona and shipped him off to the mainland." Alessa sighed for wasted opportunities.

Verona is a tribute city of Venice, of course.

"When was that?"

"About four years ago. Bertucci did not have me thrown out in the canal; he allowed me a month to make other arrangements. He was stern, but never vicious. Enrico told me more than once how the old man's war wounds caused him great pain, yet he never complained. And you tell me somebody murdered him? This is a terrible thing."

The Church would call Alessa a fallen woman, and yet I believed that she was sincere. The crusty old trooper came alive for me in her words.

"And children?"

"Very tragic. His oldest son died at sea. Another was killed by janissaries in some stupid brawl in Constantinople. Both his daughters died when the Convent of San Secondo burned. Enrico was the only one left to him."

"So tell me about Enrico," I said. The heir to the Orseolo fortune must be an obvious suspect, even if he had not been present at the supper party. "Does he engage in politics or just run the business?"

"Both. He's been very successful in politics. His father was a fighter, but he is a conciliator. The Great Council approves of men who build bridges instead of burning them, and Enrico could walk across the lagoon without rippling the water. He served a term as a lord of the night watch in his twenties, four or five terms as a minister of marine, and twice as rector of Verona. Now he is one of the great ministers."

I had not found Enrico Orseolo conciliatory in my few encounters with him. His father had commissioned a horoscope from Maestro Nostradamus. After I had delivered it and asked for payment, the old man had told me to collect from Enrico. Enrico had refused to pay and threatened to have me thrown in the nearest canal.

"I've heard him touted as a likely member of the Council of Ten," Aspasia said. "In twenty years or so he'll be elected procurator to succeed his father."

"Did he and his father get along?"

Alessa shrugged. "Fairly well, considering how different they were. He could never replace his martyred brothers, of course. And the age gap was so great. Enrico is . . ." She mused. "Enrico is hard to describe. He shows the world a cold outside, like crystal plate mail. Yet he is passionate. I assure you, he *is* passionate! I have known him to weep with happiness after making love, spilling tears on my breasts. He wanted to defy his father over me, and I had to persuade him that his career was more important than a mere concubine. And business is hard now . . ."

Neither Violetta nor I said a word. Alessa perforce continued.

"Not just the House of Orseolo. A hundred years ago the

Republic was great, and the Orseolos were great, but then the accursed Portugese found a way around Africa and now the Dutch heretics are stealing our spice trade. Every mercantile house has been declining. The last twenty years have been especially hard for some, but the old man perhaps did not see this as well as he should. He may have blamed Enrico unfairly."

"Enrico was not there that night, so far as I know," I said. "Vi?" She had thought of something. I recognized the glow of Minerva's eyes.

"Who was the girl with the old man on Valentine's Eve?"

Alessa frowned. "How should I know? Young?"

"Yes, but old enough to turn a man's wits. Not a courtesan."

"Ha! I doubt most greatly that old Bertucci ever glanced at a courtesan in his life. He disapproved of lechery. Most likely you saw his granddaughter, Bianca. Enrico has two children, Benedetto and Bianca. Benedetto is studying law in Padua, I believe."

"And their mother?" Violetta asked.

Alessa sighed. "I never met her. Her family had money, whereas Ca' Orseolo was one of the oldest houses in the Republic, fallen on rather hard times. She brought him a legendary dowry, but she never even tried to make their marriage work. So he told me." The courtesan smiled. "Believe as much of that as you want. She died about a year ago."

Even if she hadn't, an unhappy wife is more likely to find consolation with a *cavaliere servente* than poison her father-in-law. I was no nearer to finding a motive for the old man's murder.

I rose. "I must go, Reverend Mother. I have an appointment with the cardinal-patriarch, who is looking forward to hearing my confession. I am very grateful for your help. It definitely merits another kiss." I demonstrated.

"Gratitude can be overdone!" Medea dug claws into my arm. "You mustn't take up too much of the cardinal-patriarch's time. Come along."

As usual, she tried to persuade me to take the orthodox road home, because my route is even trickier in that direction, requiring a run down the tiles to gain speed for an upward leap. As usual, I pointed out that I would give away the secret if I was often seen going from 96 to the Ca' Barbolano and never in the opposite direction.

I did reach the ledge and did catch hold of the bars before I ricocheted off. Had I not, I should not be telling you this. I changed and hastened to the atelier. The Maestro had been busy, for his side of the desk was littered with books and several pages of scribbles left on my side were recognizably draft pages for next year's almanac, waiting for me to find a few hours to transcribe their snail tracks into legibility. There was also a scrawled note about Isaia Modestus, the second-best physician in the Republic, which I deciphered.

"You want me to transcribe this into a letter?"

The Maestro looked up vaguely. "What? Oh, no. Just go and ask him those questions. And hurry. I have more important things for you to do than waste time on murders."

I said, "Yes, master," very sweetly, and headed over to his precious book shelves.

He watched angrily as I recovered the *Apologeticus Archeteles* from its hiding place.

"Where do you think you are you going with that?"

"*Nasone* wants it back. He also wants some of the balm of Gilead and mustard seed ointment. This should be a good time to catch him, because the senate will adjourn after the tributes to Orseolo. He was a witness, so he may have seen something suspicious. Will it be all right if I take him the batch I prepared for madonna Polo and mix more for her this evening?"

The Maestro growled approval. "What did you learn from your friend?"

"Not much." I had not told him where I was going, but it does not take a great sage long to guess how a young man will react when given an excuse to call on his lover. I went to the alchemical bench, noticing that the jar of digitalis leaves was missing and the other jars had been spread out to hide the space. I made a mental note to dust all the shelves that evening. While spooning the unguent into a fresh container with a spatula, I narrated the little I had learned at Number 96.

"Of course the woman, or girl, was his granddaughter," the Maestro conceded angrily. "When he took ill, she got to him even before I did, and she did address him as 'Grandsire.' I barely noticed her in the book room. I had to keep answering questions."

"Even so, it isn't like you to miss a pretty girl." I got no reply. Maestro Nostradamus has no interest in pretty girls. Or pretty boys. Books, now, or a shapely alembic . . .

Back at the desk, I wrote out a label for the ointment. I also made a note in the book catalogue that the Zwingli volume had been returned to its owner, and corrected the original entry. Having replaced the catalogue in its hidden compartment, I wrapped the book carefully and tucked it in my satchel with the jar.

By the time I had done all that, the Maestro was again engrossed in his papers, quill flying, ink spraying. I left quietly, locking the door so he would not be disturbed. Giorgio and his slave gang were still at work in the *salone*—as a matter of honor the twins would have done as little as they dared while their father was away that morning. When he saw my satchel, he began to lecture them on the terrible things that would happen if they slacked off again. I saved their day for them.

"I'd like some help, too," I said. "Unless you'd rather wash floors?"

"We'd rather be burned at the stake," Corrado suggested. He is the leader. Christoforo is larger and stronger but does what his brother tells him, never learning who gets punished for it.

"Or row a galley," Christoforo added, "single-handed."

"No. I need you to find Doctor Isaia Modestus for me. You know him?"

They both insisted that they did. They were not as certain as they pretended, but everyone in the Ghetto knows Isaia.

"He may be anywhere in the city," I explained as the four of us trooped downstairs. "Start at his house; they'll give you an idea where to try next. If you can find him, then I want one of you to stay with him, but keep the other one informed where he is, understand? And that one is to be at the gate of the Ghetto Nuovo when I get there, ready to lead me to the good doctor. Your father will probably have to wait for me at the Molo for some time, so you can report to him there if your quest takes you to that end of the city. Yes," I added before they incurred Giorgio's wrath by asking, "you will be richly rewarded."

"How much?" Corrado demanded eagerly, and this time failed to move his ear faster than the back of his father's hand.

7

In no other state in Christendom could I have walked into the ruler's palace without having a pike or something worse thrust in my face, but no one challenged me as I mounted the steps of the watergate and strolled along the passage into the great courtyard. It was bustling, of course. There are always people going about the Republic's business there, and I remained invisible among them. I climbed the censors' staircase to the second story, walked along the loggia to the incredible golden staircase, and climbed the first flight of that. But that brought me to the door of the equerries' hall, and there I did have to stop and explain myself.

Six old men were waiting ahead of me, all white-bearded, black-gowned *messere*, no doubt intent on paying their personal respects to His Serenity on the death of his friend. Three equerries were keeping watch on them from a polite distance, but my luck was holding, because one of them was my friend Fulgentio Tron. There was no sign of my jailer from the morning, old *sier* Aldo Somebody.

Fulgentio wandered over to meet me with a quizzical look in his eye. We live in the same parish, are the same age, and share the same fencing tutor. He has even been known to beat me with the rapier or épée. To be honest, he lucks out quite often, but not *always*. The main difference between us is that although his family is only a minor, obscure branch of the enormous and ancient Tron clan, it has more money than the Pope. I had seen much less of him since he was appointed ducal equerry, around the last Santa Barbara's day.

"I heard you spent the night here," he murmured.

"Some of it. Nothing serious."

"Nasty rumors going around about your master."

"Nasty and unfounded."

He nodded with a glance at my satchel. "I'll try and get you in sometime before Judgement Day. Meanwhile you'll have to sit here and not fidget."

"They've changed the pictures. May I look?"

He brightened. "By all means. Come and tell me if you think this *John the Baptist* is really by Carpaccio." A love of great art is something else we have in common.

Halfway around our circuit of the walls, he presented me to the equerry in charge—who looked all of eighteen—and explained that the doge's doctor required me to deliver all medications directly to the patient but I wouldn't need more than a minute. It does help to have influential friends. Three more black robes tottered in and were seated with the rest. Then another equerry entered by the inner door.

"That means he's on his way." Fulgentio led me in that direction. "He has his own staircase down from the Senate."

"I do appreciate this," I said. "I'd have been there for hours. I hope those nine ancient worthies don't make trouble for you."

"They can't. He has to change his clothes before he sees anyone. You're not anyone." His grin held no malice.

"Thanks." In fact, as the doge's sometime masseur, I had seen him with no clothes on at all. He changes them several times a day and his choice of garb is always carefully noted. He can insult a nation by wearing the wrong socks when meeting with an ambassador. Fulgentio escorted me to the room I had visited that morning and departed with: "Jacopo will take care of you."

Jacopo regarded me with distaste, knowing that I was not good for a tip. "His Serenity may be some time. How can I help you?"

"You can bring me supper later. Luckily I brought a book to read."

Knowing which book that would be, he grimaced. I left it in my satchel and resisted the temptation to try one of the doge's silk-covered chairs. The paintings on the walls were interesting compositions by artists I did not know. I was just edging my way to the nearest one when the doge marched in, monumental in gold state robes and *corno*.

He said, "Alfeo?" in surprise and turned his back on my bow. "You came to say goodbye?" He began rearranging his draperies. Jacopo waited, holding the ducal chamber pot at the ready.

"No, Your Serenity. But I brought the unguent you requested, and the book."

"Leave them over there. Your master thinks he can defend himself against a charge of poisoning?"

"Yes, sire."

I heard a familiar sound. His Serenity sighed happily. "How? The man had a stroke, that's all. How can you prove a negative?"

"By proving a contrary positive. May I ask Your Serenity a couple of questions that may be vital to the security of the Republic?"

"And more likely are not. Ask."

"You have met the attorney Ottone Imer?"

"Yes."

"Offered a choice of refosco, malmsey, or retsina, which did you choose?"

Grunt. "I never drink retsina except with a certain friend I expected to see there. I knew he would choose it, so I did, for old times' sake. We used to drink it together years ago during the Cyprus campaign. It still tastes like turpentine."

"Yes, sire. That is the whole point."

He had completed his business. Jacopo put away the chamber pot and began assisting him adjust his draperies. It was a few moments before the doge turned to scowl at me. "What are you blathering about, Alfeo?

"Could Your Serenity have switched glasses with your friend?"

"Mother of God!" The ruddy ducal complexion paled visibly. "He really was poisoned?"

"My master believes so."

The doge sank onto a chair, official business forgotten. "What evidence has he?"

"His professional opinion, sire—his *medical* opinion." Not something he had read in the stars, I meant. "He detected symptoms of a certain drug. That is why he asks if you might have accidentally switched glasses with the procurator."

Nasone pondered for a moment. "I cannot swear we didn't. We looked at some books together."

"But you noticed no sudden change in the taste of the wine? You had no intestinal problems later, no irregular heart beat or excessive saliva?"

Mention a symptom to some people and they will at once imagine experiencing it, but Pietro Moro is the least suggestible of men, a human barnacle. "No. I hardly touched it before I spoke with Bertucci. When we had finished our discussion, I gulped down the rest and left."

"Who could have known Your Serenity would be there?"

He leaned back and glared at me. Legally doges may be

figureheads, but they usually get what they want. They do not appreciate being cross-examined by mere apprentices.

"Only Bertucci himself. This is your master asking all this, not just apprentice Alfeo Zeno wasting an afternoon to get out of honest work?"

"I am here by his leave and will report every word to him, I swear."

He stared hard at me. "We are both liable to get in trouble over this, lad. We ought to be singing this song to the state inquisitors. And they may be a lot less gentle with you than they will be with me."

I said, "The matter is still in doubt, sire. The drug my master detected can also be a physic and we have not yet learned whether or not Procurator Orseolo's physician had prescribed it. If he had, then the procurator's death might have been due to an accidental overdose."

Moro grunted again. "Listen, then. The Imer man wrote to tell me he had some rare books for sale. I sent for him and looked them over. Most were the usual monastery scrapings—tedious preaching by long-dead bores. But there were a couple I found interesting. One was a fine fragment of Virgil's *Aeneid* and the other was a play I did not know, which Imer claimed was a lost Euripides. It looked exciting, but of course I was noncommittal. I named an agent who should be invited to the general viewing and might bid on my behalf. At the end of my meetings that day, I found a note from Bertucci Orseolo confirming that he would be going to the sale in person. He had heard disturbing rumors about Imer and wondered if the books were all they seemed to be."

So that was how it had been done? The doge must have seen a reaction in my face. He paused, but I outwaited him, all eager and expectant.

"It was too late for me to be sure of getting hold of my agent to change my instructions. I decided to go and see for myself if there had been substitutions made. There had not. Your master agreed that the Virgil was a very early, very valuable copy. He said he thought the *Meleager* was just Hellenistic imitation. So did Bertucci. I was not at all sure I believed either of them, but a doge must not risk being made to seem a fool, so I had a footman fetch my agent, told him not to bid on the Euripides, and left. You're suggesting I was lured there to be poisoned?"

The valet was chalk-white.

"I think the possibility should be kept in mind, Your Serenity."

"Bah! A doge is not a king. I have no real power. Why should anyone try to assassinate me, huh?"

"Ambition, sire? Terror? If the sultan can strike you down, he can make other rulers tremble."

"Ridiculous! That's far-fetched. And I *very* rarely go charging out of the palace on a whim, Alfeo."

"Of course not, sire. But if you had been taken ill later, you might not have mentioned that you had done so. It is only a theory so far, I agree. Why should anyone want to kill the procurator either? My master believes he was poisoned in that room."

"Bah! Your master claims to be able to read the future, too. The past is usually a lot easier." Pietro Moro glared at me, his mouth moving as if he wanted to grind his teeth. He heaved himself to his feet, and paused. "I won't accept any babbling about planets, but if my old friend Bertucci really was murdered, just tell me who did it and I will see his head roll across the Piazzetta, understand? I don't care who he is!"

"I understand, sire."

"Tell Sciara when you have anything to report. Jacopo, give him a lira."

I bowed and withdrew—with my lira.

* * *

The short winter day was already ending when I boarded the gondola at the Molo.

"Where to now, Your Excellency?" Giorgio asked.

That was a good question. "No sign of those two fine boys of yours?"

"None."

"I still need to see Karagounis." He lived quite close. "But Doctor Modestus is more urgent and I must consult him before they lock up the Ghetto. I don't want to kill the horse, though." The Ghetto is at the far end of the Grand Canal.

"It's a good, strong stud horse, Alfeo. This is my job." Giorgio is far stronger than he looks. He worked the gondola out into the Basin and then began swinging his oar like a fly whisk, stooping into every stroke, overtaking everything in sight. Admittedly he did not try to sing at the same time.

There is no finer street in the world than the Grand Canal, whose waters lap the doorsteps of gilded palaces and bustle with boats of every kind—gondolas, galleys, barges, rafts, and skiffs. I have never seen it look more beautiful than it did that evening, lit by the low sun and a-sparkle in its own strange light. We passed by the Customs House and a succession of great family houses—the Giustinians', Corners', Darios', Barbaros', the House of the Duke of Milan, and many more. We swept past my birth parish of San Barnabà, where the *barnabotti* brood in their embittered poverty, and then more palaces, the new Rialto Bridge coming into sight, a single great arch of marble double-edged with shops. Beyond the bridge and around the second bend we passed the great markets, stripped now of their morning crowds, and then another magnificent parade of palaces escorted us to the Canal Cannaregio, where we turned off to follow lesser ways to the Ghetto Nuovo.

Ghetto is a Venetian word, of course, and a concept that has been copied by many other cities, but Venetian Jews fare much better than most. Christoforo saw me and came slithering through the throng that was streaming in and out of the great gate, shouting my name and grinning with delight at accomplishing his mission.

"He's still in there. Come along!"

The Ghetto is a warren of narrow *calli* and a central *campo* seething with people, almost all of them Jews in their required red hats. The buildings are higher than anywhere else in the city; there are shops and stalls everywhere, but no church, no wayside shrines. The women wear bright clothes and jewelry—rings and chains of gold—and some are very beautiful. Christoforo slipped through the crowd like a minnow, so I was hard put to keep up with him, but he led me unerringly to the door where his brother waited.

"He's still here," Corrado said. "Five floors up, he said."

I told my helpers where they could find their father and solemnly handed them four *soldi* apiece. Belatedly wondering at my chances of getting that back from the Maestro, I began my climb. At the top of the first flight up I heard and then saw the second-best doctor in the Republic plodding down toward me, bag in hand.

Isaia is narrow-shouldered and stooped—almost hollow-chested—with a permanently worried look, which he claims increases the fees people are willing to pay him. He dyes his beard gray to look older, is armed with a sense of humor deadlier than a bravo's stiletto, and plays the deadliest chess west of Cathay.

"Alfeo! Your helpers assure me that your master is well."

"Much better than he deserves. If he weren't, you are certainly the one he would send for."

"Why not a restorer of antiquities?" He showed strong

teeth in a smile. "So you must be the one with a problem. A case of the French disease, is it?" We were nose-to-nose in a dingy, dimly lit stairwell that bore a strong smell of old cooking. It was an odd place for a medical consultation.

"No. Chastity and frequent self-flagellation protect me. The Maestro wants your opinion on a case."

Modestus rolled his eyes. "The Lord's wonders never cease. This is only the third time he has done that and I must have asked his advice two dozen times. I shall be happy to do what I can. Will you tell me here, or shall we go to my house?"

"Here will do well. The subject was an elderly male of choleric humor. He limped slightly on his right leg . . ."

Isaia listened without comment, but I could soon sense that he had guessed the name of the deceased. When I had finished, he said, "Those symptoms sound to me like poisoning with the herb digitalis."

"Not oleander?"

"Possible. Digitalis more probable."

"My master's opinion also. Treatment of choice?"

He sighed. "Very difficult in a man of his years. He was already trying to vomit, so perhaps water, as long as he was capable of swallowing. The point is moot, though, isn't it? His doctor bled him that night and again the following morning, then attributed the subsequent death to old age."

"You are ahead of me," I said. "I was going to ask you the doctor's name so I could find out what medicines he had prescribed, if any."

"I am still ahead of you, but I feel unhappily close to betraying a colleague." The gloom did not hide Isaia's discomfort. "He is a good man, although he was a better one twenty years ago. He, too, asked my opinion of the case this afternoon."

"Why consult you if he believed the death was natural?"

"He was having second thoughts about it, although fox-glove had not occurred to him. When I suggested it, he admitted he had never prescribed it in his life or seen its symptoms. I advised him to take his suspicions to the Ten."

"Will he?"

Isaia laughed. "What do you think?"

But now that Isaia had confirmed that there had been murder done, I had no excuse not to do so. I could feel thin ice cracking under my feet.

"I am very grateful and will tell my master. Also, I ask a more personal favor. There is an attorney named Ottone Imer."

Isaia is much too quick-witted ever to hesitate. His pause was deliberate.

"I have heard of him." The near-darkness emphasized how resonant and compelling his voice is. Usually it is soft, a comforting bedside voice, but now I heard the steel in it, warning me off.

I said, "I heard rumors that he is heavily in debt."

Even in the Republic, which tends to listen to its purse more than its Pope, officially only Jews lend money, and moneylenders are as secretive as doctors or courtesans.

"This is important, Alfeo, or you would not ask?"

"It may turn murder into treason. That could not make the crime more serious, but it might save some innocent people from suspicion."

Isaia sighed. "Then I agree that it is important. I will ask around. They will tell me if I say it is important, and I will let you know very soon."

I thanked him, aware that the Ten's spies might take many days to dig out what I was going to learn "very soon" and Isaia's information might be better than anything they would gather.

"And now you should go, gentile," Isaia said, "or you will be locked in with us unbelievers all night and have to eat my wife's cooking and play chess with me and evict my children from their bed and worry your master."

"You make it sound very tempting, doctor," I said.

8

Giorgio was still at the quay, standing within a group of gondoliers and listening more than talking, as always. He strolled over to meet me.

"No boys?" I asked.

He gave me a blood-chilling look. "You didn't give them money, did you?"

"You think I am an idiot? A half-witted softhearted troublemaker?"

"How much?"

I dodged the question. "Not enough to buy them any serious trouble. I expect they'll be here shortly, I just have to visit the Ca' della Naves and I can walk there from here. I won't be long." I fled the field.

Like almost any father, when his sons are old enough to earn money at odd jobs, Giorgio insists they turn it in as part of the family income. Corrado and Christoforo, for instance, had been working on and off at the building project on the other side of Rio San Remo. I felt he should let them keep at least some of their wages, else why should they bother? But it was none of my business and I must not meddle in his affairs.

The mysterious foreigners who had gate-crashed the book showing lived a few minutes' walk away, so I might as well go and see them. Had I been offered my choice at that point, I would have spoken with the procurator's granddaughter, the mysterious Bianca, who had probably had more opportunity than anyone to tamper with his wine, but the Orseolo family was in mourning and I had no authority to intrude.

As I hurried through the darkening *calli* of San Marcuola parish, I worried how much things had changed the moment Isaia confirmed that the procurator's death was murder. I had a clear duty now to report that fact to the authorities. Of course an apprentice is bound to obey his master, so I might argue that I must report to the Maestro first, but I did not think that excuse would weigh very much with the Ten.

And what if the Maestro refused? If he still insisted on trying to find the killer by himself, he would be courting disaster. His efforts to unmask the murderer might well be seen as an attempt to bury evidence, not uncover it. Or we might scare the criminal into fleeing beyond the reach of justice. Then both of us would find ourselves where I had been that morning, in the Leads. If that shock didn't kill the old man outright, the disgrace would ruin him. *Sier* Alvise Barbolano would evict him, his clients desert him.

But I hate to start something and not finish it. So does he. *Half-done is do,* he tells me often enough. He had occult tools that the Ten did not, or at least would never admit to using. Even I could invoke a fiend, and that might be less dangerous than what I was doing now, meddling in the Ten's business.

And then there were the doge's parting words: *I will see his head roll across the Piazzetta.* The doge did not trust the Council of Ten to see justice done. The Ten are politicians, all seventeen of them, and the other sixteen are eagerly planning promotion to higher office. They lust after votes in the

Great Council, and if the murderer turned out to be a patrician, then the nobles of the Ten would be wary of antagonizing his relatives and friends.

I peered into the parish tavern, partly to see if the twins were there, which they were not, and also to inquire which apartment in the Ca' della Naves was infested with heretics. The drinkers gave me the information I wanted plus some seriously disapproving looks.

As I started up the stairs in the big house, I began to have misgivings. The Republic's attitude to foreigners is complicated. For centuries, pilgrims have passed through Venice on their way to the Holy Land, and there are state officials, *tholomarii*, stationed at San Marco to take care of them, to see that they find proper housing and transportation. The inns they use are carefully regulated and, although they do have to pay more for goods and services than residents do, they must not be cheated any more than the law allows. On the other hand, the senate is very wary of foreign politics. Contact between Venetian nobles and foreigners is strongly discouraged, and is actually illegal in the case of foreign ambassadors. A nobleman can be put to death just for meeting with a foreign ambassador in private. Feather was not an ambassador, but a procurator had been murdered. What I was about to do began to seem foolhardy.

I was very close to talking myself out of my mission when I heard voices just above me, one more flight up. Not just voices, but a woman shouting a barbaric guttural rant that I could barely recognize as French. I swallowed the bait and took the rest of the stairs at a trot.

Thus do the stars dictate our lives.

She was just inside the door. He was just outside it. She was one of the largest women I had ever seen, so much taller than I that at first glance I thought she must be wearing the stilt shoes of a courtesan. She was blonde, not just Violetta's bleached reddish gold, but a Germanic ash-blonde displaying a complicated sculpture of silvery curls on which balanced a tiny bonnet. A high fan-shaped collar formed a backdrop, her neckline was surprisingly demure, yet her gown was a voluminous mass of purple brocade and gold lace that would have been denounced by the Venetian Senate as absurd extravagance. It was not, obviously, a local costume. Her eyes were the watery blue of sapphires and her cheeks were flushed with anger.

He was clutching a parcel with both arms and prepared to defend it to the death. She was speaking *loudly* and *clearly*, so his failure to understand her was pure perversity.

"Madame!" I proclaimed in French, offering a gymnastically low bow suitable for reverence to a goddess. "May I be of assistance?" I added in *Veneziano*, "Shut up and let me deal with her."

She uttered a satisfied, "Ha! At last! You speak French, monsieur!"

Better French than she did. "A little," I said. "Is this oaf causing you trouble?"

"He has brought our costumes for Carnival and refuses to give them up without payment, although we had made an agreement with the seamstress."

I understood the problem already, but decided to spin it out. *"Talk back and threaten me,"* I shouted in *Veneziano* so broad that even a Paduan would not have understood. *"Slum-dwelling, dung-eating spawn of a canal rat, you insult the madonna?"*

His response flaked plaster off the walls. He was either a lot more skilled at invective than I was, or just well worked up already. Fortunately he had his hands full and I had two to wave, which evened the odds a little. I responded and we screamed at each other for a few minutes. Then I turned to the lady.

"Madame," I explained calmly. "The wretch expects to be

paid for delivering the goods, as if one glimpse of your divine beauty should not be sufficient recompense in itself. Permit me to settle the matter."

I palmed him half a lira, which was five times what he was demanding and ten times what he had expected. *"For the lesson in abuse,"* I bellowed, waving a fist. *"You have the foulest mouth it has ever been my privilege to meet."*

He thrust the package at me and slunk off as if I had whipped him, calling back curses over his shoulder. What he actually said was, *"Blessings on you,* lustrissimo, *and give the foreign mare the ride of her life."*

Hyacinth said, "Oh! What a disagreeable man! That was most kind of you, m'sieur. If you will wait a moment I will find my purse."

"I should not dream of accepting one *soldo*, madame. The honor of being of assistance is recompense enough. You are the Contessa Hyacinth of Feather, are you not, the celebrated English beauty I came to meet? Permit me." I offered another bow. "Alfeo Zeno, assistant to the celebrated Maestro Nostradamus, clairvoyant, physician, astrologer, philosopher, and sage, honored to be at your service, madame."

Even in distant England, they knew that name. A tiny frown ruffled her eyebrows. "Nostradamus died years ago."

"Not Michel Nostradamus, but his even greater nephew, Filippo. You met him two nights ago. And he has talked of little else since."

"He has?" She peered down at me suspiciously.

My hopes of being invited inside were fading. "He was at the book viewing. You spoke with him."

"Oh, that shriveled little gnome behind the table? I asked him if he was the clerk. He didn't speak like a Frenchman."

She was not the first person I had heard say so. Loyalty has always forbidden me to ask. "He is an expert on old manuscripts."

"You are selling manuscripts? Why didn't you say so sooner? Come in, monsieur, er . . ."

"Zeno."

She let me enter and locked the door, then marched me through to a roomy, but rather cluttered *salotto*, whose furniture looked as if it had been rented in the Ghetto, although I could make out little by the light of a single oil lamp. She bade me sit and brought me a glass of malmsey with her own soft, white, shovel-sized hands. She strode around like a musketeer and declaimed louder than a sergeant drilling a platoon. Statuesque, she was. She would have been right at home embracing Mars on the giants' staircase.

"Sir Bellamy went out to call on some dealers, monsieur. We had promised the servants a night off to enjoy Carnival and Sir Bellamy always keeps his word, although without Domenico it is difficult for us to manage by ourselves."

Her clothes and hair styling were wrong and I could not read her signals. It was unheard of for a lady of the Republic to entertain a man in her husband's absence and the absence of servants made the unspeakable unthinkable. Romantic near-darkness would normally turn hint into blatant invitation. Perhaps this was normal social behavior in cold, foggy England, or perhaps she was confident she could knock me senseless with a single blow if I tried anything. Who was Domenico? She was still proclaiming.

"That disgusting exhibition the other night was quite typical. If any Englishman spoke to us the way that vulgar Imer man did, Sir Bellamy would have given him a thorough thrashing. And if he didn't I would. But it is a joy to meet a man who understands French."

I suspected that many others did but were unwilling to swim against her accent. "Is it that you have traveled widely, madame?"

"Just France and Rome and Savoy and Tuscany. We

brought letters of introduction from many respectable people, including several members of the English and French nobility, you understand, but the recipients have not responded
warmly." She pouted. Her lips looked like ripe plums in the
dusk.

"You find our city appealing?"

"Most beautiful!" she said. "But the canals do smell and
the people are not friendly. Not like Padua or Verona, even.
We have not been invited to a single ball or banquet since
we arrived."

"I am sure this is only a language difficulty, madame.
Veneziano is not Roman or Tuscan."

"Absolutely unintelligible! Nothing like proper Latin.
But even when we had Domenico, the nobles never invited
us into their palaces. It is most unfriendly. And I know that
some of them are very pressed for cash just now. A lot of fine
art has been coming on the market, and Sir Bellamy represents several important collectors. He is willing to pay in
gold if the price is reasonable."

She paused to draw breath and I whispered, "Domenico?"

"Domenico Chiari. Sir Bellamy hired him to be our guide
and interpreter. He ran out on us three days ago. It makes
things very difficult."

Rich foreigners are always suspect. Either Domenico had
been spying for the Ten, or he had been taken in for questioning. "Did he take his belongings with him?"

"Well, yes, he did. Why do you ask?" Sudden suspicion
pulled rolls of flesh in around her eyes.

"People can meet with accidents and I could have advised
you on how to report the matter."

I could see no way to bring the conversation around to
wineglasses and poison. I wondered how I could lure this
bell tower of a woman and her so-trusting husband to Ca'

Barbolano so that the Maestro could interrogate them for himself. She was still galloping ahead of me—

"He walked out on us without asking for his pay. It makes our task here almost impossible. Like two nights ago, when we met your master. The book dealer had told us about the sale at Master Imer's residence. He assured us that it was open to the public, and of course Sir Bellamy was not going to disgorge the sort of money he wanted without seeing how much other people were willing to pay. The host told us to leave and was very rude about it. Sir Bellamy apologized for the misunderstanding—extremely politely for him—and offered to show the color of his money, but then he became even more offensive and ordered us out of the house at once. He asked your master to translate for him. Sir Bellamy was much offended. He is talking seriously of breaking our lease on these premises and leaving the Republic as soon as possible. The weather is appalling. Worse than England. We can make better purchases in Florence."

"Karagounis himself had invited you to the supper party?"

"Certainly. And there was no mistake, because we still had Domenico with us when we called on him."

"Lord Bellamy is a collector of books?" That seemed fairly obvious.

"He isn't *Lord* Bellamy. Why do you Venetians have this extraordinary custom of making all your nobility equal? The rest of the world has dukes and counts and so on, including England. Here everybody is *sier*. Sir Bellamy is a baronet, a chevalier."

"But he does collect books?"

"Books are one of our objectives. We have also been buying pictures and small sculptures. You said your master had manuscripts to offer?"

I had not said that, but I could think offhand of half a

dozen items in his collection that he would willingly unload on wealthy foreigners.

"He will be happy to show them if you and the baronet wish to come and inspect them. I could send his gondola—"

"Let me show you the treasures we have collected so far."

Taking up the lantern, she marched into the bedroom. I followed, wondering giddily if I was supposed to ask how long we had before her husband came home, but no, she took a taper and began lighting more lamps so she could show me paintings. There were six of them, all framed but not hung, leaning against the walls.

"I realize the light is not very good," she boomed. "And they aren't very much to show for two months' work, are they? But some real gems! This Tintoretto, for example . . ."

Maybe *school of* Tintoretto, I thought. And if the next one was a *school of* Titian, the old master had been sparing the rod too much. In the end I was quite certain that two were crude fakes and three made me very uneasy. But there was one I honestly admired. It was the smallest, so I could lift it and carry it to where the light was best.

"I still think we paid too much for that one," Hyacinth declared, bringing another lamp close enough to singe my ear. "It was the first we bought. But Sir Bellamy knows a nobleman who will pay generously for it."

Even an art lover would. A few feather shafts protruded from the subject's torso so the Church would accept that he was a martyred San Sebastiano, not just a beautiful young man tied to a tree while wearing only a dishrag. But his musculature was well portrayed and his expression saintly, not agonized or lecherous; also the canvas was unsigned, which was another reason for a cynic like me to think it might be a genuine master. It was old enough for the varnish to have developed craquelure.

I set it back in its place. "A very fine piece, worthy of Giovanni Bellini! But I am no expert in art, madame. My master has shared with me a little of his wisdom on books. When would it suit you and Chevalier Feather to come and view what he has to offer, and perhaps discuss others that he knows of?" I started to move to the door and suddenly she was in front of me.

"First tell me why you really came." She raised her lamp so she could study my face. "Two nights ago your master, if that is who he is, denied that he sold books, because I asked him. So who are you and what do you want? And don't try anything with me, boy, or I'll break every bone in your body."

The look in her ice-pale eyes was that of a Persian cat that has just caught a juicy mouse. I had misjudged her. She had been testing me. Inside all that beef there was a smarter woman than I had realized.

"I do serve Maestro Nostradamus, madame. It is true that he is not a book dealer as such, but he owns a large collection and I catalogue it for him, so I know he has some duplicates he would part with if the price was right. I have told you no lies, except to praise the pictures a little more than I should."

"But what are you really after? Were you in league with that ruffian delivery man?"

"No, madame. I never saw him before. I came to ask you which wine you drank at the Imer residence that night."

"What?" Not surprisingly, she looked surprised.

"At the viewing . . . One of the guests was taken ill later. My master is a physician and suspects that one of the wine bottles may have been spoiled. You were offered three wines when you arrived, yes?"

"I took the malmsey," she said. "Both of us did. It's what we drink at home in England. I don't care for most of the foreign stuff."

Where did she think malmsey came from? "If my master is correct, you made a wiser choice than you know. You didn't happen to notice anyone tampering with the bottles or the glasses, did you?"

"Of course not." She seemed to grow even bigger. "I was interested in the books and nothing else. *Tampering?* What business is this of your master's anyway? Why doesn't he report his suspicions to the magistrates?"

That was a very good question, for which I had no good answer. "He has his reasons, madame, which I am not permitted to—"

An explosion of consonants from the doorway spun me around. Sir Bellamy had returned. He was older than Hyacinth and surprisingly short for a man married to a woman so large; he wore clothes that looked more Tuscan than local, but he was sporting a ruff the size of a millwheel and an absurd pointed mustache, neither of which even a Florentine would have willingly been buried in. He was pale with rage, which was understandable—and he wore a sword, which was disturbing.

I bowed and for the moment was ignored.

His wife answered him in the same guttural language, which I assumed was English, but she did not seem in the least discomfitted at being caught alone with a young man in the connubial bedchamber. She gestured at the paintings and pulled a face in my direction. I caught the Maestro's name.

Feather was very loud and very furious. Hyacinth shrugged and continued to answer calmly.

"What is it that you want?" he demanded of me. His accent was not quite as bad as his wife's.

"Two nights ago, at the residence of citizen Imer, observed you a man in purple robes?"

"And two in red. It was more a coronation than a book sale. Answer me! Why do you come here pestering my wife?" He had his hand on his sword. He was fizzing with rage and he was between me and the doorway. This was no time for finesse.

I waved my hands to show that they were empty and I was unarmed. "To warn you, monseigneur, and your noble wife. The older man, the one with the purple robes and the fancy—" I had to gesture to my shoulder, for my French did not extend to the word for tippet. "Procurator Orseolo. He was poisoned at that meeting. Everyone who was present is suspect. You have heard of the Council of Ten?"

"You work for the government?"

"No, *messer*."

Feather drew his sword. "You dare come here and threaten me, you young—" Fortunately, he reverted to English, although the gist was obvious. He came towards me.

I started backing. "I am unarmed, *messer*. What you are doing is a very serious offense in this city."

"So is forcing yourself into a lady's bedroom!"

Her word against mine, although if the judges ever saw the size of the potential victim, they would laugh the case out of court. Meanwhile, the crazy *Inglese* was out for blood. I backed rapidly to the pictures and grabbed San Sebastiano to be my shield and defender, while sending a quick prayer of apology to the saint.

"Put that down!" Feather screamed. "Drop it!"

"Put up your sword, *clarissimo*. I wish only to leave in peace. You will not improve the holy man by adding sword wounds to his troubles." I kept half an eye on the doughty Hyacinth. If she got behind me, she could garotte me with her bare hands.

"Depart!" he bellowed, pointing at the door. For a small man he was both loud and ferocious.

"I will follow you, *clarissimo*. Madame, if you would be so kind as to go and open the outer door? Then you lead, *messer*. San Sebastiano and I will follow."

"Come, Sir Bellamy," his wife said. "The boy will not turn his back on your sword." She led the way, moving with majesty.

It took some more calming talk from me before he followed her, reluctantly walking backwards, not taking his eyes off me. I kept my eyes on him as I edged out through the outer door, dropped the saint at the top of the stairs where he would obstruct pursuit, and took off downward like a rat diving into its hole.

9

Carnival revelers were starting to emerge in the alleys and on the canals, the lights had been lit in the corner shrines. Christoforo and Corrado had not drunk themselves stupid and drowned, as I had feared. They were sitting in the bow of the gondola, so obviously pleased with themselves that their father was threatening to send them to confession first thing in the morning.

"I did not give them enough for that," I said. If I were mistaken, then they would need the Maestro's professional care very shortly.

"How much did you give them?" he asked narrowly.

"Didn't they tell you?"

"They said two *soldi* apiece."

Blessed Lady help me! I bit the bullet. "Giorgio, I know this isn't any of my business, but I was their age not so very long ago. My mother was desperately poor, but she let me keep all my earnings as long as I paid for half our groceries. I ate three times what she did, so that was fair, and I learned what honest work was for." I sighed and said the rest of it: "You are teaching them to tell lies."

He glowered, but he is a reasonable man at heart. "You gave them more than four *soldi*?"

"Just believe I gave them four to pass on to you. Now take us all home, please, before I starve to death."

I took my seat inside the felze, but when we were underway I beckoned Christoforo to join me—Corrado is more canny.

"How much did you win?"

His face puckered with guilt. "Me? Eight *soldi*. Corrado got six."

"And what would you have done if you'd lost it all?"

"We weren't going to gamble it all."

"You did very well to stop when you were ahead, but believe me, you will lose it all the next time. Gambling is for fools. Tell your brother I said so." I knew my advice would drive them to exactly the opposite course, because that was how I had reacted at their age. But now they must have enough money to buy a harlot of the lowest sort, so they would be better off losing it at dice. Sometimes life seems unnecessarily complicated.

Back at Ca' Barbolano, I found the Maestro gone, but my side of the desk upholstered with pages of scrawl. He works that hard only when he is seriously frustrated by something, and it invariably means twice as much work for me. He had been at the crystal ball again, too, for the velvet lay on the floor and the slate was adorned with drunken snail tracks. I left that problem until later—I tend to be prejudiced against the crystal, because it never shows me anything except my next encounter with Violetta. The Maestro says I will outgrow that. I say I don't want to.

I began by re-shelving all the books, mostly herbals and ephemerides. The reagents I had bought the previous day I stowed in the appropriate bottles, out of reach of any Angeli toddler who might stray into the atelier. After I had mixed the unguent for madonna Polo, I dusted the entire collection of bottles and shelves to leave no evidence that digitalis had ever been present.

Then I lit the lamp over my desk and inspected the litter. The Maestro insists that everything be kept tidy, but is himself the untidiest of men. He had completed three pages of next year's almanac and four scribbled horoscopes that were the routine jobs I had expected to do that day until murder intervened. He had even made all the calculations, probably more to keep his own mind occupied than out of consideration for me. A fifth horoscope, identified only as "PM," was obviously the doge and I did not like the look of his immediate future. If you identified him with the Republic itself, which was legitimate synecdoche, and the Republic as Queen of the Sea with the planet Venus, the current conjunction with Saturn was as ominous as it had been for Orseolo. The Maestro posited that the ascendant Turkish Empire should be equated with the moon in some circumstances, and in that case the aspects were even worse. If he had not yet answered Pietro Moro's mocking challenge to read the name of the murderer in the stars, at least he had found some evidence regarding the name of the intended victim. As I was tucking all the papers away in my work drawer with a bundle of routine letters, including the papal piles, out fell a letter addressed to me.

It had been opened, of course, although I recognized Violetta's scent on the paper, and he would have done so also. The contents were terse:

Lover—The ball is canceled. Come and entertain me tonight. —V

Normally I would be down the hall in my bedroom and half changed within a couple of heartbeats of reading that invitation, but tonight I had far too much work to do and too much sleep to catch up. I wrote my regrets on the same paper, sealed it with my signet, and went in search of Bruno, who was always happy to help, just to justify his existence.

I barely needed to explain. He sniffed the paper, grinned, and made the signs for *woman—belong—Alfeo*. I nodded and off he went. Sending so much beef to deliver so small a load seemed inefficient. I felt I should have enclosed a gift—something pretty, like the Michelangelo *David*.

Now I had no more excuses to delay tackling the Maestro's latest prophecy. I brought light and ink and the book to the slate-topped table. It was not as illegible as I had feared, which, as I told you, implied that the events it foretold would not be long delayed. When I had deciphered it, I didn't like it one bit.

> *Dark deeds, dark night, but bright the gold.*
> *Gold rains brighter than the eyes of the serpent;*
> *Eyes and legs a-bleeding on the* campo,
> *So unthinkable love will triumph from afar.*

Just then Corrado tapped on the door, come to tell me that supper was ready. Before I reached the dining room, I was brought up short by Bruno's smile, looming over me like a rainbow. He had brought back a reply from Violetta.

> *Cedet amor rebus, res age, tutus eris.*—V

Which means roughly that business keeps one safe from love—ominous talk when one's lover is a courtesan. I hoped that it was just another literary conceit I ought to know. (It is, I later learned, an apothegm by Ovid.)

To my astonishment, I found the Maestro already at the table. His eyes were bloodshot and I guessed he had a raging headache, but he was not as haggard as I expected after two foreseeings in two days.

The dining hall would seat fifty at a pinch, but only the Maestro and I eat in it. There I can dream that my family's fortunes never sank in the Aegean with the fall of Crete, for our dishes are finest porcelain, our knives and spoons are chased silver, as are the special forks with which we lift the food to our mouths, a custom foreigners find very strange. Colored candles burn in golden candlesticks on the snowy linen cloth between the crystal flagons and enameled beakers.

Normally I feast and my master nibbles, but that night I also had to talk; Mama's superb risotto of Rovigo veal stuffed with oysters grew cold before I was half-done. I told of my visit to the doge, my exchange with Isaia, and the bizarre English couple. Then, I hoped, I was free to eat.

Alas, no. "You saw the latest quatrain?"

I recited what I thought it said and he nodded grumpily.

"It seems to predict violence," I said. "Whose eyes and legs are going to bleed, do you suppose?"

"Mine. From now on go armed and take Bruno with you everywhere."

"You are serious?" I am his eyes and his legs, but I had never heard him admit that before.

"Have you ever known me to make a joke?"

"No, master." I suspect he tried one seventy years ago and nobody laughed. "Why me?" Not getting an answer, I continued. "What else? Unthinkable love? A rain of gold? Eyes of the serpent?"

Seemingly he could make no more sense of the quatrain than I could. He poked more food around his plate aimlessly. He had eaten almost nothing. "You know who is carried shoulder high around the Piazza San Marco, scattering gold coins to the mob."

"Yes." I reached for the wine glass I had been neglecting. He had just described the installation of a new doge. "Isaia confirms that the procurator was murdered. Do you seriously believe you can unmask the culprit before the Ten take you in for questioning?"

He did not tell me what he believed, and it was what the Council of Ten believed—and would do about it—that mattered. I tried again.

"You think there was a botched attempt to assassinate the doge?"

Maestro Nostradamus thumped the table furiously with a tiny fist. "I told you this morning that His Serenity was appealing for our help, didn't I? Whether someone is trying to murder him or he was just impetuous, he met with foreigners in a private house. If his enemies have the votes, that is enough cause to depose him, or worse. Any two of the three state prosecutors can indict him. He cannot hope to keep the Ten out of this, but the way the matter is presented may swing the vote."

I murmured, "Yes, master," and returned to my veal and oysters.

"There is more than one way to reverse an emperor. Tell me again about your tarot reading last night."

I was both surprised and gratified, for I suspect that tarot is the one occult skill at which I can better him. I went over my reading again.

"As you say, master, it may be hinting that the doge was the intended victim," I admitted, refilling my glass. "In spite of what you think of my humor, I do think that Death reversed was *Circospetto*; Raffaino Sciara just looks too much like Trump XIII. He might have brought death and in the end he did not. Justice reversed meant my night in jail, I suppose, or does it mean a murderer getting off scot-free?"

"I think the jail. Your deck must be well attuned at present."

From him any praise must be counted fulsome. Pleased, I said, "I can fetch it and try a more detailed reading."

He shook his head like a chicken ruffling its feathers. "Not tonight. You must never overwork a tarot deck."

Never having been told that before, I waited for more and there was no more. He reached for his staff. I helped him rise and he leaned on my shoulder all the way across the *salone*. He usually returns to the atelier after supper and either reads or lectures me until late, but that night he headed straight to his bedchamber and disappeared with a muttered *Godbless!*

Now was the moment I had mentally set aside to consult my tarot deck again. Why had the Maestro forbidden me to do so? The only reason he had ever given me for letting a deck rest was that it had started reporting obvious nonsense, and mine was certainly not doing that. What else could I do to help solve the murder? I could not use the crystal as he could.

I could summon Putrid. That was why the old rascal had not wanted me to lay out a tarot spread. My tarot was painted long ago by an artist of superlative skill and subtlety; since then the fears and yearnings of many owners have infused it with deep empathy. If I tried to consult it when I had a fiend in my immediate future, I might ruin it beyond repair.

The Maestro was a murder suspect and had to clear his name. He dare not risk asking a demon for help, but he would let me take that risk, because I needed help less than he did. Another reason was that I was less important and so, in a non-facetious way, relatively innocent. Summoning a minor fiend can stir up a major one instead. You never see senior condottieri fighting in the front ranks; they send the cannon fodder forward and shout encouragement from the rear, but any demon that managed to enslave the great Nostradamus would be capable of performing enormous mischief through him. All the legions of hell would rally to try it. I was mere cannon fodder.

I locked the door, then sat down at my desk and readied pen and paper. A summoning needs careful planning. Even my trivial fiend Putrid can be a terrifying apparition, and to panic and forget what comes next or change plans halfway through could be disastrous. It would do no good to demand, "Tell me who killed Procurator Orseolo," or even "Procurator Bertucci Orseolo" because there might have been several men of that name in the history of the Republic. And the fiend could just reply "his doctor," which might be true in a narrow sense. After much thought I wrote down two questions, plus the command of dismissal, which demonologists have been known to forget in emergencies, although none ever more than once. Purists conduct their summonings in Latin. The Maestro says that the fiends themselves don't care what language you use and it is better to be right than classy.

I moved a chair over to the big mirror in the wall of books. Mirrors themselves are no more magical than crystal balls, but both can be used for occult purposes, like the piece of chalk I used to draw a pentacle around myself and the chair. I sat down, tried some deep breaths, and then uttered my first call, summoning Putrid (not his real name) to be manifest in the mirror before me.

The room cooled and dimmed. It always shocks me when mere words can do that. Even the flames in the fireplace seemed to shrink, and I wished I had brought a lamp inside the pentacle with me.

I summoned a second time. Now the mirror showed very little more than my own white face with darkness behind it, and the air was filled with a nauseating stench. Think of every bad smell you have ever experienced—bad fish, cesspools, warm pig dung—add them all together and multiply by thirteen. Gagging, anxious to get the seance over with, I spoke the words a third time.

My scared face in the mirror blurred and melted into a reddish globe, which shrank back and resolved as the iris of an eye. The surrounding space cleared into scaly, scabrous flesh of an indeterminate green-purple color, like a very ripe bruise. The monster moved farther back yet, until a second eye came into view. Whatever shade or shape they choose for the rest of themselves, fiends always seem to prefer red eyes. Putrid had begun his apparition the size of a house, and even now I could see only part of his face peering in, huge as the mirror was. The less I saw the better.

"You!" he said. He slobbered and his breath stank even worse than the rest of him. "I will eat you."

I peered at my script in the feeble firelight.

"You have a nice smell of fresh sin on you, *sier* Alfeo Zeno," the fiend said chattily. "You should have been shriven before you called me. And your harlot also I will eat."

Another rule is that you never listen to fiends.

"Putrid, I command you by your true name that if there was no murderer present on San Valentine's Eve last in the room in this city where Ottone Imer the attorney displayed books to certain potential buyers, that you instantly quit this realm and return to the place from whence you came."

The fiend coughed, spraying the inside of the mirror with spit and almost choking me with putrescent fumes. My skin crawled.

"That's clever," he growled. "Thought that up all by yourself, did you, Alfeo?" He was still there, which disposed of any last hope that the procurator's death had been an accident.

"Look, Alfeo," the fiend said. "Violetta with her customers. Let me show you what she does, Alfeo. Look!"

I did not look. "Putrid, I command you by your true name that until and only until I clap my hands three times you show me in this mirror before me the murder committed by the murderer who was present on San Valentine's Eve last in the room in this city where Ottone Imer the attorney displayed books to certain potential buyers, and I further command you by your true name that when and only when I clap my hands three times that you instantly quit this realm and return to the place from whence you came."

"Damn you," the fiend muttered, but the hideous images faded from the mirror.

I was staring down into a tent. It was dim, lit by two small lamps suspended from the ridge pole, but luxuriously carpeted and furnished with elaborate chests, a divan, a silver ewer and basin. Steel mail and a sword hung on a stand by the entrance. Seemingly right below me, a man sat cross-legged on a cushion under the lamps, reading. I could see that the writing was Arabic, and needed no demon to advise me that I was spying on one of the sultan's generals. His face was hidden from me by a turban shaped like a giant pumpkin, much bigger than his head, but he wore a sleeveless tunic and a complicated, multicolored skirt that barely reached his knees. He could not be the sultan himself—unlike his warlike ancestors, he stays home in safety in Constantinople, and he would command far grander quarters if he did venture into the field—but someone of importance. What was Putrid playing at? What loophole had I left in my instructions?

The man looked up, frowning and tilting his head as if listening to something. He was dusky and weathered; he had silver streaks in his beard, but his face was lean, vulpine, and still dangerous.

The flap lifted to admit a second man. He was young, short but heavyset, swarthy and bearded, and he wore very

similar garb. He salaamed to the general. There must be
millions like him in the Ottoman Empire, from Hungary to
the Persian Gulf, from Libya to the Caucasus—fierce Muslims all, fanatically loyal to their sultan—but very few of
those would have a fiend sitting on one shoulder as this one
did. In shape the horror resembled a tailless rat with red
eyes and a grin that showed sharp teeth, but its texture was
slug-like, bluish and slimy.

The general had risen, but he clearly did not register the
fiend, because he listened calmly to whatever the visitor said.
I could not hear a word and would not have understood it if
I had. The general salaamed in response to whatever message
or instructions he had just received. He went over to the
portable table with the ewer and basin and there proceeded
to wash his hands. The visitor watched, smiling contentedly,
while the fiend hugged itself in glee and chomped its teeth.

I still had no idea what was going on; I just knew that I
could not approve of anything that a demon enjoyed so
much. No doubt there are possessed walking the streets of
Christendom, too, even here in the Republic. I was identify-
ing this one and his rider only because I was seeing them
through Putrid's eyes.

Hands washed, the general returned to the center of the
tent, knelt down with his back to his guest, and began to
pray in the Muslims' fashion, bending to touch the rug with
his forehead, leaning back to raise his arms. To my astonishment, the fiend disappeared. The visitor did not seem to notice its absence any more than he had shown awareness of its
presence earlier. What surprised me was that the Muslim's
prayers had dispelled it at least as effectively as a Christian's
would. Was the name of Allah as effective as the name of
Christ? That was certainly not what the Church taught. If
the unbelievers worshipped the Antichrist, how could their

prayers banish demons? I would be burned as a heretic if I ever suggested such a thing.

The fiends must be trying to deceive me.

The general ended his prayers and the demon reappeared where it had been before. The general sat back on his heels, his visitor walked across the carpet to him, looped a cord around his neck, and strangled him. The fiend jumped up and down with joy as the general thrashed in his death agonies. I may have cried out in horror, but if so no one noticed. I had asked to see a murder, hadn't I? Putrid had shown me the wrong one, perhaps the murderer's first murder, his initiation.

When the assassin was certain his victim was dead, he drew his sword. At that point, I admit, I closed my eyes. When I opened them again, the corpse on the floor was headless and a blood-spattered turban lay empty and collapsed beside it. The visitor seemed neither upset nor especially pleased by his gruesome task, nor by the weighty leather bag he held. He was possessed, after all, and no doubt believed he was loyally carrying out his sultan's orders. He probably was. Turning his back on his grisly work, he headed for the door—and his demon looked up and saw me.

I could not hear its shrieks of rage, but I could see them. The possessed turned again and returned to stand directly below my vantage point, but now his face was blank, his eyes lifeless. His passenger was dancing with fury, almost glowing with it, making clawing gestures at me and becoming larger, its spongy flesh swelling like dough, its eyes flaming redder. I was seized by a terrible, paralyzing, horror that it would leap out of the mirror at me.

I clapped my hands three times. The image blurred, steadied slightly, and then faded—all except those two red eyes. I yelled out the words of dismissal, but of course those were addressed to Putrid and I did not know the name of this other fiend, to which it had betrayed me. For a moment the mirror showed the two hate-filled red eyes superimposed on me and the atelier behind me. Then, mercifully, they disappeared.

10

Summonings always leave me feeling sick and unclean. Even after I had replaced the furniture, wiped out the pentagram with my dustrag, and burned my notes in the fireplace, I was still shaking like a fatal case of palsy. I kept wondering whether a hateful little slug fiend was now perched on my shoulder, invisible and gloating as it planned the horrors it would make me perform.

Back in my room, I stripped and washed myself all over with cold water. Tired though I was, memories of the ordeal would keep me awake for a long time, and I had an invitation to call on a lady who thought nothing of playing all night and sleeping by day. I dressed in my shabby burglar clothes, doused the light, and prepared to go visiting. Of course I was disobeying the Maestro's orders by leaving the house unarmed, but I could neither ask Bruno to accompany me on my tryst nor risk my death-defying leap while encumbered with a rapier. I stopped worrying about being murdered when I opened the window and discovered that the stormy weather had returned, blustering rain about, making roofs slippery, and plotting to throw acrobats off their timing. Very likely the Maestro had misinterpreted his bleeding eyes-and-legs vision and it had nothing to do with assault. I hesitated, but not for long. I *needed* Violetta too much just then, and not for lust. I needed comfort and understanding and her arms around me, her warmth and love.

So I scrambled out on the ledge and then went through the nasty contortions required to replace the bars, for I never leave the window unguarded in the night. That was not the easiest of maneuvers in such weather and the leap in darkness wrung a prayer out of me. Obviously I survived, although I banged my left knee on the tiles.

A light burned in her room, for she never sleeps in complete darkness—unless her current companion insists on it, I suppose—and I could see that she was alone. She stirred while I was undressing.

"Alfeo?" she murmured drowsily.

"Are you expecting someone else?" I asked, hoping the answer was *No*.

"No. The nobility are in mourning."

I wasn't. I slid between the sheets, into her arms, her warmth.

Jolted awake, she said, "*Eek!* You are freezing!"

"Only on the outside. I love you. I need you."

"I'm here, love. What's wrong? You're trembling!"

"Rough night. Just hold me."

The night fled, the lamp burned out, and chinks of daylight came to smile through chinks in the drapes. My knee hurt. The rest of me felt much better.

"Time to go," I whispered.

"Not yet." Helen stirred sleepily. "I have something to tell you."

"Speak, goddess."

The Ten would start asking questions soon. Thanks to Putrid I knew the murderer must be either Alexius Karagounis or his Moorish servant, but finding admissible proof would take time.

Violetta sighed and rolled on her back. "I went and saw Bianca Orseolo yesterday."

I heard Minerva in her voice. "You did *what?*"

"You heard me. Ca' Orseolo is in mourning, so after you left I went calling in my nun costume, to offer comfort."

"But she saw you at the—"

"She did *not* see me at the supper. She may have *seen* me, but she did not *look* at me, because she was busy tending her grandfather and I am a courtesan. Proper young girls ignore such women. She did not recognize me yesterday because I was a nun, completely different."

"You think that costume you were wearing would fool—"

"Stop interrupting. There are nuns who wear habits like that. I got in to see her when nobody else would have done, except other family members, of which she has none. We had a long talk. Bianca had more opportunity to see the crime committed than anyone else did, because she was at her grandfather's side all the time."

"She also had the best opportunity," I said. "All she had to do was hand him the wrong glass and he would never have questioned. Did she do it?"

"I don't know." Violetta rarely admits ignorance. As Minerva, she is much brainier than I am. As Aspasia, she is unsurpassed at judging people. "She is extremely upset by her grandfather's death . . . almost too upset. She wept in my arms. So much sorrow may be a sign of guilt, either guilt because she killed him or guilt because she is glad he died, I don't know yet. You and I are to go and see her later today."

This needed a lot of rational analysis and rational analysis was hard to achieve while cuddling the finest courtesan in the Republic—which duty compelled me to do at that moment, of course, to keep this witness cooperative. It crossed my mind that few men enjoyed better working conditions.

I made an effort to concentrate. "You told her my name?"

"No. I said I knew a man who was investigating the possibility that her grandfather had been murdered, and asked if I might bring you to ask her a few questions. The funeral is this morning. We are to see her after that, around noon."

I gulped. "You want me to pretend to be an agent of the Ten? I don't know what the penalty for—"

"Hope you never find out," Aspasia said coldly. "I made no such claim and the city is stuffed tight with the Three's spies, as you well know. If Bianca assumes that you are one of them, her mistake is quite unrelated to anything I said."

The doge had asked me to investigate the procurator's death, but he would deny doing so if the Three asked him.

"Did Bianca have a motive?"

Helen's dark eyes looked at me under divine eyelashes. "I don't want to talk any more. Kiss me."

The Maestro watched with disapproval as I laid a tray on my side of the desk. "Why are you limping?"

"I banged my knee on a tile."

"What did you learn?"

"Have you eaten?" I bowled a hot roll across to him; he caught it before it went over the edge. "The murderer is a Muslim, presumably an agent of the sultan, and probably the servant who poured the wine. He could be the Greek or, more likely I should say the man posing as a Greek, the book dealer, Karagounis. How old is he?"

"About forty."

"The man I saw was in his twenties."

"Start at the beginning."

I did. Between sips of my *khave*—a hot, black drink recently introduced from Turkey, becoming very popular—I continued through the middle and stopped when I got to the end.

The Maestro did not look happy. "You witnessed an execution. No doubt the general was a janissary, but it wouldn't matter—any servant of the sultan, from infantryman to ambassador or vizier, is a *kapikulu*, a slave, and when the sultan sends his *chaush* with an order that the man deliver his own head, then the order is obeyed without complaint or resistance. The *chaush* arrives with a bowstring, a sword, and a bag. No matter how high they rise in the state, *kapikullari* owe their lives to the sultan."

"Why did he wash his hands?"

"I have no idea. You are in grave danger. The fiend that saw you may be much stronger than the guide you were using. It may have managed to open a portal to you. You must go and make confession right away."

One of the advantages of living in San Remo is Father Farsetti. Other priests might report me to the Holy Office, but in Venice the priests are elected by the parishioners, subject to the patriarch's veto, and the good folk of San Remo had chosen a practical, broad-minded man. Even so, I wondered uneasily how long it would take to say a million *Aves*. That was what he had threatened me with the last time I confessed to practicing demonology.

"If you insist."

"I do insist! I assume the funeral is today?"

"Violetta says the service will be held this morning, but I haven't finished reporting. I have a second suspect to offer—Bianca, the sweet child you overlooked at the book viewing." I told him of Violetta's escapade. "My friend is an exceedingly shrewd judge of people," I finished. "And if she distrusts Bianca, then we should be wise to pay heed. Or do we believe only what the fiend showed me?"

The Maestro curled his lip. "I see no reason to choose between the two testimonies just yet."

"I assure you that the strangler I saw was no blushing Christian maiden, and I refuse to believe that a *kapikulu* assassin could disguise himself as one well enough to deceive her grandfather, however doddery he was getting."

"Faugh! You blather like a lace maker. If this affair were straightforward, I could have solved it in ten minutes with the crystal. By all means fold the fair Bianca to your manly breast and dry her tears. The girl may be unduly upset because she saw the glasses being switched and chose not to intervene. Speak with her father, also, the great minister. Find out where he was on Valentine's Eve, and his son also."

"Benedetto. He's supposed to be at the University of Padua."

"It's only twenty-five miles to Padua. He would have been sent for as soon as his grandfather fell sick."

I failed to see how he could have switched glasses at a party in Venice when he was miles away on the mainland, but a well-behaved apprentice does not make fun of his master's instructions. I nodded, being well behaved.

"And you still have to see Senator Tirali and his son."

"Pasqual Tirali. Master, I admit I have personal reasons for wanting to send *sier* Pasqual Tirali to the galleys, but I cannot imagine his managing to poison a wine glass and switch it with another without Violetta noticing."

"Include him anyway." The Maestro scowled across at his bookshelves. "Bring me the *Midrasch Na Zohar* before you go. You had better start with Father Farsetti. You may be able to catch him about now. And don't forget what I said about Bruno and your sword."

I left him with his ferrety nose deep in the Rabbi Ben Yohai's masterpiece. If he was willing to try cabalism, he must be really desperate.

11

Violetta and I have a longstanding agreement. I never ask her to give up her career as a courtesan, because I know how much she values the freedom it gives her, saving her from the closeted, subservient life of a "respectable" woman. Housebound boredom would kill her in a month, she says, and I believe her. Her side of the pact is never to offer me money or expensive gifts. The only exception I allow is something to wear, to mark either my birthday or the anniversary of the day we became lovers. She interprets the terms liberally, which is why I could buckle on my rapier and matching dagger of superlative Toledo steel. I covered them with my kidskin cloak, also given by her.

Bruno is the gentlest and most amiable of men. He beamed with joy when I signed that I wanted him to accompany me. Then he noticed the sword under my cloak and frowned mightily. I signed *danger* and *maybe* to tell him I was not going out to pick a fight, but when I told him to bring a cudgel, he glowered down at me like a thunderstorm, folded his great arms, and grew roots.

We often have this argument. I dropped to my knees and

clasped my hands in prayer. He scowled, lifted me bodily, and held me there until I put my feet down; but then he did go and fetch the only weapon he will tolerate—Mama Angeli's heaviest flatiron in a canvas bag with a shoulder strap. Most men would balk at having to lug something like that around for long, but Bruno barely notices the weight. Why it is a more acceptable defense than a stout stave I cannot understand and he cannot explain. I grinned, he smiled sheepishly, and off we went.

We could have run down the back stairs and gone out the servants' door. It never occurred to me to do so. Instead we left by the watergate as usual, carefully negotiating the narrow ledge along the facade of Ca' Barbolano to the corner of the building and the *calle*. It was easier for me than Bruno, who takes up much more space.

Seagulls were swimming on the strangely empty canal. This was the day of the funeral, so the city was in mourning for its procurator, and already I heard bells ringing in the distance. The Marciana porters were not working and the building site on the far side lay silent. Once we had made our way through the maze of *calli*, we found the morning crowds in the *campo* much decreased, and few hawkers making their rounds. Even the gossip session around the wellhead was thin, although there were more men than usual. We paused there to chat as neighbors do. I chatted. Bruno just smiled and nodded. Two girls teasingly warned me not to let my companion step on me, but most women are scared of Bruno.

As befits a small parish, San Remo has a small church. It is old and quaint, but it does have good stained glass and Father Farsetti is a personal friend of Jacopo Palma the Younger, who is the finest painter working in the city at the moment. Two of his early paintings hang in the church and afficionados come in droves to argue over them. There was no one arguing there that morning, but the door to the confessional was closed, so Father Farsetti was about his holy duties. I said a few prayers, including one for Bertucci Orseolo. Bruno wandered around, admiring the pictures and the glass. He does not understand churches and what happens there.

A woman came out of the confessional and I went in. Father Farsetti probably knew what to expect as soon as he heard my voice. I admitted to summoning a demon from hell and some lesser sins. He demanded to know why I had invoked the fiend, so I told him. He disapproved, of course, but he could see that an attempt to assassinate the doge justified extraordinary countermeasures. As usual, he was more worried about my sinful relationship with Violetta, but every man in Venice has that sort of problem at least sometimes. He gave me a thorough nagging, absolution, and a much smaller penance than I had feared.

We emerged by our separate doors and bid each other good morning. He gave Bruno his blessing. Bruno, who had been guarding my sword and cloak for me, just smiled politely. There were no other penitents waiting.

Father Farsetti is a small, birdlike man with a warm smile and an enormous laugh. He isn't quite up to Isaia Modestus at chess—I can beat him sometimes—but he is incredible at chess without boards, able to take on the Maestro and me at the same time and usually win both games.

"You must come and dine with us again soon, Father," I said. "Arguing with you gives my master an appetite, which he sorely needs."

He lit his smile. "That is a worthy justification for a personal pleasure. Before you go, though, I have a book on the role of political assassination in Islamic history that I think might interest you."

Without asking whatever had given him that idea, I assured him that I would enjoy reading it. And so we crossed to the side door of the church and went out that way, emerging into a small courtyard between the church nave on one side, the priest's house on the other, with the transept closing off the end. I followed Father Farsetti out.

"That's him!"

There were six of them. One of them had been keeping watch at the corner to alert the others when I came out of the main door. The other five had just been waiting. I couldn't dive back into the church, because the way was blocked by Bruno, doubled over as he followed me out. Fortunately the bravos needed an instant to react because I had appeared behind them. Had Bruno and I emerged where they expected, they could have come after us and made short work of us in the open. In the courtyard they were going to be hampered by lack of space.

My rapier flashed out. They produced stilettos, but those blades looked as long as swords to me, and bravos know how to use swords. Luckily I had left my cloak just draped on my shoulders, unfastened. I swirled it loose and leaped into the corner to have my back protected. Father Farsetti was hurled aside, his yells ignored.

I parried a slash from the man on my right and enveloped the one on my left in my cloak. My riposte took the first man in the face, but by that time numbers three and four had arrived, number two had shaken off my cloak, and Father Farsetti was bellowing for help at the top of his well-trained lungs. I did not expect to be there to welcome it. I had my dagger out and was parrying with both hands, much too busy just staying alive to attempt to injure my opponents. In theory a rapier should keep a stiletto out of range, and even two stilettos should not be an impossible match in daylight. Five most certainly were.

Fortunately Bruno was in the fight, too. He did not appear to be armed, but he was too big to ignore and when the others closed in on me, one man dallied to deal with him. Bruno swung his weighted bag overhead and smashed the man's arm before he even got within range—that was probably how it happened, because we found his stiletto and the spectators described one of our assailants supporting an arm as he ran away. Father Farsetti was doing as much as he could to get between the others and me, for even a gutter bravo will not knowingly injure a priest. They shoved him aside with their free hands.

That still left four young toughs jostling in at me, faces full of hate, steel gleaming, and I should have died, had not San Remo and Our Lady heard my prayers. Bruno must have delivered a backhand sideways swipe at one of the men engaging me, who was later found with the back of his head crushed. He fell against his companions, diverting their attack, and I am fairly sure I wounded another. Then Bruno's victim toppled face-first into me, smearing blood on my doublet and knocking all the wind out of me. I went down with him, found myself among the boots and was certain I was done for—*Eyes and legs a-bleeding on the* campo.

That I survived was again due to Bruno, who felled the third of my attackers with a punch to the back of the neck, dropping him on top of me as a human shield. Father Farsetti witnessed that, and thereafter I was protected by two bodies so that the others could not get at me. Armed with staves and hammers and even cook pots, men and boys were running in from all directions, answering the priest's continuing yells. The remaining thugs took to their heels to avoid being trapped in the courtyard. They escaped because other spectators out in the *campo* were unarmed and naturally did not tackle daggers with bare hands.

Two bodies were left behind, a flattened skull and a broken neck respectively. So Bruno killed two and wounded one, while I, the celebrated swordsman, merely wounded two. My excuse for such a sorry and unheroic showing is that I was the target and the bravos had not at first registered

Bruno as anything but a bystander. He survived only because they did not have time to react to his unorthodox and fearless assault. Had the fight lasted a moment longer, they would have made a sieve of him.

Fortunately Father Farsetti keeps the ground by the church clear of ordure and garbage. I decided I was alive. Had I been alone and unarmed, the Maestro's prediction would have been fulfilled exactly—it had certainly come close enough. Although my bruised knee had not hampered me at all in the battle, it was hurting a lot more than it had earlier. I reached down to rub it and discovered the vision had been closer to the fulfilment than I had realized. Fresh blood is always shockingly red, especially when it is one's own. I had no memory of being wounded in the calf and no idea how it had happened. One of the men falling on top of me must have still been holding his knife when he landed.

Several voices were asking, "Alfeo?" and "You all right?"

The two closest were Pio and Nino Marciana from the *casa*, who had hauled the bodies off me and were now regarding me with worried expressions. Behind them Bruno was having silent hysterics because he had hurt people. Before I could answer, he saw that I was bleeding and uttered a wordless animal cry, one of the very few noises he makes. He swept everyone else aside, scooped me up in his arms, and charged into the jabbering, yelling crowd. Bodies flew in all directions. He crossed the *campo* like a runaway horse, into the Ca' Barbolano and all the way upstairs to the Maestro, where he laid me on the desk. There is an examination couch in the corner, but he ignored that. Giorgio and a mob of descendants followed him in to see.

The Maestro laid his book out of harm's way and examined my wound.

"Your calf is cut," he said. "It's not deep. Needs a few

stitches, but no need to send for the barber. Giorgio, fetch my bag. Roll over, Alfeo."

I sympathize with embroidery; being stitched hurts. I kept my mind off the pain and my undignified posture by trying to answer all the questions and explain what had happened without saying everything I was thinking. Who had reason to want me dead? The poisoner. Why? Because I knew his face. How did he know he had reason to want me dead? Because his demon had told him so. How had his bravos known I was in the church? Same answer.

Soon I was stitched and bandaged and set on a chair with my leg propped up on another. A fortifying glass of wine was thrust into my hand and the Maestro dispensed a spoonful of laudanum to soothe Bruno, for every attempt to hail him as a hero just upset him more. Mama herself washed my blood off the desk. My best hose were in rags and my shoe needed washing also.

The Maestro hates having more people in his atelier than he can keep an eye on. He ordered everybody out and I knew he wanted to have a serious talk with me, but the Republic does not approve of dead bodies lying around. The *shirri* arrived, the local constabulary, four of them, led by Sergeant Torre the Unthinking. I find it very hard to keep my temper around Torre. He was quite capable of marching me off to jail for questioning, as if I were the culprit and not the victim.

Fortunately Torre had barely opened his mouth before another man appeared and took over—*Missier Grande* himself, the chief of police, whose red and blue cloak is the most feared sight in the Republic. Gasparo Quazza is a tall man with the solidity of a Palladio facade, and has been known to break up a riot with his mere presence. It is *Missier Grande* who carries out the orders of the Ten. He has the integrity and hardness of a diamond, a man of poor background raised to one of the highest offices in the Republic, which he serves without scruple or question. He will be the next Grand Chancellor when the present one dies or retires. He has never racked me yet. He would hate to rack me, I'm sure, but he will rack me if he has to; I'm sure of that also. He came close so he could stare down at me. He has a gray-flecked beard and wears the standard flat, circular biretta of any civic official.

I smiled up at him politely. "Who were they?"

"You tell me, Alfeo."

"I don't know who they were, *Missier Grande.*" Sometimes servility is the better part of valor.

"Why should anyone set an army on you? *Six* men?"

"I don't know why, *Missier Grande.* I'm a good swordsman, but not quite that conceited. I was attacked without warning." I was glad to hear Father Farsetti's voice outside, and then see him walk into the atelier. His testimony of events would agree with mine and be accepted without argument.

"You were wearing your sword," *Missier Grande* said. "You had your giant with you. You *expected* trouble."

The Maestro intervened. "I foresaw it, *Missier Grande.* I ordered my apprentice to go armed today. I foresaw trouble."

Quazza flashed him a look of disgust and me another. "So your defense is witchcraft?"

There he was speaking more to the audience than to me. Very early in my indenture, Quazza's daughter was abducted. The child was recovered unharmed and the offender captured by a combination of the Maestro's clairvoyance and some insanely brash juvenile derring-do by me. Unlike the doge, *Missier Grande* is no skeptic in occult matters.

"The attack was witchcraft," I said. "How else did they find me? And how could six armed strangers assemble outside the church without attracting attention from the parish residents?"

Father Farsetti broke in angrily. "They *had* attracted attention, Alfeo. A dozen local men were loitering nearby, keeping an eye on them. It was Our Lady who saved you, not the Enemy."

"Your lungs deserve credit also, Father."

"But your neighbors deserve more, for noticing suspicious strangers and keeping watch on them. I will give you a chance to stand up and thank them in church on Sunday."

"Thank you, Father."

Quazza was still admiring my smile. I assumed that was what he was doing from the careful way he was studying me.

"Who knows where you will be on Sunday, Zeno? I have two dead men to explain to Their Excellencies. I have an apprentice wearing a sword and claiming he was forewarned by witchcraft. Perhaps I should call in the Holy Office?"

"Has not Bruno done the Republic a service today?" I asked. "Who were they?"

"Hired thugs," *Missier Grande* admitted. "Common bravos."

"From the Ponte degli Assassini, or the Calle della Bissa, I expect," the Maestro remarked, sending me a smug look. Just east of the Rialto, the Bridge of Assassins and the Alley of the Serpent are the most sinister haunts in the city. *Gold rains brighter than the eyes of the serpent.* That was where one went to hire killers.

"Did they have gold in their pouches? How much was I worth?"

"Someone got to their pouches before I did." Quazza glanced briefly in the direction of Torre and his band. "You may have been worth some silver to them, but not much while you are still alive, Alfeo Zeno. Dead, you would have brought them a second instalment. Dead or alive, it is not for you to hand out justice. A few days in the Leads will afford you protection against any second inexplicable attack and possibly refresh your memory of recent events."

The *sbirri* in the background were leering. Father Farsetti was not. And neither was I, now. The threat was believable. Again I was saved by my master.

"You have two corpses, *Missier Grande*," the Maestro said wearily, as if addressing a wilful child. "If you don't know them personally, some of the *sbirri* will, or your own *fanti*. You can locate their associates and extract the name of the person who hired them. He is the one you want, yes? The problem is that they may not know his real name. No matter how much pain you inflict they may give you nothing more than a vague description."

Missier Grande sensed an offer coming. He nodded. "Continue."

"As it happens . . . You can walk, Alfeo?"

I carefully laid my left foot on the floor and pulled myself erect. I took a few steps. "The agony is indescribable, but I can hobble, master."

"Good. As it happens, Alfeo was on his way to call on a certain person who may . . . Or may not." The Maestro sighed. "We have our suspicions, but no evidence, you understand? No evidence I can lay before the Ten." Meaningful glances were exchanged. "I dare not make an accusation yet. But the person we suspect may carry his own evidence on his person, and his face may be evidence enough when you have arrested the surviving bravos. Even his reaction when he sees Alfeo still alive may be revealing. Since one attempt has already been made on his life this morning, and since my servant Bruno is too upset to continue providing protection, may I ask that the Republic provide some staunch and trustworthy bodyguard to accompany my apprentice when he makes this visit?"

Quazza is not the sort of man to grab at a deal before he

has walked around it a few times and counted its teeth. Especially a deal offered by Maestro Nostradamus. He chewed the nearer edges of his beard and stared hard. "What exactly do you mean about evidence on his person?"

The Maestro pulled back his lips out sideways. He is a superb actor the justice system lost a great advocate in him. "He may be posing as a Christian and not be a Jew."

That meant *Turkish spy* and raised the stakes a lot. It certainly took the matter out of the hands of the *sbirri*.

Missier Grande chewed for another moment and then accepted the offer. "I will send a man. An hour from now, Zeno?"

"I shall be at your service, *Missier Grande*."

"And your memory will improve in the meantime?"

"I shall think very hard, *Missier Grande*."

Quazza spun on his heel and marched out. Torre and the *sbirri* followed like sheep. No one argues with *Missier Grande*.

12

Having attended to my penance and dressed in clean clothes and shoes, one of which was decidedly damp, I peglegged down the stairs with Giorgio hovering alongside. I was waylaid halfway by a mob of Marciana women and children and had to give an expurgated adumbration of my battle outside the church, which was the talk of the parish. I arrived at the watergate at the same time as a gondola glided in to the quay. The curtains on the felze were open and inside sat Filiberto Vasco in his red cloak.

I do not like *Missier Grande* Quazza, but I respect him; he is tough but honest. I cannot say as much for his *vizio*. Filiberto Vasco is about my age, which is too young for the high office he holds; his family has too much money and he has far too much ambition. Were I *Missier Grande*, I should wear plate mail on my back whenever Filiberto Vasco came within stabbing distance. He pays court to all the women, menaces all the men, fancies himself as a wit, and knows everything. His only admirable quality is that he dislikes me as much as I dislike him.

Giorgio's services would obviously not be needed. The two

men rowing Vasco's boat wore ordinary gondolier clothes, but I should not have cared to wrestle with either of them. Nay, were I triplets, I should'st not. I limped down the steps and boarded, squirming into the *felze* with heartrending stoicism to seat myself alongside Vasco. We regarded each other with mutual distaste.

"Where do you want to go to, Zeno?"

I gave him Karagounis's address in the Greek quarter just east of San Marco. He passed it on and we shot away from the quay. The gondoliers started to sing, because they are forbidden to listen to their superiors' conversation, but they sang surprisingly well, one bass and one tenor. The *vizio* leaned back and smirked. I wondered if I could have learned to smirk like that if my great-great-grandfather had been a pirate like his. We cross swords almost every week at Captain Colleone's Monday fencing class. I am a better fencer than he is.

"I have orders to take you to the Leads, Alfeo, unless you tell me the truth and the whole truth."

"I will gladly tell you as much as I am allowed by my oath, Filiberto."

"What oath?"

"I am not allowed to say. But it was sworn to someone much higher than *Missier Grande*."

The sneer waxed. If I could do no better than that, Vasco would hear the music of a cell door closing on me.

"The well-loved Procurator Orseolo died two days ago," I said.

"What has that to do with you?" But a moment of hesitation had told me that the doge was not the only one concerned about that sudden death.

"He was taken ill the previous evening. Maestro Nostradamus was the first physician to attend him, you know, and he suspects poison."

Vasco's eyes narrowed to stiletto stabs as he calculated how to use this information for his own advancement. "Keep talking."

I had my master's leave to reveal all this. If the Greek's servant, Pulaki, matched the assassin I had seen in the mirror, then he was a Turkish agent and the murderer we sought. I was sorry that *Vizio* Vasco would get the credit for arresting him, but the Maestro would be rescued from suspicion and the case closed.

"We have a theory that the procurator was an innocent victim of a plot to poison somebody more important. No, dear friend, I am forbidden to reveal more. But we believe that a man named Pulaki, one of the wine stewards, is actually an agent of the sultan. Remove his britches and all will be revealed."

"You mean not enough will be revealed?" Vasco fancies himself as a wit.

"As the *lustrissimo* says. There is a slight chance that his master is the culprit. That is what I have to establish. If I identify either of them, I will happily accuse him and give you reason to look for the missing evidence."

"Will you, indeed?" The *vizio* smiled. Heads he won, tails I lost. What more could his shriveled little heart desire? "And on what basis will you identify either of them?"

"Call it a hunch."

He smiled. The Ten could make stones speak. "And who is his master?"

"A Greek bookseller, Alexius Karagounis."

Vasco's smile disappeared like an anvil in a canal.

I guessed why and felt a fact drop into place with the thump of a pile driver's mallet—the Ten already suspected Karagounis! That was why the doge was so concerned; he had unwittingly gone to meet with a possible Turkish agent, and he was utterly forbidden to talk with foreigners except in the presence of his counselors.

Silence fell. Under the competing songs along the canal, I could hear Vasco's brain creaking as he weighed his options. If Karagounis was under surveillance, then it would take a specific order from the Ten to arrest him and a premature move would bring the wrath of the mighty crashing down on the *vizio*. To let Alfeo Zeno interfere and then not arrest Karagounis would alert the suspect and cause him to flee. Vasco's only safe course was to throw Alfeo Zeno back in jail and report to Quazza for fresh orders.

Then he reached a decision and smiled again. "It will be interesting. If your accusation is false, you will be in serious trouble, of course."

"I am confident that my information is correct," I said, trying to look as if that were true. Now it was my brain's turn to creak. My warped imagination toyed with the possibility that Karagounis was a spy for the Ten and then discarded it. "He may have fled. I did try to call on the man yesterday, but there was no one home."

"We have ways of opening doors," the *vizio* said. He continued to smile, no doubt listening to the noises my brain was making as I tried to work out what he had worked out.

No more was said until we reached our destination. There is no way to climb out of a gondola while keeping one leg straight, and my scarlet hose was oozing blood by the time I was up on the quay. I looked skyward in dismay.

My companion leered. "Top floor, you said? You want to run up ahead?"

"If you were a gentleman you would carry me," I said grumpily and headed for the stairs. Vasco and his two *colossi* followed. There had been women standing around the door as we approached. Now there were none, but almost every window held a face or two, as if we had sounded trumpets. The *vizio*'s red cloak had worked this magic.

Somewhere around the second floor it occurred to me to wonder how long the Council had suspected Karagounis, assuming it did. Suppose the Ten had debated arresting Karagounis on the day of the Imer supper, and that very evening the doge himself had gone rushing off to a meeting with the suspect? If Karagounis had already fled the country, the doge could be accused of warning him.

Around the third floor I found another possibility, a more plausible one. What if Vasco knew that Karagounis was under surveillance but was not supposed to know? He could have been snooping in documents or eavesdropping. So now he would get the credit for catching a spy but could not be blamed for spoiling a plan he had not been told about. He need no longer worry that I was leading him on a wild goose chase. This was going to be one of his good days.

We reached the top and I pointed to the correct door. One of the apes pounded a fist on it: one, two, three . . . It opened.

I did not know the man standing there, although he was dressed as a servant and fitted Violetta's description of "middle twenties, slender, dusky, looked like a Moor." He was a scared Moor when he saw Vasco's sword and cloak.

"Your name?"

"Pulaki Guarana, *clarissimo*." He sounded more like a mainlander than a Venetian, but certainly not a Greek.

Vasco glanced at me; I shook my head.

"Take me to your master."

Pulaki resisted a push. "What name shall—"

"No announcement. Move!"

I followed with the oversized gondoliers on my heels. We crossed a dingy, cramped hallway and entered a dingy, cramped room being used as a study. It was almost filled by the desk. The man on the far side rose to his feet.

He had gone from heavyset to fat in the twenty or so years since I saw him perform his first murder. Then he had been bearded, now he just needed a shave. He was ugly, oily, and angry. Although I could see no demon on his shoulder, I would believe that it was still there until I had watched him being exorcized by a conclave of archbishops. He ignored me completely.

"Your name and station?" Vasco demanded.

Karagounis bowed a slight bow and smiled a slight smile. "Alexius Karagounis, at your service, *messer*. I have a permit of temporary residence, if you wish to see it."

"You sell books?"

The Greek smiled again, a *you-won't-catch-me-that-way* smile. "No, *messer*. I am not yet permitted to trade. But I do have some interesting manuscripts if Your Excellency would care to inspect them? Pulaki, bring goblets and wine for the noble lords."

"No wine. Apprentice?"

I said, "If you are an honest Christian, let us see you cross yourself."

Karagounis turned his oily smirk on me. All his reactions seemed curiously wrong. He had not asked our names or questioned our right to burst in on his privacy; it was almost as if he knew both of us and had been expecting us. "As a child in Greece my mother taught me to cross myself like this. Here, after I have been inducted into the truer faith, I shall cross myself like this."

I had him. Now he could not try to claim that he was a Jew.

I said, "In spite of your offer of wine, I say you are a Muslim. Show us that you are not."

"You are calling me a liar, young sir?"

"No," I said. "I believe that you had Christian parents, because I say that you are a *kapikulu*. You were born somewhere in the impoverished wilds of the Balkans. In your youth you were sold to the sultan's slavers, forcibly converted to Islam, and reared to serve the sultan. Prove that you have not been circumcised and I will apologize."

Vasco ostentatiously laid a hand on his sword hilt.

Karagounis ignored him and kept staring at me, but sudden hatred burned up in his eyes and some trick of the light made them seem to glint red. He said, "We could help you, Alfeo Zeno!"

Then he turned and dived out the window.

Which was closed. Don't try it, just take my word for it, but it is almost impossible to jump through a well-made casement, because both glass and lead are resistant to blunt objects. Either Karagounis called on demonic strength or the wooden sash had rotted after a century or so in the damp Venetian climate. Either way, he and the window vanished together, noisily. Vasco cried out in dismay and rushed around the desk. In their dash to join him, his heroes threw me against it, making me bang my injured leg.

By the time I stopped swearing I was alone, the others having raced downstairs to demonstrate their skills at first aid. I limped to the gap in the wall and peered out carefully. My companions had not arrived yet, but Karagounis certainly had, landing half in and half out of the gondola—smashing it and smashing himself and sinking it in two feet of seawater and sewage. Some spectators had been injured by falling debris and a crowd had gathered to shriek like seagulls.

I was sorry about the bystanders, but everything else pleased me. Suicide would be construed as a confession. Neither the Ten nor the gossips of the Rialto would have reason to blame the Maestro for the death of Procurator Orseolo. The doge and his friends should be able to hush up the whole affair. Vasco would probably get half his hide talked off him. I started toward the door and was distracted by a swirl of motion as the wind fluttered the papers on the desk.

I gathered them up before they blew all over the room. When we intruded, Karagounis had been transcribing or translating something. I am no expert like the Maestro, but I could see at a glance that *these* white sheets were modern, while *those* yellowed pages were densely inscribed with Greek text in a faded and antique hand. The originals were unbound, but looked as if they had been razored out of a bound book. They might be worth nothing or a lot of something.

Who owned those tatty scraps of manuscript?

Originally they must have been pillaged from a private house or cobwebby monastery in some Christian territory overrun by the Turks, or sold by starving owners for coppers just to buy food. So the sultan probably considered that he owned them, but he had given them to Karagounis to use as bait so he could get within striking distance of the doge. Karagounis had no further use for them and all his goods would be confiscated by the Republic anyway. They would end up locked away as evidence in some musty archive.

Who had unmasked the Grand Turk's agent at no small risk to himself? Who was going to reward me for this outstanding service to the state? Who had ruined a good pair of hose and very nearly been impaled in six directions that very morning? Was I to be compensated for loss and suffering?

The answers were: me, nobody, me, and not likely. Considering all the factors involved, it did seem that no one had any better right to those papers than I did. I slipped them into the pocket of my cloak and set off to limp down all those stairs, one step at a time.

13

I had no sooner paid off the gondolier outside the Ca' Bar-bolano than the Marciana horde swarmed around me to point out that I was bleeding. By the time I had finished explaining that I had just been oozing a little but had now stopped, two of the largest size had lifted me between them to chair me upstairs. Holding my leg straight out while they were doing this took enough effort to start it bleeding again. I thanked them and hobbled into the Maestro's apartment. Corrado shouted that I was hurt. His mother came flustering out of the kitchen . . . You would think none of them had ever seen blood before, let alone mine.

I went briefly to my room to shed my cloak. Then I went to report.

When I limped into the atelier, the Maestro was seated by the fireplace. To my amazement, the visitor in the green chair opposite was a nun. I blinked twice before I recognized Violetta, alias Sister Chastity, and remembered that she and I had a date to call on Bianca Orseolo.

The Maestro is enough of a prude to rank courtesans with prostitutes and despise men who pay women for sex when they could buy books instead, but he is not a misogynist—he finds almost everybody stupid and boring, regardless of gender. Violetta is well aware of all this and goes out of her way to charm him. Nobody is less boring or stupid than she when she wants to be. He eats out of her hand and would not notice if she fed him rocks.

I detoured by the desk because there was a letter lying on my side of it. It had been opened, of course.

Dear and honored friend,
The man of whom you enquired was in serious financial straits until recently, having pawned his book collection and some of his furniture. About two months ago he came into better times and paid off all his debts.

I have the honor to be
Your humble servant
Isaia

That testimony would hang Ottone Imer now, if the Ten got hold of it.

On the Maestro's side, the *Midrasch-Na-Zohar* had been closed and pushed aside, but Nettesheim's *De Occulta Philosophia* lay open beside it, so he had not given up on cabalism yet.

I headed for the tête-à-tête, collecting a chair on the way. Somehow Violetta seemed much less outrageous in her nun's costume than she had the previous day. Had I grown used to it, or had Milana altered it for her? Her sun-bleached hair was well tucked away and she wore no face paint, but it was equally possible that Violetta was merely acting *nun* so effectively that I failed to find her display of ankle and bosom as outrageous as I should.

"Bishop takes pawn." She lifted her lips to offer me a kiss, but she was Aspasia, so it was a Platonic, political kiss.

Besides, bending was awkward for me at the moment. "You are bleeding, Alfeo."

"Just another jealous husband." I sat down between them, facing the fire.

"Rook to king's bishop five," the Maestro said.

"Ah, disaster!" Violetta said. "I should have seen that! It will be mate in three, won't it? I should know better than to try to match wits with one of the greatest minds in Europe, but I do thank you for the game, doctor. You look very pleased with yourself, apprentice. Shall I leave, so that you men can talk business?"

"Maestro?"

He said, "Not at all, madonna. I know Alfeo tells you everything anyway."

He does this just to rankle me, because he knows I will leap to her defense like a dog chasing a stick.

"I do *not* tell her everything! I tell her nothing. In this case I questioned her because she was one of the witnesses, and a very observant one. She led me to valuable information about Enrico Orseolo, who had to be a prime suspect because he will be the old man's heir. Other than that, she knows no more than the public at large."

He pulled a mawkish smile. I had brought back the stick. "Would you tell her what you did with that mirror last night?"

"I haven't done so, but if you give me permission I will."

Courtesans have to be the most secretive of people, and he knows that.

"Do so, then." He leaned back to watch.

"I invoked a fiend last night, love," I said. "Dangerous but necessary. That's why I went to the church this morning." I knew she would have heard about the fight that was the talk of the parish. "The demon showed me the face of the poisoner, and today I went calling on him with Filiberto

Vasco. The spy was Karagounis, not his servant. When we questioned him he saw the game was up and jumped out a window. About now the *vizio* must be trying to explain why he brought in a dead spy. I wish him luck, very bad luck. But the case is closed. The would-be assassin was a Turkish agent. The procurator's death was an accident, when their glasses got switched. The real plot was to kill the doge, who had been cleverly lured to the meeting."

"Well, I'm sorry about the old man," Violetta said softly. "I am glad we don't have to suspect poor Bianca." She was Niobe, an aspect of her I rarely see, the sorrowing mother. Bellini or del Piombo would have taken one look at her and painted her at the foot of the cross for all eternity to admire.

"We need not bother Bianca," I said happily. "The case is closed."

"Indeed?" the Maestro murmured.

I almost fell off my chair in alarm. "Am I missing something?"

"You missed something last night," he said with quiet satisfaction. I detest that sleepy look he puts on. He was going to make me look stupid in front of Violetta.

I spoke through clenched teeth. "Instruct me, master."

"You are looking for a simple solution after I warned you the matter was complex." He bunched his cheeks into a mocking smirk. "Evil is rarely simple. Yes, I've told you that often enough, but you must also remember that, while fiends are not as clever as certain nuns, they do know their business. A fiend making a mistake would be very unlikely to commit a lesser evil instead of a greater, and yet you are telling me that the fiend-ridden Karagounis poisoned a harmless old man instead of the Republic's head of state. How very curious! A demon would be much more inclined to err the other way, like a dog spurning fresh meat in favor of a stinking heap of carrion. If the fiend had the chance—by design or by accident—to poison *Nasone* and did not do so, then the fiend must have been on the track of some greater evil. We must hope that today's incident has balked it."

Violetta was silent, watching us both without expression. She must see how the old scoundrel was baiting me.

I said, "You are telling me that Alexius Karagounis did not murder Procurator Orseolo despite what the other demon showed me?"

He nodded smugly. "The logic is inescapable. How exactly did you command the fiend?" He knew that. I had reported every word.

"First, a negative—to go away 'if there was no murderer present on San Valentine's Eve last in the room in . . .' Oh, confound it!" What I actually thought was *Damn you!* which is what Putrid had said to me.

"You have it now?"

"Well, I don't!" Violetta said loyally, probably lying to make me feel better.

"A murderer," I said, "is a person who has murdered another. The old man did not die until the following day, so the poisoner was not a murderer until then—unless he had killed someone else previously, I mean. Until Orseolo actually died, the crime was merely attempted murder. I should have specified *poisoner*, not murderer."

The Maestro picked it up. "Alfeo's tame fiend would normally have taken him exactly at his word and gone away, to mislead him into thinking that there had been no killer present. But there *was* a murderer present, one of the sultan's assassins. The demon would undoubtedly have preferred not to betray that one, because the man had the potential to do much greater evil in the future, but it had to obey Alfeo's command."

"What greater evil, Maestro?" Violetta asked anxiously.

"Hell alone knows," I said. "Karagounis was setting himself up in the city, planning to marry so he could stay here. He had Ottone Imer in his pocket. He organized the book sale so he could meet rich and important people. He must have had some long-range plan. In a few years he might have become truly dangerous."

He had already been dangerous enough to shed some of my blood that morning. He had known my name and face. Who else but his demon could have warned him about me and told him to send *bravi* after me? Or tracked me down in the church, a place I do not go as often as I should.

Violetta looked from me to the Maestro and back again. "So who did kill Procurator Orseolo?"

We both shrugged.

"It is no longer our concern," I said. "The Ten do not know about the demons. They may suspect that our information was unholy, but the Maestro's skills are often useful to them, so they prefer not to ask, and they do keep the Inquisition away. Vasco recognized Karagounis's name, so he was already under suspicion. The Ten will accept that he tried to poison the doge and failed to . . ."

My master was smirking again. "But the doge was not there, was he?"

"Not officially," I admitted. "But a man who was there later jumped out a window before the *vizio* could ask him questions. Won't the Ten accept the Greek's guilt?"

He stuck out his goatee stubbornly. "I won't! I have my reputation to consider. The real culprit committed a murder in my presence, and I want to see him die between the columns! Besides, you haven't told me why Karagounis killed himself."

Puzzled, I said, "To avoid being tortured?"

"Why should that bother a demon? Surely the fiend that possessed Karagounis could have prevented him from giving away any secrets? It would have enjoyed his agonies."

Violetta frowned. "It sacrificed the pawn for some later advantage?"

The Maestro drew back his lips in his implied smile, but I could see he had wanted to reveal this himself. "You are a much better chess player than Alfeo, madonna. Whatever the Greek was up to, and Alfeo may be right on that, I don't believe that he poisoned the procurator."

"You know who did?" Aspasia demanded.

Again he smiled. "I have known for some time, but I want to find out what more evil remains to be uncovered and I must have evidence to convince the council of Ten."

I held back an angry comment. Either he was just strutting to impress Violetta or he had let me invoke a fiend when he already knew the murderer's name.

Aspasia glanced at me and then said, "Maestro, I understand why you won't tell me who poisoned the procurator, but why won't you tell Alfeo?"

He shook his head so hard that his wattles flapped. "Alfeo's face gives him away every time. Look at him now—he's angry and can't hide it. He would speak quite differently to the murderer than he does to the innocent witnesses. Alfeo, you must visit with Bianca Orseolo. If anyone saw the murder committed, she did. And we still don't know why Pasqual Tirali went to the book display, do we? That was quite a detour if he was taking his companion to the Lido."

Violetta did not rise to the bait.

I said, "I need dinner first. Can't you see just by looking at me how hungry I am?"

14

Giorgio did not approve of a courtesan dressing as a nun; he rowed us in angry silence. I did not approve either, although I pulled down the blinds of the *felze* to enjoy the guilty fun of cuddling her. I could kiss her freely, because nuns do not wear face paint to smudge, but my talk was not romantic.

"If you are discovered, you will be whipped!" I told her. The thought of her flawless body being ripped and bruised by the lash made me feel ill.

"Nonsense!" she said. "It is Carnival! I brought a mask I can put on if I need to. And why are you wearing a sword? You can't fight on an injured leg."

"I can if I must." My calf had stopped bleeding at last— fortunately so, because I was going to run out of clothes soon. Bruno was sleeping off his laudanum, but I was resolved to go nowhere without my sword until we had all the fiends and murderers accounted for. "You would wear a Carnival mask in a house of mourning?"

She laughed and kissed my cheek. "Or I can claim to be a spy for the Ten."

I shivered. "Don't joke about it."

"I'm not one," she said, "although I suspect many courtesans are. Would it put you off your game if you thought I was taking notes for *Circospetto?*"

Of course it would, but the idea that Raffaino Sciara might spend his days perusing hundreds of pornographic score sheets made me laugh out loud. I said, "It would inspire me to even more heroic efforts." It was time to change the subject, and also the entertainment or I would become too distracted to think about business. "A question, love—Yesterday I asked you about the book viewing and you told me the foreigners' names. You even knew their address."

Suddenly I was in grave danger.

"You dare ask him and I'll tear your eyes out." Medea bared her teeth at me. She meant it, too.

"Pasqual?"

"I told you that in confidence, and only because you already knew who escorted me that night. I *never* discuss my patrons!"

"I won't mention it, I promise!"

She mellowed slightly, into a still-angry Aspasia. "He is no friend of theirs, so far as I know—and I would know. He told me about them afterwards. He said they've been turning up at auctions and making fools of themselves."

"I didn't know Pasqual collected old books."

"He doesn't. He collects antiquities—King Cheops's mummy or busts of Julius Caesar. Have you ever noticed how many famous Romans had no noses?"

I laughed and changed the subject by asking about Bianca Orseolo. One of the rewards of being a procurator of San Marco is being housed at state expense in the Procuratie, the long building along the north side of the Piazza. Although it is less than a hundred years old, it is already being called the Old Procuratie because they are building a Procuratie Nuovo on the south side. We were almost there.

Aspasia said, "She's about sixteen, and a complete innocent, reared in a convent. Her mother was called to the Lord
last year and since then she has lived with her grandfather as
a companion and, I suppose, hostess, although I doubt if the
old man entertained at all. Her father lives at the Ca' Orseolo and her brother is off on the mainland. She must be ter-
ribly lonely. Likely her duties were just to keep an eye on
the old man, because he was unsteady on his feet. And in his
head. I got the impression that he had become very difficult,
but she seems to mourn him deeply."

"Too deeply?"

Hesitation . . . "I don't know her well enough to say."

"How old is her brother?"

"Benedetto? Early twenties. Neither he nor his father was
at the Imer party, so neither could be the murderer, right?"

"I'd think so. You said Bianca had a motive."

"I did not say she committed the crime, though." Aspasia
made a moue of disapproval. "The old man wanted . . . was
insisting that she return to the convent and take her vows.
Bianca's a lively child, or would be if she got the chance. She
did not want to. Now her father is head of the family, and he
may be more understanding."

"I would certainly consider murder if anyone tried to force
me into a monastery," I said. "I would negotiate on a nunnery.
She had two aunts who were nuns, according to Alessa."

I should have known better. It was like asking the Pope
about Martin Luther. Or vice versa.

"It's *disgusting*!" Aspasia said. "Do you know that at least
half the noblewomen of this city are banished into convents
and never marry? A family's accursed honor forbids a girl to
marry down the social ladder, and very few families rank
higher than Bianca's. That same stupid honor would require
that she bring her husband a gigantic dowry, tens of thousands of ducats!"

"The law forbids huge dowries."

"But who obeys the law? No family can easily part with that sort of money. So the girl is cloistered and the family wealth stays with the sons."

And sons brought in dowries. I bear a noble name. Someday a wealthy citizen may offer me a thousand or so ducats to marry one of his daughters and sire patrician grandsons for him, a gaggle of little Zenos.

Violetta was in full flood now. "Then they wonder why their sons have trouble finding noble brides. Of course it's all right for *men* to marry beneath them, just as long as the brides have money and not too many brothers. Pasqual's father applied for permission to marry a citizen's daughter and the Great Council held its nose and approved. The marriage restored the family fortune and hasn't even hurt his political career. But Pasqual is an only child. His parents are nagging him to marry and produce an heir."

A few of the old clans have grown enormously, so there can be fifty members of the Great Council with the same family name—some fabulously rich and some mouse-poor, like me. Others trimmed the herd too small and died out.

Violetta had not done. "Do you know that some fathers have forced their daughters to take their vows at knife point?"

Yes I did, but such things are better not discussed. A mere courtesan should not speak ill of her betters. Alarmed, I said, "Beloved, just what did you say to Bianca in your tête-à-tête yesterday?"

She shrugged as if the question was completely unimportant. "I just told her a few things she did not know. She has no one to turn to, you know, no one at all. No mother or sisters to advise her. All her childhood friends are still in the convent. The Church and the state and the men in her family are all against her."

"Merciful God, woman, if you advised a procurator's

daughter to take up a career as a prostitute, they will pillory you! They'll brand you, deport you . . . I don't know what all they'll do to you!"

"I did nothing of the kind," Aspasia said stiffly. "I told you she was trained in a *convent*! What do you suppose she knows about Ovid or Boccaccio? She knows no songs but psalms. There is only one way she could entertain a man, and that is the least part of a courtesan's repertoire. I told her that she was crazy to prefer marriage, that many noblewomen are confined even more strictly than nuns. They are assigned husbands for dynastic reasons, usually much older men, and they often lack even the benefit of company."

"Thank Heaven!" I said, convinced that I was not hearing the whole truth.

"Of course I did have to agree with her that most, or at least many, young wives acquire a *cavaliere servente* to brighten their lives while their husbands are occupied with business affairs."

I shuddered.

"I also listed," she conceded, "some of the more liberal houses, like San Zaccaria, where the sisters' habits are of attractive cut and decent fabric, not just sackcloth bags, where the diet and the prayer regimen are not too tyrannical. Where they allow music and so on."

"That's all right, I suppose," I said doubtfully.

"Or San Lorenzo, Maddalena, San Secondo, and some on the mainland and outer islands that are even more forgiving, like San Giovanni Evangelista di Torcello—"

"A common brothel!"

"It has unusually relaxed views, but there are many where the sisters are allowed to entertain friends in the parlor, even friends with whiskers. And so on."

"But you did not suggest she become a courtesan, did you?"

"I answered all her questions," Aspasia said evasively. "She asked me how I got started and what sort of money one could earn. I told her about secret marriages, which the Church recognizes and the state does not, and what an outraged father can or can not do about it afterwards—especially to the bridegroom, of course. About how a girl might find a trainer and a protector . . . Useful information that she wanted to have."

I shuddered even harder. "Did you mention pox and pimps and turning tricks in alleys?"

"I told her that few were as successful as I am. Do you honestly suspect that sweet child of murdering her grandfather?"

"She had the best opportunity," I said, happy to return to the safer subject of murder. "Who else knew that he was drinking retsina? She must have been close enough to hear him choose it. The servant said he laughed. Doesn't that suggest a family joke and an audience to appreciate it?"

"How distinctive is the poison's taste?"

"We don't know," I admitted weakly. "We assume it had a strong flavor and therefore the fact that he chose that wine was important."

"If you are going to argue that way," Minerva said, "then you must explain how she knew that retsina would be available. It's rarely served even in the great houses, and I would not expect to see it offered at a party given by a citizen attorney."

"You know more about that than I do."

"Or Nostradamus."

"He doesn't get out much," I agreed. She was right, as always. The murderer must have carried the poison to the reception, so the crime was premeditated, but then to count on the victim drinking or eating something with a very powerful flavor seemed strangely hit-and-miss. "Who, apart from Imer and Karagounis knew there would be retsina available?"

"Let's ask Bianca," Violetta said as the gondola nudged against a mooring post.

I gripped her arm. "You wait here! It's far too dangerous for you to go around masquerading as a nun. Suppose we run into her father?"

"Her brother would be more dangerous." Medea struck my hand away, scorching me with a warning glare. "Just how do you think an unknown, unattached young man like you is going to get in to speak with an unmarried girl of her lineage and upbringing? On the very day of her grandfather's funeral? You are not usually so stupid, Alfeo Zeno."

"Ah, flattery!" I stepped ashore and handed her up beside me. She turned to the nearest door, and I said, "No, this way."

"You have been here before?"

"Two years ago. I delivered the procurator's horoscope." Then I had been sent around to the tradesmen's entrance, but I had argued my way up into the state rooms by refusing to deliver the scroll to anyone other than the great man himself. I had been tantalized by glimpses of marvelous paintings that I had not been able to examine properly.

This time I expected a tomb of a house, draped in mourning and silent as the streets of Atlantis, but a barge tied up at the steps was half full of furniture. Two workmen came out carrying a chest. On our way upstairs we passed a team bringing down a wardrobe.

"The family has three days to move out," Violetta told me.

"That seems cruelly soon."

"It is usual. Funeral this morning; tomorrow they will accept condolences in the palace courtyard. The Great Council will elect a new procurator on Sunday. You can be certain that vote buying and arm twisting have already begun." That was Aspasia speaking, of course.

"Surely the family will have already gone to the Ca' Orseolo?" I said.

A line of workmen ran up past us to fetch more furniture. "She said not yet." Helen wafted her lashes at the harassed young doorman who accosted us. "Sister Maddalena and *sier* Alfeo Zeno, to see Madonna Bianca."

He had certainly expected me to speak, not her, and was perhaps startled to discover that nuns even had eyelashes. Confused, he mumbled, "The family is not receiving visitors today, sister."

"Madonna Bianca agreed to receive us this afternoon."

Understandably, he went and fetched the majordomo, who frowned suspiciously at me, as if trying to remember where he had seen me before. He was older and less susceptible to eyelashes, but Helen had already lowered her veil and yielded place to Aspasia, who explained about her friendship with Bianca and their appointment for this afternoon. We were shown into a reception room overlooking the Piazza. Violetta swept forward to look out the window, while I followed unhappily, squirming at intruding on a family's bereavement—we were not even wearing mourning! Half the room had already been stripped of furniture. Two men followed us in and left with a bundle that probably contained a harpsichord. I had mad visions of being left behind, locked up in an empty apartment with Violetta.

Outside, the Piazza was being swept by damp gusts of February. Official mourning had also helped reduce the usual bustle, but the mountebanks at their stalls were still hawking their quack nostrums. The beggars were still in evidence, the hawkers, porters, priests, nuns, monks, and, of course, the inevitable crowds of aimless foreigners from all corners of the world. I could not hear their voices, but I could guess at many of the costumes—Egypt, Turkey, Dalmatia, Spain, France, Greece, England.

Leaving the depressing wintery sight, I went to admire a large Titian, a family group adoring the Virgin: two men and five youngsters, no wives and mothers allowed. Titian died when I was a toddler, so even if this were a late work, as the fashions suggested, the old man on the right was the wrong generation to be our murdered procurator. I recognized the martyred Bertucci in the heavy-jawed central figure who dominated the composition, the suppliant who would have paid for the painting. He was wearing the robes of a ducal counselor. The children were his brood as listed for us by Alessa—two youths destined to die abroad, two girls to burn in a convent fire, and Enrico. After so much tragedy, it seemed macabre to keep the picture hanging in full view. My mental image of the late Bertucci Orseolo was not yet clear enough to tell me if he had been a maudlin romantic who enjoyed weeping at the sight of his dead children, or the exact opposite, a Spartan with a marble heart and the hide of a crocodile.

Violetta joined me and went through the same reasoning. "That must be Enrico," she said, pointing to the youngest boy. "The only one of the lot still living."

The workmen had cleared the last of the furniture and were rolling up a rug at the far end of the hall, ignoring us. From the noises I could hear, the entire house was infested with them.

I was just about to head for another picture—a mythological free-for-all between centaurs and armed nudists—when a rapid tap of heels made me turn, knowing that whoever was coming was not Bianca. He was about my age; tall, self-assured, and holding his chin high as befitted a man whose ancestors had helped rule the Republic for nine hundred years. He wore a black robe of mourning with a train, a black bonnet, and a sling supporting his right arm, all of them beautifully tailored, even the sling.

"Sister Maddalena? May I ask what business you have intruding on my sister's—" Silence.

Violetta had folded back her veil again. His face turned ivory-white. My heart dropped like an anchor.

She curtseyed. "My most sincere sympathy on your loss, Bene."

"You are no nun!"

She smiled. "As you well know."

"What do you want with my sister? Why does a harlot force herself on a girl of patrician rank? She says you were here yesterday, too."

"I came to help her, Benedetto."

"Help her? Help her in what way?"

He had recovered from his first shock and was moving swiftly to anger. Had I been alone I might have taken to my heels, but I was much more frightened about what might happen to Violetta than I was about any danger to me.

Aspasia remained serene and confident. "How are you enjoying Padua?"

"What business is that of yours?"

"Who suggested you go there?" Her smile would have dissolved the stoniest heart. "Be fair, Benedetto! Admit that you have benefitted from my help in the past. When I made you welcome in my bed, you called me courtesan, not that other word."

He colored. "State your business!"

She sighed. "May I present *sier* Alfeo Zeno? Will you listen to what he has to say, please, Benedetto? Then you will see why this is important."

At a glance Benedetto assessed my best outfit as rags and me as poor trash, probably her pimp. He barely nodded to my bow.

"Clarissimo," I said, "my sympathy on your sad loss. The news I bring can only increase the pain. Your honored grandfather," and I pointed up at the painting, "was murdered."

He bristled. "I give you two minutes to justify that remark."

"One will suffice. You have no doubt heard gossip that the procurator's death was prophesied in a horoscope prepared for him by Maestro Nostradamus. Your sister may have told you that the doctor Nostradamus who came to his aid when he took ill at the supper party was the same man. He immediately recognized the symptoms of a certain poison. Whether you believe in astrology, as your grandfather did, or scoff at it like His Serenity Pietro Moro, you must acknowledge that Nostradamus is a celebrated doctor. He says that your grandfather was poisoned. I am helping him discover who did this terrible thing."

Sier Benedetto rallied. "On whose authority? Is the Grand Council so desperate for candidates that it is electing boys as state inquisitors?"

"I was instructed to make these inquiries by a close friend of your grandfather's, Pietro Moro himself."

He glanced at my sword and then said, "Rubbish! Have you tried to tell my father this? You expect me to believe it?"

Actually I did not, but I was determined to keep trying, because the alternative was excessively unappealing. "I assure you, *clarissimo*, that His Serenity granted me not just one, but two, audiences on this matter yesterday. You have heard of the Greek, Alexius Karagounis, who was selling the books?" Receiving a nod, I forged ahead, trying to seem as assured as Violetta. "This morning I called upon Alexius Karagounis, being assisted in my inquiries by the *vizio*, Filiberto Vasco."

"So?" But Vasco's name had sown a seed of doubt.

"Rather than answer our questions, Karagounis leaped out a window to his death, *clarissimo*."

Workmen with ladders had started taking down the paintings and propping them against the walls, ready for carpenters to come and crate them. I should have preferred a more private meeting place, but there probably wasn't one in the house.

Under happier circumstances, the turmoil of conflicting emotions in Benedetto's face would have been amusing. "So you consort with the *vizio* as well as the doge?"

"Reluctantly. *Missier Grande* and *Circospetto* are also cooperating. I have no official standing, but the Republic is backing my inquiries." And all of them would deny me if asked.

"*Sier* Alfeo is being modest, Bene," Violetta said. "This morning he was set upon and almost murdered by a gang of bravos."

"I am not surprised to hear it."

Wearing a sword carries certain obligations and I had taken as much as I could reasonably be expected to stand. Despite the throbbing pain in my leg, I laid a hand on my sword hilt. "*Messer*, you hide behind a claim of injury or of nervous prostration brought on by grief?"

He paled. "You *dare?*"

"My name is written in the Golden Book. Yours does not deserve to be."

"Stop that, both of you!" Medea's eyes flashed fire. "Bene, you should withdraw your remark."

He bit his lip. "I spoke without thinking, *clarissimo.*"

"And I in haste." We bowed to each other. My standing had improved.

"I have good reason to believe that the attack on me was related to the matter of your grandfather's murder."

Young Benedetto was visibly drooping under the load we had just piled on his shoulders. He made an effort to straighten them. "My father must be informed of all this. And the first thing he will ask is why the state inquisitors are employing a . . ." He looked at me in disbelief. "This *nobleman* to conduct their inquiries for them."

"It is a tribute to the esteem in which your late grandfather was held," I told him. "Do you really want your sister interrogated by the Three? Everyone is trying to head off formal proceedings that must be a harrowing experience to those involved. For example, where were you on Saint Valentine's Eve?"

His outrage did not convince. "You dare suspect *me*?"

"You think the Three will not?"

"I don't care if they do." That was juvenile bravado and unbelievable. "I was not even in the city. I was in Padua—in jail. There was a duel and I was accused of drawing first." Hence the sling, of course. It was probably a sound alibi and I would get nowhere by asking to see his wound.

"I hope you killed him?" Helen asked sweetly.

He turned to her in anger, but her smile can melt any man. It won a tiny, shamefaced grin. "I didn't get near him. But I will next time." Then he swung back to me. "If what you say is true, *clarissimo*, the Greek's suicide was an admission of guilt."

I shrugged. "My master has good reason to believe that it was not, strange as that may seem. But you are undoubtedly right if you think that the Ten are likely to accept that explanation. And in that case your grandfather's killer will escape to enjoy the benefits of his crime. Is that acceptable to you and your honored father?"

Before he could answer, I continued. "Obviously if you were in Padua that night, you were not the killer. Your father was not in the Imer house either. But your sister was. No!" I raised both hands to hold back an explosion. "I am not suggesting that she poisoned your grandfather. But she may have seen something vital. I beg you, *clarissimo*, to allow us to ask her a few simple questions. It will not take long."

Benedetto was out of his depth. He had much growing up to do yet. "Tell me your questions and I shall go and put them to her."

I set my jaw in the notch labeled *stubborn*. "My master's orders are that I speak with her in person, *messer.*"

"Then you must call on her when my father is present."

"I have only one more day to complete my investigation before I must report to the authorities. Shall I say that your honored sister refused to answer my questions?"

"That is a foul lie!"

"Then I must tell the truth, which is that she was not permitted to. Expect *Missier Grande* to come calling tomorrow." I bowed and offered my arm to Violetta.

She cried, "Oh, no, Alfeo! How awful for her!"

"Wait!" Benedetto snarled. "Did you tell her that you and I were once intimate?"

Violetta's eyes twinkled like stars. "Only once, Bene? You were never satisfied with once. But no, I certainly did not mention that to her. I never discuss my patrons with anybody."

"If I permit this, then you will remain Sister Maddalena in her presence and you will never have anything to do with my sister ever again, is that agreed—no visits, no letters, nothing?"

"Bene, you know you can rely on my discretion. Of course."

"And you will never pester her either, Zeno."

"Certainly." I bowed.

"Wait here!" His heels went clicking away across the terrazzo to the door.

"You did that beautifully, my dear," Helen purred, easing me away from the Titian as the ladder crew closed in on it. We wandered towards the empty center of the big room.

"You did more than I did. How long were you a friend of *messer* Benedetto?"

She smiled cryptically. "I never discuss my patrons."

"Then discuss his grandfather. Why did somebody hate him enough to murder him?"

I thought for a moment she would not answer, but she was just working out what she would tell me.

"He was strict, and had his own ideas. You know that rich families sometimes hire a courtesan as tutor when a boy reaches the age to study calligraphy?"

"Penmanship?"

"Joined-up writhing."

I laughed. "Yes, Aspasia."

"And physical intimacy may blossom into friendship. I recall one young man who was very upset and desperately wanted my advice. He said his grandfather was planning to launch his political career right away by entering him in the Santa Barbara's Day lottery."

Every December the Great Council admits thirty youngsters as young as twenty, the creamiest of the cream, scions destined for greatness. The odds of winning a seat are good for anyone, and I would have been very surprised if an Orseolo had failed to win, because there are ways to adjust lotteries. Putrid would do it if I told him to. You should know by now why I never would, but there are other practitioners of the occult in the Republic and some have nothing left to lose.

"The young man in question," she continued, "did not want that. He wanted to get away from home, poor little rich boy. He babbled about volunteering to be a gentleman archer on a galley. His ambition was to be a sailor, a great merchant trader like his ancestors. His grandfather would have blocked him. I suggested he ask to study law at the University of Padua. The old man accepted that compromise. It got him out of the city, at least."

"Is Benedetto a good swordsman?"

"If you mean that literally and are not just being vulgar, I have no idea. Why?"

"Just wondered."

Around any university you will find almost as many expert swordsmen as fleas. Pick a fight with one good enough to claim first blood without doing any serious damage, be first to draw so that you end up in jail, and you have an excellent alibi. I could not imagine why Benedetto Orseolo would have wanted an alibi. I am just a cynic.

15

Bianca entered on her brother's arm. She was swathed in black, even to a full veil, although I could make out enough of her features through the lace to recall Giuseppe Benzon describing her as "fiery." In fact she was gorgeous, with a heart-shaped face and eyes the size of cartwheels. She exchanged greetings with Sister Maddalena and curtseyed to my bow.

"Remember," Enrico said, "that you do not have to answer this man's questions, none of them." He scowled unhelpfully at me.

"Madonna," I said, "I am apprenticed to Maestro Nostradamus, whom you met the other night. There is reason to believe that your honored grandfather was poisoned at that reception, and we are trying to discover the culprit and bring him to justice. I deeply regret intruding on your time of grief, but you will agree that I offend in a good cause?"

She nodded, keeping her eyes downcast even behind the veil. Workmen at the far end of the hall were laying out lumber to start crating up the pictures, as if determined to make the interview even more difficult.

"Did you often accompany him to such social affairs?"
She shook her head. I waited.

"No," she whispered. "He rarely left the Procuratie any more. He was getting so unsteady . . ." More silence. "He was forced to use a cane and his right hand was bent. He called me his hands, *clarissimo.*"

"That evening, he went straight to the book viewing from this building?"

She nodded again, but this time spoke more strongly. "Yes. We went in the gondola. It is not far. He did not see well in the dark and it was raining a little. But he very much wanted to acquire some of the books. He was quite excited."

Wonder of wonders!—I had found a cooperative witness at last.

"Did he eat or drink anything before he left here? In the hour or so before?"

"It was not possible. He had been at a meeting downstairs, in the offices. He sent a clerk up to summon me and I went down to him."

"Excellent! That is very important information! I do not wish to pry needlessly, but did he say anything unusual in the gondola? Was he angry about anything, or upset?"

"No, *messer.* He spoke about one of the books, a play. He said he was convinced that it was genuine but he wanted to take another look at it. He would gladly pay several thousand ducats for it, he said. But I mustn't tell any of the other buyers he had said so."

"And what happened when you arrived at the Imer house?"

"We climbed the stairs together," Bianca said, and now she was telling the story as if eager to do so. "He was slow. Attorney Imer welcomed us, and presented his wife . . . He took Grandfather into the book room. I made my excuses to the lady and followed, because I thought he would want me with him."

"You were offered wine when?"

"Ah, before that, when we arrived."

"And you chose which?"

"I took malmsey. Grandfather had retsina."

I waited for mention of a family joke, but it did not appear. But she did! She made an annoyed sound and lifted her veil back, as if it were getting in her way. She did not quite smile at me—indeed she did not even look straight at me, which would have given her brother cause to snap at her—but I found the change a great improvement. The footman, Giuseppe Benzon, had excellent taste in feminine temperature. Pyretic, she was. She was quite nubile enough to be enfolded in my strong arms and comforted by sympathetic words murmured into her shell-like ear.

I bowed low in admiration, provoking scowls from both Medea and Benedetto. "How welcome is sunlight when it breaks through the clouds!" Such talk would be a well-deserved novelty for a cloistered beauty like Bianca. "Tell me about the viewing, then. How many people were at the table when you arrived?"

Her account confirmed the Maestro's. When she entered, he had been there, and Karagounis, and Senator Tirali, and her grandfather. Then the foreign couple had arrived and started asking the Maestro a lot of questions in a language Bianca did not know.

"And then . . . another man . . ."

"I know who you mean," I said. "An old friend in crimson robes?"

She smiled then, but not right at me. "I thought I was seeing things."

"Who was this old friend?" her brother demanded.

I could not resist saying, "That is a state secret. He came to speak to your grandfather?"

Bianca said, "Oh, yes, *clarissimo*. They greeted each other warmly. He asked him . . . The friend asked Grandfather if his health would let him come to dine at the, um, his house, and he said it would."

She had been excited by the thought that she might get to visit the palace too.

"Did they discuss the books?" I asked.

She thought for a moment. "I think the, um, other man, asked if they were all the same ones they had seen before. And Grandfather said they seemed to be. And there was one they agreed might be a fake—I'm not sure which. I think Maestro Nostradamus had been saying it was, also."

I wondered briefly how far those two old friends had lied to each other about the presumed Euripides, and if even my master's evaluation had been completely honest. Collectors can be as ruthless as hyenas. Yet the doge had withdrawn his bid after that, or so he had said. Had he been dissuaded, or had he decided to let his old friend have the treasure? Or had he lied to me?

"Madonna, can you recollect where everyone was standing?"

"That is a ridiculous question!" her brother snarled. "Bianca, you don't have to endure this."

"I am anxious to help *sier* Alfeo, Bene. They did keep moving around. They all wanted to see the books, understand, but none of them wanted to show too much interest in the ones they thought special, in case they alerted the others to their interest." Bianca was sharp, obviously. "So they walked back and forth along the table, picking them up and putting them down. The Greek man trotted along beside them, chattering all the time. *Lustrissimo* Imer came in a few times. And then another man I did not know, a younger man, and spoke with Senator Tirali. He had a lady with him."

Despite the downcast eyes and carefully flat tone, I realized instantly that Bianca knew perfectly well who Sister

Maddalena was. Bianca was a very observant young woman. Whether Violetta's nun disguise had failed to deceive her the previous day, or Violetta had deceived me, Bianca was now deceiving her pompous brother and enjoying the joke. Maybe San Giovanni Evangelista di Torcello was the place for her after all.

"That was *sier* Pasqual, the senator's son. Anyone else?"

"Two footmen came in a few times, offering more wine." She gave excellent descriptions of both Benzon and Pulaki Guarana. The outing had been exciting for her, and she had observed details that the older witnesses had missed or forgotten. "I refused more, having drunk very little. Grandfather allowed them to top up his glass once. I did not see how much he had drunk, *messer.*" She was clever enough to know what I needed to hear.

The workmen were now wrapping the pictures in canvas and rope. At least they had not started sawing and hammering.

"When you all went off to join the other guests," I asked. "Did people take their wineglasses with them?"

For the first time Bianca turned her eyes full on me. Had circumstances permitted, I could have melted on the spot very realistically.

"I do not know what the others did, *messer* Alfeo. I laid mine down so I could assist my grandfather. He drained his glass and handed it to me in exchange for his cane, which I had been holding. And he pulled a face."

"*What sort of face?*" Benedetto demanded.

Bianca lowered her eyes again. "A grimace. As if he had not liked the taste. He did not say anything. I did not ask him. *Sier* Alfeo, would it have made any difference if—"

I said, "None at all. There is no known antidote. You could have done nothing. Had you realized he had been poisoned, then a finger down the throat to induce vomiting might have helped at that early stage, but even that could be dangerous to an old man. He might well have choked. You had no reason to suspect foul play. He did not, obviously. Who has not unexpectedly found bitter lees in the bottom of a wineglass? And perhaps that was all it was."

I doubt she believed me, but she whispered, "Thank you."

"The wine was poisoned?" her brother said furiously. "The waiters have been questioned?"

"Other people drank from the same bottle," I said. "Did the procurator set his glass down while he was looking at the books, madonna?"

She nodded. "And when he moved to another, I sometimes picked it up and carried it for him, but usually he did that himself. I am certain I never picked up the wrong glass, and almost certain he never did, either. I was watching, because he was getting forgetful. That was why I was there, to help him."

Bianca had been the best-positioned witness, yet even she had not seen the killer strike. Had there even been a killer? My hopes of exposing a murderer sank to the bottom of the Adriatic Sea.

"Do not distress yourself with such thoughts!" I said. "Very few people were drinking retsina. He would have known if he had accidentally taken some other person's drink—would have known by the smell before his first sip. His death was not your fault and it was not an accident. Either his glass was deliberately poisoned or it was switched with one that had been."

"No, *messer*! If anyone had tampered with his drink I would have seen."

"Bianca!" snapped her brother. "Be careful what you say."

"She is only trying to help," I said. "Nobody suspects her." I could not imagine that angelic face belonging to a sinner guilty of anything. "She would not have made that statement if she had poisoned the wine herself! Did your grandfather have anything else to eat or drink? Antipasto?"

She shook her head. "We joined the other guests in the *salone*, but he refused more wine. At the table he took ill before the antipasto was served."

The mystery now looked more impossible than insoluble. The Maestro had been mistaken, the procurator had died of natural causes.

"You have been extremely helpful, madonna," I said. "Did anything else happen in the book room that we should know?"

She smiled. "There was a fight! Well, an argument. Our host discovered the two foreigners and asked them their names. Then he told them to leave, politely at first. The man became offensive and said he had been invited. The illustrious Karagounis was brought into the argument. Maestro Nostradamus had to translate back and forth. At one point the foreign man took out a purse and shook it in Attorney Imer's face."

Before I could ask anything more, I heard steps and looked around at the trouble approaching, Great Minister Enrico Orseolo, who had tried to beat me down from ten ducats to three for work already delivered while he was standing under a Tintoretto painting as big as the Piazzetta.

Whenever noblemen over the age of twenty-five appear in public, they wear floor-length robes, a tippet over one shoulder, and a flat, round bonnet like a cake. Magistrates wear color, all others black. As a great minister, *sier* Enrico Orseolo would wear violet instead of black, but now mourning had put him back in black, a trailing gown like his son's. Alessa had described him as cold on the outside, warm inside, but I thought of him as cold-blooded. My private name for him was Lizard, because his eyes were protuberant, heavy-lidded, creepily unblinking, while the rest of his face was gaunt and fleshless. He was said to be a politician's politician, a conciliator, a maker of deals, and I knew he was the sort of man to value agreement for its own sake, not caring whether its terms are honorable—anything was negotiable. His offers to settle the Maestro's bill had gone up one ducat at a time.

I got the full amount in the end, though.

Enrico Orseolo, the procurator's son, last survivor of the family group I had inspected earlier, Alessa's sometime patron, possible future member of the Council of Ten, came to a halt and looked us over with glassy indifference. He did not quite flicker a forked tongue at us, but I imagined it. Today he was not in a mood to compromise.

"Who are these people, Benedetto? What are they doing here?" His gaze fixed on me. "Don't I know you?"

I bent to kiss his sleeve. "Alfeo Zeno, Your Excellency, apprentice to Doctor Nostradamus, the physician who—"

"The astrologer. Yes, I remember. He took advantage of an old man's gullibility, and you were an insolent pest. What are you doing here? You, cover your face!" That last remark was directed at Bianca and the next to Benedetto. "You are supposed to be supervising the servants."

Son and daughter hurriedly departed. His Excellency turned back to me.

I began at the beginning, with his father's collapse. I did not get very far.

"*Who* poisoned his wine?"

"That is what I am trying to—"

"Did my daughter see it happen?"

"Apparently not, Your—"

"Then I am confident it did not happen at all. If your charlatan master thinks he has evidence of foul play, he should take his suspicions to the Ten. I will not tolerate vicious gossip about my family or my late father and the next time you or he meddle in my affairs, boy, I will denounce him as a mountebank to the state inquisitors."

Now he would turn his reptilian gaze on the nun. Violetta was veiled again, although I had not seen her move, but he might still recognize her as the celebrated courtesan. I had to distract him, which was easy enough. I can tolerate abuse directed at me, but I will not stand by and let people denigrate the Maestro.

"Mountebank, *clarissimo*? That horoscope you repeatedly described as a worthless piece of parchment would have saved your father's life, had you or he paid better attention to it. My master warned him to beware the coming of the lover and he was murdered on the eve of the feast of San Valentino. I would have thought ten ducats was little enough to have paid for—"

Sier Enrico was quite smart enough to see the potential for ridicule if he tried to carry out his threat. His eyes bulged even farther. "Get out! Get out of here!" He wheeled around to Violetta. "Who are you and why are you here?"

"I am another charlatan." She spoke with Medea's voice. "Your manners may be forgiven on account of your bereavement, for which I offer my condolences and my prayers. Let us go, *sier* Alfeo."

Enrico Orseolo snorted at hearing my title. He probably stood and watched us leave, but I did not turn around to look. I hate being seen off as much as any man does, but this did seem a propitious time to leave.

"Pretty girl," Medea said as we descended the great staircase.

"I suppose so."

"Suppose? I was frightened someone would step on your tongue, it was hanging out so far. And her father is absolutely charming. You are old playmates, are you, you two?"

"Something like that," I admitted. "My master has a rule

that a horoscope is confidential and must be delivered into the client's own hand. I often have to talk my way up the chain, from skivvy to footman to majordomo to people with names. And then I have to collect the money, which can take several more visits. I got to know the Orseolo household quite well."

She squeezed my arm. "In my profession we have other ways of dealing with the deadbeat problem."

"You send bravos to cut throats?"

"Not yet. So far a discreet threat has always been enough."

We reached the landing stage. Tethered boats were nodding gently on the Rio di Cavalleto. A gull standing on one of the brightly-colored posts regarded me seriously, but not without sympathy, I thought. Giorgio had tied up at a mooring several doors along, but he saw us and waved.

"I have friends who have rough friends," Violetta said seriously. "If you want to learn more about the gang that attacked you, I can ask around. I'm sure the Ten will track them down long before I ever could."

"And if they belong to some nobleman's workforce," I said, "the Ten will forget all about them." When Giorgio pulled alongside, I said, "Back to the convent, please."

16

"So now you will go on to Ca' Tirali?" Sister Chastity inquired as we cuddled once more in the privacy of the *felze*.

"I do as my master tells me," I said. "But I am convinced that the procurator was called to the Lord in the normal way. The truth may have to wait for Judgement Day. In mortal terms we have found no real motive, nor opportunity, because Bianca would have seen the crime committed."

Violetta said, "Mm?"

I pricked up my eyebrows. "What am I missing?"

Minerva pulled loose from my embrace. "I think there is an obvious motive. How much was the supposed Euripides manuscript worth?"

"Perhaps nothing, if it is a modern fake. A handsome sum if it is an ancient fake. But even if it is the only surviving copy of a genuine play by Euripides of Athens from two thousand years ago, it is still just medieval paper or vellum with ink marks on it." Whichever it was, it now rested in the secret compartment in the chest in my room. I might not get thousands for it, but I would certainly be able to buy some wonderful gift for my love, gold and rubies, the sort of miracle jewelry her patrons gave her. It was a thrilling thought.

"I think you're wrong," she said. "A unique item is not a bottle of wine or a loaf of bread, for which the state can decree a fair price. It will fetch whatever someone is willing to pay for it, and that is one ducat more than the second-most determined bidder can afford. The winner might not even be the richest bidder at the auction, just the craziest."

I followed her trail through the mental forest. "And Procurator Orseolo might have been the craziest, you mean?" In public he had been a Grand Old Man and in private a tyrant; he had been enormously rich and reluctant to pay his tradesmen; but those things were true of many noblemen. "You really think anyone would commit murder just to stop another man outbidding him on a heap of dog-eared paper?"

"I think you should finish the job, my darling Alfeo. Go and ask Pasqual Tirali the same questions you have been asking the others. He's taking me to Carnival tonight, so he should be at home now, getting ready. I have no idea whether the senator will be there or not."

"Is Pasqual a suspect?" I asked incredulously. "You were with him. Could he have poisoned the old man without your seeing?"

Giorgio's voice faded away in the ending of a verse. His oar creaked in the rowlock; other voices picked up the melody in the distance.

"I didn't notice Pasqual doing anything in the least suspicious," Aspasia said. "And I can't imagine he would murder anyone for any reason at all. But I wasn't watching his father. I don't know the senator well. He is the most charming man you can ever hope to meet, yet he has the reputation of being ruthless. I know he is a fanatical bibliophile."

"I shall certainly go by Ca' Tirali," I said, wondering if I had just been given a hint. I would try not to murder dear Pasqual in a fit of jealous fury.

The Tirali mansion is a close neighbor of Ca' Barbolano, situated on the far side of the Rio San Remo, within sight but not hail. Having delivered Violetta safely to 96, I asked Giorgio to take me there and offered to walk home.

"Not on that leg, you won't," he said. "I'll send one of the boys to wait for you. He can run and fetch me when you're ready."

Lounging in the gondola I had almost forgotten my wound, but it did hurt when I walked on it, so I agreed. There is much to be said for decadent self-pity. I disembarked and hammered the door knocker. I gave my name and the Maestro's to the doorman, expecting him to leave me moldering in the entrance hall while he plodded upstairs and returned with orders to drop me in the canal. Then I would have to start dropping careful hints about murder and the Council of Ten.

Wrong. The flunky bowed very low. "You are expected, *sier* Alfeo. If you would be so good as to follow me?"

I was so good, but I was also scared prickly as a hedgehog. I had claimed no title when I gave my name. And *expected*? I do not like being surprised when there may be murderers loose. This reception was too reminiscent of that morning, when I had been *expected* at the church.

I had never spoken with any member of the Tirali family in my life, and would have been both astonished and hurt to hear that Violetta had ever mentioned me to Pasqual. I knew him by sight, though, and he was waiting for me at the top of the stairs.

He was young, rich, and dazzlingly handsome, clad in embroidered silk jerkin and knee britches and a sleeveless robe of blue velvet trimmed with miniver, for he would not wear his formal gown at home. He had been admitted to the Great Council the previous year and was expected to have a notable career in politics, following his father. He could afford the finest, most beautiful courtesan in the Republic and charm stars down from the sky to make her a bracelet. Just looking at him, I wondered why Violetta bothered to share the time of day with me, let alone her pillow.

He came forward smiling a welcome. "*Sier* Alfeo! I hoped that was you I heard. I am Pasqual Tirali. This is a great pleasure."

"The honor is mine, *clarissimo*." I went to bow and kiss his sleeve, but he caught me in the embrace with which nobles greet their equals.

"Come in and share a glass of wine," he said. "My parents are as eager to meet you as I am." He led me across the wide *salone* whose ceiling was of gilt and stucco, supported by jasper columns. The fireplace was of black marble, the chandeliers were flamboyant multicolored fantasias from the glassblowers of Murano, and the statues were original marbles or bronzes, not copies. I noted several Romans without noses and some antique Greek urns and kraters, no doubt items from the collection Violetta had mentioned. I did not see King Cheops around, but anyone who can afford to buy such ancient junk must have a serious excess of wealth. The rugs beneath our feet were worth kings' ransoms and the paintings on the walls made me drool like the source of the Nile. I must have gaped at them as we went by; Pasqual noticed.

"You are a lover of art, *sier* Alfeo?"

"Is that by one of the Bellini family, *sier* Pasqual?"

He smiled. "It is indeed. Jacobo Bellini. Let me show you them while we still have some light . . ." Forgetting his parents waiting to meet me, he took me on a tour of the glorious, shining paintings, rattling off the artists and subjects, and several times commenting on the technique, pointing out Tintoretto's influence showing up in Titian's later work, and so on. I was impressed by his knowledge. I wanted to hate him and was charmed against my will.

Very rarely I had been flattered like this in the past, and always by people who wanted something I was determined not to give them—but *Prejudgment is no judgment*, as the Maestro often tells me.

Eventually Pasqual took me into a small but luxurious *salotto* and there presented me to the senator and his wife, madonna Eva. Giovanni Tirali was a robust man in his fifties, with bright, questing eyes and a winning smile. He looked neither ruthless nor fanatical, but Violetta had also called him charming, and there I could not disagree. He embraced me, bid me welcome, and flawlessly acted the role of a distinguished and gracious nobleman.

His wife was a silver-haired matron who still retained much of what must have been spectacular beauty. She was not of noble birth, but he had not been stricken from the Golden Book when he married her; his political career had survived and prospered. No doubt she had brought him a stupendous dowry. The Great Council can tolerate that sort of marriage.

I was assigned a seat with a view of the canal and asked what wine I preferred. A footman brought it. It was starlight on the tongue.

"We were reading some of Petrarch's sonnets together," the lady said, closing a book. "Are you a poetry lover, *clarissimo?*"

Oh, how sweet! "I love sonnets as I love the stars, madonna, and know as little about them."

"But swords you know. We heard that you had a very narrow escape this morning."

I shrugged modestly. "There were only six of them."

The laughter was convincing.

"I noticed you limping," Pasqual said.

"I think they nicked my calf, but I may have done it my-self. I was flailing quite wildly." Nicking with a rapier would be tricky.

"I expect you were," the senator said, smiling in cherubic innocence. "You were lucky that they tried to take you out with knives. Such bravos usually wear swords and know how to use them. They did not expect to find you armed, obviously."

Thanks again to the Maestro's incredible clairvoyance! But how did Tirali know all this? "They probably thought that six unfamiliar swordsmen would be conspicuous and attract the locals' attention," I said.

"Very likely. You had a busy morning. You went to see a man in the Greek quarter."

Alarm horns were blowing. What was going on here? How did he know that? "You are well informed, Your Excellency. You even knew I was coming to call on you."

He laughed. "I have friends in high places. You came to ask if we noticed anything unusual at Ca' Imer the other night?" He had a rich, sonorous voice, an orator's voice that could speak out along the length of the Great Council's hall and be audible to more than a thousand people.

Now I was more than a little nettled. "And did you notice anything?"

"I did. My son did not."

"Nor I," his wife said.

"But you were not in the viewing room, my dear, and that is what interests *sier* Alfeo."

"Why should that be, Your Excellency?" I asked softly.

His smile told me that he had been baiting me. "A friend told me." He took a sip of wine and when he spoke again he dropped the banter and changed his tone to make his next words more significant, like the practiced orator he was. "I am interested to meet you, *sier* Alfeo. I admire what you are doing. We have far too many impoverished nobles sitting around believing that the Republic owes them a living and honest work is beneath their confounded dignity. They whine in the Council, demanding sinecures and phony offices with many rewards and few duties. The career you have chosen is unusual but quite honorable. Many patricians put off their political careers until midlife and do well regardless."

I wondered if all this oil would make the floor dangerous, and if he was flattering me or just nagging his son the playboy.

"Your Excellency is most kind." Giovanni Tirali was certainly gracious, yet Violetta had called him ruthless. I found Enrico Orseolo repulsive, but he had the reputation of being a negotiator, a maker of deals. People are unnecessarily complicated.

"I mean it," he said. "I mean it! I was very shaken by Bertucci's death. He was twenty years my senior and I had always looked up to him. That evening at Imer's he seemed frail but quite competent and cheerful, and yet the next day he was gone. *Dominus dedit, Dominus abstulit, sit nomen Domini benedictum.*"

"Amen," we said in chorus.

"But . . ."

Calculated pause. My cue.

"But?" I echoed.

"That evening, when we had looked at all the books and told all the lies we wanted about what we thought of them, our host suggested we join the other guests. I emptied my glass. Pasqual, I am sure, emptied his. And Bertucci drained his. And I saw him make a face, as if it had tasted bad."

"Dregs?"

His Excellency shrugged. "I assumed so, although properly trained servants know to look out for sediment. I did not get a chance to speak to him again. I thought little of it at the time. When Bertucci took ill, later, I recalled the incident. It niggled at me. After the funeral service this morning, I sought out my friend and told him my worries. And he told me that there was a serious possibility that Bertucci had been poisoned."

Again the senator paused for effect. I wondered if he made speeches in bed to his wife. "A friend in a funny hat?"

He smiled. "Yes, that one. I asked if the Ten were looking into it. He told me that the Ten were bombardiers who blow up everything and injure the bystanders; this was a case for a stiletto. He had set Maestro Nostradamus himself on it, and his apprentice, Alfeo Zeno. And if they could not solve it, he said, then the Ten would never even get close to the truth."

I was having trouble not purring or rolling over on my back. "So much flattery is bad for my liver, Excellency. And I should not dream of telling my master what you just said. He would be unbearable."

The senator's eyes nailed me to my chair. "Was it murder?"

"I don't see how it can have been. Another witness saw what you saw, but how could anyone have put poison in his wine with so many people watching? Nobody saw that." I glanced at Pasqual.

He shook his head, somehow subtly implying that the Old Man got bats in his bonnet sometimes. "I did not see even what my father saw. I have asked the lady I was escorting and she saw nothing untoward."

Violetta had not mentioned that.

I said, "Thank you. It does seem unlikely that anyone could have poisoned the procurator without being observed. I cannot discover any motive to commit such a terrible crime. Can you suggest one?"

Three heads shook.

The senator added, "Every politician has enemies, but we do not go around poisoning people here in the Republic—not like the Borgias did in Rome. The Council of Ten has the reputation of disposing of people in that fashion, but not here in the city, only enemies living elsewhere, out of its jurisdiction. I could name many men who yearn to be procurators of San Marco, but there are very few who have a reasonable chance of being elected, and none of them was there that night. I certainly cannot imagine a man who aspires to such a job bribing someone else—a servant, say—to commit murder for him. He would pay blackmail for the rest of his life."

"I thank Your Excellency for an expert analysis. I shall report to Maestro Nostradamus that I have found nothing to indicate foul play."

"Then why," Pasqual inquired in a subtle soft voice, "did the Greek throw himself out the window this morning? Did you threaten him?"

I included his father in my reply. "You will understand, *messere,* that I do not have permission to discuss everything concerned with this case."

"Of course." The senator showed no resentment. "*Sier* Alfeo, the Senate has paid me the wonderful honor of electing me ambassador to Rome."

I congratulated him and his lady and drank a toast to them. Her smile looked genuine and probably was. Two-thirds of the Great Council would murder for that appointment. It established her husband as one of the inner circle, the fifty or so men who actually run the Republic, trading senior posts around among themselves. It offered tantalizing glimpses of a shot at the dogeship in another twenty years or so.

"When I go to Rome," Tirali said, "Pasqual will remain here to look after the family's affairs. As is customary, I shall take a few young noblemen along with me, both as aides and to teach them some of the ins and outs of serving the Republic. I especially need a personal secretary. While you are younger than others I am considering, I have been aware of your reputation for some time. I am prepared to pay a very generous stipend to a man who can be relied upon to perform his duties with intelligence, diligence, and discretion. You would rank third in the embassy."

I managed to blush. Indeed I blushed without meaning to, and much hotter than I wanted. "Your Excellency, this is a totally unexpected—"

"Stop!" He raised a hand. "Do not say a word! I can tell you that the doge himself recommended you, and so did several other men I consulted—right after their own grandsons, in every case. Your decision will influence the rest of your life, so I insist that you take a few days to consider it."

I did not want to consider it. I wanted to turn it down flat before it began gnawing at me like the Spartan's fox. He was offering me his patronage and a political career. I could never aspire to the dogeship, for that requires enormous wealth and powerful family connections, but I could become a real noble, marry a woman with money, hold office, live in comfort, be worthy of my ancestors. The prospect was giddying.

"You must excuse me, Alfeo," Pasqual said, with a glance at the winter dark looming beyond the windows. "I need to prepare for an engagement this evening. I do hope you will accept my father's offer, though. Very few of my contemporaries seem to know what real work is. I know he has tried to explain it to me many times and still it escapes me."

His oil was not quite as smooth as his father's. First-name terms so soon in our acquaintance overstepped the bounds.

I said, "Believe me, Pasqual, what he is offering does not sound in the least like real work. Your Excellency, you shall have my answer in a few days, my thanks now, my gratitude forever . . ." And so on.

Violetta had urged me to come to Ca' Tirali. Had she known what was in store for me there?

Was I being bribed to overlook a murder?

17

The senator sent his gondolier along to ferry me home, but I found Giorgio waiting for me down at the water-gate. As I dismissed the Tirali man I felt a mad impulse to tip him a few silver ducats for two minutes of his time. The Rome offer was already making my head spin like a windmill.

"No boys?" I asked as I boarded.

"They're on some errand for the Maestro," Giorgio said, adding gloomily, "I hope he doesn't pay them too much."

"I will bet you everything I own that he won't."

"No takers."

So I came back to the Ca' Barbolano as day turned to night and a shivery-cold sea fog drifted in over the city. As I reached the atelier, the twins emerged, whispering excitedly and looking dangerously pleased with themselves. They barely even noticed me. Inside I found the Maestro at the desk, crouched over a book like a black spider, as usual. Also as usual, he had not bothered to light more than a single candle. The fire had almost gone out. I poked it up and added more wood.

He looked up with a scowl. "Construe this sentence . . ."

"No," I said, sagging down on my seat. "You shouldn't read *Hermes Trismegistus* so late in the day. You know he always gives you an attack of choler. There was no murder."

He looked at me blankly. "Murder?"

"Procurator Orseolo."

"Oh, yes." He smirked disagreeably. "I am engaged in more important matters. I have discovered the real reason the ancients distinguished between the natures of Hermes and Mercury in some of their texts."

"I have discovered that there was no murder. I have spoken with everyone who was in the room. His granddaughter was at his side the whole time. Nobody could possibly have poisoned his wine. Two people reported seeing him pulling a face when he emptied his glass, but that doesn't prove anything. And besides, nobody had a motive. The poison you suspect is not available in the city. None of this may be enough to stop the Ten from taking you in and interrogating you, at the very least."

He grunted. "Those boys—"

"Corrado and Christoforo? What about them?"

"I gave them fifty *soldi*. Five each for them and two lira for expenses. Write it in the ledger."

"Saints' laundry! What did they do for you—murder someone?"

He ignored that. "You look tired."

"I am tired!" I snapped. "It has been quite a day." It had begun with six toughs trying to kill me, continued through a spectacular suicide, and ended with someone trying to redirect my entire life.

"Let me see that leg."

"It's fine."

"Show me!"

I removed my hose and spread one leg on the desk. "I shall have a scar."

"It won't be the first." He brought the candle close enough to produce an odor of singed hair. "It seems to prosper. If you don't succumb to lockjaw or wound fever, you will be as good as new. Put the bandage back on. 'If you encase your spirit in the flesh and abase yourself, saying, "I know nothing, I can do nothing; I am afraid of earth and sea, I cannot ascend to heaven; I know not what I was, nor what I shall be," then what have you to do with God?' "

"What's that from?"

"*Hermes Trismegistus.*" Gathering up his book and the candle, he hobbled towards the fireplace.

"And what does it mean?" I demanded, contorting myself to bandage my calf in the dark without bending my knee.

"It means that the procurator was murdered and I know who did it and how."

The old scoundrel refused to say more. I should not have made fun of his contempt for *Hermes*. He was allowed to insult the book; I wasn't. He did not ask me to report on my afternoon, which was a bad sign. I went to my room to freshen up.

When I came out, I was accosted by the terrible twosome. They exchanged conspiratorial glances.

"You had a good day, I hear."

"Our lips are sealed," Corrado said.

"We are sworn to secrecy," Christoforo explained.

Pause. Christoforo said, "Alfeo? How much do you need to . . . How much do the, er . . ."

"Next door . . . If a man wants . . ."

"Not *old* . . ."

They were both bright red by this time. I sighed. "That depends."

"Depends on what?" they asked together.

"On how fussy you are. And whether you want the French pox or not. Let me talk with a friend of mine and I'll advise you."

They agreed to that with relief. I went in search of Giorgio and found him alone, or almost so, for he was in his bedroom, bent over double so Matteo could hold his fingers in a walking lesson. Matteo would not repeat what we discussed, because he spoke no better than he walked.

"You should have taken my bet," I said. "The Maestro had a brainstorm."

He looked at me in alarm. "How much?"

"I don't know." I didn't, because they might have retained some of the expense money as well as their wages. "They obviously think they have enough to buy serious trouble. If you like, I can arrange it so they won't come to real harm."

No father enjoys hearing that his authority is being flouted. Giorgio turned bright red. He began with, "I'll whip their backsides raw," progressed through, "I give them ample pocket money!" and finished with, "We need that money to buy their clothes!" and talk of hellfire. I countered with French pox and similar arguments. In the end his fatherly pride won out. He agreed that this was Venice, after all, and he had been not much older than them when, and some of their brothers . . . He sighed and told me to take care of it, as long as I swore not to tell Mama.

The Maestro was still in the red velvet chair, reading. He ignored me completely, so I knew he was planning something I was not going to like, and I had a strong hunch what it would be. I wrote a note to Alessa, asking that the two bearers be given quality treatment and promising I would be good for the balance of the fee, if any. I sealed it and took it out to them.

Corrado turned pale and Christoforo bright red.

"Now?" Corrado said. "Right now?"

"You'd rather wait until they're busy and want you to hurry?"

Grabbing my letter, Corrado vanished down the stairs with his brother in hot pursuit. This was Venice.

They missed a magnificent supper. Mama's Lombardy quail with baby calamari is always divine, and that night she excelled herself.

The Maestro brought *Hermes* with him and propped it up on the table. He paid far more attention to the book than he did to his food, grumbling angrily over every page and ignoring me. I was happy enough to savor the meal and dream of the wonderful gift I would buy for Violetta when I had sold the Euripides manuscript. Rubies, I decided.

The moment I wiped my plate with a last crust and leaned back, sighing contentedly, the Maestro slammed his book shut.

"Bring a glass of water with you."

My fears were confirmed. "I'll carry *Hermes*," I said. He had enough trouble managing his staff.

He hurried off back to the atelier like a little black ant and went straight to the crystal ball on its stand, whipping away the cover. Then he adjusted himself on his chair, laid his staff on the floor beside him, and rubbed his hands expectantly. He enjoys a soothsaying as much as I detest it.

I laid the *Hermes* on the desk and the glass of water beside the crystal. "This really isn't necessary," I complained. "I can tell you everything you want to know without this."

"What color are the drapes in Attorney Imer's office?"

"I don't think there are any drapes. Why—"

"But you don't know!" he said triumphantly. "Next time I ask, you will tell me exactly. You will tell me whatever I want to know. There's too much light. Bank the fire. And lock the door so we won't be disturbed."

I laid fresh logs over the embers. I locked the door and extinguished all the lights except one candle. I cannot put myself into a trance deep enough to see the future in the crystal, as the Maestro can. That is clairvoyance. Soothsaying is speaking truth, and for that he puts me into the trance. It gives me perfect recall, so that I can recount conversations verbatim and describe everything I have seen. What I hate is that I remember nothing of what he asks or what I tell him. I lose an hour of my life, and for all I know he pries into all sorts of personal details that do not concern him.

"I thought you said you had solved the mystery?" I was moving as slowly as I dared.

"I have. I knew the answer last night, but I need evidence that will convince the Ten. Tomorrow you will take a letter to the Lion's Mouth announcing that I have the solution. Come and sit down!"

I sat opposite him. He moved the candle so the crystal glowed with fire for me. I stared into the sun, burning gold in the utter dark of space.

"You have had a hard day. You are tired. You are sleepy."

That was true, I was.

"Recite the twelve gates to alchemy, according to the learned Ripley."

"Calcination, solution, separation, conjunction, putrefaction, congelation, cibation, sublimation, fermentation, exaltation, multiplication, and projection."

"And backwards?"

"Projection, multiplication . . . exaltation . . ."

I was gone.

18

Giorgio rowed me to the Molo before dawn. Fog lay on the city like wet cement, muffling even the halfhearted slap of ripples. As we tied up, the *Marangona* bell boomed out to sound the start of the working day. It sounded right overhead, but I could barely even see my own feet in the murk, let alone the bell tower. I climbed out onto the Piazzetta, accelerated by a neck-cracking heave from Bruno, behind me. He had no idea why I needed him along, but he found this fumbling around in the dark great fun. In a moment he was up beside me. Because I had left my sword in the gondola and had not asked him to bring his flatiron, he had no worries.

I did. "I hope I won't be long," I told Giorgio.

"I can wait," he said. "It's what I do best."

"You make babies best."

"Mama does that. It's nothing to do with me."

I beckoned to my giant and set off along the loggia they call the *broglia*. This is the part of the Piazzetta where noblemen meet and do their plotting before the Great Council meets. It is where votes are bought and sold, deals made,

offices traded. It is where every young noble must wait
anxiously on his first appearance until he is beckoned in to
be introduced and suitably bribed to deliver his vote. I had
never seriously considered ever being one of them, but if
I had Senator Tirali—who by then would be former Ambassador Tirali—as my patron, then anything would be
possible.

There had been a change of plan. Until the soothsaying
the Maestro had intended to have me deliver a letter to the
Lion's Mouth, but in my trance I had told him of the doge's
command to report to Raffaino Sciara, so that was what I
was going to do. My problem would be finding him. *Circospetto*, like *Missier Grande*, keeps no regular hours. He attends the Senate and the Council of Ten, which meet in the
afternoons and evenings respectively. He had come to the
Ca' Barbolano in the middle of the night. It seemed very
unlikely he would be available at dawn. Even he must sleep
sometimes, so I would probably have to make an appointment to see him and return later.

My second problem was that the doge was not playing by
the rules.

I did mention, did I not, that the Republic likes to keep
things complicated? Since no one in government trusts anyone else, matters are arranged so that every man will have
others watching him. The Council of Ten consists of seventeen men, with a state prosecutor present to advise on the
law, and sometimes with another fifteen or more men
added, when things look so nasty that the blame must be
widely spread. The Ten's agenda is set by the three "chiefs of
the Ten," who are elected anew each month and must remain within the Doges' Palace during their terms. They
each hold one of the three keys needed to open the Ten's
"Lion's Mouth" drop box. It was to them that I ought to be
reporting evidence of murder, and if they demanded to

know why I wanted to meet with Raffaino Sciara in person, I would have to do some creative talking.

There are several ways into the palace. I had chosen to go by way of the Piazzetta and the Porta della Carta because I might have to send Bruno away and it would be easier for him to find Giorgio by retracing his steps—the Rio di Palazzo is so narrow that gondolas are not allowed to linger at the watergate. We stepped through into the great arched passage beyond, where lamplight hung like golden spheres in the fog, barely reaching the paving below. A guard slammed the butt of his pike down and demanded to know who went there. What was visible of him between his breastplate and the brim of his helmet looked thirty years older than he sounded, but I think it was just his first glimpse of Bruno that made his voice so boyishly shrill.

I introduced myself and explained that I had urgent business for *Circospetto*. We were ordered to wait. One man went into the guard room, two more came out to keep an eye on Bruno. A fourth was sent off to report to someone. Time passed. Graveyard cold seeped into my bones; fog spitefully saturated all my clothes. I wished someone would offer me a seat, preferably close to a fire.

The messenger returned and hurried into the guard room to report. Two men emerged and one of them told us to follow them, which was a good sign, I supposed. The other followed us. Halfway across the courtyard the signs became very bad when I saw that we were heading to the watergate beside the Wells, which was not the route by which honored visitors were taken to anywhere. Sure enough, we were led up the same, narrow stairs I had climbed when Sciara brought me in. They were a trial for Bruno, who had to stoop low to get through some of the brick arches.

Three storeys up we left the stairwell and entered the room

of the chiefs of the Ten, which is very splendid, especially its ceiling paintings by Veronese and Ponchini. I was given no time to admire them, even had the light been good enough. We crossed to another door and were ushered through into the room of the inquisitors, the Three. Tintoretto painted that ceiling and the walls are richly paneled, but I doubt if many of the people who visit it are ever concerned about its art. On the dais sat a single man, seemingly doing nothing except waiting for us to arrive. He was elderly and portly, with a silver beard and a heavy, weathered face, looking as if he might have been a husky sailor in his youth, now run to seed. He wore the sumptuous scarlet robes and velvet tippet of a ducal counselor, plus an unfriendly scowl.

I walked forward. Bruno stayed close to my side, but our escort must have stopped at the door, for I could not hear their footsteps. I came to a halt and waited to be announced. I wasn't.

I bowed. So did Bruno.

"Your Excellency, I am—"

"I know who you are," he growled. "Do you know me?"

"I believe I have the honor of addressing the ducal counselor from San Paolo, *sier* Marco Donà."

There are six ducal counselors, one from each ward of the city, each elected for an eight-month term. Their job is to restrain the doge, who can do nothing without the backing of at least four of them. Like the doge, they are automatically members of the Council of Ten. I did not know whose side Donà was on, because I did not know why sides were even necessary.

"I am also a state inquisitor."

Which is exactly what I had been afraid of.

The inquisitors are the Three—I did warn you this was complicated. The Three are not the three chiefs of the Ten, but a subcommittee of the Ten, consisting always of two ordinary members and one ducal counselor. The Ten may delegate any or all of their powers to the Three.

At a loss for words, I bowed again. So did Bruno, who would know only that the man in the fancy robe must be important if Alfeo was being so respectful.

"Who's he?" Donà demanded.

"He's a mute, harmless unless he's attacked."

"What's he for?"

"Armed men tried to kill me yesterday, Excellency."

"He can't help you here. Send him away."

I had arranged three signals with Giorgio: *I—in trouble— go to—home,* meant bad. *Go to—home—come—later,* was hopeful. *Everything—is well—wait,* was obviously inappropriate.

To Bruno I made the signs, *Tell—Giorgio—go to—home.* Bruno frowned and eyed the counselor. His deafness limits him, but he is far from witless and sometimes he seems to sense things by means that we more fortunate mortals cannot know. He did not want to leave me. I repeated my orders.

He signed, *You—go to—Giorgio.*

Stamp, point, wiggle two fingers, wave arm like an oar: *No!—you—go to—Giorgio.*

Point to chest, point to floor. *I—stay.*

Again I stamped my foot: *No!*

This time he nodded, to my great relief. Still obviously reluctant, he turned and headed for the door. I turned my attention back to Donà.

"State your business."

"My master sent me with a message for the illustrious Raffaino Sciara."

"Give me the message. If it is appropriate for him to receive it, I will see that he does."

I was now in considerably worse trouble than I had been two days before. To defy a direct order from a state inquisitor would be insanity beyond the call of duty, and the Maestro would certainly not expect me to try.

"Your Excellency, my master, the learned Doctor Nostradamus, has evidence that Procurator Orseolo was murdered. He knows the name of the murderer. He instructed me to ask the secretary to arrange a gathering at the house of the learned Ottone Imer, at which my master will demonstrate how poison was administered to the procurator."

"And whom will your master denounce?"

This was the problem. "I do not know, Your Excellency. He would not tell me."

"You expect me to believe that?"

Icy water trickled down my ribs. "I swear it is the truth, Excellency."

"Your master expects us to give him a free hand to slander anyone he fancies?" The old man made a gesture of impatience. "I will ask you once more. If you do not answer my question willingly, you will answer it unwillingly and at great personal cost. Who is your master accusing?"

"He would not tell me. Believe me, Your Excellency, I did ask him. I begged him to tell me. He would say only that he has very good reasons."

"Take him away and teach him better manners."

I turned. The guards who had brought me had been replaced by three very solid men in dark workmen's clothing, and with them stood my companion of the previous day, *Vizio* Filiberto Vasco, our juvenile Caesar in his fancy red cloak.

Without any open sneering or gloating, he gestured for me to accompany him. He led the way, carrying a lantern, and I followed. More heavy footsteps and lanterns came behind.

When we reached the stairs, I said, "Wait! Where are we going?"

"You know very well where we're going, Alfeo."

"But he can't do this, can he?" I could hear my voice growing shriller by the word. "Doesn't he need a vote of the Ten, or at least another inquisitor's approval?" There was an unreal quality about this experience. That I might be locked up until the Maestro came to apologize and explain had always been a risk, but we had never dreamed of extempore torture.

The *vizio* smiled mirthlessly. "All he needs is men to obey him, Alfeo. Do you want a sword point in your back or not?"

I did not. The stairs seemed shorter than I expected, but they could not have been long enough for me. The torture chamber is surprisingly large, but then it plays an important role in government. I looked around in despair.

Vasco was watching me. "Give him the tour, Carlo."

One of the jailers said, "If *messer* would come this way . . ." I was appalled at how huge he was—he could not possibly have been as big as Bruno, but I was feeling unusually small. He conducted me around the room, courteously explaining the machinery for breaking, twisting, burning, choking, wrenching, dislocating, crushing. In truth, the entire collection seemed quite insignificant, just a bag of tools spread out on the floor; all that really mattered was the rope dangling in the center.

When the circuit was completed, I was back at the *vizio*. I knew he must see my shaking hands and hear my teeth clattering. No doubt the tormentors could tell exactly how long I would resist before I broke. And when I did I would not be able to tell them what they had been told to find out. I had to speak or go mad, even knowing that this was just evidence of my terror.

"You enjoy this part of your job?"

"No, I hate it," Vasco said seriously. "I would enjoy watching you take forty or fifty strokes of the lash, Alfeo, but even you don't deserve this. Fortunately I do not have to

stay and watch what happens. As soon as you have been secured, I am free to go. Do you want to do it the easy way or
the painful way? The easy way is much better."

Coward that I was, I would do anything to postpone the
start of pain. I took off my hat and handed it to the monster
looming over me. Then cloak, doublet, shirt, until I was
bare to the waist. He took them as politely as a valet, then
turned and threw them down in a corner beside a bucket.

"You can keep your britches on," Vasco said. "For now."
He pointed to the bucket. "You need to use that?"

To my shame, I did need to use that, and all four of them
watched while I did so. Humble as a mouse, I crept back to
the rope, where they waited for me.

"If *messer* will pardon . . ." The big torturer pulled my arms
behind me and knotted the rope around my wrists and forearms, hauling my elbows together. The torture known as the
cord, or strappado, is more feared than the rack. A man who
denies his crime on the cord cannot be hanged for it afterwards. Since he will no longer have any use of his arms, that is
a doubtful blessing, and one that cannot be earned very often.

A moment's respite, then a pulley creaked and the rope
began to tighten, raising my arms and bending my torso
forward. My elbows could not bend at all at that angle, and
my shoulders very little. When my head was level with my
crotch and I stood on tiptoe, a voice said, "Tie it there."

Vasco bent close to my ear. "Resist as long as you can," he
whispered. "If you give up too easily they won't believe you,
and then it's terrible."

He told Carlo to carry on, and left, taking his lantern. I
was shaking harder than ever, teeth chattering uncontrol-
lably. Cold was a part of that, but I was scared out of my
wits and do not deny it. One of the torturers came close and
clasped my shoulder with a callused hand.

"Strong one," he remarked to the others. "We'll need weights." He gave me a playful slap on the buttocks. "Don't go away. We'll be back."

They left and the door boomed shut.

19

I thought I was alone, but could not be certain. All I could
hear was the crackle of the fire, a sound I had always considered cheerful until then. All I could see was the bucket
and my tormented feet. The room bore an indefinable
stench, no doubt stemming from centuries of every bodily
secretion imaginable. The pain in my toes was already be
coming unbearable, but any attempt to ease them threw
more strain on my shoulders. When the real torment began,
of course, they would raise me right off the floor, with or
without weights on my feet, and with or without bouncing,
whatever they chose.

The doge said, "You seem to be in trouble again, lad."

I started, and gasped aloud at the pain even that twitch
caused me. With an effort, I made my mouth work more or
less normally. "That's a very good imitation."

"I really think you should leave before those fine sinners
come back. Why don't you call on little Putrid for help?"

The voice was right beside me, but I could not see the
speaker's feet. I was in the power of a fiend from hell and yet
I felt a tingle of hope. This whole experience had been just

too bad to be true. Even the Three must have some proce-
dures to follow and one state inquisitor, acting alone, sending a witness straight to torture did not seem plausible. The
king of France can lock up a man in the Bastille on a whim,
a French count can have a peasant flogged or hanged, but in
Venice a nobleman who strikes a servant will be charged and
punished. The Republic has never tolerated despots.

"I don't believe a word you say. Go away."

A cold and scaly finger scratched all the way down my
bare back, making all my flesh cringe.

The demon sighed. "We shall see. How's this voice?"

"Senator Tirali."

"Very good! A charming man. We have great hopes for
him. Why aren't you going to accept his offer?"

"How do you know I'm not?"

"You are. You think you're not, but I am going to talk
you into it. Violetta would love to go to Rome with you, you
know."

I had thought of that, Rome with Violetta . . .

Violetta's voice said, "You can't expect a harlot to stay
faithful, darling, but you don't mind sharing me and you
know you can't ever marry me. You'd be out of the Golden
Book in a flash if you did that. We women are *so* fickle, Alfeo!
We tire of our boy toys. Another month or two, if you're
lucky, and then I will send you away and find another."

Back to the silky tones of Senator Tirali: "You need money,
lots of money, so you can be her patron and pay her. You have
that manuscript. It's quite genuine, the only surviving copy of
Meleager by Euripides. Selling it here will be very dangerous.
You'll have problems with provenance, Alfeo. Too many people know about it. But in Rome? Or even better, stop in Florence on your way there. Grand Duke Ferdinand is crazy about
that sort of trash. You'll be a rich man before you even get to

Rome. That way you can be Violetta's patron, have her almost all to yourself. And the opportunities! A trusted confidant of the Venetian ambassador? Millions, you can make there."

"I have thought of all of that," I said. "Go away. I have to say my prayers."

The demon laughed. He changed to the Maestro's scratchy old voice. "And there's me. You know where I keep my gold, Alfeo, my lovely box of ducats. Nobody else even knows it exists, so no one will look for it. You know what all my books are worth, too, every one of them. And I've left them all to you in my will."

I started to say a paternoster and was stopped by a monstrous punch on the kidney. I won't bother to describe the results—you can guess. I screamed at the top of my lungs. I was left gagging and sobbing . . . Oh, Lord! If one punch made me weep like this, what would an hour on the cord do?

"Don't interrupt me when I am tempting," the demon said in Inquisitor Donà's voice. "You need money, Alfeo. You need money to keep Violetta willing. You need money to restore your family name. Yes, it would be a shame to betray the Maestro when he's taught you so much, but he can't last much longer now, can he? You know how to use all those poisons, but a pillow will be better. When he goes to bed tonight. You're a strong lad and he's so frail. He won't have time to realize what's happening. Two minutes' work and the world will be yours, Alfeo! Wealth, women, power."

"And I won't have to come to the palace in the morning."

The demon chuckled. "Of course not! You're clever, Alfeo. That's what we like about you. You'll do great things for us—as long as you don't come here to the palace in the morning. If you do, we will be waiting for you, and this time it will be real. We will enjoy that, but you won't."

Somebody snapped his fingers.

* * *

I gasped at the blaze of light and almost fell off the chair.

My mouth was a desert. Squinting through my eyelashes, I searched for the water glass. It was empty. The fire had burned to embers. The light was a single candle, reduced to a stub, its flame reflected in the crystal globe.

"How long was I gone?" I mumbled.

"Oh, I don't know," the Maestro said. "An hour? Probably nearer two. It was very interesting." He peered at me. "Are you all right?"

"Could be worse," I said. "Need a drink."

I staggered slightly as I rose. I went to the fireplace to find a lamp, lit it, and walked unsteadily to the door. My own room was closer than the kitchen, and I had water there. It soaked into my tissues like an elixir of life; it calmed my heartbeat; it was triple-distilled dew. I knelt to unlock the chest, but my hands were still shaking enough to make me fumble, and I needed three attempts to work the hidden catch and open the secret compartment in the lid. I gasped aloud relief when I saw that the manuscript was still there. Had it not been, I might have jumped out the window.

Back in the atelier, I went straight to the fireplace and lit more lamps to make the room bright. Every shadow held a lurking demon. I needed sunlight, lots and lots of noon sun. Tomorrow was going to be foggy. I sat cross-legged on the hearth rug, hunched close to the warmth.

Thump, thump—The Maestro came stumping across and settled into his favorite chair with a sigh of contentment. "You hadn't told me about *Circospetto*."

"Sciara? What about him?" I was feeding the embers, trying to coax them into a blaze.

"That the doge told you to report to him."

"I would have told you when you were ready to report."

"Well, I was going to write to the Ten, but obviously there's political skullduggery afoot, so we'd better do what His Serenity wants."

"I am sure there is but I would much rather write a letter." Very much rather.

"No." He put his fingertips together and began to lecture. "You must seek out Raffaino Sciara first thing in the morning and tell him I need to see all the suspects back at the Imer residence in the evening. We can reenact the murder and I shall show who did it and how."

"And you're not going to tell me who, are you?" I had the flames leaping joyfully now.

"No," the Maestro said firmly. "It has to be done my way. Believe me, I do have good reasons. If I tell you in advance, then they may get the name out of you tomorrow."

"That's not impossible." I shivered at the memory, the smell of the torture chamber, the harsh bite of the rope on my wrists. "How reliable is clairvoyance?"

"Huh?" The Maestro sat up so he could peer at me suspiciously. "Why?"

"I saw a vision."

"You did? Excellent, excellent! Clairvoyance is a sign of maturity. It means you are starting to get your mind off that woman once in a while. Not for very long at a time, perhaps, but . . ." He paused, frowning. "But I put you into the trance, and I ordered you to view the past, not the future. So whatever you saw was not clairvoyance. What did you see?"

"The ultimate quintessence of unmitigated disaster. Answer my question, please. Is what I foresaw inevitable, or can it be prevented?"

"Of course it can be prevented! What use would clairvoyance be if the future was inevitable? Although," he said cautiously, "it would be more correct to say that the foreseen can sometimes only be modified, not negated. The sagacious

Zosimos of Panoplis wrote of a man who was told the or-
dained hour of his death and therefore fled to Memphis, only
to be killed there by a falling chimney pot at the time and in
the place predestined. The main thrust of a prophecy can by
diverted sufficiently, provided you can find the fulcrum, the
single crucial item that you must change to divert the turn
of events, because history is a mighty stream washing all before it and it is only when you can find the place where in-
serting a pebble . . . What are you doing, Alfeo?"

"Diverting the mighty stream," I said, feeding more paper into the hearth. "I made a terrible mistake."

My master uttered a strangled cry and groped for his
staff. "What are you burning?"

"The last surviving copy of *Meleager* by Euripides."

He whimpered. "No, no! It's priceless."

"It isn't, you know. There's one price I won't pay for it." I
threw the rest of it in as a single wad and sat back to watch
the leaves blacken and curl. I crossed my legs and balanced
my forearms on my knees. I felt better already.

"How did you get it?" he muttered, watching the fire,
not me.

"It was a present from a demon. You obviously didn't ask
me for Karagounis's last words. He said he could help me! But
he left the manuscript on his desk and a halfwit young idiot
decided that he could make better use of . . ." I explained.

"No!" Firelight made the Maestro's tears shine like dia-
monds as he watched the paper burn. "You're no thief! That
was a cleverly set trap, Alfeo. Karagounis was dispensable.
Even if the Ten did not already know about him, you had
exposed him. So his demon used his death as a powerful
charge of evil to break down your normal defenses, like setting off a mine under a castle wall. Your fiend had betrayed
you to the *chaush*'s demon, and it managed to open a portal
to you, so you were vulnerable. You were bewitched!"

That thought helped. "But if I'd listened to what he said—"

"What he said was meaningless, just to distract you from the trap. Unwittingly, you swallowed the bait the demon had set out for you. Whatever you saw in the crystal was not clairvoyance, it was a sending, a hallucination from hell. What did you see?"

"The hook. Have I broken the line, though?" I told him briefly about my vision of the torture chamber and the temptation of the Tirali offer. I did not include the demon's suggestion that I murder the Maestro for his hoard of ducats. They say you can only be tempted by your own thoughts and I had been aware of that possibility for years. We all know of dark places in our souls that we stay away from, and the Maestro must be aware of that one in mine.

He thought for a moment and then nodded, gazing wistfully at the charred mess on the burning logs. "You have repented and done penance. You spat out the bait. You should be safe now."

Tomorrow I would know for certain. "Tell me what you want me to do in the morning."

20

The fog seemed thicker than I remembered, but its salty smell and the slap of ripples were frighteningly familiar. Everything was happening as before—Giorgio rowed me to the Molo and the *Marangona* bell boomed out, just as it had in the vision. I climbed out onto the Piazzetta, aided by the same unexpected heave from Bruno, which I had forgotten. He scrambled up beside me.

"I'll be as quick as I can," I said.

"I can wait," Giorgio said. "It's what I do best."

I resisted an urge to make a joke about babies. "Keep an ear open for gossip about the murder, will you?"

With Bruno at my side, I walked along the loggia. The outer world was unfolding as before, only my thoughts were different. Now I knew I would never stand here waiting to be beckoned into the *broglia* and introduced by an influential patron. I had already written to Tirali, turning down his offer of Rome on the grounds that I owed loyalty to the Maestro; Corrado had promised faithfully to deliver the note and Christoforo to see that he did.

If I had described my vision in greater detail, the Maestro

would certainly have given me very different instructions. So why hadn't I? Why was I here? I had broken my curse by burning the book, but why not play safe and change the future completely by having someone else deliver a letter to *Circospetto*? Why risk the outcome being *almost* what I had foreseen? I did not know the answer to that. A stubborn determination to prove my courage, perhaps, or a refusal to be intimidated by evil. *Let fear deter you and the evil has won*, the Maestro says.

I hesitated for a moment at the Porta della Carta, so that Bruno went another step and turned to look for me, but then I forced my feet to move again and we entered the tunnel. The same guard shot the same startled look at Bruno, slammed the butt of his pike down on the same flagstone, and asked the same question.

I gave him the same answer. Again we were ordered to wait. Time passed even more slowly than before, because I had to fight a desperate yearning to turn around and flee away into the fog. The messenger returned eventually and again we crossed the courtyard. But now the pattern was broken, for only one man went with us, and not in quite the same direction. The moment I realized he was leading us to the censors' staircase, I took large gulps of air and told my heart to calm down, for this was the way that honored guests were taken to the halls of justice.

We had to climb just as far, but the stairs were wide and high, and thus much easier, especially for Bruno. At the top we were shown into an antechamber that leads to both the hall of the Ten and the smaller room for the chiefs of the Ten. It was presently occupied by two *fanti* guards, and the cadaverous Raffaino Sciara, *Circospetto*, in his blue robe. Our guide departed the way we had come. The future was unfolding as it should.

"Well, *sier* Alfeo?" The secretary's eyes were as sepulchral as always. "You have had a busy couple of days." Sciara smiled contemptuously, but probably a face so skull-like can smile no other way.

I bowed and admitted that I had. Bruno was staring at the murals.

"And why are you demanding to see me, *sier* Alfeo? At this ungodly hour in the morning?"

"The . . . A mutual friend suggested I should report my master's conclusions to you, *lustrissimo*."

Circospetto frowned. There were witnesses present. "The man you saw that morning?"

I nodded.

"I'm sure you misheard him."

"I must have done, *lustrissimo*. I am sorry."

"Sensitive reports are made to the chiefs of the Ten. As it happens, your timing is excellent. They were just discussing the attack made on you yesterday. They may have some questions to put to you." He pointed at Bruno, who was gaping at the Tintoretto paintings on the ceiling. "Will he remain here?"

"I could insist, *lustrissimo*, but he will do no harm if he comes. He cannot hear."

Sciara nodded and ushered me through the corner door to the room of the chiefs of the Ten, Bruno hurrying at our heels. Three men sat behind the big table on the podium; all were elderly and wore the black robes of nobility with the extra-large sleeves denoting membership in the Council of Ten. Red tippets over their left shoulders showed that they were indeed the three chiefs. They had their heads together, conferring. The papers waiting their attention were still neatly stacked and the candles in the golden candlesticks were long and unlit, suggesting that they had barely started their morning's work.

At a side table sat an equally venerable spectator in the

robes and biretta of a state prosecutor, and beside him sat *Missier Grande* Gasparo Quazza in his blue and red, solid as a marble staircase. He looked at me with no sign of recognition whatsoever, which is his way.

If the doge had wanted to keep the Ten out of the Orseolo affair, then he had failed, but at least this time I was not facing Inquisitor Marco Donà. I gestured Bruno to a corner and bowed low while Sciara gave my name. He went back to his seat beside the prosecutor and dipped a quill in his inkwell.

The right-hand chief had a long white beard; the one on the left was portly. The middle one must be this week's chairman and him I knew to be one of the Maestro's patients, Bartolemeo Morosini. The Maestro had not told him that his heart was going to give out very shortly, but a glimpse of his inflamed, choleric face in any mirror would offer a strong hint.

In the overly loud tones of the hard of hearing, he proclaimed, "You are citizen Alfeo Zeno, clerk to Doctor Nostradamus?"

"I am Alfeo Zeno, Your Excellency. I do have the honor of being listed in the Golden Book."

All three old men scowled at me for not being dressed as a *nobile homo*. I would collect no more tips from Morosini when he called on his doctor in future.

"NH Alfeo Zeno, then, but a clerk. You testify before this tribunal on pain of perjury. You were attacked by a gang of *bravos* yesterday?"

"I was."

"Do you know who they were?"

"No, Your Excellency."

"Or why they picked on you?"

I saw the portly chief wince at the directness of Morosini's question. It left me hanging over a very long drop. To mumble hints of clairvoyance to *Missier Grande* in private was bad enough. To testify about demons on oath in state records would be suicidal.

I said, "I can only assume that it was to prevent my exposing the foreigner Alexius Karagounis as an agent of the sultan, *messere*."

"The man who jumped out the window when you went to see him later in the company of the *vizio*?"

"That man, *messere*."

"And how did you know that—"

Because I was at floor level and the chiefs were up on a dais, I saw Portly's shoe slam against the chairman's ankle. He started and glared at his companion.

Portly said, "Did we not decide to close the file on the foreigner Alexius Karagounis, subsequent upon his suicide?"

The three chiefs choose what shall or shall not be discussed by the whole Council of Ten. If the doge wanted to keep his involvement off the table, his success or failure would be decided here.

Long Beard harrumphed. "We are questioning the witness Zeno about the assault on him earlier in the day. That case is not closed, but we have only his word—his admitted speculation—that there is any connection. On your oath, witness, do you know for a fact that there is a connection?"

"No, *messer*, er *messere*."

"Well, then," said Portly. "And the man was not summoned as a witness, he came here to volunteer some information. Why don't we hear what he wants to tell us?"

Morosini shrugged and gestured to Sciara to lay down his pen. "We give you three minutes, *sier* Alfeo."

Relieved, but aware that my reprieve might be only temporary, I said, "Doctor Nostradamus instructed me to inform Your Excellencies that the late Procurator Orseolo died as a result of poison administered to him the previous evening at the house of Citizen Imer. My master—"

All three chiefs tried to speak at once.

Portly had the loudest outrage: "Administered by whom?"

"He dare not say yet, *messere*. I swear," I continued quickly, "that he has not confided even to me the name of the person he suspects." The torture chamber was still open for business, one floor up.

"Why doesn't the old fool write us a letter?" Morosini shouted. "That's how these things are done."

"Because he cannot yet offer absolute proof, *clarissimo*. He is convinced, though, that if the persons who were present at the book viewing that night were to be reassembled in that same room—including himself, of course—then he would be able to reconstruct the murder, showing how it was done and who did it."

My suggestion was as welcome as a risotto of pig manure.

"Bertucci died of old age," Long Beard muttered. "We agreed we had no reason to believe anything else."

"Let him rest in peace," Morosini agreed.

Contradicting the chiefs of the Ten requires extreme tact or total insanity, and better both. I bowed. "Without questioning Your Excellencies' wisdom or knowledge in any way, my master humbly submits that he has additional evidence that he can bring to Your Excellencies' attention, but it will require the demonstration I described."

"He must tell us the name of the person he intends to accuse."

"He insists he has reasons for his secrecy, which will become obvious at the time."

I had reasons for the nest of eels squirming in my belly, and most of them were memories of that torture chamber.

These men might or might not know that the doge had gate-crashed the book viewing, but they must know that one of the men present that evening had been the new ambassador-designate to the Holy See. To have Giovanni Tirali mixed up in a murder case at this time would be as embarrassing as involving the doge himself. The chiefs *wanted* the file closed. They wanted to bury it in the bowels of the state archives. They did not want a celebrated sage throwing wild and embarrassing accusations around.

Morosini banged a fist on the table. "Nostradamus expects just us to attend his *harlequinade* or is he inviting the whole Council of Ten? How much will he charge for admission?"

"He hopes only that Your Excellencies will permit the demonstration and send some trusted observer."

The three chiefs bent heads to confer. If their expressions were any guide, they were going to send *Missier Grande* to fetch the Maestro by fast boat and order me flogged for insolence to amuse them while they were waiting.

"The old charlatan is hinting that he doesn't trust us!" muttered Portly.

Of course he was.

"I have never heard such audacity," grumbled Long Beard.

Very softly, Raffaino Sciara cleared his throat.

Portly had the best hearing. "*Lustrissimo?*"

"I believe there have been precedents, Your Excellencies. A similar case . . . *Missier Grande*, do you recall the details?"

Members of the Council of Ten are elected for one-year terms, although they become eligible for reelection after another year. *Circospetto* and *Missier Grande* know everything because they are appointed for life.

"Maestro Nostradamus has helped the Council on several occasions," the police chief said. "I can recall a couple of times when he made dramatic demonstrations."

Sciara nodded. "That case of the dead gondolier on the roof? Bizarre!"

"Incredible!"

The chiefs pursed lips angrily. Long Beard said, "What case of what dead gondolier on what roof?"

"The man had seemingly been beaten to death and his body left on a roof, which it was quite impossible for him to have reached without witchcraft."

"And Nostradamus explained it?"

Sciara shrugged. "With a pendulum, Your Excellency—a long rope attached to the nearby bell tower. There had been a drunken bet. The sage has never been proved wrong yet, but of course the man is old."

Morosini scowled. No one likes to hear hints that his doctor is senile. "If anyone did poison old Bertucci," he conceded, "then he ought to wear the silken collar."

The other two muttered agreement. I could see beads clicking on their mental abacuses—the Ten make their reports to the Grand Council, and a truly dramatic conviction would bring great credit to the current chiefs and boost their political prospects.

"You said there were other precedents, *lustrissimo?*"

Sciara smiled his death's-head smile. "Nostradamus has made some startling demonstrations in the presence of state witnesses. I doubt if the learned doctor expects the entire Council of Ten to turn up."

The chiefs exchanged glances and near-imperceptible nods.

"I see no reason," Morosini proclaimed, "for us to forbid the sort of charade the Maestro is suggesting, as long as we make clear that it is a private function. How many people would have to be rounded up?" He directed his faded eyes and scarlet wattles at me.

"About a dozen, Your Excellency. Five or six houses would have to be notified. One man and a boatman could deliver the warrants in a couple of hours."

"Why *about* a dozen?" asked Portly. "Can't you count?"

I glanced at *Circospetto*. Sciara had a sudden need to scratch his right ear, which in turn required him to shake his head, ever so slightly. I took that to mean that I was not to invite the doge.

"My master would like to have the servant Pulaki Guarana attend the demonstration, and also a certain Domenico Chiari. We do not know their present whereabouts. Perhaps the Council does?"

The chairman said, "Even we can't know everything, lad. You want warrants? I s'pose . . . Can we order the Imer man to allow this invasion of his home, *Avogadoro*?"

The prosecutor smiled thinly. "The learned attorney is certainly aware that it is every citizen's duty to assist the Council of Ten in its inquiries. As long as compliance is voluntary, verbal invitations would be adequate."

And non-compliance would be prima facie evidence of guilt of course. The chairman glanced at his companions and both nodded. Sciara took up his pen again.

"Let it be recorded," Morosini declaimed, "that the chiefs raised no objection to the petitioner organizing a private party to reenact the events at the Imer residence . . . within the existing laws governing assemblies. The petitioner was so advised, and . . ."—more glances and nods—". . . and *Missier Grande* was instructed to ensure that the proposed gathering be conducted in an orderly fashion."

I bowed, backed away three steps, and bowed again.

Bruno bowed also. *Missier Grande* strode across to open the door and see us out to the anteroom. One of the *fanti* closed the door behind us.

"Find the *vizio*," *Missier Grande* told him. "Quickly. I'll watch this door." Both men vanished out the door to the staircase. He turned back to me with an eye colder than the peaks of the Dolomites. "That man you scared to death yesterday— we had been keeping him under observation for months. The Ten nearly skinned me, because of your meddling."

For once I could think of nothing to say, so I said nothing.

"Does Attorney Imer know you want to stage a masque in his house?"

"Not yet, *Missier.*"

"Do any of the 'guests' know?"

"Not yet, *Missier.*"

He growled. "So now I'm going to have to send Vasco out with you again, wasting another day of his time as if he had nothing better to do? I warn you, Alfeo Devil-take-you Zeno, that when he came back with a corpse yesterday, the chiefs tore his balls off and made him eat them. The *vizio* likes you even less than I do. Now I will more or less be putting him under your orders, so I suggest very strongly that you do not say so! If you try to lord it over him, he may lose you in a canal somewhere, and if he does, I do not intend to lead the search party."

What Filiberto Vasco had in mind for me was forty or fifty lashes, I recalled. Perhaps ten of those had been added by yesterday's disaster; the rest had been building up over the years.

"The Maestro is very sure of himself," I said quietly. "He is certain that Karagounis did not poison the procurator and that someone else did."

Missier Grande grunted. "He had better be right. You are not to mention the chiefs, understand? You do not speak with their authority."

"If I cannot say that the Council of Ten has given its permission, then no one is going to turn up."

He growled again, longer. "Vasco's presence will tell them that."

For a moment there was silence, but it was too uncomfortable to last.

"I assume you have Pulaki Guarana locked up?" I asked.

"I will see he is there tonight."

"And Domenico Chiari, the interpreter?"

"Never heard of him." *Missier Grande*'s basilisk stare dared me to call him a liar. I didn't. "Just between us two, *sier* Alfeo, who do you think your master is going to accuse?"

I was not going to fall into that trap. Any opinion I ventured would be held against me by somebody. "I honestly do not know, *Missier Grande*. I have learned never to try and outguess the Maestro."

A glare from Gasparo Quazza would strike terror into Medusa. "If he is so frightened of having the name mentioned beforehand that he does not even tell you, his trusted apprentice, does that not suggest that the person he will accuse is someone of importance?"

Of course it did. It might also suggest that the Maestro thought the murderer was possessed. Karagounis might have died to save another demon from exposure and eviction. Mentioning that theory would land me in even worse trouble.

"Being a doctor, he regards everyone as being of importance, *Missier Grande*."

The silence was now deadly. Fortunately at that moment my dear friend Filiberto Vasco flew in, cloak swirling. He shied back when he saw me and bared his teeth like a horse. He was sweating like one, too, from his run up all those stairs.

"It's more bad news," Quazza told him. "The chiefs have agreed to let Nostradamus organize revels. The host doesn't know it yet and none of the guests will want to attend. So you have to accompany this pest around the city and make sure everybody understands they are under absolutely no compulsion to cooperate, but if they don't show up their absence will be noted. Attendance is purely voluntary, but God help those who stay away. No threats, though. Understand?"

The *vizio*'s eyes measured me for the rack. "And when do I get to extract the real story from Alfeo Zeno? Soon, please?"

"Tomorrow, perhaps. If his master doesn't pull off another of his miracles tonight, Their Excellencies will be very upset. Then I think we can certainly bring Alfeo in for questioning."

Vasco smiled hungrily. "I look forward to it."

"So do I. I'll take the first hour. Carry on." *Missier Grande* Quazza went back into the meeting room.

21

The Lord be with you, *Vizio*," I said politely.

"You may need Him more." Vasco flinched at Bruno's troglodyte leer. Bruno knew him and even had a sign for him, but he also knew that sometimes Alfeo did not like him, and Bruno disapproved of such people. Since Alfeo was presently smiling, the *vizio* must be a friend now, so Bruno was happy.

"Come along and let's get it over with," I said. "I'm fussy about the company I'm seen with."

As we went down the stairs, I explained the situation in more detail. I could hear the lash count going up inside his head: sixty, seventy . . . When we reached the loggia, he was chalky white with fury.

"You think that I am now under your orders?"

"Well, *Missier Grande* certainly told me you were, but warned me not to say so, because the news might provoke you to excessive secretion of black bile. I'm sure you'll do fine, as long as you're properly respectful so I don't have to reprimand you in front of witnesses. Your boat or mine?"

"Yours. You sank mine, remember?"

We trotted down the giants' staircase and marched across

the courtyard to go out by the Frumento Gate, directly to the Molo. The fog was still heavy, and people would loom into view and then veer suddenly when they recognized the *vizio* almost upon them. Even the normally unflappable Giorgio was startled to see his new passenger and bowed to him. I told him Ottone Imer's house, and off we went. Vasco left the outside, damp, benches for Bruno and joined me on cushions in the *felze*, sitting at my side as if he was about to bite off my ear.

"Did you see your Turkish friend?" he asked suddenly.

"No."

"Hanging between the columns, in the Piazzetta."

"It can't make him much more dead."

"I suppose not." To my astonishment, Vasco chuckled. Either he had decided to make the best of the situation or he had settled on a nice, round hundred lashes.

After a moment he asked quietly, "How did you know he was a Turkish spy?"

"Just between us two?"

"I swear."

"Too dangerous to say."

He eyed me uneasily. "You or the Maestro?"

"In this case it was me."

"You really have such powers?"

"He's taught me a few tricks."

"And those tricks won't tell you who set the *bravos* on you yesterday?"

"I can't ask personal favors, but I'm fairly sure it was because I had learned about Karagounis. The idea was to silence me before I could expose him."

"I would not traffic in such evil," Vasco said pompously.

"It's dangerous," I admitted. "I get nightmares."

Sometimes he was in them.

And yet going visiting with the *vizio* was a wicked pleasure. He might not be able to quell a riot just by appearing, as *Missier Grande* could, but he did shine with some reflected glory. People almost fell off the *fondamente* into the canals to get out of his way. Doors seemed to open of their own accord as he approached. When we reached San Zulian, I left Bruno with Giorgio and strapped on my sword. Vasco always went armed, but he truly did not need to.

Even Imer's mildewed clerk, who had tried to be officious to me two days earlier, just fell back in horror when Vasco walked in. I pointed at the far door. Vasco marched straight on through without waiting for permission and then told the attorney's client he could leave, which he did expeditiously. The attorney cowered behind his desk and listened in steadily rising fury as I explained what we wanted.

"On whose authority?" he croaked when I had done.

"Filiberto?" I said.

Vasco shot me a venomous look and then said, "You have a duty to cooperate with the Council of Ten, *lustrissimo*. Must I go back and report that you refuse?"

"The Council has ordered this?"

"I am here on *Missier Grande*'s instructions."

Imer twitched. "What time?"

I said, "An hour after Angelus will do."

"Do I have to serve wine again?"

"Not unless you wish to. But we need the same furniture and glasses and some books or papers. Also we want the servant Giuseppe Benzon present."

"Anything you say, *apprentice*." His glare would have boiled the Grand Canal. Vasco was untouchable, but I had made another enemy.

As we walked out side by side, I said. "It must be nice, having such power."

Vasco is slightly taller than I am and never misses a chance to look down on me. "Yes and no."

"What's the no?"

"I get nightmares too."

Once in a while he shows a humble streak that I find very annoying.

I told Giorgio the Ca' della Naves and made myself comfortable, opening the curtains and preparing to enjoy the journey. Vasco brooded in silence, mostly, but every now and again he would nonchalantly ask a simple question about what we were doing. I answered honestly, admiring his skill. Without ever pushing, he soon knew everything worth knowing about my meeting with the chiefs.

"So your master doesn't trust you with the name of the murderer?"

"Did yours tell you Karagounis was under observation?" I countered.

No answer.

"Do you know anything about Domenico Chiari?"

Vasco's dark gaze drilled into me. "Should I?"

"Yes. The foreign couple we're about to see hired him as interpreter and guide, so it is sure as holy writ that he was spying for the Ten. Last week he disappeared. I'd like to know if he walked out on them or was ordered to or if he's just floating face down in the lagoon, somewhere."

"You are melodramatic."

"We have seen four violent deaths in three days and I barely escaped another."

Vasco sighed. "Life is full of sorrows. I knew a Domenico Chiari. We took lessons from the same tutor, but I haven't seen him in ages. He works for a banker. I don't know if he spies for the Ten. Only *Circospetto* would know for sure."

As we walked up the echoing, musty, and scabby staircase in the Ca' della Naves, I said, "Sir Bellamy Feather has been here about two months, buying pictures and other art for collectors in northern Europe. Lady Hyacinth, his wife, is the size of a canal dredger's barge and smarter than she pretends.

They were not invited to the Imer party but they turned up anyway and Imer threw them out. No known motive to kill the procurator."

"Succinct report, deputy."

That sneer put him a few points ahead, so I resolved to try harder. I hammered on the door. We waited. It stayed shut.

"I can run down and fetch Bruno," I suggested.

The *vizio* was raising an official fist to try his luck when the door swung open, and there was Sir Feather himself, millwheel ruff, oar-sized mustache, and shoulder high. In fact he was not as small as I remembered, but then his wife was not present.

"You're late! We have been waiting," he said in his execrable French. "There they are." He stepped aside to reveal a pile of roped trunks and boxes. Then he saw me. "You again? You dare to return to this house?"

"In the flesh." I bowed. "And this is—"

"Go away before I call the police!" He tried to shut the door, but the long leg of the law intervened—Vasco put his boot in.

"*Je suis un gendarme, monseigneur.* You have a complaint against this man?" The accursed Vasco spoke French better than I did and was beefier than Feather, because the door opened despite the little man's best efforts to hold it. I know from engaging blades with him on many occasions that Vasco's wrists are stronger than mine, which is another flaw in his character.

Feather glared at both of us, as if uncertain which he hated more. "He inserted himself in this house the night before last under false pretenses and forced my lady wife into the bedroom under the deception that he wished to inspect the paintings we have collected and had I not returned opportunely might have—"

"Yes?" Vasco said breathlessly.

"Frightened her considerably."

"This is a most serious charge," the *vizio* told him, and his sidelong glance at me was suffused with pure ecstasy. Heaven had answered his prayers. "I shall need to hear all the details. I am Filiberto Vasco, deputy to the chief of police of the serene Republic." He flashed the silver badge on his belt, while steadily edging his way into the apartment, herding Feather before him.

"There is no time! My wife and I are leaving on the instant. The men coming to take our baggage are overdue."

At that moment the lady of the house loomed into view, rattling off some guttural question to her husband. Vasco's eyes widened at the sight of her. He eyed me as if wondering how a charge of attempted rape would stand up before the judges. And then, to my intense annoyance, he switched to English. He was clearly not fluent in it, but he spoke it at least as well as any of us spoke French. The other two cried out in joy and all three began gabbling in a hodgepodge of the two languages.

Another point to him! This day was not working out as it should.

I was not quite shut out, for I could guess what was going on from the French words and watching the faces. The Feathers were about to leave the city to go to Rome. But Vasco had orders to make sure that they turned up at the Maestro's party that evening and they were only foreigners, so he had all the latitude he wanted. Now Sir Bellamy had accused me of attempted rape, Vasco explained, they would have to file a formal complaint and probably stay in town until an investigation could be held.

The English are reputed to be a phlegmatic race, but Bellamy exploded like a bombard. He stamped his feet and screamed and at one point seemed about to draw his sword.

I was not worried by that, for I knew Vasco was deft enough with his rapier and I would have enjoyed rescuing him had Feather turned out to be defter. I waited, leaning against the door jamb, occasionally stifling a yawn. Hyacinth watched the argument narrowly, saying nothing.

Three men came plodding up the stairs and stopped in alarm when they saw the *vizio* and a crazy foreigner arguing with him. Vasco, who was starting to turn red himself, stepped out into the hallway.

"If you came to take the foreigners' baggage, you are not required today."

They shrugged and removed themselves without a word. He turned and the door slammed in his face with a peal of thunder. He laughed.

"Having a better day than you expected?" I inquired.

"Oh, much better! Stay here, Zeno. I don't suppose they will try to slip away without their baggage, but I must find some reinforcements." He dashed off down the stairs.

I waited, hoping the door would open. After a few minutes it did. Hyacinth peered out, then emerged fully.

"We demand to see the English ambassador!"

"I cannot help you, madame. The matter is in the hands of magistrates."

She eyed me thoughtfully. "I could reward you well if you would take a message to him. Two ducats?"

I sighed and shook my head in deep regret.

She changed signals, lowering eyelashes, pursing plum lips. "If you could help me, I should be *very* much in your debt, *lustrissimo*."

Saints protect me! I imagined a tussle with those great limbs and hastily thought of Violetta instead. "It would do no good. The *vizio* has gone to fetch guards. If you try to leave the city, you will be stopped, madame. I am sorry."

She went back in and slammed the door.

Vasco reappeared at the bottom of the topmost flight of stairs, beckoning me to go down to him.

"All arranged?" I asked. "That was quick."

He smiled smugly. "All arranged."

Venice supports nothing like the great police forces found in most cities, but the Council of Ten has agents everywhere. Without doubt someone was already carrying word to the palace and others would keep watch so the Feathers did not slip away.

As we walked back to the gondola, I asked, "Am I to be charged with attempted rape?"

"I hope that can be arranged," the *vizio* said happily. "It will depend, I suspect, on what happens this evening. If we need a way to solve our Alfeo Zeno problem, and the Feathers need permission to leave the city, something can be worked out to our mutual satisfaction, if not to yours."

"Certainly not to mine," I agreed. "An automatic death sentence, commuted to ten years in the galleys?"

"I wouldn't count on that last bit if I were you."

Another point to him.

I said, "You mentioned that you shared a tutor with Domenico Chiari. What subject were you studying?"

"English and German."

"Why?"

"You think I got this job entirely on my good looks?"

"Obviously not." He had gotten it by being somebody's nephew, but it would be petty to say so. "So Domenico was planted on the foreigners to spy for the Ten, but he only admitted to knowing French, not English, so that he could eavesdrop on their private conversations?"

"That's very obvious, Alfeo. Quite simplistic."

"I'm sorry," I said. "I'm just a dumb *monseigneur*. And has Domenico Chiari now returned to his normal job at the bank, spying on foreign currency transactions?"

We arrived at the mooring and had climbed into the gondola before I received an answer. I told Giorgio to take us to the Ca' Orseolo. When I joined Vasco in the *felze* he said:

"I don't know what's happened to Domenico. He's not a close friend of mine, but he is a friend. That's another reason the Feathers will not be leaving Venice today."

22

C a' Orseolo fronted on the Grand Canal, naturally. It was too old to be one of the truly splendid palaces, but it still gave off a reek of money that annoyed me intensely when I remembered all the trouble I had had collecting the Maestro's fee for the ill-fated horoscope. Two large cargo barges were tied up at the watergate when we arrived, and Giorgio had trouble docking. Although Florence is a greater weaving center, Venice trades in wool from England and Flanders, cotton from Egypt, silk from Cathay. I knew that Ca' Orseolo was one of the principal importers of finished fabrics, and I counted ten men unloading bales. Inside the *androne* I saw stacks of furniture that had probably just arrived from the Procuratie.

By myself, and especially after the previous day's spitting match, I would have needed the backing of a brigade of musketeers to get close to any member of the family. I had dear Vasco instead. Without hesitation he strode into the *androne*, headed straight to a man issuing orders, and demanded to be taken at once to the noble Enrico. And so he was, with me smiling happily along at his side. We did not even have to go upstairs. The Lizard and his son were closeted in a counting room nearby with an elderly clerk and a dozen massive ledgers. None of them was wearing formal mourning, so grief had been stoically set aside in favor of tallying up the inheritance. Or possibly young Benedetto was being given a lesson in the family business. His sling still hung around his neck, but did not contain his arm. That hand held a pen, and he was making notes. A fast healer, obviously.

Father and son stared in blazing disbelief at the intruders, from Vasco to Zeno and back again. Vasco stepped aside with a flourish to give me the stage. The clerk tactfully scuttled out, closing the door.

I bowed with grace. "Your Excellency . . . *sier* Benedetto . . . I am deeply sorry to have to intrude on your grief again. I did inform Your Excellency yesterday that officers of the Republic were supporting my investigation of your honored father's death." I paused so Enrico might comment. He merely laid his arms on the desk and stared at me with his bulging eyes like Jupiter aiming thunderbolts.

I continued. "This evening, one hour after Angelus, the persons who were present in the Imer residence on the evening of the thirteenth will assemble there again, at which time my master, Doctor Nostradamus, will demonstrate how and by whom your father was murdered. Since your daughter was one of the witnesses, we request that she attend."

Enrico waited to see if that was all, then snake-eyed my escort, "You are the genuine *vizio,* Filiberto Vasco?"

"I am, Excellency."

I wondered if the great conciliator was about to offer us a deal, something involving only half my head on a plate.

"I wanted to be quite sure. The swindler beside you intruded on our house of mourning yesterday claiming to speak for the Council of Ten and accompanied by a prostitute masquerading as a nun. He created a disturbance, even threatening to draw on my son, who was unarmed. I am surprised by the company you keep, *Vizio*."

Vasco's day just kept getting better. How he managed to keep from giggling I could not imagine.

"I am deeply shocked to hear these charges, Your Excellency. They are most serious and I am certain that the Ten will react with great severity."

"Is he a *nobile homo* as he claims?"

Vasco sighed. "Regrettably, yes, at the moment, but even if he escapes the gallows, he will certainly be stricken from the Golden Book when he is sent to the galleys." He gave me a warm smile. "His master does have permission to stage a reenactment this evening, though, and action against both of them will have to wait until after that is completed. I expect that *Missier Grande* himself will be there, and will certainly oblige a minister of your eminence by taking Zeno into custody as soon as the farce is over. I may report that your daughter will attend?"

I was keeping an eye on Benedetto, who looked troubled. Alfeo with the *vizio*'s backing was a much more credible threat than Alfeo without.

His father said, "As a member of the *Collegio*, I take grave exception to this harassment in my time of sorrow. The Council of Ten has approved the farce you describe?"

Vasco would not have arrived where he had without some natural skill at obfuscation. "The chiefs raised no objections to Maestro Nostradamus's proposal, but they granted him no immunity either. He and Zeno may both be vulnerable to prosecution for malicious mischief, at the very least."

"I will see that both are charged," Enrico said, giving me a venomous look. "My daughter will be present."

As we walked back out to the watergate, Vasco said, "If you have any sense, boy, you will start running now and not stop until you are somewhere in the hinterland of the King-dom of Prester John, wearing a heavy beard."

"You enjoy this prospect?"

"It helps me bear the sorrows of life," he conceded.

I told Giorgio the Ca' Tirali.

For several reasons I dreaded my coming meeting with the new ambassador. For one, although my letter had turned down his incredibly generous offer, no doubt I would find a gracious and courteous reply waiting for me when I returned to Ca' Barbolano. For another, I strongly suspected that he was possessed, like Karagounis, because his offer had not just been incredible in itself, it had come very soon after I was snared by the manuscript. And for a third, even my impudence does have limits. Tirali senior was one of the inner circle of government. As one of the six great ministers, Enrico Orseolo was another, of course, but Vasco and I had not been demanding that he attend the meeting, only asking that he send his daughter to it.

I had no need of the *vizio* to gain admittance, because the doorman granted me noble honors. He deeply regretted that Ambassador Tirali had already left for the palace, but *sier* Pasqual was in residence. If the *clarissimo* would be so kind as to follow . . . He led us up the great staircase and left us in the imposing *salotto* while he went to report our presence. I headed for a Palma Vecchio I had admired the previous day.

Vasco could hardly have missed the difference in my reception. He strolled over to join me. "Friend of the family, are you?"

"Neighbor," I said, peering at the brushwork with my nose almost on the canvas. "I feed the cat when they're out of town."

He said, "Hmm?" and after a moment, "Have you any theories on *why* your lunatic master is being so diabolically secretive about the name of the murderer?"

"Yes. What's yours?"

"There are those who mistakenly believe," he murmured, "that the Council of Ten, while often insanely suspicious of members of the nobility it thinks may be plotting treason with foreigners, is sometimes not as assiduous as it should be in charging the same aristocrats with purely criminal behavior. If your master shared this seditious misapprehension, then he might think that he could force the Ten's hand by exposing the culprit in public."

"That assumes," I said, "that he intends to accuse a noble. It also assumes that the Ten already know or suspect the culprit and have decided to let him off by accepting the Greek's suicide as a confession of guilt, and that the chiefs of the Ten do not like this travesty of justice and seized upon my master's offer as a way of frustrating the will of the majority. You are jumping to a huge heap of conclusions, *Vizio*."

"So what's your theory?"

"That he was telling the truth when he said that an accusation would not convince but a demonstration would."

"That's all?"

"No." I backed away so I could admire the composition from afar. "He's also a real Pantaloon who loves showing off."

"He will be walking a very high wire tonight, then."

Before I could counter that, Pasqual Tirali strolled in, looking frowsty, as if he had been dragged out of bed and had dressed in a hurry. I wondered if he had been partying all night with Violetta and thrust the thought out of my mind. Although this was an unconscionable hour to call on a patrician playboy, he embraced me and acknowledged Vasco's bow with a gracious nod.

I explained our mission.

He frowned. "You told us yesterday, Alfeo, you had found no evidence that the procurator's death was due to foul play."

"I would still say so, but my master disagrees. He insists that he will unmask a murderer this evening."

Pasqual smiled the irresistible Tirali family smile. "Then we must not miss the excitement. My father is very busy just now, getting ready to take up his new position, but I will tell him. How long will it take?"

"I should hope no more than an hour, Pasqual."

"And you wish me to bring the same lady who was my companion that evening?" His face showed no sign of mockery or secret knowledge. If he was aware that he shared Violetta with me, then he was a stunningly effective actor.

"If you would be so kind."

"It will be a pleasure. My mother?"

"No, he asked for only those who were in the viewing room."

"Knowing my mother, she may not take no for an answer." Subtly, he began moving us toward the door. "My father was very disappointed when he received your letter this morning, Alfeo."

I mumbled my apologies.

"I know he sent you a reply leaving the offer open if you ever change your mind."

That made me feel even more ungrateful, of course.

The inevitable question came as Vasco and I descended the marble staircase. "What offer?"

"The cat. He wanted me to look after it while he's away in Rome."

"This is my sty," I said as we approached the Ca' Barbolano. "Giorgio will take you on to wherever you want to go. You

won't mind if I do not invite you in? The neighbors would
be shocked."

"I understand entirely," Vasco countered. "In my job I
have to consort with the worst sludge imaginable. We shall
meet again this evening, I expect. But hopefully not for the
last time."

I said, "Amen to that. I do so enjoy our little fencing
bouts."

As I emerged from the *felze*, I caught Giorgio's eye and
signaled *Hurry back* in Bruno sign language. Giorgio merely
nodded, a gesture that means the same to Bruno and me as
it does to everyone else in the world except Greeks. With
Vasco aboard, the gondola sped off along the canal.

Our arrival had gone largely unnoticed, because the Marciana battalions were all out on the quay, having a screaming
match with the workers on the building site opposite. Insults and obscene gestures flew back and forth. I was amused
to notice that Corrado and Christoforo were over there,
yelling abuse as loudly as anyone at their Marciana friends on
this side. I did not bother to inquire the cause of contention.
Just because this was Venice, I suspected. I sent Bruno off
upstairs and leaned against the door jamb to judge the invective. The Marciana army won by default when the foremen
opposite managed to drive everyone back to work.

Giorgio returned in an astonishingly short time, flitting
his gondola along the Rio San Remo like a seabird. He
pulled in to the quay and I lurched aboard. I would like to
say I leaped aboard, but my leg was throbbing again. In fact
he caught my wrist just before I fell overboard.

"Where did he go?"

"The Rialto."

"Fast as you can!" I shouted, flopping down on a thwart.
I almost never ask that of Giorgio and he responded with a

wild swing of his oar, spinning the gondola on its axis to great shouts of rage from other boats going by, and then shooting it back the way he had come like a musket ball.

I knew exactly why Vasco had gone to the Rialto, but I had very little hope of finding him. The Rialto area is the commercial heart of the whole Republic. It has the only bridge over the Grand Canal, is where the banking is done, where most foreigners lodge, and where the great food markets are—hardly surprising that it is constantly crowded.

Giorgio shot the gondola in between two others in front of the Palazzo dei Dieci Savi and shouted "That way!" I scrambled ashore and hobbled as fast as I could along the Ruga degli Oréfici, which was packed with people heading home for their midday meal. The bankers mostly congregate near the church of San Giacomo di Rialto, scribbling in ledgers laid out on tables under the porticos. If Domenico Chiari was about the same age as Vasco and myself, as Vasco had implied, then he would be no more than a clerk, a junior who might be sent off on errands anywhere in the city. So Vasco might have drawn a blank and headed back to the palace to report to *Missier Grande*.

But he hadn't. San Giacomo answered my panted prayers, and I caught a glimpse of a red cloak. The *vizio* was standing by a pillar, having a friendly tête-à-tête with a man of our age, but shorter, pudgy, and bespectacled. The crowds had observed the cloak and left a clear space around them. Even so, the two men were conversing in whispers. Fortunately Vasco had his back to me, so I was able to approach unnoticed and come to a stop right behind his shoulder. I leered like a shark at Domenico so he could not help noticing me—eavesdropping is beneath my dignity and honor unless I can do it unobserved.

He flinched. With his eyeglasses balanced on an almost comically snub nose, he looked very owlish.

Vasco whirled around and bared fangs at me. "What do you want?"

"A chat with the illustrious Domenico."

"Go away!" the *vizio* said. "Or I will arrest you as a public nuisance. Dom, never answer any question this character ever asks you. If he pesters you in any way at all, throw him in the canal."

Chiari smiled nervously. "I don't think I could do that without help."

"A lot of help," I suggested.

"Would four scriveners and two tallymen suffice?"

Oh? A wit!

Vasco was not amused either. "Go away, Zeno."

I shrugged. "A very few questions, quite harmless. Does he spy for the Council of Ten?"

Chiari, regrettably, failed to turn pale or flinch guiltily. He laughed as if that was the funniest suggestion he had heard in years.

Vasco said, "That is none of your business. I have to put up with you, but I will not allow you to harass my friends. Now go!"

Fun is fun, but if I concealed information just to score points off Vasco, I would be handing him a stick to beat me with in future. Besides he was several points up on the morning.

"Truce?" I said. "Just listen while I ask him a couple of questions. Whether he answers or not, you will be glad you did."

"No!"

"He's lying to you. Upon my honor and as I hope for salvation." I crossed myself.

We have cooperated in the past, Filiberto Vasco and I, although not often. We both hate doing it, he probably more than I, but he knows I play fair. I am not always so sure about him.

He scowled. "Truce then, as San Marco is my witness. Dom, this is *sier* Alfeo Zeno and you are still not required to answer his questions."

Chiari peered politely at me over his eyeglasses. "How may I help you, *clarissimo?*"

"*The Miracle of the Holy Cross,*" I said. "Painted by Titian. You advised *sier* Bellamy Feather when he bought it?"

This time his response was more guarded. "I translated for him during the negotiations. I do not pretend to be an art expert."

"But you are a Venetian? You speak like one. You must have recognized the bridge in the background of that picture."

"It looked much like the Rialto, but artists—"

"I remember the new Rialto bridge being completed," I said. "So must you. When did Titian die, *lustrissimo?*"

"I don't recall, *clarissimo*. I am not—"

"1576."

If I could see the sparkle of sweat on his forehead, Vasco certainly could.

Chiari said, "I think the picture is in the master's style, painted by one of his pupils, *messer.*"

"No doubt, but it purports to be signed by him. How much did Feather pay for it?"

"I don't remember."

I had no need to ask more questions. He was pale as ashes and Vasco scarlet with fury.

"What are you implying, Zeno?"

"Truce, remember? One or two bad fish in the net I could understand, but the Feathers' association with *your friend* turned out to be astonishingly unfortunate for them. The lady showed me six paintings, and only one of them was any good. *Your friend* must consort with very unscrupulous dealers. Does he spy for the Ten?"

Vasco said, "Yes," through clenched teeth. Domenico gaped at him in horror.

"So when a rich foreigner and his wife arrived and rented a luxurious —"

"No!" Chiari squeaked. "His bankers in London wrote to Ca' Pesaro before he even arrived—"

"Immaterial," I told Vasco. "Ca' Pesaro reported the London request to the Ten—or the Ten opened their mail, perhaps. Probably both. House Pesaro was told to assign *your friend* to the Feathers, because very rich foreigners are suspect. He discovered they had more money than knowledge, and no evil intent whatsoever. He proceeded to swindle them blind, feeding them the sort of junk that is painted only to dupe tourists. He may even have embroidered his reports to *Circospetto* to make the Feathers seem dangerous enough to justify watching. What sort of kickback did the forgers give him, do you suppose? Half? A third? Then either the Bellamys found out what he was doing and threw him out, or the Ten decided that they were harmless and pulled him off the case. I remind you, my dear Filiberto, that while we Venetians are the world's hardest bargainers, we do always keep our word. Swindling customers is just not in the cards."

Vasco was snarling. "Have you finished?"

"Certainly. I proved my point, didn't I?"

"The truce is ended. Get out of here."

"Do I have to report this thief to the Lion's Mouth?"

"I will take care of him. Get out!" Vasco repeated furiously.

Domenico Chiari crumpled to the ground in a dead faint, causing heads to turn. Spectators cried out in alarm, with undercurrents of anger against the bullying *vizio*. I bowed with an ironic flourish and left Vasco to deal with the situation.

About ten points to me.

As I limped back across the *campo*, I reflected that I should have played my hand a little more subtly. I had not discovered the truth about the Feathers' visit to Karagounis. They had insisted that the Greek had invited them to the Imer book viewing; he had denied doing so. No doubt Domenico Chiari had arranged that misunderstanding for his own purposes. Well, although Karagounis was beyond questioning, Chiari was not and the Ten's tormentors would soon strappado the truth out of him.

"You're looking happy, Alfeo," Giorgio said, as he rowed us sedately along the Grand Canal.

"It's been such a wonderful morning! I haven't had so much fun since I was four years old and pulled wings off flies."

"Now you pull feathers off the *vizio*?"

"*Darling* Filiberto!"

"Be careful of him, Alfeo. He's a dangerous enemy."

"He's a wonderful enemy. He never stops trying."

"That's what I mean," Giorgio said.

It was too early to call on Violetta, so I went upstairs to see if the Maestro had opened and read my letter from Ambassador Tirali.

He had, of course. Then he had used it as a bookmark, so I had to ask him where it was and he had to find it for me. He was still deep in his pursuit of Hermes and Mercury. While reporting on the last couple of hours I tried to bring some order to the incredible clutter he accumulates the moment my back is turned.

He nodded. "Satisfactory. There are some letters to write,

and . . . About tonight . . ." He fixed me with a scraggy eye. "Wear your sword."

He knows perfectly well that wearing a sword at night is illegal.

"Certainly, although I wouldn't be much good with it. My leg still hurts."

"I mean for appearances. How much would it cost to dress you like a real noble?"

"I am a real noble." I let my annoyance show. "You really did rummage about in my memories last night, didn't you?"

He managed to seem surprised. "I asked you only questions relevant to the murder, nothing private. My point is that I can't shout. I can't overawe people. I need you to keep control of the meeting tonight. You have to look the part. Clothes talk. How much?"

"You want me to control *Missier Grande*, his *vizio*, a great minister, an ambassador, the ambassador's son, an attorney, and possibly the entire Council of Ten?" I said, awed. "I am humbled by your trust. Perhaps the doge would lend me his *corno*? To dress me as a noble from scratch would take at least a week, but the Ghetto's pawnshops are full of good stuff. I could look there and have things altered to fit. Four or five ducats. Ten would be better. Otherwise it will look pretentious and fake."

He swallowed as if it hurt. "Go and do it. Enter it in the ledger."

"As what?"

"Maintaining appearances. Hurry before I change my mind."

23

Bruno has his own strange ways of knowing things, and when I returned to the casa with my worthy apparel, he became excited and asked if the Maestro was going to need him later. When I nodded, he ran to get out the carrying chair and strap it on. For the next two hours he wandered about wearing it, a menace to the Barbolano artwork every time he turned around.

But eventually I was ready too. Blue has always been my best color. It sets off my sultry good looks, or something. I had chosen a doublet of peacock blue silk, embroidered in gold, with a wide white ruff collar, puffed sleeves tied at points with silver ribbon and frothy white linen peeking out through the slashes. My buttons were nuggets of amber shaped like pears, and amber strawberries decorated my belt. Below a very low waist I sported matching knee britches and white silk stockings tight and sheer enough to reveal every wrap of the bandage on my calf. My fur-trimmed short cloak of silver brocade hung on my shoulders so as not to conceal my sleeves; my bag-shaped bonnet stood half a yard high. I hoped Violetta would be able to control herself when she clapped eyes on such splendor. With a last minute adjustment to the hang of my rapier and dagger, I minced out into the *salone* in my gold-buckled shoes.

Christoforo cried out and dropped to his knees. Corrado and Archangelo came running to see what was wrong and were even more overcome, falling on the floor, writhing and moaning. Then came a torrent of younger brothers and sisters, Mama herself, and Giorgio in his best red and black. Giggling at their clowning brothers, the small fry began bowing and curtseying. The merriment stopped when a steady thumping announced the arrival of the Maestro in his black physician robe—even the twins mind their manners near him, having been warned so often that he might turn them into frogs. Which the rest of us think would be an improvement, mind you.

Bruno rushed over and knelt to offer the chair. I went to assist, moving carefully in case my cloak fell off and shamed me. The Maestro eyed my radiance with intense dislike.

"How much did all that cost?"

"About twenty ducats, I suppose. It isn't brass and glass, you know."

He said, "Obscene!" and clambered awkwardly into the chair.

As soon as he was settled, I tapped Bruno's shoulder to let him know he could now rise, and the three of us followed Giorgio downstairs. It was a fine evening and Carnival revelers were out already, boatloads of them singing along with their gondoliers, even on sleepy Rio San Remo. The Maestro and I made ourselves comfortable in the *felze*—I having some trouble managing sword and bonnet, I admit. Bruno sat in the bow to block the view as only he could. Giorgio pushed off.

"The twenty ducats, master? I can enter them in the ledger?"

The old miser chuckled. "Enter whatever you spent. But tomorrow you must take the clothes back to the Ghetto and get whatever you can for them. Enter that in the ledger as a credit."

I can never fool him. We have played out this farce before, when he wants me dressed up, and I always solve the problem the same way. I went across the *campo* to the Ca' Tron San Remo, home of my friend Fulgentio, now ducal equerry. As I told you, he and I are the same size, and fortunately he was home. When I explained that I needed to shine before some important people, he at once rang for his valet and told him to dress me. I refused to cooperate until I had made Fulgentio promise to take the clothes back the next day and not try to make them a gift. He agreed unwillingly, grumbling that he rarely got to wear decent things now, having to spend all his days and half his nights disguised as a gargoyle in equerry rags.

The Maestro has no idea how humiliating this is for me. I keep promising myself that next time I will take him at his word and actually spend some of his golden hoard. So far I never have. He would weep.

I got down to business. "Master, I need instruction. You have deciphered the rest of the quatrain? The gold and the eyes of the serpent were about the attempt on my life. But *unthinkable love triumphs from afar* sounds like a clue to the murder."

"It may well be so."

Resisting a temptation to grind my teeth or punch out his, I said, "I tried a reading before we came out."

"Tarot? Old wives' nonsense."

"It may well be so."

"Bah! What did it tell you?"

"For question, subject, or present I dealt out Fire, Trump XV. That puzzles me. It obviously doesn't represent me, or

you, or a murderer." Fire shows a tower being struck by
lightning, with a man and woman falling from it. "Can it
mean danger to the Republic?"

He chuckled. "Not in this case. I'm glad you weren't stupid enough to reject it and start over. Tell me the rest of it."
Obviously he already understood more than he was going to
tell me, but at least he was showing real interest and had
stopped scoffing.

"For past, problem, or danger, I turned over the two of
cups. That one seems easy. It must represent the two glasses
that were switched."

"Or the two waiters?"

I grunted, not having thought of that possibility. "For
future, objective, or solution, I got Trump XII, the Traitor,
reversed. And that I most certainly do not understand!"

The Traitor depicts a man suspended from a tree by one
ankle. Hanging his corpse upside down is the traditional
Italian way to disparage a traitor, but in my deck the Traitor
seems alive and happy in his odd position and has a mop of
golden hair like a halo. He is not just a convicted criminal.

"What did I teach you about XII?" my master murmured
cautiously.

"That it may represent a change of loyalty or viewpoint,
or a rebirth, because we all take our first breath upside down.
But *reversed*? What does that mean? No sudden change of
viewpoint—we were right all along?"

After a significant silence, my master said, "In this case I
think it may be a warning not to jump to premature conclusions. What else did you find?"

"For helper or path, I turned over the two of staves,
which I do not understand at all. And for the warning, the
snare to be avoided, I got the jack of swords, which tonight
ought to mean me." Jackanapes of swords, perhaps.

The Maestro was nodding. "That's very good! Excellent,

an excellent foretelling. You are becoming quite skilled with tarot." Praise indeed!

"But why the jack of swords as the warning? Am I going to commit some fatal error?"

He chuckled like a hen calling her chicks. "I shouldn't think so. The program seems reasonably foolproof. Perhaps the jack of swords may mean someone else. Benedetto Orseolo, for example?"

"It would be a lackluster match, even if my leg wound is worse than his shoulder's. What does the rest of the spread mean?"

"It tells you who committed the murder and how I shall reveal the truth. Think about it."

I resisted an urge to throw the old mummy into the canal. Bruno would just rescue him, and I might get Fulgentio's outfit splashed.

At the top of the stairs, Bruno knelt to let the Maestro dismount. Ottone Imer was waiting there for us in his black attorney's gown, and I was amused to see his mouth twitch a few times when he registered my sartorial apotheosis. I could almost imagine his brain turning from the Apprentice page to the NH page. The Maestro had been right, as usual—*clothes talk*.

I granted our host a small bow. "I see you have done us proud, *lustrissimo*." The hallway was cramped, but he had not spared on candles. Wine bottles and goblets of crimson glass were arrayed on a table, and the servant Benzon was waiting there. He was staring wistfully at my gold and amber.

Imer said, "Welcome back to my house, Doctor Nostradamus. I hope this will be a happier visit than the last. May I offer you wine?"

"No. You did not the last time, not when I arrived. I

hope we can duplicate the last time as closely as possible. Of course people will probably not arrive in the same order. I dislike standing . . ."

Imer conducted the Maestro into the dining room. Bruno, I noted, had shed the carrying chair and was taking it away to some nether corner of the house, probably the kitchen, where he would wait as patiently as a mountain all night, terrifying servant girls by smiling at them. I saw no reason why I could not try a glass of wine. I went over to Benzon.

"Blessings on you, Giuseppe. You have the same wines as last time?"

He nodded. "Yes, *messer*."

"Which one is poisoned?"

His eyes narrowed. "All of them, Alfeo. Which one would you like?"

I had told him to call me Alfeo. I laughed. "The arsenic. I'll try the retsina, please." As he poured me a generous glassful, I said, "You may have your friend Pulaki back to help you shortly."

"He's no friend of mine," Benzon said sulkily. "I never saw him before that night."

I took a sip and grimaced. "You weren't joking about the poison."

"And I wish you wouldn't! I didn't poison anybody!"

I realized that he was terrified, a midget caught up in a clash of titans. I apologized. "You don't have anything to worry about," I assured him.

"No? You swear that?"

"Not unless you poisoned the old man. Maestro Nostradamus knows who did and is going to expose him. So you can relax." Unless the tarot's two of cups meant the waiters, of course.

Imer came stalking out of the dining room. "Doctor Nostradamus wants the guests shown into the *salone*," he told Benzon, "and not served wine until later." He noticed my wineglass, but did not comment on it. "How many will be coming, er . . . *clarissimo?*"

I made a graceful gesture with the glass. "I don't know exactly. There were thirteen in the room on the thirteenth, but two are dead—the procurator and Alexius Karagounis. I doubt if the doge will appear again, but someone else can play his part. I expect Great Minister Orseolo, *Missier Grande*, and possibly his *vizio*. Perhaps others from . . ."

Imer drew breath sharply; his mouth twitched. In his blue and red robe, *Missier Grande* was mounting the stairs. Gasparo Quazza is an ominous sight at any time, yet it was his young companion I watched, the Greek's servant Pulaki Guarana. He moved with difficulty, one hand gripping the balustrade and the other heavily bandaged and held tight against his chest. He wore the same clothes he had worn the previous morning, but they looked the worse for wear. So did he, face pallid under a heavy beard shadow, eyes sunk in deep wells.

Imer uttered a croak of welcome. I laid down my glass and bowed to *Missier Grande*.

"I am only here to observe," he told Imer. "This man is a state prisoner. He has agreed to cooperate with the evening's procedure."

Pulaki nodded as if he would agree to anything that would delay his return to prison.

"And I am merely following *sier* Alfeo Zeno's orders," Imer twitched, dissociating himself from anything horrible that might happen and probably would.

Missier Grande turned his regard on me. It traveled from my cap to my shoes and back up to my eyes. "So what orders do you have for me, *clarissimo?*"

I find jokes from Gasparo Quazza unnerving. "I believe that all you have to do is observe, *lustrissimo*. What action you take is up to you. The meeting will be held in that room there. So far only my master is here. Will Domenico Chiari be attending?"

"No. He has other business." I wondered if Quazza's eyes had always been that cold or if his job had made them so. He turned and walked into the dining room. I heard him greet the Maestro.

"What did they *do* to you?" Benzon whispered.

Pulaki just shook his head, unwilling or unable to say.

"We don't need you yet," I said. "Go and wait in there, please." I pointed to the *salone*, and he limped away while the three of us stared after him in horror.

All states use torture, of course. The confessions it extracts come with no guarantee of truth, so its main value is to incriminate people—either the victim or others—and terrorize all the rest. Was Domenico Chiari even then twisting on the cord with blocks of stone tied to his feet? In the Republic such questions are never answered and rarely even asked.

Now the suspects were starting to arrive, all determined not to keep the Council of Ten waiting. The Tirali men were first—Ambassador Giovanni in scarlet robes, *sier* Pasqual in black. They were steadying Violetta between them as she teetered up the stairs on her ten-inch stilt courtesan shoes. She was a grounded angel in a silver brocade gown, glittering with precious gems, her red-gold hair piled in two horns, her low neckline exposing peerless breasts padded to ride high. Her eyes widened when she saw me. I thought I recognized Aspasia behind them, calculating the political significance of my finery. If clothes spoke, mine were saying surprising things that evening. I kissed the ambassador's sleeve. He was too gracious to ask, but he was definitely puzzled, wondering why his intelligence on me had been faulty.

Pasqual named Violetta to me as if we had never met. A glint of Medea's smile warned me to be careful, but I had to live up to my debonair persona.

"I have heard tales of madonna Vitale and thought they were only myths. Now I see that they are legends."

Aspasia's response was instant. "Your subtlety flatters my wits, *messer*!"

"Alas, your wits are faster than my wit, madonna."

"I keep my wits about me and they introduce me to others."

"To wit?"

"To who? To you, *messer*."

"Can you keep up with this sort of play, Pasqual?" the ambassador asked.

"Usually." Pasqual was eyeing me thoughtfully.

Clothes talk, but mine had run out of funny things to say. I asked the Tiralis to wait in the *salone*.

And already the Orseolo contingent was approaching, three figures draped in mourning. I had expected Enrico to escort his daughter, but was surprised he had brought Benedetto. Bene had his sling on again, so perhaps he just wanted to remind everybody of his alibi. Unarmed, he did not look like a good candidate to be the jack of swords. Bianca, alas, was veiled and shrouded. Displayed as she should be, she would give even Violetta competition. I introduced Imer to the men, we both kissed the minister's sleeve, and I sent them all off to the *salone*.

The heady sense of power I obtained from ordering a great minister provoked me to smile broadly when I turned to the stairs and realized that Filiberto Vasco had arrived in time to see me do it. He was escorting the northern barbarians.

I made them welcome. "You all know the learned Attorney Ottone Imer, of course . . ."

Vasco started to translate, but milord Bellamy did not wait for him.

"This outrages me! I have sent complaints to the English ambassador."

"I hope it will be over very quickly, *messer.*"

The foreigner's absurd horned mustache quivered. He began to gabble and Vasco rattled off a translation. He was good. "We were due to leave today. The boatmen we had hired insisted on payment. The carriage waiting on the mainland will want an extra day's money. Who will compensate me for these losses?"

There are times when my humor gets the better of my discretion. I pointed to the *salone*. "In there, *messer,* is *sier* Enrico Orseolo—the elder of the two men in mourning weeds. He is one of the six great ministers of the Republic. More even than the doge himself, the great ministers run the government. Why don't you go and present your problem to him?"

That, I thought, ought to put the chickens in the fox house. As Sir Feather offered his wife his arm, the big woman disconcerted me yet again.

"How much for your outfit, Alfeo?"

"You want me to quote it as a complete set or item by item?"

"Every stitch." Either she had the strangest way of flirting I had ever met, or her wheels were well off center. I could engage verbal rapiers with Violetta, but the foreigner's signals confused me.

"Perhaps you and I can discuss that after the meeting?" I said, half expecting her husband to whip out his sword and start yelling at me. He just took her elbow and steered her away.

I noted with amusement that the buzz of conversation from the *salone* ceased abruptly when the foreigners entered. I smiled at Vasco, who was practicing looking intimidating but had a long way to go.

"You are also welcome, *Vizio.* The guests are assembled through there, and *Missier Grande* is in here." I turned to Imer. "*Lustrissimo*, that should be everybody." I was wrong.

Imer was not looking at me. He was staring aghast at the stairs. Majestic in his scarlet robe and patriarchal white beard, Ducal Counselor and State Inquisitor Marco Donà was ascending at a measured pace. I clenched my teeth tightly so they would not start chattering. The last time we had met, he had sent me to the torture chamber.

24

In my demonic delusion, the old man had been grim and menacing. Present in the flesh, he was paternal, condescending. He nodded benignly when Imer groveled to him, bleating how honored his house was and how he would brag of this visit for years.

Donà almost patted his head. "This charade is an imposition, citizen, and your cooperation is appreciated." But then the old man turned cynical eyes on me as I bent to kiss his sleeve. "And you must be the philosopher's apprentice."

I had met him in nightmare; he had never met me. "Alfeo Zeno, Your Excellency, honored to be at your service."

"Mm? It looks as if the Council of Ten should be investigating the permissible scale of physicians' fees. What do you think, attorney?"

"And the sumptuary laws also, Excellency," Imer murmured.

"Definitely the sumptuary laws."

The Council of Ten, its three chiefs, the three state inquisitors, the doge—I had no idea what political currents were flowing and who was on whose side. This was definitely not a moment to create waves. I replaced my bonnet at a more sedate angle. Humble was in.

"I borrowed these clothes for the occasion, Your Excellency."

He nodded. "From your friend Fulgentio Tron." He was warning me that I was under surveillance and the Three knew everything. They might know who had poisoned Procurator Orseolo and prefer that no one else did. "I just came to see if your master can make good on his boast. You are about to begin?"

"At Your Excellency's convenience. You wish to meet the other guests?"

"I think I know them all. Those I have not met I can guess. Where is *Missier Grande*?"

I would have bet a month's wages that Gasparo Quazza was standing just inside the dining room, eavesdropping on all the arrivals. If so, he moved quickly. By the time I had bowed the inquisitor through and followed him in, *Missier Grande* was seated in a chair several feet from the door.

The dining room had been made by joining two smaller rooms and was awkwardly long and narrow, but our host had again been generous with the lighting, loading his Murano chandeliers with lamps. Most of the floor space was taken up by what seemed to be one long linen-draped table, but must in fact be several set end-to-end. A few books had been laid out at intervals along it to represent the Karagounis manuscripts; sixteen chairs stood along the far side, on one of which sat the Maestro, leering at us as we entered. The sixteen on the nearer side had been pulled back against the wall, and it was one of these that had the honor of supporting *Missier Grande*. He rose to acknowledge the inquisitor, his face giving no hint of whether or not he was surprised to see the old man there.

Donà gave him a quick nod and said, "No, do not rise,

doctor," to the Maestro. "I trust you will make no wild accusations you cannot prove?"

The Maestro's face turned sulky. "Your Excellency forbids us to proceed?"

"Not at all." Donà chose the chair behind the door, where he would not be visible to persons entering. He sat down heavily, as if his feet or ankles hurt. "No, I wish to see justice done. The official view, I can reveal, is that the supposed Greek, Karagounis, was an agent of the sultan and had set up a complicated trap to murder the doge. Poor old Bertucci somehow got the wrong glass." *And to suggest otherwise may be unwise.*

"That is certainly a theory I considered, Your Excellency." The inquisitor raised silver eyebrows. "And discarded? You intrigue me already. You have no objections to these proceedings, *Missier Grande?*"

"None, Excellency. I have known the Maestro to astonish us before."

"Carry on, then."

"Alfeo?"

"Master?"

"Since the doge did not come, either you or *sier* Benedetto will have to stand in for him." From where the Maestro sat he had seen everyone going past the door.

Donà chuckled—ominously, of course. A state inquisitor cannot possibly chuckle otherwise. "That should be my role, surely? We mustn't raise the Orseolo boy's hopes too high before he has even taken his seat in the Great Council. And we must not distract *sier* Alfeo from his duties as Carnival King."

He obviously enjoyed being one of the dreaded Three, and I did not like the way he was muscling in on my master's production. Had *Circospetto* Sciara told him what was going to happen this evening? Or told the doge so the doge had told Donà? Had the Ten assigned the case to the Three, or was Donà there without the knowledge of Bartolemeo Morosini and the other chiefs of the Ten? And who could stop an inquisitor doing almost anything he wanted anyway?

"Your Excellency is gracious," I said. "With your permission, I will sound the trumpet." I stalked out and headed to the *salone.*

There I found three separate groups, sitting well apart and conversing in whispers—the three Orseolos, the two Tiralis and Violetta, the Feathers and Vasco. The unfortunate Pulaki sat by himself, with eyes closed and face twisted with pain. Imer had been waiting in the hallway and followed me in.

I apologized for the delay. "We had an unexpected arrival. Pulaki, please go and help Giuseppe with the wine. I know you have only one good hand, but I'd like you to watch and see that everything happens in the same order as last time." I waited until he had gone. "At the original viewing, the guests entered the dining room in the following order: Ambassador Tirali first, then the procurator and madonna Bianca. Your Excellency, will you represent your father for us?"

Lizard Enrico nodded with poor grace. Bianca, I was happy to see, had raised her veil to expose her angelic child-woman face.

"Then came *sier* Bellamy Feather and madonna Hyacinth. You spent some time discussing the books with Maestro Nostradamus, I believe. *Vizio*, you will interpret for them, please? And the next man, as you all know, was the doge, incognito. He will be represented this evening by State Inquisitor Marco Donà."

I wished I could watch all the faces at once, so that a sudden pallor might identify the murderer for me. I did not see one. Hyacinth demanded a translation from Vasco.

I continued. "*Sier* Pasqual, you and the lady were next.

That completes the ensemble, except for Alexius Karagounis, who cannot be with us this evening because he is tied up on the Piazzetta. Will you stand in for him, please, *sier* Benedetto?"

He shrugged his shoulders, sling and all. "If you will tell me where to go."

"That will be everyone's problem."

"This is not going to work, you know," Pasqual told Violetta. "We all moved around too much. I suppose the person who demonstrates the worst memory must be the murderer? Come, my darling, let's go and carnival."

I stood at the dining room door to direct the dance. Wineglass in hand and escorted by our host, Ambassador Tirali swept by me, red senator and black attorney.

"You introduced me to Maestro Nostradamus, did you not, attorney? But the Greek was here when I came in."

Benedetto Orseolo was summoned and inserted as Alexius Karagounis.

"Then you left, attorney," Tirali continued. "I walked down there and worked my way back up to about here. And the accursed Greek kept following and yattering at me."

Benedetto smiled. "Yatter, Your Excellency. Yatter, Your Excellency."

Tirali laughed. "You'll do well in the Senate, my boy. I was about here . . ."

He turned and I nodded to Minister Orseolo. As he entered with Imer, I noticed that the glass he carried was empty. He might scoff at tales of murder, but the Lizard was taking no chances. A moment later Bianca followed him in, flashing me a smile that raised my heartbeat significantly. She joined her father-grandfather. Imer went out again to greet more imaginary arrivals.

Missier Grande had disappeared, which seemed odd if he had come to oversee the reenactment. The actors on stage had a brief argument over who had been standing where. I waited until they reached agreement, then nodded to Vasco to bring in the Feathers. Bellamy stalked by me without a glance. Hyacinth paused, looked me over, and fluttered her eyelashes at me before continuing into the dining room. Vasco, coming behind, shook his head at me in disbelief. I wondered if she had been flirting with him, too. How crazy was she?

"Englishmen need more encouragement," I explained quietly.

He very nearly smiled.

Now there were eight people in the room and it was becoming obvious that Pasqual had been right—the Maestro's plan was not going to work. It had been four days, and there had been no reason to memorize the choreography of a casual social meeting, or just when who said what to whom.

"My turn now?" murmured the inquisitor, who had been sitting close to the door all this time.

"I think it must be, Your Excellency—or may I address you as 'Your Serenity'?"

Donà heaved himself up and approached the table. The Maestro directed him to a place.

Hyacinth spun around, moving very fast for so large a woman. She barked an objection, which Vasco translated: "The Greek was here. I was not so close."

Benedetto stepped into place between her and the doge-substitute. I saw his lips shape, "Yatter?" but he did not say it.

I turned to the still-crowded hallway and located our host. "Attorney, did you recognize the doge when he arrived?"

Imer riffled his feathers. "Of course I did. You think I am blind? But before I could even bow to him he told me he wanted no ceremony. He had just come for a second look at some of the books and would stay only a few minutes."

"Thank you." That explained why the doge had entered the dining room alone.

The actors had agreed on where they should be. Violetta was disturbingly close to me, her perfume all around me, whispering promises. She said something to her patron, pointing at Benedetto.

Pasqual murmured agreement and raised his voice. "We think the Greek was standing closer to the doge when we came in." He entered, Violetta on his arm.

I watched the players dance in the masque, but I had returned to my old opinion. It seemed quite impossible for anyone to have switched glasses with the procurator, or with the doge if he had been the intended victim. When the disagreements wound down I caught the Maestro's nod and looked for Imer again.

"Now, *lustrissimo*. This is where you threw out the foreigners."

Imer nodded and strode past me, heading for the Feathers. "Now I ask you to leave."

"It is where you *ordered* me to leave," Bellamy countered. "It is where you insulted me. But we did leave. Come, then, Hyacinth, my love. Are we permitted to go now?" he demanded of Vasco.

Vasco replied in English, but he pointed at me, as Carnival King.

"That is not what happened next," said a new voice. Bianca spoke up for the first time. "His Serenity left first."

"That is correct, *messer*," said a quiet voice at my elbow. It was Pulaki.

"Excellent," I said, and beckoned him forward. "We have a new witness. Speak up."

Pulaki advanced one step and looked nervously around the room. He spoke to the inquisitor. "I heard voices raised in anger and looked in. His Serenity came out and told me to go to the *salone* and fetch a gentleman he described. I have forgotten the name, Your Excellency."

"Good, good!" Donà said. "Then, as doge, I leave now. Are the rest standing about where they were then?"

Pulaki hesitated. "I only saw . . ." He pointed at Imer and Feather. "I did not notice anyone else, Excellency."

"Well, that's a help." The inquisitor removed himself from the group and headed for a spectator's chair. "Carry on, puppet master."

I thanked Pulaki, and he left with obvious relief. His intrusion had been out of character for a servant, and even more so for a man fresh from the tormentors. Was he desperate to cooperate in any way he could, or was he just obeying orders?

Imer showed the Feathers out into the entrance hall and Vasco followed. Behind them, the meeting became confused. Perhaps everyone had been distracted by the loud foreigners, but no one seemed at all sure where anybody had gone after it. The Maestro queried Bianca, who had not left her grandfather's side, but even she could not be sure who had spoken with him later.

"This is a waste of time!" the great minister complained loudly. "If I wanted to celebrate Carnival, I would do it in the Piazza or on the Lido. Marco?"

"I seldom agree with you in the *Collegio*, Enrico," the inquisitor said, "but I certainly do this time. I can't see what more you hope to achieve, doctor."

The Maestro spread his tiny hands in resignation. Perhaps only I, who knew him so well, guessed what was coming. "Nothing more, Your Excellency. I have demonstrated what I set out to demonstrate. Didn't you see who committed the murder?"

"There is no poison in this glass!" Orseolo snapped, turning it upside down. Then he realized that he had made a very stupid statement. "And I did not see how or when anybody could have put any there."

"Because you rarely set it down," the Maestro retorted. "Your father, examining books with a crippled hand, did not cherish it so closely. Alfeo, would you bring the others in, please?"

Turning, I almost walked into monolithic *Missier Grande*, who was standing right behind me, watching over my shoulder. But everyone else out there was listening too, so all I had to do was step aside and let them file past me. I beckoned Benzon and Pulaki to join us, since they also qualified as suspects. No one objected to their presence.

Missier Grande closed the door and stood in front of it, arms folded. Imer and Benzon began pulling chairs closer to the table. The four nobleman finished up in front of the Maestro like children before a teacher, but the rest of us were content to sit back against the wall. I certainly was, because I found myself next to Violetta. By purest chance, of course. She ignored me, attentive to the odious Pasqual at her other side.

"You will forgive me," the Maestro said with a hint of malice, "if I point out that everyone who was in this room that night had to be a suspect. For example, the person who had the best opportunity to poison the procurator's glass was his granddaughter, who never—"

"You dare suggest such a monstrous thing?" her father roared.

"No," the Maestro said mildly. "I am not suggesting that she did so. I am merely arguing that, since nobody witnessed the terrible deed, we must set aside all preconceived ideas and proceed by a careful analysis of the evidence, regardless of where it may lead us. I am sure His Excellency

the inquisitor, and attorney Imer, and *Missier Grande* . . .
and the *vizio* . . . will all confirm that this is the only way to
make out a case against anyone. I could quote the immortal
Aristotle, universally recognized as the paradigm philosopher, and the polymath Roger Bacon . . . but I digress."

He put his fingertips together and I braced for a lecture.

25

T he means were obvious from the start," the Maestro said. "Even before he left this house I knew that the procurator had ingested poison. I knew the name of that poison. There is no known antidote. Any physic other than time and rest would have been hazardous in a man of his age, so I recommended none. I knew from its effects that the drug had almost certainly been administered in this room, and madonna Bianca later confirmed to my apprentice that her grandfather had eaten nothing for some time beforehand.

"Most crimes have an obvious motive, but this one did not. The procurator had reached the pinnacle of his political career, his honored son now supervised the family business affairs, and most of his old enemies have long since preceded him to a better realm. The minister will understand that I speak in generalities when I note that family members are generally more likely to have motives for violence than strangers are, unless we include footpads and pirates, who are not in evidence in this case. I trust that Ambassador Tirali will take no offense at an observation that poison seems an extreme way to eliminate a rival bidder in a book sale."

Vasco was whispering a translation to the Feathers. The Maestro paused to let him catch up.

"I am happy to learn," Ambassador Tirali remarked, in a heavy-handed parody of the Maestro's style, "that my notoriously voracious acquisitive bibliophilic instincts are not suspected of leading me into mortal sin. As I told *sier* Alfeo yesterday, a political motive seems equally improbable. So why was Bertucci murdered?"

The Maestro was not about to spoil his own enjoyment by telling him that, not yet. "I could see no ready answer. Sir Bellamy and his wife are strangers, visiting our city to buy art, not to murder our national heroes. Our host here and the servants seem equally improbable killers. I was forced to wonder if the intended victim could have been someone else, such as our Most Serene Doge Pietro Moro. When the book dealer Karagounis was exposed as a Turkish agent, this explanation suddenly became worthy of serious consideration. The doge testified to Alfeo that he chose to drink retsina, which he rarely touches, simply because he knew the procurator would be here and would choose it. So an accidental switch of glasses must be considered.

"But consider the complications required! The doge should not have left the palace without his counselors. He should not have consorted with foreigners. He did so, he told Alfeo, because at the last minute he received a note from his old friend warning him that the books actually sold might not be those he had been shown."

"I object!" The howl came from Ottone Imer.

Nostradamus dismissed his complaint with a wave of his hand. "I do not say that was the case, attorney. I merely report what the doge said, quoting a note from the deceased, who might, just possibly, have been deceived by a deliberately planted rumor. Or the note might have been forged. But the chances that this too-complicated trap would lure the doge here in person were extremely remote, and even if he did decide to come and see for himself, why go through all the legerdemain with poison and retsina—a wine the doge was very unlikely to choose anyway, so far as a man like Karagounis could know?"

"I told him," Imer grumbled. "I told him no one would want it, but he insisted on bringing some."

"Quite. As I was saying, to a Turkish agent the poison would be an unnecessary complication. An ambush in a dark doorway would be far more effective. So you see, Your Excellency—" now the Maestro carefully addressed the inquisitor "—although the official theory cannot be absolutely disproved, it requires a lot of unlikely suppositions. *Pluralitas non est ponenda sine neccesitate,*[1] as the saintly Brother William of Ockham taught us."

Donà did not comment. He did not look very pleased, either, from what I could see of his face from where I was sitting. I glanced at Violetta, and she was smiling quietly at no one in particular. So she had seen the answer! I wondered whether she had applied Aspasia's sensitivity or Minerva's logic.

Having trashed the official government verdict, the Maestro pressed on. "*Vizio,* ask Sir Bellamy for me: When he and his lady visited Karagounis at his residence to view whatever books he had for sale, did he offer them wine?"

Translation . . . Bellamy nodded.

"Retsina?"

Hyacinth pulled a face and said what Vasco translated as, "The madonna says that whatever it was it tasted terrible."

"You see," the Maestro continued happily, "we assume that the poison could not have been concealed in the other wines—although this is not certain, because no authority

[1] Keep it simple.

I have consulted gives a recipe for isolating venom from the leaves and I have not had time to carry out my own experiments. But very few people have a taste for retsina. So the question becomes, who else was drinking retsina that night?"

"I tried it," Pasqual said. "But I promise never to do so again. And while I have the floor, I will point out that I never stood next to Procurator Orseolo. There was always at least one person between him and me."

"Oh, this is a stupid waste of time!" Minister Orseolo made as if to rise. "If you have an accusation to make, then make it now. Otherwise my children and I are leaving."

"Two minutes more, if you please, Your Excellency. I think some of you know whom I am about to accuse?"

Violetta said, "Yes."

Orseolo sat back again, glaring at her. Just about everyone else was frowning, except Bianca and Benedetto, who both looked horrified. There was a murderer in the room?

"Very well," the Maestro said. "One more digression and I am done. The poison in question is not available for purchase in the city. *Sier* Alfeo established this for me the next day. That means that the murderer obtained it from the mainland or from even farther afield and the crime was planned long in advance. Unfortunately, this information is not as useful as one would like. Madonna Bianca, for example, would seem to have no opportunity to acquire the herb in question, even if some demented nun in the convent had taught her its properties. But her brother attends university in Padua. I assume he came home for Christmas and . . . No, I am not suggesting that the procurator's grandchildren conspired to murder him! I am just pointing out that the poison could have been acquired, given time, by almost anyone in this room. It tells us only that the motive was not a sudden impulse. Either the murderer planned the crime well in advance . . ." He paused, enjoying the attention like a child performing for family friends.

"Or?" Minister Orseolo demanded.

"Or the murderer is a professional killer, Excellency." The Maestro stretched his lips in a smile. "Madonna Bianca, are you certain that no one put poison in your grandfather's glass?"

She was by far the youngest person in the room, reared in the shelter of the cloister, but she held her chin high and was not intimidated. "I did not say that, Doctor Nostradamus! I said I did not see it happen. But I was keeping an eye on his drink, in case he forgot it. I should have seen if anyone had tampered with it."

"Except once. You noticed the doge leaving, because he walked out when the attorney and Sir Bellamy were having their shouting match. They made so much noise that a servant looked in to see what was going on. That was the only moment when everyone was distracted and the substitution would have been safe."

I watched faces, as many as I could. I saw realization and even some nods. Imer was twitching again.

"So who," the Maestro said, "would have known that there would be a convenient ruckus? Who could have obtained the poison somewhere outside the city and had it ready to tip into a glass or switch glasses? Not Feather himself. All eyes were on him. But his wife fits these requirements."

Hyacinth snapped something at her husband.

"No!" Feather jumped to his feet and gabbled a tirade at Vasco.

The *vizio* translated. "Sir Bellamy denies that his wife did so and demands that the English ambassador be summoned."

All eyes settled on State Inquisitor Donà in his splendid scarlet robes, presiding like a judge. He stroked his beard a few times. In his way, he was as much a showoff as the Maestro.

"Tell the foreigner to sit down while we hear more of this."

The Maestro bowed his head in acknowledgment. "Your Excellency is kind. Of course there are questions I must answer. How did she know that retsina, or something equally pungent, would be on offer that evening? How did she know that the procurator would be present, how did she know he would choose the retsina if she had never met him? What possible reason can a visiting art dealer have to murder a senior officer of the Republic? And how did she and her husband come to gate-crash the party?"

"I did not invite them!" Imer shouted. His chair was against the wall at the far end from me, so I could not see him well. I could hear the panic in his voice easily enough. "And neither did Karagounis! I accused him of it. He denied it. He said they had come to his apartment and he had shown them some other documents. He had not told them about the auction and *did not* invite them to my house! I had told him that nobles would not come if there were foreigners present. I told *him* not to come, but he did."

The Greek had not trusted his local hireling.

Vasco's whisper droned in translation. Both Feathers started shouting denials before he was even finished. He calmed them down and translated.

"Monseigneur Bellamy insists that this is not true. The Greek did tell them that they would be welcome. He invited them to come and dine, to view the books and bid on them, and to meet important people."

The Maestro nodded. "But that invitation would have had to come through the interpreter, Domenico Chiari. What went in may not have been what came out. Today Alfeo exposed Chiari as a swindler. I trust, Your Excellency, that he was taken into custody and questioned about these events?"

Only the Maestro would have the audacity to cross-examine a state inquisitor. Donà stared very hard at him while the rest of us held our breath. Finally he said, "The man Chiari has confessed to art fraud and is currently naming his accomplices."

I had sent him to the torture chamber. I said a hasty prayer for both of us.

"But," Donà continued, "despite careful interrogation, he persists in denying knowledge of the murder. He claims he did not even know about the viewing planned for this house and could not have told the Feathers about it."

The Maestro shrugged. "It is *sier* Bellamy's word against his. *Vizio*, pray ask the foreigner if he is truly married to—"

Bellamy did not wait for a translation, and his French improved dramatically. "No! I am her servant. We do not share beds. She paid me to pretend!" He jumped up and moved his chair well away from Hyacinth.

Hyacinth was not the sort to remain silent. She burst into an excited babble of French, English, and Latin.

When she paused for breath, a very unhappy-looking Vasco said, "I cannot remember all that, Your Excellency. But she denies using poison. She says she never met the procurator before and would not know him if she ever met him again. She came to Italy to buy art and she pays her secretary to masquerade as her husband because single ladies traveling alone may be molested. Domenico told her the book viewing was open to everyone. And she again asks to see the English ambassador."

The inquisitor nodded, but I was certain that the Maestro's accusations had not surprised him. He or someone in the Council of Ten had worked it out. Two people working together are much more effective than one alone. I should have seen that for myself without having to have my nose rubbed in it, and now I could understand her clumsy efforts to flirt with me as a desperate effort to find any available ally to help her escape from the trap.

The inquisitor said, "You have brought serious charges against these persons, doctor. Can you also supply us with their motive?"

The Maestro looked offended. "Certainly."

"Then will you—"

"Lies!" Hyacinth shouted, on her feet, towering over both her husband and even Vasco. "I demand the ambassador!" She had taken two quick strides towards the Maestro before Vasco grabbed her arm and stopped her. To my regret she did not flatten him on the floor with a single punch; did not even try, in fact. Realizing I was on my feet with my sword out, I sheathed it and sat down.

"Silence!" Donà said. "*Missier Grande*, have the foreigners taken to the palace and lodged in the Leads as witnesses in a case of murder. They may have one cell or two, as the woman chooses. You may tell them that their ambassador will be informed in due course."

Missier Grande opened the door and called in two *fanti*, large young men wearing swords. He nodded to Vasco. No one said a word. Even the Feathers seemed to be shocked into silence. They vanished out the door with the *vizio* and the guards.

But just before the door closed, I caught a glimpse of more *fanti* standing outside. And also two slender youths I knew very well, Christoforo and Corrado Angeli, wearing matching grins as wide as the Grand Canal. My tarot had prophesied help coming from the two of staves—who else but the gondolier's twin sons?

26

The room settled. Only *Missier Grande* remained stand-ing. The mood had changed, the dark clouds of worry rolled back to reveal the pearly sunlight of the Adriatic. It had been the foreigners all along.

"Now," the Maestro said happily, "we can forget Domenico Chiari and the Feathers' visit to Karagounis. It is probably ir-relevant, except that it may explain how the woman knew——or could gamble——that there would be a strong-tasting wine like retsina on offer. No doubt Karagounis proclaimed its excel-lence. I cannot prove the details of their conversation, of course. How can we ever know what a spy told a thief to tell a murderess? I expect her secretary-husband will prove to be a cooperative witness. So, if you will give me the benefit of the doubt on that point, we shall proceed to the question of how she could be sure her victim would choose the retsina, so that her plot would work."

"And her motive," the inquisitor said.

"Ah, yes, motive." The Maestro rubbed his hands. "And yet there is one small puzzle that remains unsolved. For a private gathering, the book viewing was curiously infested with gate-crashers. The doge had not been invited, nor had the Feather woman and her escort. Nor had you, *sier* Pasqual. *Clarissimo*, why did you go out of your way that evening to come here, bringing your charming lady with you?"

Pasqual threw back his head and laughed, seemingly quite unworried. "But I was invited, doctor! Not by our host, I grant you. By my father."

The ambassador favored him with a rueful glance and then addressed the inquisitor. "So it is all my fault, of course! But my son does speak the truth in this case, Marco. I know old manuscripts. I knew at a glance that the supposed Euripides had been copied out in the late twelfth or early thirteenth century, almost certainly by a Greek monk. The hand is distinctive and the paper characteristic. The document was valuable in its own right, therefore, as an early copy of much earlier copies, but when had the original work been written? I asked Pasqual to come and look at it because he is a much better Classical Greek scholar than I am. I wanted to know if it read like something Euripides might truly have written."

"Ah! And what did you decide?" the Maestro asked.

Pasqual appraised the company and then looked to his father.

The ambassador sighed. "Tell them."

"Yes, father. I told him I was certain it was genuine. The imagery, the vocabulary, the flow of language—all cried out that this was a work of Athenian genius. And another thing! A few lines from the play have been preserved in works by other writers, as you are probably aware. Just glancing through it, I chanced upon the famous one about cowards not counting in battle—and the wording was not quite the same! A forger would certainly have been careful to include the known version, to give his fake a semblance of authority."

"What does this have to do with the murder of Bertucci Orseolo?" barked the inquisitor.

Pasqual smiled. "Nothing, so far as I can see."

"Nothing," the Maestro agreed. "I was just tying up a loose end. I already knew that His Excellency the ambassador was not guilty, because he volunteered the information that he had seen the procurator pull a face after draining his wine. You, *sier* Pasqual, asked Madonna Violetta if she had noticed the same thing, and the timing of your query required that your father must have asked you the same question *before* rumors of poisoning started to circulate. That is not the action of a guilty man, nor one who suspects his son of being guilty."

"*Motive!*" roared the inquisitor. "Why did that woman put poison in Bertucci's wine?"

"Motive?" said the Maestro. "Ah yes, motive. I require another demonstration, a very brief one this time. If all the gentlemen present would kindly stand along this table, facing the door? *Missier Grande* has some witnesses he wishes to bring in to identify the real murderer. Thank you."

Playing fair, the Maestro obeyed his own orders, struggling to his feet and leaning on the table before him. Violetta took Bianca's hand and together they moved to the far corner, out of the way. The rest of us moved like galley slaves—promptly and in unison—until we were lined up as required. All except the state inquisitor. Marco Donà moved to a chair against the wall, so he could study the faces in the lineup. His acceptance of Hyacinth's guilt had been so quick that he must have known exactly what was going to happen, but now he seemed more wary. If he did not know who was going to be denounced this time, then the Maestro must have cooked up this demonstration with *Missier Grande* after we arrived, while I was welcoming the guests.

And Giorgio must have gone back to Ca' Barbolano to fetch the twins. How did they fit in?

Who was next? Whom did Inquisitor Donà suspect? In his ducal counselor's red robes, he was sitting directly opposite me. Beside me stood Ambassador Tirali in his senatorial red robes. Was it mere coincidence that we had lined up like this? Did Donà suspect *Tirali*?

The demon in the illusion had claimed that Tirali was possessed, but what demons say must never be trusted. They can turn around and speak the truth to deceive, though, and Tirali's bribe to me had come at a very convenient moment. He had known that the poisoning must have happened in this room, he had known about the attack on me, even that the *bravi* had used knives and not swords. He had known I would be coming to call on him. Had the doge really revealed all that to a man who had been present at the scene of the crime? Surely Pietro Moro would not be so indiscreet?

Charming, Violetta had called Tirali senior, but also ruthless. What motive could he possibly have to order the murder of old Bertucci Orseolo? So that he could buy the Euripides manuscript to give to the Pope for the Vatican Library?

That was utterly ridiculous.

Missier Grande was still by the door. "If Your Excellency permits? The two persons outside have been assured that they are required only to tell the truth and will not be punished for it in any way."

Donà said, "Let's get it over with."

Quazza opened the door, peered out, then stood aside.

It was neither of the Angeli boys that entered, though, but a man in his twenties, wearing his church best, obviously a laborer and a scared one.

Missier Grande closed the door behind him. "Do what I said. Take your time and don't be frightened."

Pulping his cap in both hands, the man walked along the

line of us and then turned and walked back again. It is amazing how much guilt that sort of inspection can generate. I searched my soul all the way back to puberty. I didn't bother going farther than that, because my earlier memories are less interesting.

"Well?" *Missier Grande* said. "If you recognize him, point."

The man raised a very shaky hand and pointed. Nobody said a word, but Bianca stifled a gasp.

The first witness was dismissed. The second had more confidence, although he was only a youth, little older than the twins. Grinning cheekily and without even removing his cap, he strolled along the line. He, too, stopped in front of Enrico Orseolo.

"Him, *Missier Grande*."

"Are you sure? You haven't looked closely at all of them."

"No, him. I'm sure."

The door was closed behind him. We returned to our seats, mostly in the same places, but I strolled along to the end, where I had a better view of them all.

The great minister stretched out his legs and crossed his ankles. It was a bizarrely informal pose for a Venetian magistrate. "Well, *Missier Grande*? Who were those men and what am I supposed to have done?" He was admirably calm. His children, flanking him, looking considerably more frightened than he did.

Inquisitor Donà said, "Maestro Nostradamus?"

Fingertips went back against fingertips. "Yesterday morning, assassins tried to kill my apprentice. Such things happen in the Republic, but rarely in broad daylight, and it would be stretching belief to dismiss a connection between that assault and his inquiries into the procurator's death. At that time very few people knew that he had begun asking questions about it. The doge did, but it was at his suggestion that I had set Alfeo to work on the matter. Alfeo began by consulting a physician I respect, and a couple of personal friends. All of those we trust. He also called on the Feathers. Bellamy, if that is his name, drove him out at sword point." The Maestro chuckled. "It is an interesting, but probably immaterial, question as to whether the alleged *sier* Bellamy is naturally so irascible, or if he has been acting so at every opportunity on the woman's orders in order to justify the outburst he staged in this room four nights ago.

"I was already confident that the Feathers as a team had committed the crime, but I did not know why. Without a motive, they were unassailable, so why should they have been sufficiently worried by a boy's questions to attempt a second murder? By his own admission, Alfeo had no authority and fled from Bellamy's threats. They are strangers to our city. They had met me, but a senescent bibliophilic doctor should not seem dangerous, even if they knew of the spectacular clairvoyance I demonstrate in my almanacs and horoscopes. How would they find their murderous assistants in time? They had acted extremely fast to prepare such a trap overnight.

"Many great houses employ large staffs of manual workers—boatmen, warehousemen—and sometimes employ them for wrongful purposes. It was more than likely that Alfeo's attackers came from such a source, but two of them had been killed and thus would be missed by their workmates. Although the Council of Ten has sometimes been accused of turning a blind eye to misbehavior of the nobility, this case was clearly related to the death of a senior magistrate—the doge knew that, even if no one else in the Ten did. I could be confident that inquiries would be made in both Ca' Orseolo and Ca' Tirali. The fact that both Your Excellencies were available to attend this conference is evidence that the thugs did not come from either of your workforces. I hasten to add that I would not expect either of Your

Excellencies to be so foolish as to involve your own workers in a criminal affair already being investigated by the Ten.

"So the would-be assassins, despite their lack of swords, had been drawn from the ranks of *bravos* who lurk in the dark corners of our fair city. I should know where to send Alfeo to hire such vermin and I expect most of you would. But would foreigners know this? Unlikely! So they must have reported to a local, an accomplice, who took fright and arranged for my investigation to be hamstrung by the loss of my mobile assistant. Perhaps I was supposed to be frightened off by such terror tactics.

"I already knew that the Feather woman was the murderess. How had a married woman, staying with her husband in a strange city, passed word at night to—I assumed—another man? I surmised that Feather was not her husband and her local accomplice would turn out to be a lover."

The Maestro peered around as if looking for argument, but no one spoke.

"So how did he set up the ambush? Walk into any parish in the Republic, other than your own, and start asking questions about a resident, and in moments you will find the local men around you six deep, asking counterquestions. Someone who already knew the victim by sight would have to identify him, either to the entire gang or to one member of it. One member would make my problem more difficult, for two men gossiping on a corner or in a boat are not remarkable. But the attack went off so fast that there had been no time for elaborate preliminaries. The whole gang must have been standing by, ready to pounce as soon as their prospective victim was pointed out. A lurking gang should have been noticed.

"No doubt the Ten's agents in our parish have been making inquiries, but my gondolier has a pair of sons with wearisome amounts of youthful energy. As residents, they can ask questions, so I set them to work. They met with no success in our parish, but they are resourceful and they were lucky. Some days the boys do odd-job work at a building site directly across the canal from my residence. On the morning of the attack, as you will recall, the town was in mourning. The builders were not working, but a man and a youth were on watch, with little to do. At dawn they noticed a gondola full of men loitering on the canal just beyond the bridge near our watergate. So many men with time on their hands seemed unusual enough to attract their attention.

"The boat stayed in place for about an hour, they said, and then suddenly approached the Ca' Barbolano. No doubt these predators expected their quarry to embark in my gondola as he usually does, and were prepared to give chase to some distant place where the crime could be committed. The plan went awry, because Alfeo went along the *calle* to the *campo* instead. Six of the men disembarked and ran after him—and that was very curious behavior! It is not surprising that the witnesses remembered. The boat departed, bearing its gondolier—and you, Your Excellency."

Bianca cried out and clapped her hands over her mouth.

Benedetto said, "No! That is—"

"Shush, both of you!" their father commanded. "This is total rubbish. My government duties keep me far too busy to go wandering around at random. I have not been near Ca' Barbolano in months and I never saw that woman before the night my father took ill. How much did you pay those louts to identify me? Did you explain the penalty for perjury?" The politician was about to start bargaining.

The room was very quiet. I expected the inquisitor to comment, but he did not.

"You served two terms as rector of Verona," the Maestro said. "And the woman mentioned Verona to Alfeo. You summoned her or she followed you here, to Venice. You knew that your father would choose retsina if it were offered. He walked with a cane, had a crippled hand—easy to describe to someone who had never met him. You killed him without even being in the room! And you knew Alfeo by sight, because you had ordered him out of the house several times rather than pay a trivial debt. When he went to her house and started asking—"

Orseolo rose to his feet. "Slandering a member of the *Collegio* is criminal sedition. Marco, you have known me for years. You cannot believe this. Why should I murder my own father?"

The inquisitor's face was grim indeed. "The law does not care why, but I expect Doctor Nostradamus can tell us why. We must hear the rest of what he has to say."

The Maestro bunched his cheeks in an antiquated pixie smile. "Because his father discovered he was throwing away his political career on a woman. You may be able to find witnesses who have seen him visiting the Ca' della Naves. A similar thing happened a few years ago, when his father forced him to dismiss a courtesan he was supporting, a woman who goes by the name of Alessa. Granted His Excellency is now a widower, and can reasonably be expected to take a mistress; but that Feather woman is a foreigner and he is a senior minister in the government."

Which would make their intrigue treason under Venetian law. Such love is unthinkable, as the quatrain had said. The least penalty Orseolo could hope for would be dismissal from political office and loss of his place in the Golden Book. Exile or the gallows were possible.

Bianca and Benedetto were on their feet, saying, "Father! Father, you—" but Enrico bellowed for silence.

"You are a clever devil, Filippo Nostradamus. May you

burn in hell for all eternity!" he put his arms around his children. "I am sorry, my darlings. Yes, what he says is true."

"Father!"

"You are admitting the charge?" old Donà demanded, horrified.

"I admit it. My father was a tyrant, and I have never been able to stand up to him. There was a time when I could make him see reason, but lately he had become close to irrational. Yes, I met Hyacinth in Verona and we fell hopelessly, madly, in love, like adolescents. My term of office there ended and we had to part, but we found we could not live without each other. A few months ago I wrote and urged her to come to Venice. We were happy again, briefly, until my father learned of her and swore he would expose us. He was immune to all argument. The murder was my idea. I talked her into it. Show her mercy if you can."

Bianca was weeping, Benedetto ivory-white with shock.

"Take your sister home, Bene. Look after her. Be a better brother than I have been a father."

For *fire* read *passion*, the tower destroyed, the man and woman falling.

Missier Grande opened the door. Enrico Orseolo released his children and walked out. The Lizard could not negotiate a compromise this time, not on a charge of parricide. Quazza followed him out. It is not every day that a great minister needs to be escorted to jail.

It was over. Brilliant! The Maestro can still amaze me.

"That concludes my case, Your Excellency," he said.

Donà remained slumped in misery. He had expected Hyacinth, but never Enrico. As members of the inner circle of government, the two men must have known each other and worked together for decades. Apart from any personal loss, the scandal of a great minister confessing to the murder of his own distinguished father was going to shake the city harder than the earthquake of 1511.

I walked along to the inquisitor. After a moment he realized I was standing there and looked up with a scowl.

"Your Excellency, may the man Pulaki Guarana be released now? He obviously played no part in the murder. From the look of him, he must have told you everything he knows about Karagounis, and he could benefit from medical attention."

He shrugged. "We do seem to have concluded the evening's business."

"Not quite, Your Excellency," said Filiberto Vasco.

I had not noticed him return. He was smiling. He was smiling at me.

The inquisitor said, "What?"

"We have not yet solved the problem of the books."

My bowels felt as if I had swallowed an anchor. I had forgotten the jack of swords, but of course no card in the tarot deck would be a better fit for the *vizio*. Vasco, not Benedetto, was the snare to be avoided. The palace cells might have to admit a fourth new guest tonight.

Donà frowned. "What books?"

The *vizio* bowed. "Your Excellency will recall that at the meeting of the Ten at which I had the honor of reporting on the suicide of Alexius Karagounis, His Serenity inquired what had happened to the books exhibited at this address on the night of the thirteenth. Acting on instructions from *Missier Grande*, I examined the literary material I had removed from the deceased's residence. I identified all the antique papers and submitted them for His Serenity's inspection. He ordered that they be kept in secure storage until the Council of Ten could make determination of their ownership, but he also confirmed that one was missing, a unique copy of a lost work by Euripides. His Serenity described it as 'priceless'."

His Excellency muttered, "Bloody books," under his breath. "Go on."

Vasco continued, smiling at me all the time. "I went upstairs, Your Excellency, to the Leads, where the manservant Guarana was being interrogated. I added the missing book to the list of questions he was required to answer."

"And what did he say?"

Pulaki had crept closer and now fell on his knees, groveling before the inquisitor. "I said everything, Your Excellency, everything I know! You think I would have not told about a stupid book when they were doing such things to me?"

"What he claimed," Vasco said happily, "was that the deceased, Alexius Karagounis, was working with that very manuscript at the time I called on him in the company of *sier* Alfeo Zeno. I recall clearly that there were papers on his desk. When the spy jumped out the window, I ran downstairs with my men. Regrettably, I left Zeno there unsupervised."

"I couldn't run," I said. "I had a sore leg."

Everyone ignored that.

"When I returned," Vasco continued, "both Zeno and the papers had gone. I accuse NH Alfeo Zeno of stealing a document that the doge himself describes as priceless."

This was obviously my cue to do some fast talking, but I felt as if I were standing on mist. "Oh come, Filiberto, you can't hang me any higher for priceless than you can for just pricey."

"You admit your guilt?"

"Never! What His Serenity told me was that it was worthless. He cancelled his bid for it."

"But you did steal it?"

"No, I did not." That was true. I had been bewitched into

taking it. Regrettably, that would not be a promising line of defense. "I suggest you dredge the canal for it. The entire window had gone and there was a strong wind blowing. We were up high, remember? Papers were whirling around when I left. Besides, if you torture a man he will say anything he thinks will make you stop. Can you read and write, Pulaki?"

Wide-eyed the boy said, "No, *messer*."

"But you can identify an antique Greek document lying on a desk, seen casually from across a room, when you are standing behind four other men?"

"*Messer*, they were crushing my fingers in the pilliwinks! Bone by bone . . ."

"No more questions," I said. "If they did that to me, I'd confess to burning the Library of Alexandria."

Vasco widened his leer by four teeth. "You removed nothing from the desk before leaving the room?"

"No," I said. The Jesuits lost a great casuist in me. I had *not* removed *nothing*.

But I was not a good enough liar to deceive the *vizio*. He had me cornered and knew it. No one would ever believe I had burned the book. Even the Maestro could not testify on oath that he knew for certain what he had seen me cast into the fire. I had told him it was the *Meleager*, but I could have been lying. I was doomed and if he tried to support me, he would be doomed too.

The *vizio* glanced around. "Where is our host? *Lustris-simo*, will you please bring a Bible or some holy relic so that *sier* Alfeo can give us his sacred oath?"

Even if I perjured my immortal soul, he could still arrest me.

The Maestro said, "Have you a home to go to tonight, Pulaki?"

The footman was almost out of his mind with terror. He

took a moment to find the speaker and understand the question, but then he shook his head. "I am from Mestre, *lustrissimo*. I have no money for a gondola."

"Your Excellency," the Maestro said, "this man needs medical attention. Will you release him into my custody for tonight, please? As a personal favor?"

The old rascal was taking a serious risk by coming to my rescue, which is what he was doing, because Marco Donà was another politician who knew how deals were made. He looked from the Maestro to me and back again. He could guess where the book had gone and he knew who collected books. He also knew that Pulaki was merely a decoy and I was the real favor being requested. If I were put to the question, by morning I could be made to confess to *eating* the Library of Alexandria and would implicate my master and everyone I knew. I would say anything at all to make the pain stop. If the inquisitor wanted to, he could take this chance to retaliate against the man who had forced him to destroy his friend Enrico Orseolo.

I'm sure he thought of it, but he didn't do it. "And then, I suppose you will send the Republic a bill for medical services?"

The Maestro winced. "No bill, Excellency."

Donà nodded, satisfied. Who cared about a moldering old manuscript? This was a way to reward the Maestro for service to the state without cost and without the embarrassment of having to admit what service had been provided. "Take him. Send someone to the palace tomorrow and we will issue a release. *Vizio*, you cannot accuse *sier* Alfeo on such flimsy evidence."

Filiberto Vasco flushed scarlet and showed us every last one of his teeth. They were nice, strong teeth. I thought he was going to sink them in my throat.

"We can interrogate him!"

Donà scowled. "Are you telling me how to do my job, boy?"

Vasco crumpled. "Of course not, Your Excellency!"

I was saved. Christoforo and Corrado were standing in the doorway with eyes and ears wide open. They are not as stupid as they often pretend.

"Tell Bruno it's time to go home," I told them. "And warn your father we have an extra passenger."

27

By the time we reached the Ca' Barbolano, another winter squall was thrashing the city, hurling rain in faces. Pulaki had succumbed to an ague, a reaction to the end of his ordeal. I had to help him up the stairs. Giorgio and his sons stayed behind to stow the oars and cushions and lamps in the *androne.* Bruno ran all the way up with the Maestro on his back, and had to wait for me to arrive with the key, because everyone else had gone to bed.

We took Pulaki into the atelier and put him on the examination couch. I lit lamps while the Maestro dosed him with laudanum and proceeded to unwrap the bandage on his mutilated hand. Two fingers were so horribly crushed and swollen that the only thing to do was apply leeches and wait to see if they could reduce the swelling.

"Did they do anything else to you?" I asked.

He mumbled about his back, so I helped him out of his doublet and shirt to uncover a bandage adhering to three circular burns where the torturers had branded him. Only time was going to heal those, but the Maestro did the best he could with ointment and a fresh bandage. Eventually he managed to pick some fragments of bone out of the crushed fingers and splint the entire hand. By that time the laudanum had put Pulaki almost into coma, and I thought I would have to go and waken Bruno to move him. We managed, though, the two of us reeling across the *salone* like a drunken snake.

When I had made him as comfortable as he could be in the guest bedroom, I went to check on the Maestro, who was not far off having a reaction himself. It had been a strenuous night for the world's most sedentary scholar.

As I was helping him into bed, I said, "A remarkable performance, master."

"It went well."

"And much as you expected?"

"Fairly close," he muttered. "Water, if you please."

I fetched a jug of our best mainland water, imported from the Brenta. "Without your clairvoyance I should never have believed that a man like Orseolo, with so much power and wealth, would throw it all away on a cow like that Hyacinth woman."

The Maestro yawned heavily. "Foresight helped, but simple logic would lead you to the correct answer."

"Yes," I said, smiling to myself. "It was quite obvious after you pointed it out." At the door, I added a quiet, "God bless," but heard no reply. Probably he was already asleep.

I headed for my own room with a sigh of contentment. I replaced my rapier and dagger atop the wardrobe, and shed all Fulgentio's finery, folding it with due respect. I was in bed and just about to blow out the lamp when I heard the watergate doorknocker.

The night was not over yet.

Barefoot and wrapped in my cloak, I went out to investigate. From the top of the stair, I could see old Luigi's lantern far below me, and hear him talking through the spyhole. He looked up and saw my light.

"A lady," he called. "To see the Maestro."

"Anyone with her?"

"No."

I knew who the lady must be. "Let her in and tell her I will come down right away." I hobbled back inside to find clothes of my own to wear—and my sword, of course. When I left the apartment, I locked the door behind me.

Veiled and muffled against the storm, the visitor stood beside Luigi, fidgeting nervously with her hands. She reacted with dismay when she saw me coming down alone.

"I came for Doctor Nostradamus!"

Reaching ground level, I bowed to her. "I am reluctant to waken the good doctor, madonna. He is very old and tonight was a strain on him. We can talk in the boat."

"No, I must see him. It is urgent!"

"If your concern is a medical matter," I countered, "then surely you should have sent a gondola to fetch your family doctor?" Thanks to the Maestro's teaching, I am as competent at first aid as most doctors, but the city health department, the *Sanità*, does nasty things to laymen who practice medicine. "If it is a matter of mistaken identity, then I can help you as much as he can, and certainly much sooner."

"It is extremely urgent!" She wrung her hands.

"Then let us move quickly." I glanced in exasperation at blabbermouth Luigi, who was hanging on every word. "I know why you have come, madonna. You wish to tell the Maestro that he pulled the wrong ballot out of the urn this evening."

She nodded in shocked silence.

"That was no error," I said. "No one was deceived. Did you come here alone?"

"Just the boatman."

"Then we must hurry. Luigi, lock up after us." I heaved on the bolt. "I can explain exactly what happened."

"You are very kind, *sier* Alfeo."

In happier circumstances I would have made some gallant retort. As it was, I just offered my arm and squired her out into a drenching gale that made us stagger even in the loggia. Her gondolier was waiting there and helped us board the tossing boat. The weather was at least as bad as on the night Sciara hauled me off to the Leads, as if the Orseolo affair must end as it had begun.

I huddled into the *felzo* beside her. Obviously her gondolier would overhear nothing of our conversation in such a wind, but I decided to wait rather than have to repeat it all when we reached the Ca' Orseolo.

"You and your brother will have to be very brave," was all I said. I put an arm around her. She did not object. Indeed she cuddled closer, and soon I realized that she was weeping on my shoulder. That was probably the best thing she could do, so I just sat and held her in mournful silence all the rest of the way. The world can be very unkind.

Ca' Orseolo was as full of darkness and spooky echoes as Ca' Barbolano had been, but the night watchman was younger and more impressive than Luigi. He avoided looking straight at me, although he must have been tortured by curiosity. We removed our cloaks; Bianca unveiled. Telling the doorman to stay at his post when he wanted to play link boy to light our way, she took the lantern from him and handed it to me. We went up to the *piano nobile* together. It was a strange and creepy experience, that silent trek through a great palace with a girl I did not know and had hardly met. She was overloaded with grief and I was half out on my feet with fatigue.

We reached a door that must be our destination and I opened it into a blaze of candlelight, the mood abruptly changed. Bianca cried out in horror and rushed over to the fireplace. I closed the door hastily and followed, but one glance told me there was not enough blood to worry about. The room was a small *salotto*, luxurious but cosily intimate, reeking of wine and wood smoke. Benedetto sat on the floor before the fireplace, surrounded by bottles and holding a dagger in his right hand. His left forearm was bare and his wrist had bled enough to ruin the rich silk Turkish rug, but not enough to damage him.

I caught Bianca's shoulder and eased her away from him. "Don't spoil your gown. I've seen nosebleeds worse than that. Find me a handkerchief, and I will bandage it for him."

I knelt down to peer into Bene's blurred and reddened eyes. He stared back at me resentfully, not quite unconscious but close to it. I was tempted to offer him a lesson in anatomy—blood vessels run lengthwise and he had cut cross-wise, which is the wrong way to do it if you seriously want to rush into the afterlife.

"Can you move your hand like this? Your fingers?"

He could and did, once he had worked out the meaning of my questions.

"You have done no serious harm, just a scratch." I accepted the handkerchief his sister had brought. "A quill pen and a bucket would be a good idea," I told her. "And a pitcher of water, if you please." As soon as I had tied off the bandage, I took one of the wine bottles and smashed it on the fireplace. "You cut your arm on the glass," I explained, but he was too drunk to understand.

Bianca efficiently brought bucket and feather. Taking Benedetto by the hair, I pulled his face over the former and pushed the latter down his throat. I steadied his head while he vomited. After a few repeats, when he seemed to have brought up as much wine as he was likely to, I released him and gave him water to rinse his mouth and drink. When he had done, I moved the bucket to a more pleasant distance. I tipped the rest of the water over the bloodstains on the rug. It was already ruined for Ca' Orseolo, but some humbler family would appreciate it.

Then I selected a chair. Benedetto leaned back against another, making no effort to rise. Bianca sat down between us. She looked at me and smiled wanly.

"Thank you, *sier* Alfeo. I am very grateful."

"My pleasure. I wish I could do more to help you both. Are you going to try again, *messer*? Do we need to set servants to watch over you?"

"The Ten are going to garrote me," he mumbled.

I was surprised that he was still capable of understanding such problems. "No they won't. The Ten delegated the matter to the Three, or the inquisitor would not have come. And the Three seem likely to let you go. I am truly sorry about your father, but you must not waste his sacrifice."

"He didn't do it."

"Of course he didn't, but he did send the bravo to kill me and the penalty for that is death. The two watchmen told the truth. I know Maestro Nostradamus very well, and he would never suborn witnesses." Quite apart from ethics, it would be an insanely stupid crime.

I was directing my words to the boy but meant them for his sister, who would remember them in the morning. She nodded; I continued.

"The Maestro knew that the Feather woman murdered your grandfather. He was there, he recognized the poison, and logic told him that she must have done it while her companion created a diversion by shouting at the host. I should have worked that out for myself. Once he explained, it was very obvious.

"But the Feathers had no known motive and she had used a very potent and obscure toxin, not some crude rat poison.

The logical conclusion was that they were hired killers, acting for someone else. *In which case the true murderer was not there that night!*"

That took him longer, but Bianca understood, and her eyes were wide with horror.

"In other words," I said, "the rest of the people present were innocent. Who was not present who had a motive?" A lurid imagination might have considered blaming the Council of Ten or even the papacy, which has had a reputation for using poison ever since the days of the Borgias. I did not bother going up those blind *calli*.

"I never asked your father where he had been that evening, and I am sure his duties as great minister could have been arranged to provide him with an excellent alibi, had he known that he would need one. Besides, if he had wanted to kill your grandfather, he would have taken much less risk by administering the poison himself, at home. But you, *sier* Benedetto, were not only in Padua, miles away, you were in jail that night. Your alibi, *clarissimo*, was much too good! It could have been arranged very easily, though, at the cost of a dribble of blood and a little pain. You at once became the obvious suspect."

He blinked owlishly.

His sister said, "That's absurd! He wasn't in the city. Why did he need any better defense than that?"

"Because he did not know how the killers he had hired were going to strike. He knew the likely day, but not the means they would choose. He probably expected *sier* Bellamy to jump out of the shadows and attack the old man with a sword. A fast boat down the Brenta can bring a man from Padua to the lagoon of Venice in a couple of hours. He could kill a man here and be home in Padua by morning. So clever *sier* Benedetto arranged to spend the night in a Paduan jail, well out of suspicion's way. I expect he set up an immovable alibi every time the procurator was due to leave the Procuratie.

"When I worked that out, I was convinced, but such logic would not stand up in court. Having demonstrated that your father had tried to kill me, the Maestro accused him of the murder that did succeed. No doubt he expected the Three to take over the case at that point and discover the real truth by interrogating the Feathers. But your father accepted the blame for both crimes. Obviously his confession was a lie and he was sheltering one of you, his children. Possibly both of you, but if you had wanted to kill the old man, madonna, you could have done so at any time. You could have stumbled on the stairs and tripped him."

Her eyes flashed. "I wish now that I had!"

So did I. "But you didn't. That left your brother."

"Why do you say my father's confession was an obvious lie?"

"Because it was ridiculous. A great minister certainly knows all about the Council of Ten, and the Council of Ten most certainly keeps its unwinking gaze on ministers. He could never have hoped to have an affair with a foreigner and keep it secret. Never! At best he would be stripped of his office and sent into exile. At worst he would die as a traitor. I don't suppose he ever set eyes on Hyacinth Feather before tonight."

I also had great difficulty imagining Enrico Orseolo losing his head over a woman like Hyacinth Feather, but love is blind and my opinions were not evidence. No matter—by elimination, the mastermind had been the drunken sot on the rug at our feet.

"It was me," he said quietly, staring at the fire. "I found the foreigners in jail in Padua, charged with conspiring to murder a rich old woman. I paid for their defense by selling some jewels our mother left me last year. She did not leave them to

Bianca, because Bianca was destined for the convent. I got the foreigners off and promised them more money if our grand-sire died before Easter. I told them all about him, everything I could think of."

I had guessed that. "Even his taste in wine?"

He nodded. "But he almost never went out. Not even to the Senate any more, just to sales of books or paintings. I suggested they pose as buyers to meet him. Bianca knew nothing about the Feathers, I swear!"

"But I kept writing you helpful letters," Bianca said bitterly. "Day after day. I told you about every chance I got to go out, every trip to the market or the book dealers. I told you everything that was planned. I had nothing better to do than write you letters and dream of the next time Grandsire would take me to an art auction. That's how that awful woman knew everything, *messer*—I told Bene and he told her."

"When did your father find out?" I asked.

For a while Benedetto continued to stare into the fire as if he had not heard me. Then he muttered, "The night you went to the Feathers and started asking questions . . . You scared them. Bellamy came to see me and told me I must pay them right away so they could leave Venice. I had no money with me. I went and wakened Father. I confessed. He knocked me down, he was so furious. I got up and he knocked me down again. He said he would have heard by then if the Ten suspected murder, but he said we must stop Nostradamus. The old man was too clever, he said. If we could just remove you, then the man would be helpless and we would be safe. He paid Feather something to get rid of him. Then he and I went out together, to see some men he knew. It was not an area for a man to go alone."

"But why kill old Bertucci anyway?" I asked. "Just because he was getting old and cranky?"

Benedetto turned to look at me for the first time. His eyes were still bleary but a sudden rage seemed to sober him. "Not for me. For Bianca. Because he was a tyrant! A despot. I could put up with him jerking my strings for a year or two more. But if he forced her into taking her vows, that was a life sentence! You know what they would do to her? She has to lie on the floor and be covered with a black cloth, while they sing and pray over her—three times they do that. And they take away anything pretty like embroidery. And then they cut off her hair, while the whole congregation watches. Every nun in the convent comes and cuts off a lock of her hair and throws it on the ground. Snip, snip, snip . . . They wrap her in sackcloth and put a crown of thorns on her head . . ." Bene began to weep. "And it's forever! She's locked up until she dies. Do you wonder she was terrified? The old man was crazy. He should have been locked up, not her. Father would never stand up to him, no matter how bad he got."

So it was all his sister's fault? What pathetic trash he was! He could not even kill himself properly. Bianca was sobbing too, silent tears flowing down her cheeks. In her place, I would have taken up the fire irons and made a clean sweep of the Orseolo males.

And that was the unthinkable love of the quatrain. I am certain that there was nothing carnal about it, just brotherly love carried to the point of madness.

It was time to go, or I would fall asleep in my chair. "Your father is trying to save you. He can only die once, so he took all the blame. I knew he was lying. The Maestro knew he was lying, and Inquisitor Donà knew he was lying—but he accepted the confession. You've got your life back, Benedetto Orseolo. Try to put the rest of it to better use."

"You mean that?" Bianca whispered. "The Three won't send *Missier Grande* to arrest him?"

"I don't think so. Donà will have to talk the other two inquisitors into it, but I think they will go along." The Lizard would make his last deal.

"You're wrong," the boy said. "They won't hang father for trying to kill you. The Ten will take his money instead."

Bianca stared at me, waiting for my comments. This was the crux of the problem. Shamefully, there are precedents. More than one noblemen convicted of murder has offered to pay an enormous fine instead and the Council of Ten has accepted it.

"That's impossible now," I said wearily. "He's confessed to treason and parricide. They can't overlook those crimes. If you interfere now, you'll probably get both of you hanged. Sweat it out, boy. Your penance begins now." I hauled myself to my feet. "If your gondolier is still awake, madonna, I would appreciate a ride home."

28

No matter how thick the drapes or what horrible hour of the night I go to bed, I cannot sleep past dawn. It is a curse upon the Zenos—my father had it also, or so my mother used to tell me. It was almost noon before the Maestro came huffing and thumping into the atelier. I had been at work for hours and his side of the desk was papered with examples of my peerless italic hand. Much to my amusement, Mama Angeli arrived right on his heels, bringing a steaming mug of dark fluid. The Maestro refuses to admit that *khave* is beneficent or even nontoxic, but he indulges when he has to, and this day was one of those days.

I was tempted to bid him a cheerful good afternoon but he was so obviously in no mood for chaffing that I resolved not to speak until spoken to. I went back to work. After a while he picked up some of the almanac pages, the legible copies I was making for the printers to set.

He said, "Bah! This is wrong. You are a line out on this table, all the way down the page." He was restored to his usual self.

"Good morning, master."

"Is it? I shall need all these sheets redone before you break for dinner."

"Yes, master. We had a visitor last night after you went to bed—a lady who disagreed with your apportioning of the blame."

He gave me the sort of look I associate with spiders, except that spiders' faces are too small to show details. "I hope you told her to go home and count her blessings."

I reported what had happened. He had been looking forward to explaining to me why Bene's alibi counted against him, and was peeved that I had worked it out for myself. He was disgusted that the boy had not been arrested.

"I accused the father to try and shame a confession out of the son. I never expected Inquisitor Donà to accept such nonsense! You really think the Council of Three will let the boy get away with murder?"

"Yes. I think he will be left to live with his guilt."

The Maestro shook his head. "I cannot see why they should connive at such a deception."

"Family," I said sadly. "The Orseolos provided some of the first doges, centuries ago, and Bene is the last of the line. His father must have foreseen the possibility of things turning out the way they did and warned him not to interfere if he took all the blame on himself. Inquisitor Donà understood that. Benedetto's penance is to let his father die and live to carry on the family name."

"I will never understand the Venetian nobility!"

"Neither will I, master. That's why I work for you."

Nostradamus pulled a face. "You almost ended up working for hell. You ought to go and see Father Farsetti again, just to be on the safe side. Think how valuable a boy of your talents would have been to the demons!"

Now it was my turn to bristle. "In what way?"

"Oh, many ways. You could have been hell's man in the

Vatican. Or you could have thrown the Republic into chaos by testifying that you supplied the doge with heretical books."

"If you mean his *Apologeticus Archeteles* . . ." Of course he meant that.

The Maestro bunched his cheeks in glee. "Why do you think he asked me to look after it for him? And because I told you to record it as mine, did you think I was trying to steal it?"

He was definitely back on form. "Of course not, master." I reached for my pen. "Those sheets you are holding are correct. I always double check your calculations. I found two mistakes in May and one in June. That was why your drafts were a line out. I mended them."

Where does a story end, exactly? Some stories go on for a very long time, like buildings. The Orseolo saga had been going on for centuries. I just visited for a few days, and this was where I left it. From now on they must manage without me.

A few backward glances through windows, perhaps—

Before noon Giorgio rowed Pulaki over to the mainland and saw him safely to his parents' home in Mestre. The Maestro was confident that the loss of the use of two fingers would not handicap him greatly.

Two days after that, the bell called the *Maleficio* tolled in the campanile of San Marco to announce an execution. Corrado and Christoforo were downstairs and out the door in a flash. They returned an hour or so later to describe the proceedings with as much lurid detail as anyone was willing to hear. Having seen the Feathers arrested at Imer's house, they had now watched them being beheaded between the columns on the Piazzetta. You would have thought from listening to them that they had solved the murder and brought the villains to justice all by themselves.

The Feathers had been tried in secret, but I draw your attention to the curious behavior of the English Ambassador in the meantime. The English Ambassador did nothing in the meantime. He made no outcry at all—no appeal to the *Collegio* or the Senate, nothing—so he must have been satisfied that they deserved their fate.

The following dawn revealed a gallows between the pillars, and a body dangling from it. Giorgio and Mama heard the news in the Rialto market, and I had Giorgio row me to the Piazzetta to confirm that it was indeed the corpse of Enrico Orseolo. I could tell from the stains on his clothes and the marks on his neck that he had been strangled while seated— they tie you in an iron chair, put a silken rope around your neck, and turn a handle. Only then had he been taken out and hung up on display. This form of execution is typical of the secretive ways of the Ten, but at least it is private, and the victim is not exposed to the mockery of the mob. Orseolo had been suspended right way up, so he had not been convicted of treason, as he might have been. My tarot had predicted the Traitor reversed, meaning that the world was upside down, or perhaps even that the hanged man had earned his halo.

I think that's all.

No, not quite. One final backward glance . . .

One siesta time a week or two later, Violetta poked me and said, "You asleep?"

"No, just planning my next move. Pawn takes queen?"

"Mate in two against any defense." She snuggled closer. "Did I tell you about Pasqual?"

"You have never told me one word about that disgusting and hateful man."

"I can this time, because it's not confidential. He is going to marry Bianca Orseolo."

I came awake with a start. "I always admired his taste in women. Seriously?"

"Very. He saw her twice at the attorney's house and was smitten. He's agreed to a very modest dowry, considering her station. Everyone else cut the family dead when Enrico was hanged and poor Bene has no experience of running a business. Pasqual will help him."

"And help himself too?" Pasqual Tirali was quite clever enough to have worked out the significance of Bene's excessive alibi and then bleed him of everything he possessed for the rest of his life. Even in bed I can be cynical. Try me.

"I think he'll be fair," Helen said. "And marriage is what Bianca wanted, foolish girl. If I were married, I couldn't be here with you, could I?"

"Why not?"

"Oh, you know," she said vaguely. "The wedding won't be for a couple of years yet, after the ambassador comes home. Pasqual is still my patron."

"I will kill him."

"But Lent is over and he has to go to a meeting tonight. You know how bored I get without a man around to amuse me."

Of course. I had been attempting clairvoyance with the crystal again that morning. I still could not create prophecies of epic importance as the Maestro could, but I had foreseen myself enjoying a very memorable evening.

GLOSSARY

androne a ground-floor hall used for business in a merchant's palace

atelier a studio or workshop

barnabotti impoverished nobles, named for the parish of San Barnabà

Basilica of San Marco the great church alongside the Doges' Palace

ca' (short for *casa*) a palace

calle (pl. *calli*) an alley

campo an open space in front of the parish church

cavaliere servente a married woman's male attendant (possibly gigolo)

chaush an equerry of the Turkish sultan

Circospetto popular nickname for the chief secretary to the Council of Ten *clarissimo* "most illustrious," form of address for a nobleman

Collegio the executive, roughly equivalent to a modern cabinet—the doge, his six counselors, and the sixteen ministers

Constantinople capital of the Ottoman (Turkish) Empire, now Istanbul

corno the distinctive cap worn by the doge

Council of Ten the intelligence and security arm of the government, made up of the doge, his six counselors, and ten elected noblemen

doge ("duke" in *Veneziano*) the head of state, elected for life

ducat a silver coin, equal to 8 lira or 160 *soldi*, and roughly a week's wages for a married journeyman laborer with children. (Unmarried men were paid less.)

fante (pl. *fanti*) a minion of the Ten

felze a canopy on a gondola (no longer used)

fondamenta a footpath alongside a canal

Great Council the noblemen of Venice in assembly, ultimate authority in the state

kapikulu (pl. *kapikullari*) a servant (in effect a slave) of the sultan

khave coffee (a recent innovation)

Leads prison cells in the attic of the Doges' Palace

lustrissimo "most illustrious," honorific given to wealthy or notable citizens

messer (pl. *messere*) my lord

Missier Grande chief of police, who carries out the orders of the Ten

Molo the waterfront of the Piazzetta, on the Grand Canal

Piazza the city square in front of the Basilica of San Marco

Piazzetta an extension of the Piazza, flanking the palace

Porta della Carte the main gateway into the Doges' Palace

salone a reception hall

salotto a living room

sbirri constables

soldo (pl. *soldi*) see DUCAT

Ten see COUNCIL OF TEN

Three the state inquisitors, a subcommittee of the COUNCIL OF TEN

Tuscan the language of Florence, which eventually became modern Italian

Veneziano Venetian language, similar to Italian

Vizio *Missier Grande*'s deputy

Wells prison cells on the ground floor of the Doges' Palace